STORM RIDERS

A NOVEL

Craig Lesley

PICADOR USA / NEW YORK

Picador® is a U.S. registered trademark and is used by St. Martin's Press under license from Pan Books Limited.

For information on Picador USA Reading Group Guides, as well as ordering, please contact the Trade Marketing department at St. Martin's Press.
Phone: 1-800-221-7945 extension 763
Fax: 212-677-7456
E-mail: trademarketing@stmartins.com

Interior art © Jasmine/PNI

Book design by Katherine Nichols

Library of Congress Cataloging-in-Publication Data

Lesley, Craig.
    Storm riders / Craig Lesley.
      p. cm.
    ISBN 0-312-24554-8 (hc)
    ISBN 0-312-26398-8 (pbk)
    1. Fathers and sons—Massachusetts—Fiction.   2. Fetal alcohol syndrome—Patients—Family relationships—Fiction.   3. Indians of North America—Alaska—Fiction.   4. Adoptees—Massachusetts—Fiction.   5. Tlingit Indians—Fiction.
I. Title.
PS3562.E815 S76   2000
813'.54—dc21   99-055046
                                                                CIP

First Picador USA Paperback Edition: February 2001

10 9 8 7 6 5 4 3 2 1

For

Katheryn Ann Stavrakis

and our daughters

Elena and Kira

Acknowledgments

The author wishes to thank Iva GreyWolf and the Tlingit people of Angoon for their friendship, hospitality, and assistance with this project.

Thank you also to the many dedicated classroom teachers who approach children resembling Wade with generous and cheerful spirits. Sharon Edwards, Larry Frank, and Merry Gilbertson deserve special recognition for their efforts.

High praise to the foster and adoptive parents who light their candles against the darkness. Ruth Anne and Dennis Swartout stood as beacons in a storm.

And thanks to the friendly staff at Old Harbor Books in Sitka and to other book people who have encouraged me along the way.

Finally, a salute to editor Diane Higgins, who offered many great suggestions, and yet another thank-you to Binky.

STORM RIDERS

1

Amherst, Massachusetts, 1977

Mrs. Kagita held out a small child's pink plastic raincoat. She stood beside the playground gate anxiously calling first in one direction, then another. Her lustrous black hair hung down her back like a raven's wing.

Clark Woods couldn't hear her call Yukiko's name but he read her lips through the rain splatters on the pickup's windshield. *She ought to keep better track of that kid,* he thought. The engine still idled. Paul Simon sang "Slip Sliding Away."

He was slow to shut off the engine because he had to face his mother, Grace Woods, and Wade White Fish, his foster son, in the cramped apartment at Puffton Village, a single-story maze of tiny apartments reserved for graduate students and their families. "Married student housing" the University of Massachusetts called it, but the students' term was more apt and cynical—"divorced student housing."

Climbing out of the pickup, he balanced two pies and a block of Vermont cheddar as he kicked shut the door. Raindrops struck the top pie's cellophane cover. Moving toward Mrs. Kagita, he asked, "Are you looking for Yukiko?"

She held the raincoat toward Clark as if presenting an offering. "Yukiko gone." She nodded at the empty playground.

The gate into the fenced playground stood ajar.

"She's all right, Mrs. Kagita," Clark said. "Probably with the other kids." In the distance a group of eight or ten children raced along the weed fields beside the marshes backed up from the Connecticut River. He recognized Wade among them in his orange-and-white U-Haul cap and a navy blue sweatshirt. He wondered what had happened to his new maroon J. C. Penney coat.

"You look this way," he said, indicating the apartment buildings away from the children. "I'll check out those kids. Go," he said, gesturing broadly and speaking more loudly than he needed to. Seventy feet from the playground, a high culvert drained rainwater into the murky slough. Some days, the apartment kids played near the culvert's mouth building muddy roads or gigging frogs. As Clark crossed the lawn to the culvert's edge, a wind gust lifted the wrap covering the pies. "Nuts," he said, afraid the crust would get soggy. Suddenly rain whipped into his face, sheeting his glasses. He wiped them on his shirt-sleeve and looked down to the trampled mud at the culvert's lip seven feet below him. No kids. He smiled. For once, Wade hadn't found the muddiest place in Massachusetts. The older running boys and the weedy fields had attracted him more. He double-checked the swamp's edge. No sign of Yukiko.

"Back to reality," he sighed, approaching unit L-26. He and his girlfriend, Natalie Kravtchenko, had just returned from Vermont, where they had spent the day viewing magnificent fall colors. In Dummerston, they visited with tourists and purchased pies baked by local churchwomen.

As Natalie had gazed at the hazy mountains and valleys, Clark had admired her obsidian eyes, the eloquent gestures of her long hands. She had a reserve about her, a mystery; and she was dark and exotic. Almost as beautiful as his ex-wife Payette.

.   .   .

Inside the unit, his mother was reading *Sunset.* She wore a light cotton dress and three sweaters. Her right ankle was swollen from a recent sprain, and the skin was stretched and shiny.

"Hey, Mom," he said. "Try a piece of Vermont apple pie." He set the pies on the small kitchen table.

"Those look wonderful. Did they have any peach?"

"No, it was the apple festival."

"Sometimes they put too much cinnamon in apple pie." She set her magazine on the sofa. "Well, sit down and tell me about it." Grace slapped her knees. "Start talking! I'm excited to hear!"

"Later," he said. "It's getting awful wet out there."

She peered out the window. "Wade should come in. He was getting soaked, but he was having such a good time. I thought, why not let him just go ahead. I can do the laundry tomorrow. Look." She pointed to a pile of Wade's clothes near the back door.

"Jesus, look at the mud on his new coat!" Clark wondered why his mother had let him wear the coat out to play.

"He had to change all his clothes and I made him put on rubber boots. The leather boots were all caked with mud. I never saw a boy could get that muddy. Not you."

"You're getting addlepated," he teased. "Remember when I rode steers through the mud and manure with Danny Freeman?"

"Just lucky you weren't killed," she said. "I was mad enough to throttle you myself."

Clark pulled on a gray-and-red UMass sweatshirt. "Have you seen Yukiko? Her mom's looking for her."

His mother limped to the table, pinched off a tiny piece of crust and put it in her mouth. "Mmmm," she said. "I'll bet they use lard." She shook her head. "I saw her earlier playing out in the rain all by herself. I just figured her mother took her back inside."

"Guess not," he said. "I'm going to check with the boys. What about Michelle? Sometimes she watches her."

Grace pinched another section. "Her father came and got her for the weekend. She's in Lowell. I feel sorry for that girl. Split in half like Solomon's child." She glanced at the rain. "Bring Wade in. He's wet as a priest at a picnic."

* * *

As Clark followed the bobbing U-Haul hat in the high weeds, he realized Wade was off a distance from the other boys whacking at the grass with a thin stick. The boy was so intent on his task he didn't see Clark approach until he grabbed him in a bear hug. "Got you, Spiderman!"

Wade kicked and flailed but Clark held tight. The boy's arms and legs were so long and thin he really did resemble a spider.

"Let go. Let go. I saw a rabbit!"

Clark released him and he kept swinging the stick. Each time he whacked the weeds, beads of water flipped into the air. "He was a big rabbit. The others saw him, too. He's hiding around here somewhere close. You got to help me look."

As Wade glanced up, Clark saw the streaks of clear snot running from the boy's nose. He recalled how Wade had green or yellow snot coming out of his nose for the first six months he had come to live with Clark and his ex-wife Payette.

"Undernourishment," the pediatrician had said at Oregon's Crippled Children's Hospital after Payette and Clark had brought the little boy down from Sitka, Alaska. "Chronic ear infections; the drums are pretty scarred so he's lost a little hearing. We see that a lot with Alaskan Natives." The doctor had prescribed antibiotics, vitamins, a stable home life. Payette took notes. Ninety minutes to assess six years of harsh Alaskan life. Learning disabilities and emotional handicaps, the result of his mother's hard drinking and abuse by her boyfriends. "But you'll see vast improvement," the doctor promised. "You'll be amazed." He shook Clark's hand and patted Payette's shoulder.

"We'll chase after that rabbit later," Clark said. "Right now I'm looking for Yukiko. Have you seen her?"

Wade took a couple more swings. "That rabbit is hiding real close."

Clark noticed the stick had a pointed end. "Let me see that, pal." He gently took the stick from the boy's hand and set it down. He kneeled so he could look Wade square in the face and rested his hands on the boy's shoulders. "Have you seen Yukiko, Wade? Her mother is looking for her and needs to give her a coat. It's important because the rain is getting cold. You've got your sweatshirt and hat on, see? Let's find Yukiko and then come back after the rabbit."

Wade nodded. "She might get too wet and catch a cold."

Clark explained the situation to the other boys and they scattered to look also.

"Maybe she's over there," Wade said, pointing to another section of swamp farther from the student housing. "She was there earlier, I think."

"Today? That's a long way." Clark glanced back at the boys hurrying around helter-skelter. He decided to take a quick look where Wade was pointing, but when they searched that area and called Yukiko's name they got no response.

"So, listen, Wade. Are you sure you saw her over here today?"

The boy shook his head and then his face brightened. "See what I found. It's a surprise." He pulled a red-and-yellow fishing bobber out of his pocket. A piece of line and swivel were attached to the bobber. "Can we go fishing? This is where I found the bobber, right there." He pointed. "A good surprise, huh?"

"A great surprise," Clark said, examining the bobber. "But I think there are better places to fish than this. Maybe we'll go tomorrow. Right now we need to find Yukiko. It's getting dark."

"There's a flashlight in the truck," Wade said. "If it works." His lower lip stuck out and he dropped his head. Clark wondered if the boy had been fiddling with the light again, breaking it. Wade couldn't keep his hands off tools or lights.

"Okay, we'll get the flashlight and then we'll find Yukiko. Good idea." He touched Wade's arm.

"This sure is a cool bobber," Wade said, turning it over and over in his thin, nervous hands.

"It's a dandy all right."

. . .

Clark was relieved to see Mr. Kagita back at the playground. He spoke much better English than his wife and had been studying electrical engineering at UMass a couple of years. He wore a jacket and tie. Mr. Kagita seemed to be scolding his wife, but then he smiled as Wade and Clark approached.

"Did you find Yukiko, Mr. Woods?"

Clark shook his head. "Not yet. We better get some other adults to help look."

"It's getting very dark. I'm worried about her." He said something to Mrs. Kagita and she hurried into the apartment. He was now holding the pink raincoat.

"I'm just getting a flashlight out of the truck."

Mr. Kagita followed him to the pickup. Clark felt a little embarrassed by all the clutter behind the pickup seat: Coke cans, Fritos bags,

Snickers' wrappers, jumper cables, screwdrivers, and wrenches. He found the big four-celled Sportsman lantern and switched it on. It cast a beam for a good fifty yards. Back home in Oregon, a lot of people he knew used them for poaching. He handed a smaller flashlight to Mr. Kagita.

"You go that way," he said, pointing to the right side of the village. "I'll take the left. Ask some other adults to help." He grabbed Wade's hand. It was slick and cold.

"I want to hold the light," Wade said.

"Not now. Maybe later."

The rain had stopped temporarily but the wind stiffened and Clark felt chilled. *If I catch a cold because Mrs. Kagita was goofing around watching* Charlie's Angels, *I'll be pissed,* he thought. "Yukiko's probably in one of the houses right now," he told Mr. Kagita, who was pointing the flashlight beam at them. "Most likely somebody took her in since it's starting to get dark. Knock on some doors. I doubt she went far."

Clark knocked on the doors of lighted apartments. Columbus Day was a holiday in Massachusetts, and undergraduates had left. The older men remaining in Puffton had scruffy beards or owlish glasses. The women seemed gaunt and strained, the children unruly and unkempt. *No wonder they call it "divorced student housing,"* he thought. "We're looking for Yukiko Kagita, a little Japanese girl about this high." He indicated with his hand.

"Green rubber boots," Wade added. "She has rain boots."

Clark smelled Hamburger Helper, Rice-A-Roni, spaghetti. The living rooms were not much larger than most kitchens. The kitchens about the size of closets. Several adults offered to help look. One man got so excited he carried his fork and water glass outside.

Few of the graduate students had flashlights, a neglect that frustrated Clark. *Of course, this is the East,* he thought. No raccoons or polecats slipping around at night. No changing tires on long stretches of desolate empty highways.

He held on tightly to Wade's coat sleeve, not wanting to lose the boy and add to the confusion. He had only made his way to the G section, and it seemed to be taking forever. The place was a maze. *Only a university could construct such a tangled mess,* he thought.

He paused halfway through the G section of Puffton, trying to decide whether to push on to the main road or go back toward the Kagitas and the playground. *Surely no one had kidnapped her,* he thought. She had just wandered off. Something dark flashed across his mind. Back in Portland, a distraught Japanese mother had poisoned her children with carpenter ant pesticide. Two had died and the third suffered irreversible nerve damage. *Bad stuff like that doesn't happen in Amherst,* he thought. A stolen bicycle, cows on the road, a drunk music major singing opera on the library steps. Quaint and charming, the Amherst police reports made fun reading and he'd clipped out the better ones to send to his uncle Roy back in Oregon. He recalled Roy's Silverado pickup with the bumper sticker which read, "Support Your Local Search and Rescue. Get Lost."

He smelled drifting smoke from town fireplaces and felt comfortable in spite of being wet and concerned about Yukiko. Amherst was almost three thousand miles from Oregon, but small towns were small towns—sleepy and safe. Not much had happened in Clark's hometown since Speed Pierson threw a giant carrot through the movie screen because Elvis wasn't singing enough in *Flaming Star.* Rather than pay to repair the screen, the owners shut the theater down. After that, the kids had to drive to Portland for a movie.

Clark smiled at the memory. As soon as they found Yukiko, he'd tell the Kagitas some colorful hometown stories, maybe offer them pie and tea.

In the distance, he heard sirens and his pulse quickened as the wails grew closer.

"Here comes an ambulance," Wade said. "And police cars. Wow! A big fire engine! That's cool, huh? They're going to help look."

It seemed as if every rescue vehicle in Amherst was turning into Puffton. "Now we'll get a little help," Clark said. He figured one of the Puffton residents called in the missing girl. "Come on, Wade."

Emergency vehicles blocked the apartment road near the playground. Clark had expected the rescue teams to fan out through the complex, but the activity remained close to the playground. As he arrived, two firemen in yellow coats and hip boots knelt by the culvert, peering into the water.

Clark was going to tell them he had already looked there when the older fireman scrambled down the slippery bank beside the culvert. "Get the goddamn oxygen over here!" he yelled.

Clark felt his chest tighten and he gripped the boy's hand. The second fireman went over the side and a tight knot of firemen, police officers, and ambulance personnel assembled near the culvert. Spectators crowded closer but a plainclothes officer in a blue raincoat waved them back. "Stay clear," he warned. "Give these workers room. Move back now, folks."

"Is she in there?" someone asked.

"No, they're just looking."

"Hey, I can't see anything."

"Louis. Come here. I don't want you watching this." Susan Lemke grabbed her boy by the arm and pulled him back toward their apartment. He tried to kick free, but she held him tight.

"Yukiko. Yukiko. Yukiko," Mrs. Kagita said over and over. Mr. Kagita tried scrambling down the bank but a policeman grabbed him by the jacket.

The fireman clambered up, cursing the muddy slope. He held on to what appeared to be a wet bundle of clothes. Clark saw a flash of green and yellow, then black hair and a porcelain-white doll's face. "What the hell."

"They found something," Wade said. "Is that her?" He moved forward but Clark held his wrist.

The fireman and three ambulance workers blocked Clark's view.

A yellow helmet fell to the ground. In a few moments, two ambulance medics rushed toward the vehicle carrying a small stretcher. The child's feet appeared to be kicking but she only wore one green boot. Clark felt relief to see the movement.

Mr. Kagita still held on to the pink coat. The plainclothes officer helped the adult Kagitas into the police car and they sped off after the pulsing red light of the ambulance.

As the fireman retrieved his helmet, Clark noticed he was bald and appeared older than Clark had imagined. A couple of younger firemen thumped his back. "Good eyes."

"Why isn't there a fucking fence back here?" the fireman said. "Fucking cheap college."

Wade pulled at Clark's arm. The boy was smiling. "Don't worry, Dad. They can fix her at the hospital."

Clark held Wade close a minute, then rubbed his bristly crewcut under the U-Haul hat. "They can do miracles all right, buddy. I'm sure she'll be fine."

"That man's right," Russell Lemke said. "We need a fence to protect our children. I'm going to start a petition."

Several people offered to help Lemke collect signatures, but Clark started back toward the apartment. He didn't like Lemke or his son Louis, who often quarreled with Wade over toys.

Away from the crowd, still hanging on to Wade, Clark offered a silent prayer. Even so, he felt sick, blaming himself for a near disaster. While he was off chasing after Yukiko, she had wandered out from a hiding place, or come around a corner, and fallen into the water. He should have stationed someone there. Water, cars, drop-offs. Those dangers hurt kids. He could hear his uncle Roy's warning. "When you're lost or confused, don't move around. That's when you get into big trouble. Stay put and chances are you'll come out fine." Clark felt embarrassed at his greenhorn mistake, but at least they'd found her. She couldn't have been in the water long. Clark tugged Wade back to the apartment.

．　　．　　．

"What a commotion," Grace said. "I burned the pork chops running out to look. All those sirens and lights. When I remembered I'd left the burner on, I ran back in. So they found the little girl okay?"

"They took her to the hospital," Clark said. "She'll probably be fine." He crossed his fingers for luck. "I saw her legs move."

The kitchen was smoky and Grace had opened the back door. The burnt frying pan lay outside in the grass. Four burnt pork chops were on the Corelle plate.

"Just sit down, you men. I'm all shaken." She fanned her face with a potholder.

"She's fine, Grandma," Wade said. "Don't worry."

"Oh, I do hope so," she said. "With children, you can't be too careful. What a racket. Now you take off your wet clothes and sit down to enjoy some of this meat." She emphasized the final *t* and had done so ever since Clark was a boy and they ate three meatless meals a week to save money.

"Wash your hands, Wade. No telling what's in that field. I saw a dead cat one day. You're likely to get cholera. That's what your great-uncle Herb got—in the Canal Zone. He was dead in a week."

Wade washed and sat at the table. "You should have seen the fireman, Grandma. He had big boots and a yellow hat just like the man in *Curious George*. And he was swearing, too, about needing a fence. Maybe I can help them build one."

"Public servants shouldn't swear. He's a bad example." She shook her head. "Clark, why don't you offer thanks tonight. I'm just so glad that you're both here and that everything is okay. Wade, bow your head so your father can offer thanks."

Clark bowed his head and mumbled thanks, then prayed earnestly that Yukiko would be all right. "I'll go and check on things in a little bit." Later, he planned on driving to Northampton to see Natalie. Frequently he spent the night with her or at his small study apartment behind the Amherst post office.

"Me too," Wade said.

"You stay put tonight, buddy. I think those firemen have things under control. Anyway, you need a warm bath. You're soaked from head to foot."

"I'm so thankful we're all here safe and sound," Grace said. Her eyes glistened. "A nice little family."

2

Ruby, Oregon, 1976

The first time Clark remembered seeing his natural father, Emmett Woods, was after Clark turned fifteen and was crushed and dragged by a Fox peppermint chopper. He spent five months in the Prineville hospital, the first two weeks hovering between life and death. Emmett had decided to see his son before he died, but by the time he came, Clark had started to recover.

Hooked on morphine and hanging on to life by his thumbs, Clark believed his father still looked exactly like the young soldier in the photograph Grace kept. Emmett lifted baby Clark high into the crotch of a Bing cherry tree on Lincoln Street in The Dalles. Grinning as if he owned the world, service cap tipped at a rakish angle, the soldier hoisted his son toward heaven. Clark had studied that photo hundreds of times, marveling at the service pins depicting his father's heroic performance in the Battle of the Bulge.

"Your father didn't have a mean bone in his body," Grace had told him. "But after all the fighting, he was numbed. Left us cold when you were just a baby. He suffered shell shock," she added, as if that accounted for the soldier heading over the hills, going AWOL from family responsibilities and child support.

In the photo, Emmett didn't seem to be suffering. He appeared happy, vibrant, glad to be alive. However, Clark nearly died of shock when his father showed up in Prineville. The doctors were furious at the old man for almost killing his son just by his unexpected appearance.

Recognizing his father in the hospital, Clark felt the world slide—

the giddy falling away from the tree. Morphine buoyed him up. Clark extended his maimed right hand—three fingers chopped at the second knuckles, all swollen and seamed with black stitches.

Emmett grabbed the left. "Southpaw, just like your old man."

Clark slipped back into the morphine haze but knew the visit was real enough after he found a water-ringed twenty-dollar bill underneath his bedside glass and a scrawled note: "Buy some cigars, when you can light 'em."

"That's the price of fatherhood," he said later. "About a dollar and a quarter a year." But the note struck Clark's bloodcord, and he vowed to look up the old man once he got out of the wheelchair. He waited many years, making him twenty-five when he drove Wade and Payette to the hardscrabble settlement of Ruby.

. . .

Skiffs of March snow surrounded the yellow pine stands, and a harsh wind scoured the basalt hillsides. The late winter sun shone with a hard white light. Gray smoke rose from one of the bachelor trailers on the frayed edge of town. Clark knew what Payette was thinking: The shabby chartreuse-and-silver trailer in this forlorn landscape resembled the cramped Tlingit houses in Angoon, the picker shacks she had known in Hood River when her father lost his fishing boat and was reduced to orchard work.

"Look at that Jeep!" Wade said. "Cool."

An old Willy with torn seats rested in the two-track driveway blocked by a bronze El Camino with black-and-gold California license plates.

"Out-of-town company," Clark said.

"Maybe this isn't the best time to visit." Payette paused. "Are you sure he lives here in this god-awful place?"

Clark shut off the engine. "My old man visited me once in the hospital. Now I'm paying him back."

"We better not stay long," she said. "Don't plan on spending the night."

"Just going to have a family picnic," Clark said, referring to the large wooden cable spools set up as lawn furniture.

The big man who opened the trailer door resembled Clark's young father blown up to six and a half feet, three hundred pounds. "Hello, Clark. Haven't seen you in a while." He spoke with nonchalance, as if Clark had dropped by last week, but Clark had never seen his half-brother. "Furman," the big man said three times as he shook hands with each of them. "I'm Clark's brother."

"This is my wife Payette and our boy Wade."

Furman nodded at Wade. He gave Payette a long look. "It's good to meet the little lady." When he followed them inside, his weight made the trailer jiggle.

· · ·

Emmett sat on a wooden chair watching a snowy picture on a small black-and-white Zenith. His tanned limbs were as gnarled as a wind-swept juniper. "You from the Jehovah's Witness?" he asked, squinting.

"It's Clark and his wife," Furman said.

"Hello, Emmett." Clark held his voice steady. "My wife, Payette. This is Wade." He took the boy's shoulder, but he squirmed loose.

"You met Furman," his father said after a minute. "It's a damn re-union." He stood and shook hands with each of them. "I never thought I'd live to see the day."

"You're lucky you caught me home," Emmett said after sitting. "I just got out of the Vets' Hospital. Walla Walla and then Boise for more tests. Fever, sweats, chills. Every bone ached."

"What was it?" Payette asked. "Asian flu?"

"With the Vets', you never know," he said. "They called it Colorado spotted fever and turned me out. I dug out a couple swollen ticks last trapping season. They crawled off the coyotes, I guess."

To save on propane the old man was burning a lot of Ponderosa in a small circular heating stove lined with aluminum sheets to reflect heat. Emmett was dressed in thermal underwear, a wool shirt, fleece-lined vest, and a Carhartt jacket. "Some days I can't get warm. Bug is still working me over."

Clark heard the toilet flush, and after a minute, a small nervous woman came out of the bathroom. She had ratted dyed black hair up in a bouffant but the top peak was mashed. Behind glasses decorated with rhinestones, bloodshot brown eyes flitted over each of them. She smiled but seemed ill at ease.

"This is my wife, Jami," Furman announced, clearly proud of her. "Here's my brother Clark, the college professor. His wife, Payette. That skinny fella is their boy."

"Goodness, it's nice to meet you. Forgive me for being a little spacey," she said. "We drove straight through from California on No-Doz and I'm still high as a hawk." She paused. "For heaven's sakes, didn't anybody offer you something to drink? What's wrong with you, Furman Woods?" She crossed to the refrigerator and selected beer and soft drinks for everyone, then took a chair. "You must all be parched. And Emmett keeps this trailer boiling." She frowned at Furman. "I can't believe your backwardness sometimes."

He grinned. "I got you to watch over me, honey."

"He'll be my death," she said to Payette. "But the Lord won't let me go easy."

"I'm a heavy burden," Furman said, smiling at his own joke.

Jami ignored him. "The thing is, Clark, as soon as I knew your father was feeling puny, I decided Furman needed to take his vacation time. We hustled up to help. Furman and Dad have been splitting wood, greasing the traps, fixing up that old Jeep. Even been talking about going fishing, once the ice is broke up on the John Day."

"We could eat a mess of trout or a spring steelhead," Furman said.

"I knew our visit would give Dad a lift. I'm a care provider for the elderly and I know a little about cheer. I sure do." Her head bobbed up and down as she talked. She turned slightly. "What do you do, Paulette?"

"Actually, it's Payette. Right now, I'm an assistant manager of an art gallery. We specialize in Indian art. Northwest tribes, primarily."

"I knew you were Indian," Jami said. "You've got such high cheekbones. I'm one-sixteenth Cherokee myself. My grandmother's side. So are you Cherokee, too?"

Payette shook her head. "My mother's Tlingit from Angoon. My dad's mostly Tlingit and a little Umatilla. His people fished up near Sitka."

"That's sure fascinating," Jami said. "Maybe you can write those tribes down for me. I don't think I can remember. I've been diagnosed with a little dyslexia."

Furman slapped his knee. "I don't know much about the art game. But it must pay pretty good. I've seen the prices on some Indian art. Too rich for my blood."

"You can spot bargains if you've got the eye," Payette said. "I like finding new artists. A lot of the young North Coast Indians are copying traditional methods. They make beautiful masks and dancing tunics."

"I'm in law enforcement," Furman said. "We get a lot of Indians."

Furman was a jailer in a California county facility. "I think of myself as my brother's keeper." He grinned. "I keep those boys from running like rabbits when they get itchy-footed." He talked slowly and Clark remembered how his aunt Manila told him Furman had gotten a little slow after being hit by a car speeding through Ruby. "Sometimes I get suicide watch," he said. "Men and women both. Have to play cards or checkers all night. One was a judge's wife in a divorce deal. She shot him five times with a twenty-two—that's how much she wanted to keep their sons." He shook his head. "She should have used hollow points."

His eyes twinkled. "Hey, you people like guns? Look what I just bought to pack fishing. Never know when a bear might show." Furman reached into a kitchen drawer and unholstered a Colt Trooper .357 Magnum. He spun the cylinder and dry-fired toward the refrigerator.

Jami bent over covering her ears. "Put that damn thing away, Furman Luke Woods. You know I'm nonviolent."

He handed the pistol toward Payette, clearly trying to impress her. "You a scaredy cat?" he said. "Kinda big caliber for a little lady."

She took the pistol and broke open the cylinder, checking to make sure the chambers were empty. She cocked the hammer and pointed out the window, pulling slowly on the curved trigger until the hammer released with a dry click. "You'll shoot straighter if you cock the hammer first. It's hard to hold a Colt Trooper steady on a full trigger pull." She handed the pistol back to Furman butt first.

He studied Payette. "The little lady knows her way around firearms. Better not go catting, Clark. Anyway, don't get caught."

Clark watched Payette sip her soda. She had been deer and moose hunting with her relatives in Alaska. Once she had shot a marauding brown bear near Angoon. "I don't plan to."

Clark couldn't have explained all his reasons for driving six hours to see his father. Part curiosity, part blood tie, and wanting to show the old man he had come out okay even though Emmett had left him and his mother flat. By showing up, he was proving something. He had married one of the prettiest women in Oregon and he was taking care of a tough-luck boy. So part of it was saying "in-your-face" to the old man. But he felt something else, too. Not love, but an old blood hunger for some kind of knowledge about his father, even if he was a strange semi-hermit who lived miles from nowhere and trapped coyotes. "He's in the fur business," he used to joke when people asked him. Let them figure out what it meant. "My parents wholesale fruit and manage orchards," Payette had countered, meaning they picked crops in Oregon after they moved south from Alaska.

Emmett's knotty pine paneling held a calendar from Oscar's Sporting Goods depicting a cougar about to pounce on a bighorn sheep. Deer and elk seasons were highlighted with red pen. Nails held Jami and Furman's wedding picture, a postcard of the Tillamook Lighthouse and Wade's school photograph.

Clark had sent the postcard on his honeymoon shortly after he took a job at Two Rivers Community College. He had intended to send Emmett a notice of his marriage, although he didn't want the old man showing up for the ceremony because in recent years his mother never talked about his father without resentment. Later, when he and Payette brought Wade from Alaska, Clark sent the boy's photo, scrawling on the back: "Your foster grandson."

Emmett watched Wade out the window as the boy pretended to drive the battered Jeep. "I don't like the way he's reefing on that gearshift," he said. "You boys better go see about him."

Furman stood quickly, but Clark took his time. He wasn't moving just because Emmett thought it was a good idea.

"We better have dinner soon anyway," Jami said. "I feel like making my famous oyster stew. Furman, why don't you and Clark go up to the store and get some oysters? Take the boy. That way Payette and Dad and I can talk and get a little better acquainted."

At first, Clark thought he had heard wrong. He couldn't imagine oysters in Ruby.

· · ·

Four people greeted Furman on the quarter-mile walk to the Ruby market. "Hey, big fella," one said. "I still remember those three touchdowns you scored against Condon."

Furman introduced Clark and Wade each time. "This is my brother, the college professor, and his boy." He never mentioned the townspeople's names and later told Clark he couldn't remember. "I never forget a face, though. That's a good trait in law enforcement. Some guys use eight or ten names, but they keep the same nose and eyes."

"What did you think you'd do when you were out of high school?" Clark asked. "Police work?"

"Move to Baker where you still got mountains. Get a job in the mill. Buy a Firebird. A bunch of hunting and fishing stuff." He seemed excited for a moment, then said, "But the mill's cut back. How about you, Clark?"

Keep it simple, Clark thought. "First car I bought was a Camaro."

"Six or eight? What kind of tranny?"

"Eight," Clark said. "A three twenty-seven. It was quick, though. Four on the floor."

"That's what I wanted," Furman said. "But I got an El Camino so I could haul stuff. That little pickup came in handy because after I finished with the Marines I got into a special program for law enforcement at Blue Mountain Community College. Then I got that job in Weed. Met Jami when she came to visit her boyfriend. He was stealing money and jewels from the people in the old folks' home." He shrugged his shoulders. "Can you believe it, picking on helpless old people? When he got out, I run him off to another county." He paused. "Jami's in a damn good field. Everybody's growing old. By the year two thousand, half the U.S. population will be over sixty-five. Dad's there already."

· · ·

A forlorn-looking sheetmetal grasshopper about the length of a pickup stood in a weedy lot across the street from the Ruby Market.

"Look, Dad," Wade said. "I never seen a bug that big."

"You should come for Grasshopper Daze," Furman told Clark. "We got a parade, rodeo, little fairgrounds, barbecue, duck derby. Hell, people come all the way from the Tri-Cities. One year the governor flew in by helicopter. It's always the last week in July."

Wade ran over and climbed on the grasshopper's thorax, then started kicking its wings with his boots. "Hey, cut it out," Clark said.

"He can't hurt that thing," Furman said. "Half the kids in town heave rocks at that glitterbug."

· · ·

Near the checkout counter, heat lamps were warming roasted chicken, burritos, and jo jos. Clark wrinkled his nose at the stale grease smell.

"We get great burritos in Weed," Furman said. "It's the Mexicans." In his huge hands, the quarts of fresh oysters seemed small. He inspected their labels. "Jami's oyster stew—that's a feast."

"Are they okay?" Clark asked. He didn't want to get sick from eating bad seafood, and Ruby was a long way from the ocean.

Furman squinted at the expiration dates. "Good and cold, they keep a couple weeks. We got three days left."

"Beats two," Clark said, still trying to figure how the almost-fresh oysters found their way to Ruby. He carried two six-packs of beer, one of 7UP, and a screw-top bottle of white wine for Payette.

Clark set his drinks on the counter, figuring he could take any extra liquor back with him.

"Charge this grub to Emmett, would you, Betsy?" Furman said, and the girl behind the counter nodded. She was pretty in a small-town way, and Clark wondered if she was the owner's daughter.

She bagged the groceries. Winking at Furman, she said, "Just pay by the first." To Clark she added, "In Ruby, no one's a stranger twice. Hurry back."

When the men stepped outside, Wade was whacking at the grasshopper. With each strike of his two-by-four, patches of ice fell off the insect.

"Stop it, Wade! You're like a damn vandal," Clark said. "Sticks can be dangerous."

"That silly old grasshopper broke up a lot of marriages," Furman said. "Probably cost me my first."

"How's that?"

"Well, you go to county fairs and rodeos towing that bug behind your Ford half ton and it makes you feel a little special. Then you have to stay awake nights watching so no clodhopper from Condon gets the bright idea of painting it purple or writing 'DDT' on it. You start thinking you're important, see, and you get the swelled head."

"I hadn't thought about it," Clark said.

"Sure. Small-town girls start hanging around, like Betsy there, and you chat them up. Let's say maybe they get a little flirty-skirty. Harmless enough. But sooner or later, a wild one shows up. Trouble with a capital *T*. That's how it goes. Like I said. The first Mrs. Furman was the jealous type."

He thumped Clark's back suddenly. "Thank God for unanswered prayers. I got down on my knees—imagine a big man like me—and prayed for Melva to come back. But she took off with a sugarbeet farmer from Idaho. Had himself a brand-new cherry red Thunderbird. That was Melva's favorite color."

Pulling a quarter from his pocket, Furman told Wade, "You run ahead. Tell Jami to boil the milk. Uncle Furman's coming with the oysters and beer."

As Wade ran off, Furman chuckled. "Boy's fast as hell. Seems eager to please, though. You got your hands full, brother. Payette's a looker and plenty smart. Beauty and brains make a tough combination." He whistled. "Tricky to keep in line."

Clark resented the brother-to-brother remark and the advice. He didn't need a jail guard telling him how to run his life. Even so, he wondered what had happened to Emmett and his own mother. She could have been one of the small-town girls who stopped to admire the grasshopper. Maybe fighting World War II, trapping coyotes and squiring the grasshopper around had been the biggest events in the old man's life. Of course running off on Clark's mother, abandoning both of them, counted. Somehow, payback had occurred when Emmett's second wife, Furman's mother, ran off with a younger man to California—where all loose objects rolled. He wanted to mention it now, but sized up his half-brother's heft and decided to drop it. Instead, he said, "No shit. All women can be tricky."

When they were still a block from the trailer, he heard a dull thunk and then another. As they got closer, he saw the old man and Wade outside throwing a hatchet into a big block of Ponderosa pine.

Emmett had nailed a Red Man tobacco can lid to the wood as a target. Scars were visible around the lid, but no one had hit it directly. Skids in the snow marked wild throws.

"When I'm through teaching the kid, he can nail a coyote at fifty yards," Emmett said.

Furman handed the sacks to Jami inside the trailer and took off his blue quilted jacket. "Let me show you how it's done." Seizing the hatchet, he let fly. It grazed the stump and skittered another forty feet before clinking against a piece of basalt.

The boy retrieved Furman's wild throw like a bird dog after a stick.

"You're going to wreck the hatchet head," Emmett said. "Dull makes it useless for kindling."

"That damn thing's heavy," Furman said. "But I'm starting to warm up."

Clark limbered his right shoulder. At first he couldn't remember the last time he'd thrown a hatchet, but then he recalled the Fourth of July celebration when he longshored in Ketchikan. Sugar Henry, a Tlingit dockworker with no teeth, had won the hatchet-throwing contest, beating all the lumberjacks. His victory had surprised everyone except Sugar and Clark, who had seen him work lumber loads with a pickaroon. "I carve a lot of totems," Sugar explained later as they worked swing gang. "Raven, Eagle, Bear. Got to make them just right or the old spirits get mad. Sometimes I'll take a break—throw the hatchet to let off steam."

As he warmed up, Clark remembered the afternoon Sugar had taught him to throw. The Tlingit never mentioned Clark's chopped fingers. "Spit on the hickory handle to reduce friction. Close one eye and hold your breath. Turn sideways." Sugar showed his dark gums. "Pretend that fucking target is the deck boss and throw hard. You'll never miss." Taking a sugar cube from his shirt pocket, he pressed it between his lips.

Now Clark threw. The hatchet stuck, quivering in the soft golden pine. He had nicked the Red Man lid.

"Beginner's luck," Furman said.

"He's only got half a hand," Emmett said.

Jami stood in the doorway, her arms crossed, an anxious look on her face. Clark could tell how dead set she was against this kind of activity. *This is folk art,* he thought—Ruby ax throwing—just like the miners in West Virginia who tied their wrists together and then beat each other to death with ball-peen hammers. Payette's face appeared briefly at the window. She seemed amused.

After supper, Emmett added four Ponderosa chunks to the fire and studied the flames. Sparks drifted up the flue and popped against the screen. Clark felt hot and unbuttoned the front of his flannel shirt. Emmett returned to the kitchen table and opened a fresh 7UP. "I thought Payette and Wade might like to hear a story," he said.

"Sure," Payette said. "But I'm so full it might put me to sleep."

"Not this one," Emmett said. Firelight played in his eyes, and when he spoke, he reminded Clark of the storytellers he had heard in Saxman, the Tlingit settlement south of Ketchikan. "George Stubblefield and I were way up Copper Creek, building fence," Emmett said. "Old man Nisbet got all stove up and couldn't ride his horse into the deep canyons anymore to round up stock. So he had hired me and George to fence off some canyons.

"We did it right—split the juniper posts, hand-stretched the wire, looped and stapled each strand. We slept in an Army surplus tent George had. Fifty miles round trip to Ruby, so we only came back once because George forgot his ulcer medicine.

"At nights, George went down and fished the deep pools in Copper Creek. Caught some nice-sized brookies. He mentioned seeing some trees knocked over in a funny way, but we figured it was blowdown. Sometimes those winter storms get wild up there and the wind shrieks like a banshee.

"One morning, just about two, we heard this loud thump-thump-thump way down the canyon. We got up to take a look but it didn't figure—something making that loud stomping noise in the dead of night. 'Maybe a rock slide with a big boulder banging downhill,' George said. It didn't sound like that exactly but we were tuckered and just went back to bed."

"You never heard anything like that before?" Jami asked.

"Never," Emmett said. "No sir." He shook his head for emphasis.

"The next night we heard the thumping again, closer this time. George loaded the lever-action Winchester he kept around for camp meat. That rifle was so old there was more blue than barrel.

"'Don't get excited, George,' I said. I got my big lantern from outside and we took a look around the camp, the top of the canyon. Nothing.

"Then George said kind of quiet, 'I never heard rock slides two nights in a row.'"

"What happened then?" Furman tugged his ear. "Damn but Dad tells a good story! I love hearing him. Don't you, Clark?"

Clark hesitated. "He's something, all right."

Emmett continued. "We got back to sleep, fitful, keeping one eye open—and about four A.M. heard this awful screech close to camp—then real loud thumping again.

"'A bear's got something,' George said. 'Ripping it apart.'

"I flashed that light around our fence line and then I saw these yellow eyes—not anything like a bear's. And right then I smelled a horrible stink. God awful—even my rotten fish coyote bait doesn't smell that bad.

"George might have been about to shoot, but he lowered his gun. 'It's the devil,' he said. 'The devil's come. That smell must be brimstone.'

"'No sir,' I said. 'That's a Bigfoot. Put the rifle down, George.' I tell you, it was odd. Here I've been trapping all my life—caught everything except a cougar and a wolverine, but I didn't want anything happening to Bigfoot.

"I shone the light back in that direction, but it was gone. We heard it crashing away. George climbed in the pickup, goosed the engine, and turned on the heater. I couldn't get him to come out.

"'Let's go home,' he said. 'Right now!'

"'Wait till morning, George,' I said. 'Then we'll see.'

"Dawn came in about an hour and you could tell where that old boy had knocked over a tree maybe eighty yards from camp. I finally coaxed George out of the truck, but he wouldn't set down that rifle. 'You can't stop a Bigfoot with that peashooter,' I said.

"'If I wing you, I can outrun you to the truck,' George said. 'You can deal with the devil or Bigfoot or the mad bear—whatever the hell that is.' We went over by the broken tree. The ground was all tore up—but you couldn't see a distinct track—not like those plaster casts they show on TV.

"When it was light, I found a tuft of hair on a strand of barbed wire. He must've stepped right over that thing but snagged his crotch. The hair was a funny reddish brown color, just a little yellow thrown in. I put it in some wax paper and buttoned it in my shirt pocket. Later I showed the hair to Ralston Phelps, the forest ranger for this district.

"'Maybe a cinnamon-colored grizzly,' he said.

"'This hair's lots coarser,' I said.

"'I'll send it to the state lab.'

"'No,' I said. After that, I gave it to George and he showed it to Cora. When he died, it got lost."

"So you don't have any real evidence?" Payette said.

Emmett shrugged. "I know what we saw. My word's good."

Furman slapped his knee. "I wish I'd been there with my big old H&H Magnum. Kablooey! I'd have taken him out. Hell, we used to think that grasshopper was a big deal. Imagine getting a Bigfoot. I'd freeze his ass, get a big refer truck, then chauffeur him to Reno, Vegas. Wouldn't the women stare though? I might have to get a big old fig leaf to cover that thing that ain't a foot. Everybody'd pay to see *that*!"

"Furman, you're getting carried away." Jami pretended to hit his shoulder. "I'd like to go to San Francisco, New York City."

"You should have sent it off to the state department of wildlife," Clark said. "Get some specialists out here." He'd heard a lot of Bigfoot stories, and he was skeptical of them all.

"Why would I do that?" Emmett asked. "Who wants a bunch of professors running around mucking things up? This is some of the prettiest country I know."

"Don't you want to be rich?" Furman asked.

"Not really," Emmett said. "But I could use a pickup."

Wade had stayed calm during Emmett's story but leaned toward the old man, listening. Emmett reached across the table and thumped the boy's shoulder. "I'll bet this little wrangler could out-wrestle a big stinky Sasquatch," he said. "You got Bigfoot up there in Alaska? All Indians got some monster or another."

"We got whales," Wade said. "Nothing's bigger than a whale."

.   .   .

Squashed next to Furman at the small Formica table, Clark suddenly became claustrophobic. His T-shirt seemed tight around his neck, and he started gulping overheated air. Everyone was too close. He smelled Furman's sweat, Jami's heavy perfume. She was talking about a stroke victim when he shoved back his chair.

"I got to get some fresh air," he said. "Feeling woozy."

"You look peaked," Furman said.

"Stick out your tongue," Jami ordered. "You do look way over yonder. I hope these oysters weren't tainted."

Furman wasn't moving, so Clark stuck out his tongue.

"It's all coated," Jami said.

"He had two bowls of stew," Payette said. "You made it with evaporated milk."

"I just need to walk a minute," Clark said. "Move, Furman."

"Hell, we were all just getting comfortable," Furman said. "I thought Dad might tell another story." He stood.

Grabbing his coat, Clark left the trailer. Outside, it was dark. Venus hung above the basalt peaks of the Strawberry Mountains.

"You all right, Clark?" Emmett asked, following him outside. "I brought you a cap and some gloves. Ninety percent of the heat goes right out the top of your head and I'd say it's about ten below freezing."

Clark put on the hat but jammed the gloves in his pocket.

They walked past the edge of town beyond the last lights. The old man said, "I was stuck in the Vets' during elk season. Otherwise I'd send you home with a couple of good elk roasts. Some steaks, too."

"Thanks for the thought," Clark said. He was feeling better.

"Sure," Emmett said. "Did you get your elk this year?"

"No," Clark said after a minute. Then he lied. "I put in for a special hunt in the Starkey Unit, but I didn't get a permit."

"I drew one for Murderer's Creek," Emmett said. "Couldn't use the damn thing. What are you shooting, anyway?"

"A thirty-ought-six Remington pump."

"You should shoot a bolt action," his dad said. "They're more accurate. I knew that even before I went into the service."

"Maybe." Clark exhaled, watching his breath rise then evaporate in the dark. The pump seemed fine to him. He had killed six deer and one elk, but he wasn't keen on hunting big game anymore.

"Did you know I was in the Battle of the Bulge?" Emmett asked. "I served under Patton."

"Grace has a picture of you wearing a uniform." Clark didn't mention his father was holding him.

Emmett nodded. "That was a long time ago. I thought about writing it all down, my service stuff, but I never got around to it." He paused, as if waiting for a question, but Clark kept silent.

Emmett didn't speak either. He stopped and brushed snow from a granite rock. After sitting, he took a pack of Chesterfields out of his jacket. "Don't tell Jami about the smokes or she'd have a conniption." He offered one to Clark, and he took it, even though he didn't smoke.

The old man lit both cigarettes with a cheap lighter, then slipped the pack and lighter in his pocket. "I plugged two Germans, maybe three. The last one slid behind a rock and my unit had to move out, so I couldn't tell." He toed a pine branch. "Sometimes you'll strike a rattlesnake hard, but it slithers way deep in the rockpile. You don't know if you finished him or not. The other two Germans stayed down for good."

"I know about the rattler," Clark said.

"Now it seems like a movie," Emmett said. "I used to watch a lot of war movies. John Wayne. Audie Murphy. But in the movies, guys shout or take a long time to die. These three were quite a ways off, in an open field, except for the one rock. I rested my rifle on a tree limb and squeezed off five shots. Those Germans were just dark humps in the snow. No sound but the wind."

"Did it bother you?" Clark asked. "Grace said you had shell shock." He realized his mother had probably invented a reason for his father's taking off, but he wanted to ask.

"Not really," Emmett said. "They killed a bunch of our boys. One played football for Heppner. Some surrendered, and they killed them, too. Patton told us to fight like wildcats." He stood and brushed snow off his pants. "I killed fifty-seven elk so far," he said. "Plugging those fellows wasn't even like that. You never got up close. You never got blood on your hands."

He stamped his feet. "I'm not planning on going yet," he said. "But I want you to have my rifle when I cash in. It's a Winchester bolt action. Just remember it shoots a couple inches high if you're closer than fifty yards."

"What about Furman?" Clark asked.

"You're the oldest," Emmett said. "I figure it goes to you."

Clark didn't know how to tell the old man he didn't hunt deer anymore. And he didn't care about Emmett's rifle or the old man's gesture. He had come this far without Emmett's help.

"All right," he said. He figured when Emmett died, Furman and Jami would get there first and take whatever they wanted. Clark was relieved that Emmett hadn't asked him to go hunting. *I only hunt with people I trust,* Clark thought.

3

Amherst, 1977

When the doorbell rang at 11 P.M., Clark saw two large men standing in the rain. He recognized the one in the blue raincoat as the police officer he'd seen by the culvert. Hatless, the man hunched his shoulders, trying to keep the rain from running down his neck and inside his collar. The older man wore an olive jacket and a brown tweed cap. Both had muddy shoes and pants legs.

"I'm Sergeant Hawley from University of Massachusetts, Public Safety," the man in the blue raincoat said. "This is Lieutenant Cooper from the Commonwealth State Police. Okay if we come in a minute? We're here about the Kagita girl."

"Of course," Clark said, opening the door. He wondered what they wanted. "How is she? I've got a boy myself so I was plenty worried. Officers, this is my mother, Grace Woods."

"I'm very pleased to meet you," she said. "What an ordeal."

Cooper and Hawley nodded at Clark's mother. "This is the right place then," Hawley said. "All these apartments are kind of confusing. Mostly, I deal with trouble in the dorms. Attempted suicides. Assault. That kind of thing." He sneezed, then took a big yellow handkerchief out of his pocket and blew his nose. "What a night. Miserable weather."

"I could get you some tea," Clark's mother said. "Take off the chill."

They shook their heads. "We just had some coffee," Cooper said.

"Any more drinks and I'll be up all night." He looked down at his shoes and the muddy traces on the carpet. "Sorry about the mess. We're making some general inquiries," he said. "Something like this, we hate to see it happen at the university."

"How's the little girl doing?" Grace asked. "I hope she's back home safe and sound."

"I went out a couple times," Clark said. "No one seemed to know much."

He and his mother sat on the couch, but the men selected wooden kitchen chairs. Neither took off his coat.

Cooper leaned forward. "We hate to bring unpleasant news, Mr. Woods, Mrs. Woods. I'm sorry to say the little girl didn't live."

Clark was stunned. "What happened? I saw her legs kick when they took her to the ambulance. Did she go into shock?"

Grace moved her hand to her mouth, then took it away. "Her poor parents. My heart goes out to them." She dropped both hands to her lap. "It's just so sad."

"I swear I saw her legs move," Clark insisted. "Damn it to hell!"

Hawley shook his head. "Maybe the ambulance people jostled her. I doubt she was alive when they fished her out of the water." He took out a pen and notebook. "I know this is difficult, but could you please tell us a little about the Kagitas? The sooner we follow up on a tragedy the better. Was the mother in the habit of leaving the girl by herself?"

"What?" Clark was still bewildered by the news. She couldn't have been in the water that long. He felt sick that he hadn't posted someone to watch the culvert or stayed himself. "What did you ask?"

"Did the mother leave the girl alone in the playground?" Hawley asked.

God, Clark thought. *Were they trying to blame the mother? She must be wild with grief and guilt. What kind of crap was this?*

"Not really," he said.

"I'd call her a good mother," Grace said. "She keeps that girl neat as a pin." She caught herself. "Kept her. Spit and polish, not like some of the people around here."

"Anyway, Mrs. Kagita can see right out her kitchen window," Clark said.

"So she did leave her in the playground all by herself while she was inside? Maybe watching television, going to the bathroom." Cooper seemed eager for the answer.

"Not that much," Clark said. "She kept a pretty close watch."

"Would you say she left her alone for ten minutes at a time? Five?" Cooper balanced his tweed cap on his knee. "Shorter? Longer?"

"I don't know," Clark said. "Not more than five usually."

"One of her neighbors described Mrs. Kagita as pretty quiet," Hawley said after writing something down. "This is a new country for her and all. Must get pretty hard."

"I've talked with her several times," Grace said. "She doesn't speak much English, of course. But I wouldn't call her depressed, not at all. She has a lovely smile, actually, and she just doted on that girl." Her brow furrowed. "Of course, she was a little lonely. Who wouldn't be in a strange new place?"

"My wife's from Tennessee," Hawley said. "She gets plenty homesick even though my boys keep her busy."

He leaned forward and slipped the handkerchief into his rear pocket. "Mrs. Kagita. Well, you can imagine how it hit her. We've had to put her on suicide watch."

"You can't blame her," Clark said. "It was a goddamn tragic accident. Somebody left the gate open—kids are in and out, in and out. Yukiko wandered off. There should be a fence so they can't fall off the culvert."

"At this point, we don't know if she fell," Hawley said. "We're trying to determine exactly what did happen."

"She fell," Clark said. Surely they didn't think the mother was to blame.

"I feel just terrible," Grace said. "I believe I'll have some tea myself." She stood and walked stiffly toward the kitchen.

"I expect they'll put up a fence now." Hawley consulted his notes. "Mr. Kagita said a girl named Michelle Scavese sometimes watches her, but she didn't today."

Clark nodded. "Michelle's with her father this weekend. The parents are split. She's in Lowell."

"Now your boy, Wade. Did he play with the little girl today?"

"I don't think so," Clark said. "She's too young for him." He paused. "Mom? Was Wade with Yukiko at all today?"

"No," she said from the kitchen. "He was riding his bike until he got so muddy. After that he was in the fields playing with the other boys. His clothes are just caked with mud."

"You know those bikes," Clark said. "No fenders. Throws a streak of mud right up his back. That's the part he likes best."

Hawley nodded. "Tell me about it. I got three boys. Cooper here, he's a bachelor." He looked at Clark. "So you think maybe one of the kids left the gate open."

Clark nodded. "Seems likely. When I got back, Mrs. Kagita was standing beside the open gate holding Yukiko's raincoat."

"And where were you before, sir?"

"Dummerston, Vermont. The apple pie festival. I got back about five-thirty, I guess. Mrs. Kagita was looking for Yukiko then."

"Did you help her, sir?" Cooper moved his cap to his other knee.

"Sure. Wade was playing down in the weeds with the other boys, chasing rabbits with a stick. Maybe there wasn't a rabbit. He gets notions sometimes." Clark scratched his chin. He had been in a hurry that morning and rushed shaving. "I may as well say this. I checked out by that culvert first thing when I got back from Vermont. She wasn't there."

Hawley stopped writing a second. "What time would you say that was again?"

"Close to five-thirty. It was getting dark. Some of the older kids play there and it's slippery and wet. I just took a look, but she must have wandered back there later. I feel terrible. If I had put somebody there to watch . . ."

"If it makes you feel better, she was probably already in the swamp," Hawley said. "Murky water. Getting dark. She'd be easy to miss."

"No," Clark said. "I don't think so. I fish all the time and see plenty of water."

"My son's a teacher," Grace said, clearly proud. "But he also writes stories about fishing."

Hawley wrote something down. "Anyway, then what did you do?"

"Well, like I said, Wade was out in the fields so I got him and told him to help me look. The older boys took off, too. I started going house to house—maybe for fifteen or twenty minutes . . . and then I heard the sirens."

"You and Wade and the boys were looking all that time?"

"That's right. We took a quick look farther out—near where that second drainage ditch comes in. Wade found a bobber there."

"A what?" Cooper asked.

"A bobber. A yellow and red fishing bobber. He's excited about going fishing."

Grace shook her head. "That boy loves water," she said. "But nothing's better than playing in mud. I had to change his clothes earlier. Now he's got another set dirty. He's so active."

"I'm curious about the boy's actual mother," Hawley said. "Where is she? Are you divorced or separated?"

Clark didn't like the question. "It's a confusing story," Clark said. "He's my ex-wife's cousin. When she left, he stayed with me."

Hawley paused. "Is he from the Commonwealth of Massachusetts originally?"

"No. He's Tlingit from Alaska. So was my ex-wife. The tribe let us have him when his father was killed. His real mother's an alcoholic."

"You got to spell Tlingit," Hawley said, and Clark did.

Hawley kept writing but Cooper's eyes glinted. "It's a peculiar setup," he said. "Real peculiar."

Clark shrugged, trying to appear nonchalant. He'd never bothered telling the Alaskan or Oregon authorities Payette had left him. "My ex-wife's back in school getting an advanced degree. So he's staying with me for now."

"You're in school, too," Cooper pointed out. "That's a lot to handle."

"I've got it covered," Clark said.

"I'm helping my son out," Grace said and brightened. "I took early retirement just to watch over little Wade. I was tired of working anyway. Thirty-six years."

"Is that right?" Hawley said. "Congratulations." He turned toward Clark. "Just a couple more questions, sir, and this one is tough." He paused. "When your mother described Wade as pretty active, would you say he was hostile in any way, that is, aggressive toward others?"

Clark swallowed. "No," he said flatly. "Absolutely not."

Cooper worked his mouth a little. "See, we were talking to one of your neighbors earlier and he said his boy and yours got in a mix-up over a bike. He told us Wade smacked his kid pretty hard."

Clark flared. "That's Russell Lemke, and his kid is spoiled rotten. The neighborhood tattletale."

Cooper pressed. "The thing is, Mr. Woods, this witness says your boy Wade also tried to push his boy off that culvert a couple days ago. Tried pretty hard, according to the kid."

Clark sat a little straighter. He hadn't heard about that. When he glanced at his mother, her face showed surprise.

"Officers," she said. "Wade was as good as gold all day. He rode his bike. He played in the fields with the boys having a grand time. As for hitting somebody over a bicycle, you must think back to when you were boys. My brother Roy shot my mother in the stomach with a BB once because she wanted to take away his air rifle. He kept shooting the neighbors' cat. Roy aimed right through the kitchen screen door. It drew blood, even though she wore an apron over her dress."

Hawley quit writing and cocked his head to one side.

Cooper placed his cap on the couch. "I hope he got a thrashing."

"And then some. When my father got home, he whipped Roy good and threw him in the chicken coop. It was dark and the chickens all flew at him pecking peanut butter off his chin. Those chickens were wild about peanut butter—it was the chunky type. No. Now that I think about it, it couldn't have been chunky. But Roy had red welts on his face from those chicken pecks and more welts on his behind."

Hawley looked at her with curiosity. "You understand we're not accusing the boy of anything. Even so, Mrs. Kagita was pretty adamant in saying Wade was responsible. She was extremely upset, you understand, and the doctor gave her a shot, but she kept repeating Wade's name. Anyway, we'd like to talk with the boy. Clear things up."

"He's asleep," Clark said. *What did she mean by responsible?* he wondered. *Leaving the gate open?* "He's taken his Ritalin and he's out cold."

"Rit-a-lin. Now that's for hyperactivity, isn't it," Cooper said. "Too much activity."

"It calms him some," Grace said.

"He's not much more active than most kids," Clark said. "The doctors say he gets too much stimulation. After playing hard all day, he's usually out like a light."

"Could you wake him?" Cooper asked.

"I doubt it," Clark said.

"Give it a try," Hawley said. He took out his handkerchief again and blew his nose. "Damn, but I'm soaked. When I get home, I'm going to take some vitamin C."

Clark didn't like the idea of disturbing Wade. If he awakened suddenly, he might become frightened, say crazy things. On the other hand, Clark felt that if the police officers saw the boy—his small stature and long thin limbs—they'd realize he wasn't threatening and not insist on talking with him. He was also pretty confident the boy wouldn't rouse from his sleep. "Whatever you say." Standing, Clark stepped toward the bedroom. "He's in here."

Both men followed as far as the bedroom door. Cooper's loafers squeaked.

Wade was wearing his "Sesame Street" pajamas and had kicked back the covers, including the raven blanket that served as his comforter. Grace had resewn the red felt bird onto the blue wool after Clark brought the blanket down from Alaska.

"Hey, Wade," Clark said, bending over the bed. "Can you wake up? A couple of men are here." *Don't wake up,* he thought. Placing his hand on the boy's shoulder he made a show of jiggling it, but tried to absorb most of the movement with his wrist.

The boy stirred but didn't waken. He said something that sounded like "fish."

The two men stood in the doorway, blocking the kitchen light. Cooper stepped into the bedroom but Hawley shook his head.

"Are you too sleepy to get up?" Clark leaned over the boy as if to protect him. He used his body as a shield, blocking Cooper's access.

Wade rose and threw his arms around Clark. "A big fish ate my bobber." For a second he seemed to be waking up, but Clark willed him back to sleep. Wade sank onto the bed again and rolled over toward the wall.

"We can talk to him tomorrow, I guess," Hawley said. "How old is he?"

"Nine," he said, knowing the boy was small and seemed younger.

"We need to take his clothes and boots," Cooper said.

Clark flushed with anger and shook his head. "I think you've gone far enough. How about a search warrant? I already told you guys I looked below the culvert and she wasn't there. I fish out west, big water. Yukiko wasn't there. Are you listening?"

Hawley acted concerned. "I got it all down in my notes, just like you said, but you can understand our position, too. See, this is university property you're on, so we have the right to be here. We're just asking for your cooperation."

Grace pulled out a kitchen drawer and handed the men two paper bags. "No one has done anything wrong and the sooner you officers figure that out the better. An accident is an accident without you adding to the heartbreak."

Clark started to protest but he was sure the men were following a false trail, too. "I want all his clothes back in good shape," he said. "That's his school coat."

"Don't worry," Hawley said. "We could give you a receipt."

"That isn't necessary," Grace said. "You men should be helping that poor Kagita woman."

Hawley bagged the muddy clothes, boots, and jacket.

"Thank you for your cooperation, ma'am." He turned to Clark. "Let's say ten o'clock. You can bring the boy then. Ten o'clock sharp."

"I heard you." Clark closed the door hard behind them.

Grace sat at the kitchen table warming her hands on the teacup. "Those men are quite misguided. Wade was as good as gold all day long. Poor Mrs. Kagita." She shook her head.

"You don't know anything about that Lemke kid and the bike?"

"I'm sure they've just exaggerated the whole incident. You should have seen Wade today, honey. He was so cute when I had him change his clothes. I was vacuuming, and he climbed on the vacuum, just clung to the handle and rode all around the front room. I wish I had pictures of that. You know what he said? He was so dear."

Clark shook his head.

"He said he was riding a big whale. Wasn't that cute? Not a horse but a big whale. I suppose they don't have many horses in Alaska, come to think of it."

• • •

After the officers were gone, Clark studied Wade asleep on the bed. A thin line of drool strung from the corner of his mouth to the pillow. Clark recalled how pitiful the boy had looked when he first saw him in Sitka. Malnourished, frightened, orphaned, he had resembled a small huddled animal. Now his long thin arms were crossed on his chest. He appeared scrawny, but the boy had strength. His scarred hands were always moving, his fingers tinkering with tools, twisting off buttons, taking apart mechanical equipment. Payette had flown into a rage when she found her Seiko watch disassembled, the front wheel of her Firebird wobbling because Wade had loosened the lug nuts. "If this keeps up, one of us is going," she had told Clark.

Clark pulled up the bedcovers, smoothing the blanket across the boy's shoulders. He touched the faint stains on the wool. The cops would have thought coffee or chocolate, but the bloodstains came from Nibbles, a brown and gray guinea pig the special ed teacher in Two Rivers sent home with Wade for Easter vacation. Wade had delighted in Nibbles, who got his name from tugging on the children's clothes as they held the pet in their arms. All the children in Wade's class were designated Emotionally Handicapped or Learning Disabled, and caring for the class pet was one of their rewards for good behavior.

At home, Wade changed its water and gave it huge clumps of weeds. Clark was amazed at how much the pig could eat. Clark helped Wade change the cage's newspapers and wood shavings, and even let Nibbles explore Wade's bedroom until Payette discovered the puddles of urine. "That thing's nothing but a glorified rat," she said.

One Saturday morning while she worked at the art gallery, Clark was alarmed to hear frantic squeals mixed with the loud TV noises coming from the boy's bedroom. Racing in, he found Wade clutching a struggling Nibbles to his naked chest. Both of his bony arms squeezed the pet tight.

"Let Nibbles go, damn it! Can't you see you're hurting him!" He tried grabbing the boy, but Wade twisted toward the wall, crushing the pet tighter to his thin rib cage. Blood leaked from Nibbles's nose onto the bedspread and poop was smeared against Wade's belly.

"*Let him go!*" Clark grabbed the boy's arms, but they held the pet like steel bands. Wade squeezed tighter as Clark tried to free the animal. The pig squealed frantically. Finally, Clark grabbed the boy's ear, almost lifting him completely off the bed.

"Aieeeee!" Wade screamed and released Nibbles. The boy covered his ears with his hands and faced the wall, taking deep gulps as he sobbed.

More blood seeped from the pet's nose onto the bedspread and sheets. It no longer squealed but the little rasping coos disturbed Clark even more. The shape was wrong—flattened—and Clark knew its bones were crushed. Nibbles crawled feebly—then stopped.

"God damn it, Wade. What the hell were you thinking?"

Still turned to the wall, the boy kept sobbing until Clark got up and turned off the TV. "Don't touch him," he warned. He took the leather gloves from his red-and-black Filson mackinaw hanging on the back porch, then got some clean newspaper, strapping tape, and one of Payette's shoe boxes. When he returned to the bedroom, Wade was leaning over the pet, stroking it lightly with one finger.

"Wade."

The boy lifted his head and his face seemed filled with sorrow. "Nibbles bit me." When he held up his left arm, Clark saw the white teeth marks, the bloody smear on the inside of the bicep.

"You'll be all right," Clark said. "But Nibbles is hurt bad. Do you understand?"

"I'll—be—all—right," Wade said between gasps. "You—fix—him—Dad?"

Clark didn't say anything but put on the gloves. "He's hurt too bad."

Wade started crying again. "We—were—watching—*Sesame—Street*. I wanted him to see Big Bird." Wade tried to pick up the wounded animal, but Clark seized his hands.

"Listen, Wade, I've got to take Nibbles someplace. Help me by getting dressed. I mean right now, okay?"

"Everybody's going to hate me," Wade said. "All the kids will hate me."

Clark noticed that Nibbles's rasping had gotten worse. "He's really suffering, guy, so I've got to help him out. Here's what we'll do. If you get dressed and quit crying, we'll drive into town and get another guinea pig. You can pick him out. Maybe we can find one that looks exactly like Nibbles at Scamps Pet Home." Clark took the boy's chin in his gloved hand and lifted his face a little. "I'll bet you can't even tell the difference."

Wade's eyelashes were stuck together from all the crying and his nose was running. "What are you going to do with Nibbles?"

"I said I'd take care of him. And you can help me after a little while, but you've got to stop crying and get dressed."

He picked up the guinea pig as gently as he could. Nibbles made tiny squeals and Clark vowed to get it over with fast. "There's some clean jeans in the top drawer. Hurry up now."

Inside the bathroom, he latched the door, taking off the left glove to work the hook and eye. He put the plug in the sink and turned on both faucets, making the water warm because he figured that would cause Nibbles the least pain. He could bash its head in with a shovel outside, but he was afraid Wade might see. He didn't think the pig would last much longer in any case. The pink-rimmed brown eyes were growing glassy.

When the sink was two-thirds full, he turned off the water.

Wade had the TV on again, way too loud. The *Sesame Street* voices throbbed inside Clark's head. "Turn that fucking thing down!" Kicking the wall a couple of times, he got no response.

Nibbles didn't struggle at all so maybe the warm water had been a good idea. Its mouth opened and closed, revealing rodent teeth. Clark considered the bite on Wade's arm. Bats, skunks, coyotes, foxes, and racoons were the worst rabies carriers; dogs and cats if they ran wild. Rarely a squirrel. Guinea pigs were no problem. "Thank God for small favors," he muttered.

When he saw a couple of air bubbles rise from the animal's mouth, Clark remembered drowning kittens with his junior high friend Dawson, whose parents were too cheap to get their cat spayed. He and Dawson would give away all the kittens they could from the Thriftway on Saturday afternoon. Dawson's father made them drown the rest in a bathtub, then bury the dead kittens in the vacant sagebrush lot nearby.

Clark hated Dawson's father, who always smelled like Black Jack chewing gum and English Leather. Frequently, he cracked dirty jokes as they drowned the kittens.

"Son of a bitch," Clark said, turning his head from the pig. He tried thinking of something pleasant. Once Dawson's father had taken the boys hunting for thunder eggs out on the Priday Agate Ranch. They had found good ones along with jasper and petrified wood.

Finished, Clark took off his right glove and wrapped the small soggy animal in newspapers. After placing the bundle in the shoe box, he wrapped the box tightly with strapping tape.

When he checked on Wade, the boy had managed only his underwear. He had quit crying and seemed absorbed in the show. Clark turned off the TV, then unplugged it. "Finish getting dressed," he said. "You can help bury Nibbles and then we'll go to Scamps." He thought having Wade help dig a hole would be good. At his school they were always harping on the importance of consequences.

*   *   *

"Can Nibbles get out of the box?" Wade asked outside. He had finished digging the hole. Clark held the taped shoe box in his hands. "No," Clark said. "Nibbles is dead now."

"Are you sure? He was moving when you took him."

"Yes." Clark set the shoe box in the hole. "Cover him up, Wade." As Wade shoveled dirt, Clark said, "You hurt him bad when you squeezed him. You mustn't squeeze anything like that again. Not even a small dog or a cat. Do you understand?"

Wade nodded and thumped the back of the shovel against the loose dirt. "But if he can't get out, why did you tape the box so tight?"

Clark didn't answer for a moment. "I just thought it was a good idea. Sometimes a coyote comes and eats a dead animal."

Wade shook his head. "I don't want a coyote to eat Nibbles. That might hurt him."

"Jesus," Clark said, uncertain how much of this Wade understood, if anything. "A coyote won't get him." He didn't want Wade digging Nibbles up either. He decided to rebury the animal later—someplace deeper in the woods. He'd cover it up with branches and leaves.

"We did a pretty good job," Wade said, after they'd stuck a small stick cross in the ground. "Can we hurry up and go to Scamps?"

They purchased a smaller animal with almost identical markings and Clark washed the sheets and pillowcases. The blanket went to the cleaners. That evening when Payette came home, Wade was excited to show her the new pet. Clark told her Nibbles had an accident. She said, "You handle it."

He put on a tie and sports coat Monday morning when he and Wade took the new pig to school. Miss Radditz was a former hippie who wore wire-rim glasses and pounds of turquoise. In the late sixties she had belonged to a commune near Taos and the other members had ripped off her valuable jewelry. In Two Rivers, she wore all her best pieces in case anyone broke in.

"That's a downer," she said when Clark told her Nibbles had an accident. "I hope that didn't freak out Wade."

*   *   *

Clark closed Wade's door, then leaned into it, lowering his head, pressing both palms against its flimsiness. Nothing seemed real to him or permanent. The shabbiness of Puffton Village, the bedraggled and self-absorbed graduate students, even the surly, unwelcome cops. He knew this much. He was twenty-nine years old and somehow his life had arrived here—totally different from anything he had expected.

Lifting his head, he saw his mother, weighty as an anvil, sitting at the kitchen table shuffling through some papers Wade had brought home from school. Most were just wild colored scribbles, but his teacher had written Wade's name at the top of each in a small, clear hand. One was a mimeoed sheet that had a gold star like a western badge pasted in one corner. "Improvement Today—Good Job, Pardner." On the line below the heading, the teacher had written, "After a pretty tough morning, Wade stayed on task all afternoon."

"Isn't this nice?" Grace said, handing the paper to Clark. "He's earned three awards in the past two weeks."

"That's something all right." He set it onto the small table. "Those cops really pissed me off."

Her cheerful look disappeared and she asked, "What are we going to do, son?"

"I'm calling Payette," he said.

"That awful woman," she said.

4

Sitka, Alaska, 1974

Clark didn't know much about Payette's uncle Maynard White Fish or his boy Wade until he and Payette flew to Sitka for Maynard's funeral.

"Good thing someone had the sense to bury him in Sitka," Payette said. "I wouldn't go near Angoon. It's so backward, they still believe in witches."

Clark knew her strong dislike for her childhood village. One photo he'd seen showed her standing barefoot in front of a small yellow shack holding the handlebar of a rusty tricycle. Her hair was chopped off unevenly. "The Baptists just came to town and cut all the girls' hair," she had explained. "They claimed the devil would grab your long hair and drag you away." She squared her shoulders. "When I got old enough, I ran farther away than the devil could ever drag me."

The people who attended Maynard's funeral were a hard-case lot. Aside from the fact they were Tlingit, they resembled Clark's family.

"Fucking orca followed the salmon right into the fish trap," Sampson Frank said when he talked with Clark after Maynard's service. "Whale ate lunch, then figured out he was trapped. Those cannery Japs on the tender shit their pants when they figured it was an orca down there."

Sampson dropped his cigarette butt onto the wooden porch and ground it out with his patent leather black shoes. He took another from the pocket of his outsized corduroy sports jacket and loosened a silver raven bolo tie. Coatless, he didn't seem cold in spite of the near-zero temperature, but shivered when he mentioned Maynard, his brother-in-law.

"Shit. I should have gone down to cut that whale loose but I already walked the fish trap that morning. Got rid of two big old sea lions chomping salmon like crazy. One swam up and banged me for interrupting his lunch." He lit another cigarette and flicked the match off the porch, then squinted at Clark. "See, it was Maynard's turn and those cannery guys wanted that whale out pronto."

Clark held his left hand against his ear as Sampson talked. The plane's rapid descent into Sitka had caused his ears to plug and the left one hurt. He vowed to get a woolen cap with ear flaps.

"Maynard and I probably cut free a dozen whales this season. Any one could have fucked us up. The big ones can't swim in the trap opening, but the little ones still go five or six tons." Sampson glanced in the steaming window at Payette talking with some of the Tlingit women who had attended the funeral. "I never would have recognized her in a million years. She was a scrawny, scab-kneed little thing when she left Angoon." He finished the cigarette and flipped it into the snow. "I feel like crap about Maynard."

"It's a mess," Clark said. "No sign of Wade's mother?"

"The land otters dragged her off," Sampson said. "She's not coming back."

Clark nodded, even though he didn't fully understand Sampson's remark. Some old Tlingit superstition held that people who disappeared were changed into land otters.

"Payette said she's in Anchorage somewhere."

Sampson shook his head. "She's my sister, and I don't have a clue. The cops in Anchorage can't find a butt in a bathtub. And the asshole game wardens here closed down that whole fish trap operation, pretending like they just figured out we was using chicken wire and drop lines."

Clark had learned that the old-timer Tlingit fishermen in remote villages like Kake or Angoon still used some of the chicken wire maze traps that covered as much as half an acre instead of the modern gill nets required by new laws. However, the wardens turned a blind eye as long as the fishermen hired divers to "walk the traps" and release sea lions or whales that became entangled after following the salmon into the mesh. Foolhardy guys like Maynard and Sampson went down with an underwater torch and two pairs of wire cutters.

"When a wire cuts deep into the blowhole, whales get freaky," Sampson said. "Divers got to have more guts than smarts. Once I had a whale with wires digging into the sex slits. That was awful.

"They die if you don't cut them loose quick," Sampson said. "And if the wire draws too much blood, the sharks come. Sometimes the torch hits their eyes and makes them go crazy." He moved his hands as if holding wire cutters. "Find their white bellies first and cut the wire clear. Watch the light. Then you get on top and cut their backs free. That's tricky. Once they start feeling those wires come loose, they go wild—like a bull through a blaze."

No one knew exactly what happened to Maynard underwater, but the whale had driven him against something and crushed him. The water pressure burst his blood vessels and internal organs.

"Took me forty minutes to find him in that black water and bring him up," Sampson said. "When I got him on the tender deck, and we took off his helmet, his eyes were bulging out." The big man shivered. "I thought they were looking at me." He held out his hands so Clark could see the shakes. "I still got the spooks."

Sampson stamped his feet and blew on his hands. "Now I'm too unsteady to carve on that totem me and Maynard was carving. The spirits are still trying to come out of the wood. I've got to help carve a bunch of totems for Angoon because ours got destroyed a long time back."

Clark studied the partially carved cedar log in the front yard. Ice and snow obscured the unfinished features, and he couldn't tell what animals the two men had been carving.

"Time for coffee," Sampson said. "Let's go inside before those fat women eat all the cake. Did I tell you about the orca that dragged the moose down?" Sampson put his hand on Clark's shoulder. "Right out by the pulp mill on Crescent Bay. These two moose were swimming across, and an orca dragged one down for supper. I'm not shitting you now . . ."

* * *

A photograph of Maynard and Amber sat on the television set inside the trailer. His arms circled her waist and her head rested against his left shoulder. Amber had been a pretty woman, but her face's puffiness gave away her hard drinking.

"Amber had a difficult life," Sampson said. "Maynard, too. Both of them would drink and fight, then one would take off to Juneau or Ketchikan. If Amber was in the city, she'd find a boyfriend to support her. Sometimes he'd beat up on Wade. Did you see the scars on Wade's hands?"

Clark nodded.

"One of her boyfriends put his hands on a hot plate," Sampson said. "Maynard and Amber both loved that squirrelly kid in their own ways. Neither would admit the boy was touched. His howls scared the neighbors, and the city cops shipped him off to a dozen foster homes. She'd sober up, find an old minister or a new caseworker, and try again. Somehow, she always got him back." He shrugged. "Amber and Maynard would be lovebirds again until they started more drinking."

Clark puzzled over the contrast of human ugliness against the backdrop of Sitka's beauty. The silent snow blanketing the dense spruce forests; twinkling ship lights on Crescent Bay; Mount Edgecoomb shouldering white. Humpback whales spouting, their black majestic shapes rising from the frigid sea. None of the beauty had touched Amber or Maynard. As for their loving Wade, Clark only had Sampson's word.

.   .   .

After the service and gathering, Clark explored the picturesque town. He took photos of the totem poles, the fishing fleet in Crescent Bay, St. Michael's Russian Orthodox Church. At the Sheldon Jackson Museum, he was fascinated by the Native Alaskan art—shamans' masks and rattles, cedar screens and bentwood boxes, Tlingit hats and tunics. The bold red-and-black designs featured ravens, wolves, bears, and killer whales.

Clark stopped in front of a sealskin diving suit the Tlingit whalers had once worn to finish killing then begin butchering the wounded whales. Made from the waterproof hide of a harbor seal, the suit would accommodate only a small man, perhaps a hundred and fifty pounds. Clark shuddered as he thought of how little protection the suit would provide from the freezing waters, the frantic threshing of the dying whale still fighting the harpoon.

He wondered how Maynard had felt in the heavy canvas diving suit, the brass helmet, weight belt, and weighted shoes as he plunged through the black water to free the killer whale.

Voices stirred Clark and he shook his head. Outside, the light had changed. Checking his watch, he realized he had half an hour before meeting Payette at the Tyee Hotel lounge. She had planned on spending the afternoon visiting the local art galleries while waiting to see if Alaskan Children's Welfare managed to locate Wade's mother in Anchorage. Before leaving the museum store, he bought Payette a dark stone pendant that was half otter, half woman.

"Argillite," the clerk told him. "From the Queen Charlotte Islands. Only a dozen old Haidas know the quarry's location. They call it Slate-chuck."

"Pricey," Clark joked. "My wife should like it."

Outside, ravens croaked from the tall cedars and disturbed the snow as they settled in high branches for the night. Among the Tlingits, the Raven clan was one of the most powerful. Old legends claimed shamans transformed themselves into ravens and practiced supernatural powers. Two of the large birds flew over Clark's head and fixed him with their beady black eyes. Perhaps it was just superstition, but Clark thought the birds seemed ominous. When he saw a small church, he decided to go in.

．　　　．　　　．

St. Peter's by the Sea Episcopal Church remained open twenty-four hours a day for meditation and prayer. A huge stained-glass window depicting Christ holding an anchor caught the last rays of the sun. After brushing the snow from his boots with a stubby broom on the porch, Clark stepped inside. A metal coin box above the guest register had a scrawled sign, SAILORS' RELIEF FUND. Clark dropped in a ten-dollar bill and signed the register. After his name and address he added, "A prayer for Maynard White Fish and Wade."

Inside, the church was warm and comfortable. The floors were Alaskan white pine and the pews hewed from cedar. Clark chose a pew halfway to the front and studied the emerald green altar cloth draped across the communion table. He imagined the local churchwomen had embroidered the large yellow salmon and nets that decorated the cloth.

He didn't fold down the kneeler, since he wasn't an Episcopalian, but he bowed his head and offered a prayer for Maynard and the boy. He remembered listening to Bill Willbroad, their landlord in Oregon, reciting Bible verses as he trimmed the Noble firs on his Christmas tree farm adjacent to their rented house:

"As ye have done for the least of these . . ." Christ's words from Matthew.

.   .   .

When Clark first saw Wade, the boy cocked his head to one side, then the other, and thrust his head forward, as if deaf. If he spoke, it was gibberish or the high whining of a pup. The night before Maynard's funeral he whimpered from the tiny bedroom. Clark couldn't wake Payette because she took sleeping pills so he wandered across the hall, drowsy and half expecting to find a dog. Wade's thin hands clutched a dark blanket with a faded raven design. He rocked back and forth whimpering and seemed not to notice when Clark entered the room.

"You better get some rest, buddy." Clark didn't know if the boy understood him or not but he spoke in a calm voice. The boy stuffed part of the blanket in his mouth, muffling his cries. Black eyes stared from his gaunt face.

Outside, perhaps half a mile away, the lights from the pulp mill cast a reddish glow, and the pungent smell seeped through the trailer's cracks. Steam rose from the illuminated stacks into the black sky. When the salmon weren't running, Maynard worked swing shift at the mill.

"Can't you sleep, son?" He sat on the edge of the bed, and after ten minutes, Wade reached for Clark's good hand. He held the boy's hand gently, feeling the thick white scars on the boy's palm.

"I feel sorry for the kid," Clark muttered now inside the church.

Then he remembered his mother's struggle to raise him by herself, the empty promises of the few men she ever bothered to date. They talked about taking him fishing or to the movies but never followed up, and eventually Clark stopped hoping they would.

The last sunlight twinkled through the stained-glass window, striking the green altar cloth. The golden fish and nets seemed to glow.

Clark heard a door shut in the vestibule but no one came into the church. He glanced down, surprised to see that his hands were still folded. Cupping his hand behind the plugged ear, he said, "Couldn't quite hear you, Big Fella." Fastening his jacket, he walked out into the cold dusk, wondering what Maynard had been thinking when the whale carried him into the black and crushing depths.

•   •   •

Payette waved at Clark through the lounge window. Soft candlelight backlit her sculpted features, her ebony hair—and he felt a surge of pride. He overlooked her vanity, the high MasterCard charges for wigs, cosmetics, and clothes. When he'd tried bringing up the bills, she had said, "I've got to look smart," referring to her job selling art at the best gallery in town. "Customers don't buy expensive art from a frump. And I'm getting seven percent commission now." She pointed to a couple items on the charge statement. "Anyway, these are yours. You spend a lot on sporting goods."

Payette adorned her long neck and dark arms with turquoise and silver, a couple of very expensive necklaces. She had learned about makeup and jewelry in Hood River High School. "I showed those rich girls up plenty," she said. "The boys always came buzzing around me. 'If she's brown, she won't turn you down,' they thought, but I wouldn't let them get in my pants just because their fathers had orchards and the boys drove expensive pickups."

Clark liked making love to Payette, enjoyed her physical beauty, but recently sensed the mechanics of lovemaking instead of the passion. When he was gloomy, he worried about not having children. "I wouldn't make a good mother," she said. "Got too darn much living to do. I plan to travel light."

"You can travel with children," Clark pointed out.

She frowned. "I remember how my mother got with my sisters. A watermelon with legs. She could hardly move, and my dad chased off catting around."

"I wouldn't take off," Clark said.

"All men are the same," she said. "The little head does the thinking for the big head."

She took the pill regularly even though it blotched her skin and darkened the thin line of her mustache. Every two weeks she applied cream bleach to her upper lip. The first time Clark had seen her he was surprised. "I've been drinking buttermilk," she said.

.   .   .   .

Inside the Tyee, he dropped into an upholstered chair across from her. "What are you having?"

"Coffee Nudge. It's so darned cold."

He signaled the waiter for another. "Look what I got you." He reached in his pocket and handed her the carved pendant.

"A *Kooshdaakáa*," she said. "It's adorable. Did you know it was Tlingit?"

"I saw some at the museum. The legend says the *Kooshdaakáa* help lost fishermen."

"If the otter women are hard up for a husband, sometimes they lure them to their watery graves." She laughed. "You got the tourist version of the legend. Most Tlingits are scared to death of otters and blame them for stealing children." She took off the turquoise necklace she was wearing and slipped on the dark pendant. "Lucky for you I'm not superstitious. How does it look with this dress?"

"Great," he said. "You look great."

"If I had a Raven pipe made out of this stuff, I'd be rich," she said. "Only two exist, and the British Museum has them locked up."

She paused. "I got some things, too. Tremendous bargains. Without the summer tourists, the shops are practically giving away the art." She took several packages from her shopping bag. "Look at this scrimshaw billikin carved from a walrus tooth. It's illegal to hunt walrus anymore or use this kind of ivory. Something like this only goes up in price."

She showed him several other carved pieces, pointing out their intricacies with her long slim fingers. "But this is one of the best," she added, holding up a bear claw necklace with Chinese trade beads. "If art like this ever came through our store, the owner would snap it up." She also had two bright paintings of Inuit village children playing the blanket toss, as well as a Chilkat blanket woven from goat hair, moss, and yellow cedar bark.

"That's something," he said, thinking of the bills.

"Here's the museum piece. You'll never find anything like this."

The ivory object resembled the blade of a large, double-edged hunting knife with carved notches and designs along the sides.

"Is it for some kind of game?"

She chuckled. "You could say that. It's a whale penis. Very rare. In the remote villages, young women carved them in the menstrual huts. Here's the best part. The gallery owner knocked off a hundred dollars when he found out I was Tlingit."

He sipped his Nudge and nodded his head, trying not to diminish her enthusiasm. He knew she had a terrific eye for art and most of the items she purchased at galleries had gone up in price. Occasionally, they got an offer to buy back the works of artists who had been "discovered." She called the purchases "investments," but she always kept them. "The stuff looks terrific," he said. "I just hope we can afford all these bargains."

He said it with humor, but her dark eyes snapped. "I'm going to get what I want, Clark. You only go around once. Now that I've got salary plus commission, I make almost as much as you do teaching."

He spread his hands. "Okay, let's not argue. I said they were terrific."

"That's settled then," she said. She licked the traces of whipped cream at the corners of her mouth. "Anyway, we've got to make some sort of plan about Wade. Sampson's away fishing all the time. They couldn't even find Wade's mother in Anchorage. One of her friends thought maybe she took off to Ketchikan, but no one in Angoon knows anything. Maynard cared about that boy. Even if he is sort of pathetic, he'd hate to see him carted off to another foster home."

He ran his finger around the rim of his cup. "I was thinking we might have children of our own sometime."

She frowned. "Don't count on it, Clark. You know my feelings on that subject."

He bit his lower lip. Her stubbornness always puzzled him. His own mother had been one to adjust, to compromise, to make do. Maybe the boy would be good for them. He had always wanted children, perhaps just to prove that he could be a father—responsible in a way his own father was not. And he thought a child, even a damaged child, would help bridge the drift he was starting to feel between them.

"Like you said, we only go around once." He lifted his cup. "Let's give it a shot."

"It's got to be fifty-fifty." Payette lifted her cup but didn't touch the rims. "Just because he's my relative doesn't mean I'm going to carry the full burden."

"My mother will be happy to help out some," Clark said. "When she's not working. You know how Mom always wanted to have more children."

"I think you mean grandchildren," Payette said. "Anyway, I don't know how much I want your mother involved."

Clark moved his cup to touch hers. "In for a penny, in for a pound."

* * *

When they flew south two days later, Clark put the boy by the window so he could see out. Wade was wearing a red halibut jacket, stiff new jeans, and shiny cowboy boots Payette had bought at the Sitka mercantile. "I don't want him looking like a bum. Anyway, his old stuff smells like fried fish or something."

The boy stared out the window ten minutes, but then he began panting like a dog, his face pressed to the Plexiglas, his tongue lapping.

The man in the seat ahead turned around to stare.

"Make him stop that," Payette said. She was studying a book on Native Alaskan art. "He's making a slobbery mess."

Clark took Wade's shoulder. "Hey, Wade. Cut that out."

Suddenly, the boy screeched so loudly Clark was surprised and let go of his shoulder.

"Shit," the man in front said. He had bumped his tray, spilling orange juice across his pants.

The stewardess hurried over. She tried giving Wade a deck of cards and another pair of wings, but he wasn't interested. His hands covered his ears, his eyes squeezed shut and he continued screeching. Everyone on the plane was watching.

Clark gripped the boy's shoulder and tried pulling him to his chest, but the boy arched his back.

"Hey, buddy. Look there. I see some big deer on that mountain."

Wade took a breath, then screeched louder. Clark was aware of someone leaning over him—the stewardess, he thought—but Payette had unbuckled her seat belt and stood. She raised the heavy book as if to smack the boy on the head.

"Stop it. Stop." Clark groped in the beverage glass for some ice cubes and shoved them in the boy's open mouth.

Surprised at the cold, Wade stopped. His eyes flew open. Putting his head against Clark's shoulder he began to sob.

"Is your boy going to be okay?" the stewardess asked when Payette sat down again.

"He's not my boy," she said, opening the book. "Ask him."

5

Two Rivers, 1975

"Wade's deaf in his left ear," Clark told Dr. Brooks, who was administering the hearing tests. "When he listens to the radio in the truck or watches television, he always cocks his head and puts his right ear next to the dashboard. Then he squints his eyes, concentrating."

During the six weeks he had been with Clark and Payette, the boy had calmed down a little, but he never stopped moving or fidgeting his hands. His teachers complained that Wade disrupted the class by throwing toys, playing with the water faucets, opening and closing cupboard doors. They explained that he wouldn't listen or follow instructions.

"His teachers say he won't pay attention," Clark said. "A hearing aid might help."

"We'll be able to determine if he needs one," Brooks said.

Wade kept turning around to wave at Clark. Clark smiled, waving back to reassure him that everything was okay. *It was okay,* Clark thought to himself, *or soon would be.* He was convinced the doctors would figure out a strategy to help Wade learn better. After that, he'd have suggestions to offer the teachers.

"He's not applying himself," the teachers had reported. "One day he'll recognize shapes, but the next day we have to start over. He confuses colors, too. Red is for apple; yellow for banana; orange."

Orange. Banana. Apple. Clark wondered how often Wade had seen fresh fruit. The tiny trading post in Angoon didn't carry any, according to Payette.

Clark had prepared Wade for the day of evaluations at Crippled

Children's Hospital. He had a bath, haircut, wore stiff new brown cords and a new green flannel shirt. His black cowboy boots were polished. He had squirmed and squirmed when Clark tried to wash his ears, and Clark believed the boy had a history of painful ear infections.

Wade kept fiddling with the headphones and the objects on the table. He had taken off the headset and shook his head vigorously.

"Tell him he's got to keep them on," Brooks said.

When Clark opened the door, Wade jumped up and gave him a hug. He buried his head in Clark's stomach and clung with his thin arms gripping Clark's waist.

"I'm cold."

"Hey, Spiderman," Clark said in a calming voice. "This is what I want you to do. Put these on and sit still." Clark placed the earphones over his own head, then tapped each side. "Right over your ears."

Wade snatched at them, jerking them from Clark. "Mine!"

"Ouch!" Clark's ears hurt and he rubbed them. "Now listen. The doctor will tell you what to pick up." He arranged the toys on the table. A blue boat, a plastic ice cream cone, a miniature walk and wait crossing sign, a fish, a silver airplane.

"Listen hard and follow the doctor's instructions."

He left the booth, closing the door quietly. Through the observation window, he saw Wade lean toward the toys, turning his head so his right ear faced them. He rocked back and forth, back and forth in the chair, and rubbed both hands against his knees.

Clark agonized over the extent of Wade's damage, but he wanted to get to the bottom of it. "There's nothing like knowing," his uncle Roy had always said. "Even if it's bad."

The doctor turned on a switch that said RIGHT. "Wade, this is Dr. Brooks. If you can hear me, raise your hand. Good and high. Let's see it now. How high can you reach?"

Wade didn't respond.

"You tell him," the doctor said, shifting so Clark could reach the microphone.

"Wade, raise your hand!"

Wade twisted his head until he was squinting at Clark. Slowly he raised both his hands and put them on top of his head. He started to take off the headset.

"Don't take that off until I tell you!" Clark said.

Wade lowered his hands.

Brooks grinned at Clark. "You got a way with kids." He glanced at the instructions in front of him and began to give Wade the material. "Put the silver fish beside the blue boat."

Wade did as he was told, and Clark felt a little surge of satisfaction.

"Lift the ice cream cone to your mouth."

Wade did, pretending to lick it.

"Fly the airplane over the boat."

The plane swooshed above the boat.

"Put the crossing sign beside the fish."

Wade didn't do anything.

Brooks leaned closer to the mike. "Wade, put the crossing sign beside the fish."

The boy picked up the fish, but ignored the sign. Brooks took a note on the chart.

Clark touched Brooks's arm. "He's from a little village in Alaska. They don't have crossing signs. They don't even have stop signs."

Brooks smiled slightly, shaking his head. "There's a dog in the drawer," he told Clark. "Take the sign away and put the dog on the table, would you?"

In the booth, Clark found the dog and took away the sign. "Good job," he told Wade. "We're almost finished." He tousled the boy's hair.

Brooks set the switch on LEFT, then glanced at Clark. "This is where you think he's got a problem?"

Clark nodded. "He can't hear out of that ear."

"Wade, lift your arm," the doctor said, but Wade didn't move until Clark leaned toward the mike.

"Wade, buddy. If you can hear me, lift your arm."

Wade slowly lifted his arm.

"He might be guessing," Clark said. "Following the pattern."

"You should have my job," Brooks said. "Kids do that a lot, actually. Wade, pick up the dog and pet him, would you? He's been lonely in that dark drawer."

Clark started to repeat, but Wade lifted the dog, then set him back down without petting.

The boy likes dogs, Clark thought. *Maybe it was a coincidence.* Glancing at Brooks's notes, Clark saw a question mark.

"Fly the airplane over the dog."

Wade picked up the airplane and made a couple of swooshes past the dog.

"I don't believe it," Clark said. "Try something else."

"Put the fish in the boat."

Wade did.

Clark shook his head. "I was convinced he was deaf in that ear."

The doctor nodded. "Kids who have been abused a lot or sick all the time frequently act deaf or autistic. That's why we have the tests."

Clark was elated that Wade wasn't deaf in his left ear. However, he also felt sad because the boy had been so mistreated that he feigned disabilities. Still, Clark was convinced that as Wade spent more time with him and Payette, as he grew more secure, and his trust increased, Wade would blossom and his general good disposition would win over his teachers and classmates.

Through the rest of the day, Brooks administered test after test to Wade. Clark was pleased with most of the results, but he disagreed with the IQ scores, which classified Wade in the mildly retarded category with a score of sixty-five.

"A lot of that might be cultural, don't you think?" he asked Brooks.

The doctor shrugged. "It's a small factor, maybe, but he has a really hard time following a simple three-instruction sequence or remembering a word series like 'cat, marble, car, quarter.'"

Clark glanced at his watch. "It's late. Maybe he just got tired. Anyway, he's so much better than when we got him. Night and day, really."

Brooks put his hand on Clark's shoulder. "You and your wife are doing a terrific service, Mr. Woods. You should be proud of yourselves."

Outside was a sign which said: SAVE A CHILD AND YOU SAVE A UNIVERSE.

.   .   .

Clark and Payette had rented an old farmhouse that overlooked the Columbia River. When she finished her gallery work, she sunbathed naked behind the weathered barn. Cattle hadn't been on the land in years. Willbroad, their landlord, had planted his acreage in Christmas trees—Douglas firs, Nobles, Grands. Clark liked walking the windrows between the shoulder-high firs admiring the way Willbroad came through the trees every day, trimming their shapes, putting yellow tags on the ones he planned to harvest.

Willbroad had left sixty acres of timber behind the old farmhouse, and in spring, trilliums grew in the shady spots, then wild irises. Near the house and barn seven lilac trees cast their scent. Most weekends Wade explored the woods, bringing back odd-shaped rocks and cones, deer bones, a snakeskin. He seemed at home in the outdoors, and at times, Clark almost forgot the calls from flustered schoolteachers.

Payette planned on canning but never seemed to have time. In late August, she put up some peach jam with sweet Yakima peaches. As she worked over the stove, the steam kinked her hair, and a thin line of perspiration clung to her upper lip. Four gnarled apple trees behind the house bore hardy autumn apples, and she bought a food dryer from the grange. The food dryer ran day and night, and paying the electricity bill cost more than buying dried apples at the store. "Live and learn," she said, laughing.

Breezy days, Clark sat on the basalt bluffs and watched the green Tidewater barges move inland wheat downriver, farm machinery up to the interior. Pleasure boats threw up rooster tails of spray. They planned to buy a boat and a beach cabin, but first their own home. "We're saving up for a down payment," Payette told everyone. When she bought a Pontiac Firebird, Clark worried about the mounting bills.

Sightseeing planes flew over the Larch Mountain wilderness and up as far as Multnomah Falls and Hood River. One Sunday afternoon, Grace had wanted them all to go with her on a hike to the top of Beacon Rock, but Clark and Payette stayed home together. "She's actually bought whistles," Clark said after sending Wade off with Grace. "A whistle for everyone."

"What for?"

"In case someone gets lost. She read in a book that you can wear out your voice shouting, but not with a whistle. She's completely equipped. Whistles, water bottles, and a hat, so the sun doesn't get you."

"I'd rather shrivel in the sun like a prune than hike with your mother," she said.

They had the entire afternoon to themselves. She put on her dark glasses and lay naked on her back, spreading suntan oil on the fronts of her legs, her thighs, belly, and breasts. She had put Sun-Lite in her dark hair, too, and he noticed a few honey-colored streaks. He began to harden and touched her breast, just below the almond-colored nipple. "Not yet," she said. "I just want to laze here awhile."

"Okay," he said. "Let me know when." He rolled onto his back and felt the sun on his face. Under him, the earth was hard and the grass smelled dry.

After a while he dozed. He was awakened by her breath in his ear. "When," she said, tugging his earlobe. She put her mouth closer, blowing slowly. "When."

She lay back, still wearing her sunglasses. He took her right nipple in his mouth and began working his tongue against the underside. She was sweet and salty at the same time—coconut oil and sweat. His penis grew hard against her hip.

She ran her fingers across his forehead, massaging his eyebrows, feeling the pulse at his temples, then stroking the back of his neck. He was ready to swing over on top of her but she whispered, "Don't move." Her hands pulled his head against her breast. "Stay still!"

He heard a high whistling above the trees.

"Sons of bitches!" she said.

A shadow crossed the weathered barn. Turning against the sun, he recognized the silhouette of a small plane, engine silent, gliding over the big pines. After passing the far end of the Christmas tree field, the plane's engine started.

"The bastards will be right back," she said. "They were here yesterday."

Already he could hear the plane climbing, gaining altitude for another near silent glide.

She dashed naked toward the house.

"It's just some guys out gawking." Shielding his eyes with his right hand, he stood naked in the sun and watched the plane head toward him, this time riding the updrafts above the Columbia. When the plane reached the edge of Willbroad's trees, he heard the kitchen door open and saw Payette running into the yard, still naked but carrying his Remington .30-06 pump.

"What the hell are you doing?" He started toward her, but she lowered the barrel and he stopped. Raising the rifle, she took careful aim, not a warning shot, and squeezed off a round. After the loud *crack,* he didn't hear anything else and prayed for a miss. Then the dry quick clack of the pump action, and another shot. This sounded different and he guessed she hit a wing or the fuselage. She squeezed off one more shot, a definite hit as the pilot tried to start the ignition.

The plane was past them, across the road and out of sight behind the big trees.

"Are you crazy? We're going to have the sheriff out here now. You can't go shooting at planes."

"I'm not a damn peep show," she said. "Anyway, do you think some weekend ace wants to tell his flying buddies he got chased off by a naked woman?"

"You might have killed somebody."

"I know what I'm doing." She pumped the action again, ejecting a shell. "Everybody in Angoon is prepared for bears."

* * *

When he followed her into the house, she had locked herself in the bathroom. Water ran in the tub.

He rapped on the door. "What's wrong?"

"Leave me alone," she said.

"Come on out."

"I need time to myself," she said.

Clark felt strange talking to the closed door. "Is it Wade?" he asked. "He's getting better."

"Tell that to the people at his schools! Four conferences in the last month."

"You only went to one."

She didn't say anything for a minute. "I can't stand your mother. Everybody wants something from me all the time."

"God damn it, Payette, come out so we can talk!"

"I'm going to shoot through this door," she said.

When he realized she still had the rifle, he retreated to the kitchen and took a beer from the refrigerator. After a while, he stopped listening for sirens and watching the road for brown and tan sheriff's cars. Later he heard the shower running, and he waited for her in the bedroom.

"We need some curtains for these back windows," Payette said when she came in. Her face appeared calm. She sat at her vanity, combing out her long dark hair. "One of the gas cans is missing from the garage, and I think the neighbor boys might be coming through the woods at night. I saw footprints right outside the windows."

"Probably Wade," he said. "He's all over the place."

"Not Wade. Bigger shoes."

"All right then," he said. "Buy some curtains. I don't think anybody saw much, even if they were looking. It's so dark." He paused, noticing she was still upset. "Why are you so shook?"

"I can't stand peepers and perverts." She put down the brush and turned toward him. "In Angoon they had awful little BIA houses scrunched on top of each other. An old coot named Garvey lived right next door to us, just a few feet away. He spied on us all the time. My sister Pauline hit puberty early, so she had the worst of it.

"I swear I could smell his sour breath at night. In the morning, he'd watch us leave for school, licking us with his eyes.

"When Mom hung out our clothes she had to put our panties under the sheets. Otherwise Garvey came over and stared at them. He got a lump in his pants. I didn't even want to put my underclothes on because he made them seem dirty."

"Couldn't you report him?"

She laughed but it was angry. "You haven't seen Angoon," she said. "Anytime we tried taking the ferry to Juneau, Garvey followed us. We couldn't get away from the creep."

•   •   •

In late September, Willbroad tagged more of the trees he intended to harvest. Each day, he'd park his battered International Harvester pickup at the side of the field and walk the windrows. One day, he stood outside the house, his gimme cap tilted back so Clark could see the untanned line of his forehead.

"You want some coffee?" Clark asked.

"Where's the little fella?"

"He's at school today," Clark said. "Payette dropped him off on her way to work."

"I guess she's working hard. I never see her car."

"She's taking business classes at Portland State. She'll probably run the gallery in another year." He could tell Willbroad had something else on his mind. "What's up?"

"I was wondering," Willbroad said, pausing to rub his chin, "if a fella was to go and tag all those trees again, you think you could stop that little guy from ripping off the tags?"

Stepping onto the porch, Clark gasped when he saw thousands of marking tags scattered on the ground between the rows of trees. "Hell. I never knew he did that. I'm sorry."

Willbroad shook his head. "He started way at the back of the field, I guess. Been undoing my work for days."

"Maybe he could help you retag the trees—sort of a consequence."

Willbroad toed a pine needle on the porch. "Don't know if I can afford his help. I got to finish by November."

.   .   .

ADA REALBIRD, Ph.D.
CONSULTING CLINICAL PSYCHOLOGIST

In addition to her phone numbers and address, the card had a picture of a tan and yellow meadowlark. *Sturnella neglecta,* Clark thought, slipping her card into his wallet. Half the Western states had selected the meadowlark as their official bird.

Dr. RealBird appeared Indian, about forty and slightly stoop-shouldered. Her dark eyes were huckleberry blue.

"I'm sorry Wade's file is so incomplete, Mr. Woods," she said. "In addition to reading what's here," she tapped the thin file, "I talked with Miss Radditz, his LD teacher at Two Rivers. I'm afraid the other school stuff got misplaced in the shuffle."

"Do you know exactly how many schools, Doctor?" Clark scooted his chair closer and leaned toward her. "First, the district tried mainstreaming Wade." He raised one thumb. "It lasted three days. Then came Learning Disabled classes." He raised a finger. "Emotionally

Handicapped. Developmentally Disabled. The Education Service District program exclusively for minorities. All complete flops." He closed his hand. "Now this. Naturally, every administrator and program director emphasizes the importance of *stability*. All this stability in the ten months he's been down from Alaska."

Dr. RealBird offered a knowing smile, and weariness lines creased her mouth and eyes. "Too many bureaucrats," she said. "Too many specialists who never saw a student."

"Total crap," he said. "I forgot to mention you're the fifth school psychologist I've talked with—the first one without a beard."

"I shaved this morning," she said, running her fingers over her cheeks and chin. "Smooth now, but I kind of miss it. Anal retentive, I guess."

Clark hesitated, then smiled. "Right." This one at least had a sense of humor.

"So what did the others say about Wade?" She touched the file with her right hand. "I've just got one psychologist's sketchy report."

"They didn't say much," he said. "Two of the great experts never laid eyes on Wade but just interpreted reports from his teachers. Another tried wrestling with him, claiming Wade needed to compensate for 'deficit affection.' I warned that guy to knock it off." Clark leaned toward her. "Have you spent any time with Wade, Doctor? Actually laid eyes on the boy or talked with him?"

Usually, the experts backed away from the direct question, but Dr. RealBird locked Clark's eyes and steadied one fist under her chin. "Not as much as I'd like, Mr. Woods, but I wouldn't meet with you, or any other parents, if I hadn't observed the child first. We're all overworked—too many desperate kids and frantic parents—but my grandfather was a Lutheran minister and dosed me good with Protestant guilt." She paused. "I know what you're thinking. Yes, I'm mostly Indian. Crow and Assiniboin."

When he leaned back a little, she laughed. "I'm a psychologist, remember. I'm paid to know what you're thinking."

"Ah," he said. "Not paid too much, I hope."

"Definitely not too much. But was I right?"

He hesitated. "I was thinking you didn't look Lutheran," he said.

Regaining partial balance, he asked, "But I was also wondering exactly *how much* time with Wade?"

She didn't drop her gaze. "Three hours observing the entire class. Two half-hour sessions with Wade. It's a little hard to hold his attention." She raised her eyebrows. "So am I the best of the baleful lot?"

He nodded. "Congratulations. Where'd the school system find you?"

"They didn't. I found them when I came from Montana a year ago. I don't work for the district. I just consult with them, handle a few referrals."

She glanced at the wall clock. "The meter's ticking, so we should talk about Wade. He bit the Heidimann girl pretty hard—twice. Any idea why he gets into these dog routines? All kids do it, of course, but usually stop by age four or five."

Clark shrugged. "He likes animals. Sometimes he barks and snaps when he's tired or too stirred up." He could have told RealBird about Grace and Wade playing Waggles and the Dog Catcher, a game they made up from a children's book. She was the dog catcher and Wade a stray. She chased him around her apartment with a dishrag tied onto a yardstick as a pretend net. Once when Clark came to pick Wade up, he was in a barking frenzy and Grace was so sweaty and florid Clark feared she might have a stroke. He had insisted they stop playing Waggles. "He doesn't get into that dog stuff at home anymore," he said.

"What about the raven?"

He shrugged. "I'm not sure what you mean."

RealBird stood and spread her arms, then tucked them like wings. "He climbs on the desk and pretends to be a large powerful raven. Don't worry. I'm not climbing up. He thrusts his shoulders forward and turns his head. A look comes into his eyes, and when he croaks . . ." She snapped her fingers. "Sounds just like a raven, I swear."

Clearly she had been impressed by the imitation, but Clark hadn't seen it. He wisecracked. "Maybe he's been reading Poe." She knew, of course, Wade couldn't read.

She didn't smile. "I'm being serious. Are his people Raven? Ravens are very powerful among the Tlingit and Haida."

"Yes," Clark said. "His mother's Raven, but she's abandoned Wade, and his father's dead."

"You see, sometimes Indian healers are able to help with these children. I've seen it happen. You might want to take him back to Alaska at some point, put him in touch with his tribe. Your wife's from Alaska, too?"

Clark nodded. "Tlingit from Angoon," Clark said. "But she doesn't stay in touch with them."

"It might help to put the boy back in contact," she said. "Tribal background is pretty important."

Clark tightened his mouth, imagining what she got paid for this. First bearded wonders and now feathery mumbo-jumbo. *Wade's trouble started in Alaska,* he thought.

RealBird seemed to be waiting for a response. "I'll keep it in mind," he said. *No one knows a thing,* he thought. Uncle Roy had been right when he said, "The sun wakes up the world and every dumb bastard fakes it until sunset or payday."

Clark leaned back, satisfied that the appointment was almost over. Seven minutes to go. He may as well get his money's worth. Another joke. "Sometimes Wade chews all the buttons off his shirt and swallows them," he said. "Of course, they manage to work their way out in a couple days. But my wife doesn't sew and I'm spending a lot of money at the Greek tailors . . ."

RealBird's face flashed anger. "I'm not a fool, Mr. Woods." She stood, and when she went to the open window, Clark noticed she walked with difficulty. For a minute, perhaps two, she stared out, back turned. When she spoke, her voice seemed to be coming from another place—as if carried by the wind on a clear day. "How long does a young Indian man live in Montana?" she asked. "Life expectancy, I mean."

Clark was about to guess sixty when she answered her own question. "Thirty-eight. Alaska's even worse. And they don't all die driving to church."

Outside, a breeze caught the large oak limbs and he heard the leaves rustle. Somewhere two squirrels chattered.

"The dead ones are lucky in some ways, I suppose. No more craziness or abuse. The worst are the Walking Ghosts. People-who-are-not-people. Warm Springs is full of them. That's the state mental hospital. Most are worse than dead.

"At a distance, the frame buildings look pretty—green grass, trees and picnic tables against the tan wheatfields and summer blue skies. It's just a warehouse, a holding facility. The cyclone fence wire gives that away, but you don't see the wire from the freeway. People breeze on by thinking about fishing or watching horses running in the wide meadows.

"Inside, the young people are badly disturbed. They masturbate constantly, set fires, repeat compulsive actions. Sometimes, the big ones rape and kill the smaller ones. Then they go to prison in Deer Lodge.

"That's a relief in a way, like death, because you don't see them anymore. They're placed in Warm Springs after drug overdoses, crime, prolonged abuse. They've lost their spirit, their spark. The younger they are, the worse—because they're going to live longer."

But not much past thirty-eight, Clark thought. *Not living like that.* Outside, clouds covered the sun, obscuring RealBird, and Clark felt a chill breeze from the window.

"Roxanne Pretty-on-Top stayed three years," RealBird said. "Winters were the worst. She stood by the fence, staring beyond at the snow fields, tilting her head, listening. At times, she'd drop to her knees and scoop handfuls of snow, pretending to fill a box." RealBird sighed. "This went on and on. Winters are long in Montana. They break your heart.

"We discovered she had buried her babies in the snow, filling their tiny mouths until they choked and stopped crying. Twins. Every winter she heard them calling. Their cries were louder to her than the bitter winds blowing down from Canada."

Clark wished she'd shut the window.

RealBird turned, facing Clark and holding out her hands, as if to touch him. "Roxanne tried climbing the fence. She had to reach those babies. She sliced her arms and hands to shreds with glass shards, and it took the doctors hours to sew her back.

"Before they dragged her away, she drew patterns in the snow with her own blood, then insisted everyone look. 'See Jesus? Now he's trapped in here with us, Ada. Bloody Jesus.'"

Clark felt chilled as if a fog had settled in his bones. When he spoke, he expected to see his own breath. "This isn't about Wade."

She lifted a finger. "Maybe it is. The point is, in spite of all that, Roxanne had a spark. She was one of the few—and they saved her."

Clark didn't say anything.

"Only a few have the spark, a spirit that's not completely snuffed out by the drugs and the abuse and the poverty and the self-contempt. Ritalin doesn't save them." Her voice became quiet. "Or any of the experts, God help me. Not even well-meaning ministers like my grandfather."

She took a deep breath. "Good homes and love may not help enough either. I'm sorry if you don't want to hear that, Mr. Woods. No one does."

"It needs a miracle," he said. His own voice sounded husky.

"You might call it a miracle," she said. "Sometimes the medicine people come in and perform the old ceremonies. Nothing official, of course. The state wouldn't pay for that. . . . Even the tribal officials look down on the old longhairs. But on icy winter nights, you can hear the old ones chanting and see the torchlights as they cross the snowy fields toward the fence. They're inside—no one knows how. No one recalls opening the double-locked doors, and you can smell the burning sage, the tobacco. Gourds rattle and the prayer sticks go click, click, click. They give the sick person a new medicine bundle, a new *Weyekin* guardian spirit. The old ones blow and chant over the sick child, their breaths fanning that spark . . .

"Roxanne went home in May," she said. "Later she graduated from college. She wrote me three letters. I can't explain it, but I've seen it."

"All right," Clark said, still lost in her words. He pictured dark and disturbed children gazing from behind cyclone fence line.

"I need to see these other people right now. But we'll talk about Wade again. I've seen that spark in Wade, Mr. Woods. He's worth saving."

When he took her offered hand, they shook lightly, and his mind seemed to clear for an instant. He was thankful Wade seemed different from the hard cases she had described. He thought Wade had a spark, too. Puzzled, he wondered if Dr. RealBird were Roxanne.

"Did you leave Montana because of the tough cases?" he asked. "I mean, did that work wear you down?"

"No. I don't mind hard work." She paused. "If you promise not to tell anyone else, I'll tell you."

"I'm not much of a gossip," he said.

"I left because my ex-husband started doing rock-and-roll lip synch," she said. "That was the last straw. I couldn't have a drink in Butte without worrying about running into him. Who wants a big Chippewa cop up on stage doing Roy Orbison or the Righteous Brothers?"

Clark grinned from the surprise of it. "You're not kidding?"

"Cross my heart." She made an X on her chest with her finger. "What could I do? The woman psychologist who couldn't handle her crazy husband. His mid-life crisis, or whatever it was. Even our daughter was embarrassed. She transferred to Rocky Mountain College just to get away from her dad." Dr. RealBird opened the door and he stepped out.

"Did you try the medicine people on him?" Clark asked. Her husband's situation seemed relatively easy.

"Of course," she said. "They put bundles under his bed, behind the front seat of the pickup, even close to his old record collection." She spread her hands. "We tried everything. Zip." She put her finger to her lip. "Mum's the word."

The Fitzgeralds waited nervously on gray upholstered chairs. Their boy Michael, one of Wade's classmates, wore a contraption that resembled a football helmet and frequently banged his head against hard objects. "I feel fine! I'm happy. Do you feel fine? Are you happy?" he repeated over and over whenever Clark saw him talk.

Sometimes at home, Wade mimicked the Fitzgerald boy. "I feel fine!" he shouted and banged his head against the wall. "I'm happy!" A harder bang. Clark or Payette usually stopped him before he could complete the second routine. A couple of times, he had knocked loose plaster, showing the lath beneath.

Stepping into the bright afternoon sun, Clark squinted. The autumn breeze had died. No clouds obscured the sun. He wondered what kind of encouraging words the poor Fitzgeralds expected to hear.

If Dr. RealBird could make them believe Michael had a spark, she was a real spellbinder. *I'm being too cynical,* he thought, reconsidering Roy's words. Maybe the doctor didn't know everything, but he figured she knew something.

. . .

Payette sat in the kitchen nook, nursing a cup of tea. She had awakened very early, showering and putting on makeup. In front of her was a large book: *Masterpieces in Modern American Art.* She wore a dark blue suit that Clark didn't recognize and a white silk blouse. A turquoise and silver squash blossom necklace adorned her throat.

Clark poured coffee and sat across from her. Distracted by the necklace's expense, he jarred the table with his knee and some of her tea slopped.

"God damn it, Clark. Don't be so fucking clumsy!" She quickly scooted away from the spilled tea and stood beside the table while he got a sponge to wipe up the mess. Some tea had gotten on the book, but it had a plastic jacket sheet.

"Take it easy," he said, tossing the sponge back toward the sink. "You're so incredibly beautiful I just wasn't looking where I sat. You're a knockout."

"Good." She remained standing, waiting for the water to dry. "That's how I planned it." She turned over the book. A little tea had gotten on the cover, making a brown, quarter-sized half-moon.

"Where'd you get the book?"

"Downtown at the Portland State Library. I used your staff card. If there's a fine for that stain, you did it anyway."

"Thanks a lot," he said, but he wasn't angry. "What's it about, all this study and a new outfit?"

Satisfied the table was dry, she sat down again. "No big deal, Lucille. I'm getting a raise. Anyway, Nordstrom was having a sale."

"You didn't buy that necklace at Nordstrom. It looks like old pawn. Beautiful work."

She lifted her chin and touched the necklace with her forefinger and thumb. "You like it then?"

"Very much." He tried not to think about the cost, but he knew you couldn't buy jewelry like that for under five hundred dollars.

She smiled and reached across the table, squeezing his hand. "Now don't get mad. I had to charge most of it, but it's an investment in my professional wardrobe. All the women that go anyplace in art dress well, but you need to have your own style, too." She touched the collar of the blouse. "Other women know right away if it's silk or just cotton."

"Good thing we both don't need professional wardrobes," he said. "A corduroy coat and denim shirt get me by." He tried being humorous but she took him seriously.

"You're not downtown," she said. "At your teaching job, just about anything goes."

"How much was that necklace, anyway?"

She shook her head. "That's for me to know and you to find out. Anyway, here's how you can look at it. You don't have to pay any more. You just pay a little longer."

Clark glanced at his watch. "I owe, I owe. So off to work I go."

She came around to his side of the table and gave him a long kiss, letting her hand drop to his lap. "Lucky for me, you're not a dwarf," she whispered into his ear.

He held her wrist. "I'll give you half an hour to stop that." Her heavy perfume, the scent of lipstick turned him on.

"Later, cowboy." She gave his crotch a quick rub, then pulled away. "Rose is having a group of gallery owners from back East visit our gallery today, and I've got to be on my toes. Now they've realized there's money in it, they've decided to carry Indian art. We're going out to dinner so I'll be late."

"Good luck," he said. "Maybe I should get Wade up to kiss you."

"Ooh, ooh." She made a face and shook her hands. "Keep him away for now. I don't need him messing me up before I go downtown."

.   .   .

She got home at ten, a little tipsy. After hanging up her good clothes, she put on gray sweatpants with a matching shirt, her black-rimmed glasses. Wade gave her a quick kiss and she told him she'd missed him.

"I learned a new song in school," he said. "Do you want to hear it? It's about a big old bear."

"In just a little bit." She patted his back. "You take a bath because I need to talk with Dad a minute."

Clark had built a fire and cleaned up the front room, putting away Wade's toys. The kitchen was clean, too. He'd made Hamburger Helper with macaroni and cheese—Wade's favorite.

"So how did it go?" he asked Payette when they were settled with glasses of wine.

She put her hand to her forehead. "Artsy-fartsy pains in the ass. The day went okay because Rose and I explained Indian art to them, mostly Northwest Coast. They were really impressed by the masks and the dancing sticks, some of the Tlingit screens and carvings. I had them right here." She tipped her palm toward him.

"You're terrific with people. Where did you go to dinner?"

"L'Auberge," she said. "The name's French and as soon as they served the salad, I could tell it would be terrific. They don't cut the lettuce. They *tear* it by hand. That's how you tell a good restaurant, Rose says. 'Torn lettuce. Somebody out in the kitchen is working hard.' We had five courses, ending up with cheese. That place was classy. And Rose paid."

"I've heard L'Auberge is really good," Clark said. "Teachers can't afford it."

"The food was great. But those art people made me uncomfortable, the way they sat around comparing pedigrees from back-East schools. They chitchatted about museums and their collections." She mimicked them. "'The Whitney is *adorable,* if you like Calder.' 'I prefer the Glick because they don't allow children running around and you can get some peace.' 'Have you seen those stained-glass murals in the Modern?'" She slugged back some wine. "They kept on and on, really pushing it. Then they started on the museums in France. The Monets at L'Orangerie. Versailles. And then they bragged up French food."

She poured some more wine.

"That's kind of how art is," Clark said. "Lots of snobs. But you can stand up to anybody."

She settled back staring at the expensive Navajo rug above the fireplace. "The way they looked at me, I could tell they thought I was a hick from Alaska. One woman came right out and gave me a big sweet smile, flashed her blue eyes, and asked what I thought of the Indian collection at the Peabody. She was just trying to trap me, make me feel bad.

"But I got her. I told her they'd stolen a lot of second-rate stuff, but the best collections were at the Heard in Arizona, the Provincial Art Museum in Victoria. If she wanted an *adorable* small collection, I said she should try Sheldon Jackson in Sitka."

Clark laughed. "What did she say?"

"Who cares? I shot her down like a mad dog." She raised her glass, eyes flashing.

. . .

Payette went in to supervise Wade's bath and Clark waited in bed. After a few drinks, she usually wanted to make love, especially after a good dinner.

"Brown bear, brown bear, looking at me," Wade sang. "Brown bear, brown bear, what do you see? I see a green frog, looking at me." He went through the yellow duck, black dog, and brown cow. Payette sang with him and they sounded good. Clark liked listening to them. Wade was way off key, but enthusiastic.

"Red fox, red fox, what do you see?" she sang.

"I see a penis head looking at me," Wade sang, then burst into chortles.

Smack! Smack! Smack! Smack!

As he jumped from bed, Clark heard Wade screaming and kicking the water with loud splashes.

When he burst into the bathroom, Clark saw Payette holding both of Wade's wrists high above his head with one hand while she spanked him with the other. He had red blotches on his butt and upper legs.

"You little freak! Don't you ever do that again." Payette looked ferocious.

Through the blubbering, Wade said, "I won't. I won't, Mama. I promise. I promise. Stop it."

She shouted into his face. "If you ever do that again, you won't sit down for a month." She dropped him into the tub, but he didn't sit. He rested on his knees leaning forward and protecting his rear end with his hand. "I won't, Mama. I won't. I promise."

"Tell the little freak to go to bed," she told Clark as she stormed out the door.

Forty-five minutes passed before Clark got Wade settled. He put some cortisone cream on the red blotches and told him it should take out the sting. "Where did you learn that, anyway?"

"The kids thought it was funny," Wade said.

"Better not sing it that way again," Clark said. He didn't think Payette would listen to Wade sing it again anyway, after that blowup. She had a way of holding grudges.

When he went into their bedroom, Clark saw Payette propped up on two pillows. She slept deeply, glasses still on, snoring slightly. He removed the glasses gently. Without them, she appeared less fierce, her features softened.

*   *   *

The next morning, she slept late. Clark made Wade be quiet until the school bus came.

"Is Mom still mad at me?"

"No," Clark said. "But she's very tired."

"Am I a freak? Maybe she'll give me away to the circus."

"Of course not. She just said that because she was angry."

"I don't want to leave," Wade said. "I don't want to leave with a circus."

Clark knelt beside the boy and pulled his shirt collar out of the sweater. "No one's joining a circus." He tousled Wade's hair. "They're afraid you might scare off the lions." He gave him a hug. "Even if the gypsies offer me lots of money, I won't let them take you."

Payette stayed in the bathroom a long time. When she came out, she looked ill. He tried kissing her, but she put her hand in front of her mouth. "Leave me alone. I just threw up."

"Too much French food," he said. "Living too high on the hog."

"Too much Wade," she said. "Is he gone?"

Clark nodded. "He was afraid the circus would get him. Somehow he knows that's where freaks are. He made a pretty good connection there, don't you think?"

"I hope he's traumatized for life," she said. "What if he said 'penis head' in front of Rose or some of those people from the East? They'd wonder what the hell we were doing raising him."

"He's getting better," Clark said. "Anyway, I don't think they're heading out to our home."

She snorted. "Not this place. Maybe if we had a better house."

She fixed tea and got a low-cal yogurt out of the refrigerator. "Do me a favor, would you?" She slumped at the table and stirred the yogurt.

"What is it?"

"Call Rose and tell her I'm sick. Anyway, I worked overtime yesterday." She stuck out her tongue. "What does it look like?"

"I don't know. Kind of coated, I guess."

"I saw myself in the mirror," she said. "I looked like the wrath of God."

"You just had too much to eat and drink. You look beautiful," he said, even though she was a little peaked.

"I don't need a lecture." She tried a spoonful of yogurt. "These strawberries taste like chemicals." She threw the yogurt into the garbage. "Just call Rose, okay? Please."

*　　*　　*

When Clark and Wade got home late that afternoon, she was in better spirits. "I went back to bed," she said. "I didn't get up until one." She was preparing a pot roast and wore a blue apron that said: THE COOK'S IN CHARGE. She had peeled two dozen carrots for the roast because she loved cooked carrots.

"So it's all right to have Wade come in?" Clark had instructed him to stay outside awhile, until he could determine what her mood was.

She glanced out the window at the boy who was pulling his red wagon away from the woodpile after loading it with kindling. She smiled. "What an eager beaver. No, more like a manic monkey. He's all arms and legs, tiny little body and butt. I guess I shouldn't have gotten so mad." She put the roast in the oven, and when she stood up, Clark put his arms around her, squeezing her and rubbing her belly.

She winced. "I'm kind of tender." Moving his hand away, she said, "Sorry about that. I just hurt a little."

"The rich food probably irritated your system," he said.

She took his hands. Her eyes grew bright with excitement. "Sit down. I want to tell you about something."

"Did you get a raise? We can pay off that necklace faster."

"Better than that. Do you remember me talking about John Two

Coyotes? He's come into the gallery and talked about going back to school?"

"Yeah, I think so." The way she'd talked about John before, he sounded like a smooth operator, so Clark didn't feel too excited.

"Well, I sent off for that information on the special Harvard Program for Indian students. I want you to look these over." She handed him an envelope with a lot of brochures and a page of explanation.

"A Master's in Education," he said. "But you don't want to teach."

"What difference does it make?" she said. "It's a Master's from Harvard. That's all you have to say when someone asks about your pedigree. If I can get in, I can learn a lot about art back in Boston."

"What about a bachelor's?" he said. Payette had gone to Southeast Alaska Community College, but didn't have an undergraduate degree.

"That's the beauty of it," she said. "They give you credit for prior learning experience. John told me all about it. He doesn't have a bachelor's either."

"I'm not sure I get it," Clark said. He was just skimming the brochure. The program was designed for Indian students and Harvard was providing them with an opportunity to earn a master's, then go back to reservations or the public schools and do a practicum. "Don't you need an actual bachelor's?"

She shook her head. "I called. They were very interested in me because they have hardly any people from Alaska. I'm Tlingit; I've got prior experience; and I've got an associate degree. Now all I have to do is write an essay and take the Miller's Analogy exam." She paused. "Would you help me with the essay?"

"Sure. Of course." He had always wanted her to succeed, but something about the program at Harvard confused him. He didn't understand how they could award a master's to people who hadn't earned a bachelor's. "What about the money? We're kind of maxed."

"The tribe will pay for most of it," she said. "I can borrow the rest."

For the next several weeks, she worked on her application and essay, and she studied for the Miller's Analogy exam.

"Darn, this is hard," she said frequently, but he kept drilling her on practice questions. Twice Clark and Payette met downtown with John Two Coyotes, who told them, "The main thing is—you have to say that you want to go back and *help* your people. They eat that up. I've talked to Crows from Montana and Northern Cheyenne from Wyoming. They all say it works like a charm."

When she mailed off her application, Payette said, "Keep your fingers crossed." That night at dinner, the three of them said grace and she asked for help.

Wade fell asleep early, and they made love for the first time since she'd started her application. Earlier, she'd said she was too tense. Now, after they had finished, she said, "That helped me relax."

Outside, rain pelted against the bedroom windows. Roof run-off splashed down the gutters and drain. Only a little illumination came into the room, provided by the back porch light. Clark felt they should both sleep well.

"Thank you for helping me," she said. "Do you think my essay was okay?"

"Perfect." He looked at her large dark eyes. "You're going to get in. I'm sure of it." He crossed his fingers for her.

"I really want this," she said. "How can you be so sure?"

He cupped her breast in his hand. "Maybe I don't make a lot of money, but I damn well know how to write an essay, even with suggestions from Two Coyotes." He ran his fingers over her ribs.

"I like your confidence, cowboy. Now I'm going to try to sleep." She paused, and her stomach made a noise. "Listen to that!"

"You've been awful nervous about this thing. I think it'll settle down. They're having free flu shots at the school next Thursday. Maybe we should both get one, what with Wade around."

"That little germ carrier's been pretty good lately," she said. "I know we shouldn't have put a TV in his room, but at least I got my application finished."

. . .

"This isn't a good time," Payette said. "Not for me."

"Of course it's a great time," he said. "It's a new step, like buying a house. Everybody's afraid to sign the mortgage papers, but then they say 'I wish I'd done that sooner.' It just takes awhile to get used to the idea."

"Don't be ridiculous. Having a baby isn't anything like buying a house. I'm the one signing these papers, not you."

He was exasperated. "Okay, look. That's just a comparison. I realize it's not the same."

"I regret even telling you," she said. "I knew you'd get all hysterical. Dr. Jacobs will do the procedure next Thursday. I just thought you should know."

"Procedure? That's a great term for an abortion." He rolled down the car window so he could get some air. They were sitting in a parking lot near Jake's Famous Crawfish. She had suggested dining out to celebrate her acceptance into the Harvard program, but now he realized that she also had been setting him up to break the other news. "Why did you see Jacobs anyway? You don't even like him. You told me he makes you take off your bra and panties every time you go to the office, no matter what. You said he's an old lech."

Her face was set in stone. "I know he'll do what I want," she said. "He'll get a nice fee from your insurance."

Clark had started going to Jacobs because he was quick to prescribe antibiotics or sleeping pills. When the doctor had found out Clark was from eastern Oregon, he showed him photos of a large cattle ranch he had purchased near Pendleton. The doctor and his wife, both wearing new silver-bellied cowboy hats, sat on Appaloosas. "Black Angus make a cozy retirement," he said. Clark figured that inflated insurance and Medicaid charges helped purchase the herd.

"Look, you're not thinking straight. This *is* a good time. My job's going okay. You just got a raise. My mom can help."

"I'm not having this baby," she insisted. She stared out the window at flashing neon signs advertising luxury cars. "I'm not getting attached to this baby. It's been too long even now, but I wanted to wait until a good time to tell you."

Clark had an idea. "You know what? I think you actually want this baby, down deep. That's the real reason you waited."

She clenched her fists and lowered her head, face turned away. "I knew you wouldn't understand. I don't want a baby now. It was an accident." She brought her fists to her forehead. "Damn it! Damn it! Damn it!"

He put his hand on her shoulder. "Stop it, Payette."

"I should never have gone off the pill. My face was getting blotchy and I wanted to lose weight. Now look what happened."

He slid over toward her and she leaned against him. "We can think this through. You can have the baby and go to Harvard next year. We'll save enough money and I'll go, too."

"On your salary? I'm not waiting," she said. "It wouldn't do any good." She wiped her eyes, smearing mascara on her cheeks and the palms of her hands.

"Don't you see? It wouldn't be fair to Wade. I'm not a good mother to him. I know that. But this baby would be different, and I'd love it, because it's mine and yours. Maybe I wouldn't be the best mother, but I know I could do better than mine did." She seized Clark's shoulder and squeezed until he wanted to shout. "I'd resent Wade even more, and I can't stand him now. And I'm afraid I'd grow to resent the baby, too, if I don't get to go to school. I can't sleep. I can't think."

Clark held her close and told her everything would be okay. "We can sort it out tomorrow," he promised.

However, in the morning she remained as adamant about going through with the abortion. "Talk doesn't solve anything," she said. "It just makes things worse."

While she was at work, he called Reverend Anderson, the Presbyterian minister who had performed their wedding and offered to help with counseling whenever they needed it. Clark tried explaining the situation over the phone but nearly became tongue-tied with emotion.

"You and Payette need to establish goals and priorities," Anderson said. He sounded a long way off, and Clark cursed the rural phone company for not providing better service.

"There's not much time," Clark said. "She's scheduled an abortion for Thursday."

"That is a difficult issue," Anderson said after a pause. "Both of you should be involved in the conception, birth, and raising of a child."

Clark wrote *"involved?"* on a sheet of notepaper, then stared at the word. He couldn't fathom what the word on the notepaper had to do with the flesh-and-blood issue.

"She won't listen to me. I thought maybe if we came up there . . ."

Anderson seemed pleased to have a specific suggestion. "Of course, if you can persuade her, I'd be more than happy to talk with you both. I still remember how charming Payette was when I met her. And beautiful." Another pause. "Yes, both of you coming for a chat would be ideal. Just call and we'll work out a time."

"If she refuses to drive up there, would you talk to her on the phone?"

"Any time. In the meantime, you pray for God's guidance, and I'll be praying, too, as soon as we hang up. In fact, why don't we pray together. Just bow your head and we'll ask Almighty God to lead us."

While Anderson prayed, Clark listened but didn't close his eyes. He wondered if Anderson's eyes were closed. While the reverend continued praying, Clark stretched the cord and sat on a chair. He didn't think much of the prayer. Somehow the minister sounded too superficial, too unctuous. His words seemed general, not addressed to Clark's problem. Maybe it was the lousy phone.

When Anderson said "amen," Clark also said "amen," and his word echoed on the line. He hung up the phone, baffled by Anderson's lack of outrage. What kind of minister was he, anyway? Clark felt as if he'd called about a teeth cleaning appointment or an oil change.

· · ·

Clark tried guilt, love, anger, bargaining, hurt, but Payette remained unmoved. Finally, he was too exhausted to try any longer. She seemed closer to relenting that night in the truck than at any other time, and he tortured himself with doubts about not changing her mind then. What could he have done? Surely some action or argument would have worked.

She slept with her back to him, the extra pillow over her head. Each night he lay awake thinking of what he could do or say to convince her. One night she kept talking in her sleep, but he couldn't make sense of it.

The night before the abortion, after she had packed a small suitcase, she said, "I don't want you there for the procedure, but please come afterward." Then she added, "If you love me, you'll support me in this. I'm sorry we don't agree."

He wondered how she'd act if he was in her situation, but that comparison didn't exactly work. "I'll be there," he said. "Right after I drop Wade off."

• • •

At the hospital, his anger ebbed when he saw her lying in bed, terribly pale. She wore a blue-checked hospital gown and a matching elastic cap. A unit of blood was going into her arm.

She lifted her hand and smiled weakly when she saw him. "Thanks for coming, sweetie." Her voice sounded parched, and he felt tenderness for her. "Would you hand me that glass of juice? I'm so thirsty."

As she took the glass he offered, Clark imagined—just for a moment—her hand smoothing the hair of their child. He blinked away the image.

"Something unexpected happened," she said. "It's hard to believe."

"Are you all right?" He held onto her hand and kissed her dry lips.

"When I came in I felt so awful I almost fainted. The nurses were prepping me for the operation, and they had to shave me. I remember how cold the shaving cream felt and they teased me about being pretty hairy down there, making their job tough." She paused, handing him the glass. "I think I dozed off. Maybe not. I was out of it."

She didn't say anything for a moment, but took her free hand and blew her nose with a hospital tissue. "Then this pain came—so bad, I think I passed out. When I came to, they told me I had a miscarriage."

"A miscarriage?" He studied the glass in his hand as if he'd never seen one before. Orange pulp remained in the bottom. "You had a miscarriage?"

"Something was wrong with the baby, I guess. They didn't let me see it. But I had a lot of bleeding. This is my second unit of blood." She tried a joke. "I sure hope whoever gave it has lots of energy, 'cause I feel like crap."

"I'm sorry," he said. "What was wrong with the baby?"

She lifted her head. "It's better this way, don't you think? You've been so upset, it made me sick. Don't you think this way is better?"

"I think it is." Clark wanted to believe her, but he wasn't convinced that it really was a miscarriage.

A nurse came in and checked the blood. "How are you feeling, honey? I think you're looking a little perkier."

Payette nodded. "I always feel better when my husband's around.

This is Clark Woods. He works up at Two Rivers College. He's going to take me home as soon as you say I can ride."

The nurse smiled and shook his hand.

"She looked pretty pale when I came in," Clark said. "I guess she had a miscarriage. Lost a lot of blood."

"She hasn't broken the blood bank, yet," the nurse said. "She's made a big withdrawal."

"Is that heavy bleeding common with miscarriages?" he asked.

"I'm a floor nurse," she said. "You'll have to ask the doctor."

Dr. Jacobs seemed in a hurry when he made his rounds. He hadn't taken off his overcoat, and his long gray hair was combed back, imitating wings above the ears. He reeked of sweet aftershave. Hai Karate, or Jade East, Clark thought. The doctor resembled a dissipated Mercury.

"How are you feeling, darling?" the doctor asked Payette. "You gave us a scare, but you're looking chipper now. We can probably send you home tomorrow morning. I just want to keep you here overnight, for observation."

"She's going to be okay, then?" Clark asked. "After the miscarriage, is everything okay?"

Dr. Jacobs looked at Clark as though he'd seen him for the first time, even though Clark had been a patient over five years. He gave Clark's knee a pat with his pink, pudgy hand. Gray hairs sprouted below the knuckles.

"We gave her a couple of units of blood and she'll be fine. These . . . uh . . . miscarriages can be nasty when they're that far along. Next week, she'll need to come into the office for more tests, but I think she'll be shipshape. I've seen a lot of these."

He headed for the door. Clark felt heat rising from his neck to his ears. He wanted to block Jacobs's way and grab the wings, then bang the doctor's pink skull against the wall. He wanted to take the fetus and jam it down the doctor's lying throat until the old lech babbled the truth.

*   *   *

In mid-October, Clark took Wade fishing on Eagle Creek. "You guys are driving me nuts," Payette had said. "Get out of the house. I need time to study."

Fall steelhead were running and Clark purchased two dozen Steelie lures, figuring Wade would go through them pretty fast. They hiked in at dawn to be the first on the water, and were already shivering from the wet dew at seven. Clark practiced casting in a deep pool, showing the boy how to work the Steelies through the current. "That's not a fish," he explained when the spinning rod's tip bobbed. "It's the Steelie hitting fast water."

Wade hooked a snag or dragged bottom every few casts and Clark showed him a couple tricks for getting the lure free. When one refused to unsnag, Clark pointed the rod tip along the taut line and backed away until the monofilament snapped. "Point the pole straight at the snag," he said. "Otherwise, you might break the tip. Sometimes, you're going to lose it, buddy." He tied on another swivel. "Now a fish has a red-and-white lawn ornament."

The water was too deep to cross, so Clark fly-fished the holes below Wade, letting the bright flies drift past the grassy hummocks along the creek. He tried dries and wets, weighting his floating leaders, but only had two missed strikes that morning. His arms were sore, his right shoulder and wrist tired. He remembered what Roy had said. "If you're trying too hard, lower your standards. Take a long break."

He and Wade ate lunch at eleven. Payette had packed bologna sandwiches, apples, beer, and 7UPs. All tasted good. "How many lures you got left, buddy?"

Wade mumbled something, spitting out some food. He chewed openmouthed in spite of constant instruction, and Clark tried not to look too carefully.

"How many? Wait until you swallow."

After a few seconds, Wade held up one hand and two fingers. "Seven."

Clark took the boy's right hand a minute. The raised white scar tissue that covered his palm was tough as leather. Now Clark noticed a line cut on the boy's right finger. "Don't let that line work against your finger all the time," he said. "Hold your pole like this."

Wade pretended to have a big fish. He strained at the effort. "I want to take a steelhead home to Mom," he said.

"We're just warming up," Clark said. "Letting the fish grow."

Taking out his pocketknife, he sliced one of the apples that grew on the three trees behind the house. *This was a MacIntosh,* he thought. He thought of Sherwood Anderson's grotesque small-town characters and how he compared them with the gnarled but sweet apples in abandoned orchards. *Wade was like that,* he thought—a little misshapen but basically sweet.

He found a napping spot and lay down for a while. When he awoke, the sun's slant showed it was past noon. To Clark's surprise, Wade had not returned to fishing but drew in the sandy gravel bars with a pointed stick.

Clark studied the drawings over Wade's shoulders. The boy worked intently. He had traced a line picture of waves, a few stick people, and some large fish. Three of the people seemed to be holding onto the fish fins. He wondered how much Wade remembered about his father's death, if anything.

A pretty good drawing, Clark decided. It reminded him of the native art in the Sitka museum. The Tlingits had drawn similar pictures on sealskin drums and raven rattles.

"That's good," he told Wade. "Some of those fish are darned big. I hope to catch a monster like that this afternoon."

Wade scuffed the picture out with his boot.

"Did you ever see a fish that big? Maybe a whale?"

Wade shook his head. "Not for a while. The weather's too nice here. Whales come around more in storms."

*   *   *

At three, Clark hooked a big steelhead. He felt the hard strike, the solid shock as he set the hook. "Fish on!" The fish raced through the deep blue-green water, heading downstream. The reel began to smoke and Clark wished he had a tungsten drag. He floundered a few yards along the bank, heading after the fish, taking care to keep the tension on but not enough to break the line.

"You got one, Dad! You got one!"

Half turning his head, Clark saw Wade splashing through the water. "It's a monster, Wade. Get the net."

The big fish turned before it reached the cascades downstream, then swam back and forth in the deep pool. Twice it leaped, and Clark marveled at the dime-bright color, the red and yellow fly hanging from its jaw. He had caught bigger fish, but never on a fly rod.

After playing the fish another ten minutes, he figured it was tired. The fish held to the bottom of the pool. "Wade, get below me a little on that gravel bar. Right there just past that snag. Hold still! When the fish is over the net, lift up." He waited until the boy splashed below him. "Hunker down and stay still. Now listen, don't bump the fly or the line with the net, okay. You might knock the fish loose."

He concentrated on keeping the line taut, not too much or too little. As he backed away from shore, the fish nudged toward the bar. *Six pounds, maybe seven,* he thought. He could barbecue the fish outside, adding a little lemon and brown sugar.

The spent steelhead rolled on its side and the current carried it toward shore. "Easy, Wade."

In spite of Clark's warnings, the boy lunged toward the fish, sweeping the net through the water. Panicked, the steelhead threshed sideways, and Clark felt the line go slack. He prayed the fish was in the net, but Wade lifted it clear of the water, dripping and empty. The fish disappeared into the pool's green depth, the bright fly still visible in Clark's mind.

"God damn it," Wade said, slapping the water with the net. "It got away, Dad. That damn fish got away."

Clark sat on a sun-bleached log. His legs felt rubbery and his stomach queasy. The slack fly line drifted in the current, but he didn't care. He was sick with disappointment. He shouldn't have thought about the cooked fish. That brought lousy luck.

Wade was wet nearly to his crotch. His right arm was wet, too, and hung limp from his side. His lips twisted but he didn't say anything.

"Didn't you listen? You can't lunge at a fish like that," Clark said. "They panic. Now that fish is gone. Damn it, Wade. You cost me that fish."

After a while, Clark stood. *No point in blaming the boy,* he thought. In his fishing vest, he found an old bag of M&M's. He ripped open the corner and ate a couple. They tasted like stale chocolate. "Come here, Wade. I've got a surprise. Close your eyes and put your hands out."

Wade approached slowly. He held out his hands and Clark started to pour M&M's into the open palms. The boy's eyes were squeezed tight and he jerked back suddenly. "Don't hurt me, Dad. I'm sorry."

A dozen M&M's plopped into the water, sinking like bright pebbles and drifting downstream.

Wade's hands were behind him. He trembled with fear and two tears streaked his cheeks.

Clark's heart overflowed with sorrow and love. He wanted to touch the boy, but he was afraid. "These are just M&M's," he said. "Do you want to hold the bag?"

Wade took the bag when Clark offered it and poured a few into his hands. He finished one palmful, then tried another. His tears dried. "Mom's going to be disappointed, huh."

Clark touched the boy's shoulder. "I doubt it. She never expected us to catch anything."

. . .

Pots and pans lay scattered across the kitchen floor, and dark blood pooled on the counter near the sink, then streaked down a closed white cupboard to the floor.

"We've been robbed!" Wade yelled, running from room to room. "Dad, we've been robbed! Where's Mom?"

Clark let out his breath. The blood came from a two-pound package of hamburger venison thawing on the counter.

Wade returned to the kitchen. "My room's okay, I think." When he noticed the blood, he began to cry. "What happened to Mom? Mom! Mom!"

Clark gripped the boy's shoulders. "Look. The blood is from the meat. That's all. See the package?"

Wade wiped his nose with his sleeve and shuddered twice. "Your bedroom's a mess, Dad. A big mess. Mine's okay."

Payette's wardrobe was gone and her vanity along with the wigs, wig holders, and drawers of cosmetics. Clark's clothing remained in the closet although some had been scattered and trampled on the floor. Her pillows and Marimeko comforter were gone, along with most of the sheets and a couple of new Pendleton blankets.

The worn black-and-white sofa bed remained in the front room, but the walls and shelves were bare. He remembered the afternoon they had tapped the walls, searching for studs to hang the heavy transformation masks of Eagle and Killer Whale.

"She didn't get the fireplace," he muttered.

The vacuum cleaner and all the attachments were missing from the storage closet. On the hallway floor, he found a strip of ermine and realized she'd taken her dancing costume; the copper-decorated dancing tunic, sealskin drum, the rare Chilkat blanket woven from moss and mountain goat hair.

Remembering how beautiful she looked and how gracefully she danced, he felt nauseous at the loss and moved toward the kitchen to get a drink of water. He drank two glasses, then splashed cold water on his face.

The cupboards above the sink held chipped dishes and glassware. Some still unopened wedding gifts stood outside the kitchen bins: two fondue pots, a patio buffet server, a chafing dish shaped like a fish. She'd left the bulky food dryer.

Wade held up a 7UP he'd taken out of the refrigerator. His hands trembled and he had spilled soda all down his shirt. "Mom's gone away," he said, "hasn't she."

"Just for a while," Clark said. Maybe he could talk her into coming back.

Taking the big flashlight from behind the pickup seat, Clark studied the driveway and front lawn. Someone had backed a small truck up to the door. Several cigarette butts smeared with lipstick littered the porch.

In the bedroom Wade was trying to hang some of Clark's trampled clothes. A worried frown twisted his forehead and his mouth hung open. Squinting his right eye, he turned toward Clark. "Do I have to leave, too?"

Clark knelt and hugged the boy, who stiffened against the affection. "No. Of course not," he said—hoping it was true.

•   •   •

Clark sat on the front porch watching the early sun evaporate the heavy dew on Willbroad's Christmas trees. The season before, Willbroad put up big signs along the main road and people stopped to cut Christmas trees and take hayrides in the back of a trapwagon the old man towed with his pickup. Payette had decorated their tree with red and white bows, then let Wade put on striped candy canes. They had to slit the cellophane wrappers near the cane's crook so they'd hang on the heavy Noble fir Willbroad gave them as a present. "You're pretty good neighbors," the old man said.

After they had set out Wade's present marked "from Santa," they had drunk Amaretto and made love on the sofa before the applewood fire. Clark tasted the sweet strong liquor on her breath.

Now as Clark watched the steam rise off his cup of coffee, he wondered about this year's Christmas.

About eight-thirty, he saw the red Firebird turn onto Stormer Road and pull into the driveway. Payette wore jeans, black cowboy boots, and sunglasses. He noticed her large nipples pressed against the thin red sweater and he felt kicked in the stomach. He hated himself because he was glad to see her.

He didn't know what to say, but Wade saved them by bursting through the door. "Mom! We were afraid you'd been kidnapped. Where'd you go anyway? Dad checked all the motels. Where's all your stuff?"

Kneeling, she pulled him close and kissed him quickly. She ran one hand through his hair. "You need a haircut." She stood, took a Kleenex from her pocket, and wiped the lipstick off Wade's face.

He grabbed her leg, pressing his cheek against her side. "Mom, I don't have to move again, do I?"

"Don't be silly," she said. "Go inside and get ready for school, so Clark and I can talk."

"Are you coming back?" he asked. "I cried last night."

She didn't answer for a moment. "You know, Wade, I've got to work extra hard and study for school right now. It's a long drive from here, and I thought I should move a little closer."

"Why? You got a good car," he said.

She slapped him twice on the rump. "Go on now. Get ready."

"What the hell's going on?" Clark asked when the boy was inside. "I drove around half the night looking for you. Just imagine how Wade felt when he came home and found the place tossed. What were you thinking?" He gripped his coffee cup with both hands.

"Keep your voice down, Clark. The neighbors don't need to know our business." She folded her arms across her chest. "Can you spare a cup of coffee? It's colder than I thought."

"Do you want a sweater?"

"Just coffee."

She had left most of the cups from their trips, he noticed. He brought her coffee in a cup that said "Sitka Raven's Brew,"

She stood at the edge of Willbroad's field and plucked a white fall daisy from among the weedy border. Setting her cup down, she twined it behind her ear, Hawaiian style. "It's so beautiful out here," she said. "As close to paradise as I'll ever come."

"It is beautiful," he said. "What are you talking about?" He reached for her arm, but she edged away. "Please come back," he said.

"I can't," she said. "I just can't. Wade sucks out all my energy."

A blue jay scolded from the top of the barn, then flew into the tall firs.

"He's a load," Clark said. "But he's getting better."

"The summer's gone," she said. "Look how yellow the blackberry leaves are getting."

"You made a great cobbler," he said. "I wish I had some now."

"I used a half a pound of butter in that cobbler," she said. "It went straight to my thighs." After picking up her coffee, she turned away from him. "I can't live with you anymore, Clark," she said. "Even without Wade. That's the truth."

His coffee cup and hand seemed separated from him. He couldn't move the cup to his mouth. Steam evaporated before his face.

"Did you hear me? I tried falling in love with you, but I can't. And because of Wade, I can't even invite people from work out here. I don't even have time to study. I'm not happy. Can't you understand that? I'm not going to get trapped."

His eyes focused on the three apple trees between the barn and blackberry thickets. At night, deer trailed through the high grass to feed on the fresh windfall and the gnarled apples hanging from lower branches. A week earlier, Payette and Clark sat out in the old Fred Meyer lawn chairs sipping beer and watching a doe and her twin fawns eating. Even now he could smell the apple scent drifting on the air. "You're just upset," he said. "Everybody has a few doubts about commitments from time to time."

"I'm sorry," she said. "You're one in a million, but I don't love you."

He got the coffee to his mouth, even though his hand was shaking. The warm liquid helped him speak. "You never loved me? Even that night we drank Amaretto in front of the Christmas tree?"

She hesitated, then said, "I don't feel right. I don't love you the way I should, and when we make love, I feel bad." She set the coffee cup down on the ground. "I'll check on you guys. I still care . . ."

"Listen," he said. "We can send Wade back." He was ashamed at once for saying it. "We used to be fine. Remember how excited you were hanging those masks? The strain is too much right now. Cut back your hours at work, or some of your classes."

"I can't send him back," she said. "I feel guilty enough already. You send him back, if you want."

He held out his hands. "Think about it, Payette. We can't just let everything slip away."

"I don't care," she said. "I just need to be left alone awhile. I want to be myself." She got in the Firebird and started it.

"That's a crock of shit," he said "Who helped you move, anyway? Who messed up our house?"

"Some friends from work. That's all. There's no one else."

He kicked the driver's door. Not hard enough. He kicked it again, denting the side panel. She backed faster and he chased after the car, but staggered, losing his balance.

.   .   .

Coffee had slopped on the front of his khaki pants, soaking the crotch and right thigh. "What the fuck!" Clark hurled his empty cup as far as he could, and it landed a dozen rows deep in Willbroad's Christmas trees. He found Payette's cup and threw it, too.

Furious, he slammed into the kitchen, carrying out armloads of cups and glasses, anything that might have touched her lips. He flung them into the rows of trees. Most landed with a thud but occasionally one broke. The white porcelain cups remained in the cupboard because she had refused to drink out of them. "This place isn't a diner," she said.

After fifteen minutes, he felt wrung out and slumped on the porch.

The sun climbed higher, illuminating the dead branches and clippings. They glowed a fiery red brown and Clark wondered if they'd burn, perhaps ignited by the sun's rays through a piece of broken glass.

Wade's hand rested on Clark's shoulder. "Are you finished being mad?"

"No," he said turning around. Recognizing the fear in the boy's eyes, he added, "I guess so. For a while."

"The school bus left already."

"Is that right?" No children were gathered at the small red bus hut where their lane joined Springwater. "Forget school today. We've got to bring in the apples."

They took turns climbing the ladder. When Wade climbed high into the branches, Clark turned his head to keep bark chips from falling in his eyes. As he moved the ladder, he watched his footing. Yellowjackets feasted on the rotten apples and he wanted to avoid being stung.

By noon, they had gathered three buckets and four boxes of the MacIntosh and Jonagolds. Fallen apples remained on the ground for the deer.

Wade tired of helping as soon as they moved inside, but Clark made him help for half an hour, then let him go outside to play in the woods. All afternoon, Clark cored and sliced apples, loading the twelve-shelf fruit dryer. The extra boxes of apples he carried into the cool basement to prepare another day.

They ate Chinese food in town and returned to the empty house carrying leftovers in waxed containers. Clark found comfort in the low hum and glow of the dryer, the room alive with the scent of apples. After Wade was asleep, Clark opened the dryer, sprinkling cinnamon and sugar on four shelves of apples. The instruction booklet suggested different flavors for variety.

During the night, he awoke several times and shambled into the kitchen, sitting at the breakfast nook and studying the deep shadows under the apple trees. He knew the deer would be bedded for the night but felt good knowing they could return for the fallen apples as they wanted.

Late and groggy, he awakened, forgetting at first all that happened. Stumbling out by the stove, he saw the empty breakfast nook, the cold coffeepot. For a moment, he felt sick. Even so, as he made coffee and reheated the Chinese leftovers, he found some comfort in the dryer's steady hum.

After he drove Wade to school and scribbled an excuse, he stopped at the local grange for plastic bags to seal the apples.

Returning home, he saw Willbroad's old white International Harvester pickup on the dirt road adjacent to the tree field. Sunlight caught the glint of the old man's shears and he waved companionably as Clark honked. On his front porch, Clark found almost two dozen glasses, plates, and cups, three with broken handles. Somehow, he was pleased to see most of them returned unbroken, and he washed each one carefully, then replaced it in the cupboard.

For the next two weeks, he dried apples, occasionally nibbling the fruit even though he had lost his appetite. He filled the plastic bags half full, then added Fresh Fruit as the instructions suggested. He squeezed out all the excess air and closed each bag with a tight plastic twist. Finished with the apples, he unplugged the dryer, satisfied that he had preserved all he could.

6

Amherst, 1977

"I read about it in the paper this morning," Doyle said. "Sketchy details but it seemed like an accident."

Michael Doyle had a receding hairline and a dark mustache. Clark liked his eyes—steady and warm—and his bulk. Clark was used to large, confident men in Oregon, men who talked with one cowboy boot resting on the fence line, or one ruddy left elbow jutting from a pickup window. Take away his suit, give him a squint and sunburn, and Doyle might have become one of those strong ranchers.

When he had called Payette at Harvard, she insisted Clark find a lawyer, and a legal service hotline had suggested Doyle. After listening to Clark's brief account on the telephone, Doyle had agreed to see him later that morning.

Now in the office, Doyle filled three pages of a yellow legal pad with notes. "You did the right thing by coming to see me," Doyle said. "Sometimes the police get a little overzealous, especially with kids like Wade."

Clark was glad he didn't use the word "retarded." "They wanted to talk with him at ten."

Doyle looked at his watch. "Don't worry," he said. "I'll call Hawley and arrange things. Let's wait and see what they got. Wade's only nine. I don't think they'll do much until the coroner files his report a couple days from now."

"They took all his clothes," Clark said. "Was that okay?"

"That's their job." He gave Clark a reassuring smile. "And you did the right thing by coming to see me."

Doyle stood and looked out the window. "Fall goes fast around here. Last night's rain beat hell out of the trees." He returned to his desk. "They can talk with Wade tomorrow or the next day, after things settle down a bit. Right now, it wouldn't hurt to have him in school. Keep things normal. I imagine it's pretty tense around the apartments."

"You aren't kidding. Is it all right to leave the state? Go up to Vermont and look at what's left of the leaves?"

"Sure. Take a cooling-off period. Just check back in an hour or so and I'll tell you what Hawley says. He's not a bad guy. I see him at the kids' soccer tournaments."

Clark shifted so he could look out the window. His mother and Wade were in the Chevy pickup half a block away. The driver's door opened and closed, so he figured Wade was messing behind the wheel. "I guess I can take him to school."

"He likes school, right? One of the reasons we moved to Amherst was the good schools."

"Sure. They've got him in a special program. You can imagine they don't get many kids like Wade in Amherst."

Doyle laughed. "Amherst is loaded with specialists," he said. "All overqualified and underpaid. I'm going to come out and talk with Wade a minute." He took his raincoat off the rack.

Clark put on his jacket. He nodded at the law degree on the wall. "I see you went to Michigan. I used to work in Traverse City."

"Pretty place," the lawyer said. "My wife's folks have a cherry orchard on the peninsula. The developers are hounding them to sell every day. Chop it into view lots. It'll be a shame when they sell."

"You didn't grow up in Michigan?" Clark asked. "You don't sound like it."

"Worcester," Doyle said. "That explains the accent. I did my undergraduate work at Holy Cross, but I wanted to go West. Just not too far." He chuckled. "I loved Michigan. I'm one of five Catholics in the whole country who hates Notre Dame."

"Did you play football?"

"Linebacker in high school. Now I just coach soccer." He picked up a photograph of a girls' soccer team. The players wore red jerseys and blue pants. "My daughter Stacy," he said, pointing at the blocky girl next to him. "Sent her to goalie camp this summer, and she was pretty good. The other girls called her 'Dead End Doyle.'" He set the picture down. "Defense," he said. "If the other team can't score, they don't win."

*   *   *

The boy ran through the small park, kicking the piles of leaves, then covering himself and leaping up, brushing off his dark sweatshirt. Clark sat on the gazebo steps and chewed a piece of Juicy Fruit. He threw the wrapper onto the ground. *Vermont is too damn clean,* he thought. He imagined summer people gathering for family picnics and volleyball games, relatives kidding one another and making small talk about babies and children. Probably this little community had a band. People would gather on warm evenings, spreading blankets on the grass or unfolding chairs, listening to the band play summer favorites while fireflies winked in the dusk. *A normal life,* he thought. *Just normal might work.*

At dusk Clark realized he had left his flashlight in the apartment so he crossed the square to a hardware store and bought a two-celled Eveready. The store had some Tonka dump trucks on sale and Clark bought a big yellow one for the boy. He figured Wade could fill it with leaves.

"That's some bargain for nine ninety-five," the man said. He wore a gray apron with stitches that spelled "Floyd." "We figured to sell them to tourists, but summer's been gone awhile."

Clark gave him a twenty for the flashlight and truck. Taking out his pocketknife he cut the plastic strips that held the truck to the box. "You can keep this fancy packaging," he said.

The man grinned, nodding out the window. "That boy sure likes those leaves. Old Harvey, the park manager, will have to rake piles again tomorrow, but he don't mind. Wind usually scatters them plenty this time of year."

"We'll leave some for the wind," Clark said. "Can you recommend a place to eat? Just good home-cooked food?"

"Try the Miss Flo Diner," the man said. "I'd get the chicken and dumplings, and Flo makes the best apple pie in town."

Clark tried the flashlight, then dropped it in the pickup. Wade was excited with the dump truck and started filling it with leaves, making rumbling noises, then rolling the truck over in pretend crashes. "This dump truck does crazy wheelies, Dad. Watch."

After ten minutes, Clark grew tired of the crashes, the occasional collision with a tree. "Don't wreck up that truck." He thrust his hands into his jacket pockets. "I'm getting some chicken and dumplings, Spiderman. You want to come eat?"

Wade shook his head. "I'm working on a big job here." He made wild truck noises.

Clark glanced at his watch. "It's getting dark," he said. "We got to head back in about thirty minutes. Look, I'll be at the diner right across the street. I'll bring you some chicken and dumplings."

"Too mushy," Wade said. "How about a hamburger?"

"Whatever."

The diner's windows were filled with witches, black cats, and ghosts. Red and yellow Indian corn decorated the door. Clark ate the chicken and dumplings, then ordered for Wade. After paying for the meals, he headed into the park. Now it had grown dark and colder.

"Hey, Wade. Time to go," he called.

No answer.

"Let's move it. I got your hamburger."

After tossing the hamburger on the pickup seat, he quickly searched the park but couldn't find Wade. He checked under the gazebo and toed the piles of leaves, thinking the boy might be hiding. To his surprise, his toe nudged the dump truck, completely covered in leaves.

Checking the gazebo again, he found only the gum wrapper he'd left. Where the hell was Wade? He carried the toy truck to the pickup. Across the street, he saw the diner bathed in yellow light, the harvest of Indian corn adorning the doorway. *He got cold or went in to use the bathroom,* Clark thought.

But the men's room was empty. At the counter, Flo shook her head. "I saw him playing out there earlier," she said. "But now it's dark."

Alarmed, he got the flashlight out of the truck and jogged back to the leaf pile where he'd found the truck. At least it resembled the same leaf pile. The leaves were scattered and he couldn't distinguish one pile from another.

"Wade. Damn it, if you're hiding, come out right now. It's time to go."

Across the street, a man and a woman came out of the diner. They looked toward the park a minute, then got into their car. The exhaust from the car's tailpipe evaporated into the cold air.

Clark wondered if Wade headed up the wrong street. Maybe he got the restaurants confused. Entering town, they'd seen another place to eat, a hamburger joint with high school kids wearing lettermen's jackets. He decided to check it out and headed for the truck.

A wild scream filled the air, and something struck Clark's neck. Dazed, he froze, then whirled, lifting the flashlight to strike. He recognized the boy scrambling up from the ground.

"God damn it, Wade! What the fuck are you doing?" Clark took a couple of deep breaths and lowered the light. "What a jackass stunt!"

"I wanted to trick you, Dad." Wade's face gleamed with delight. "I was up in the tree, hiding. When you came under it, I jumped!"

"Don't ever do that again!" Clark touched the welts where Wade's fingernails had scratched his neck. "Get in the damn truck."

Flo had stepped outside the diner and peered toward them.

"Everything's okay," Clark yelled in her direction. He grabbed the boy's arm.

Wade still jumped with excitement. "You were really scared, Dad. You thought it was a monster."

7

Amherst, 1977

An orange, a rice bowl, and a yellow chrysanthemum made a tiny shrine on the top of the culvert. They had appeared the morning after Yukiko's death. No one had added anything else—no flowers or pictures. Like most people, Clark didn't know what to do, but he planned on sending a spray to the funeral.

Hawley asked the questions. The day had turned warm and he took off his navy blue blazer, holding it by the collar loop. He folded his sunglasses and put them in his shirt pocket so he could look directly at the boy. "Wade, I'm just going to ask you some questions and you answer the best you can, okay?" He patted Wade's shoulder. "Your dad's close by here and so is Mr. Doyle. Your grandma's right inside. You know what telling the truth is, Wade. Lieutenant Cooper and I just want you to tell the truth." When Wade nodded, Hawley asked. "Now, did you play with little Yukiko, the Japanese girl?"

"Sometimes. Not very much," Wade said.

"She was too little," Clark said. "Wade's a lot older."

"Why don't we just let the boy talk," Cooper said. "That would be better."

"Fine," Clark said.

"Think back, Wade. Two days ago." Hawley opened the gate on the playground and they went in. "Yukiko was in here. Were you in here, too?"

"I don't know," Wade said. His brow furrowed. "When?"

"The day Yukiko got hurt. Two days ago. What about then?"

"I don't think so," Wade said.

"Maybe you were in here with Yukiko and left the gate open," Hawley said.

Cooper squatted so he could see eye-to-eye with Wade. "A boy in a hurry to join his friends might leave the gate open. Sometimes, I leave a gate open myself. Maybe Yukiko followed you out."

Clark studied Doyle. The lawyer seemed miles away. His head was tilted back slightly as if he were enjoying the October sunlight. *This wasn't about the gate,* Clark thought. Anyone could leave a gate unlatched. They were trying to place Wade with Yukiko.

"Look." Hawley unlatched the gate and stepped outside. He walked twenty feet and stopped. "I forgot and left the gate open. Simple. A little mistake. I'll bet something simple like that happened. If you left the gate open, that's not really your fault."

"Everybody leaves gates open," Cooper said. "You know what? I've got a big black Labrador retriever named Ace, and when I leave the gate open, he tips over the neighbors' garbage. What a mess." He laughed and the boy laughed, too.

Turning to Clark, Wade asked, "When we get back home, can we get a dog?"

"I think we can," Clark said. Right now, he wished he were back in Oregon.

"So you might have left the gate open, like everybody else does." Hawley worked the gate a few times, moving it back and forth, open and shut. "Nobody's perfect, right?"

Wade nodded, but didn't say anything. He tried the gate himself. His arms seemed terribly thin, his hands loose and nervous.

"Maybe we should walk over there, closer to the water," Hawley said. "That might help you remember. Can you count the steps? How many steps from the playground to the culvert?"

Wade concentrated on counting. "Twenty-two," he said.

The five formed a tight group, crowding the space at the top of the culvert. Clark was certain one of them would kick over the rice bowl or knock the orange into the water.

"That's not very far, is it?" Hawley said. "Let's say you came over here and looked at the water. Yukiko might just tag along, right? After all, you're the big guy."

"Here's the thing," Cooper added. "We don't want any more kids to get hurt, so we're going to put a big fence all along here. Then no one else can get hurt in the water. That's a good thing, right?"

Wade nodded. "I like the water, though. How will I get down with the fence?"

No one answered.

The swamp shimmered in the angle of light and Clark saw a small boat's windshield wink a quarter mile off. Maybe someone was out fishing, or just cruising around. For a moment, he thought of the college girl from Michigan he used to love and her parents' boat out on Traverse Bay. After water skiing, they'd lain beside the boat, putting down two towels to keep off the coarse sand. A wave of regret swept over him. If he'd had the sense to marry her, none of this would be happening. Now he had the feeling that all of his life was out of control.

"Let's picture this a minute," Hawley said. "You and the little girl were up here on top of the culvert and you bumped her—by accident—and she fell into the water. Is that what happened?"

Clark stared at Doyle, expecting him to object to the question, the way lawyers acted in movies, but he just stared out toward the river.

"Wade? Is that what happened? An accident?" Hawley touched the boy's shoulder.

Wade hadn't said anything. He bent down and peered at the water, about seven feet below them.

"Your dad said you found a bobber. I sure like fishing." Hawley pretended to cast. "Did you find that bobber close by here? This looks like a good spot. In fact my boys used to fish right here when they were younger. I'm sure they caught a big trout right here."

"You tricky son of a bitch," Clark muttered and glared. Cooper reached for his arm, but Clark stepped away.

Hawley knelt close to the boy. "I'll bet you were thinking about fishing."

Clark turned to Doyle and the lawyer shook his head. *This guy's useless*, Clark thought. He noticed how frail Wade looked, the sag to his shoulders. Now Wade had that puzzled, worried look, the kind he got when he knew he was in trouble but was figuring out what to say. *Jesus, don't let them get him*, Clark prayed silently. Wade wasn't some little cute blond kid, a professor's son. He was dark and clumsy and looked guilty.

"You come here to think about fishing, don't you?" Hawley pointed to the swamp. "I see a big fish now. You come here a lot, don't you, Wade?"

"Wade, don't answer," Clark said.

As Cooper moved toward him, Clark half-turned, putting his finger near Cooper's face. "You're going to be looking at about ten Indian lawyers," he said. "That's big trouble for you. I should have hired an Indian lawyer to start with." He felt a flush rise in his neck and face. Cooper was ruddy, too.

Clark turned toward Hawley. "You never caught a fish in your life. Nothing but trash fish in water like this, you phoney." Clark expected to take some flak, maybe even get arrested for interfering with an investigation, but he was fed up.

Then Doyle spoke, and his words seemed to calm everyone. "Let's have the officers finish their inquiry," he said. "There's no point in dragging this out too long. Let's just see what happens. We're not in court."

"That's what we're trying to do, Doyle," Hawley said. "Okay, Mr. Woods? No more interference."

"Cut the crap, then."

"All right," Hawley said. "Look, Wade. See where I'm standing up high away from the water. Show me where you like to stand, where the kids play. Go ahead, son."

Wade scrambled down the bank and stood to the left side of the culvert's screened opening. "Here," he said. "Sometimes, I bring my trucks down to play in the mud."

"Who played down there with you?"

"Screwy Louis," he said after a minute. "Michelle came down a couple of times."

"What about Yukiko?"

Wade shook his head.

"You mean Yukiko never stood here, where I'm standing? Now tell the truth, son."

Wade toed the mud. Clark didn't know what the boy would say. He'd seen Yukiko there a couple of times with the other kids.

"Sometimes Michelle brought her," he said.

"Show me how fast you can get back up here, Wade." Hawley shifted his coat to his other hand as Wade scrambled up the bank. "This is a hell of a spry kid," Hawley said. "Like a mountain goat."

Wade grinned. "I can run fast, too."

"Point to where you found the bobber. I'll bet it was down there right where you were standing."

Wade shook his head. "No, it was way over there." He pointed across the fields near where Clark had seen him wearing the U-Haul hat.

Hawley's lips thinned. "All right. But you know, Wade, people told us you were here playing that afternoon. And guess what? We found your boot tracks in the mud, so you must have been here, right? Louie's dad says you found the bobber around here. Louie wanted one like it when you showed him. Is that right?"

"I think so," Wade said.

"Now you're telling the truth," Hawley said. "Good boy. That's a brave thing to do, Wade. Your dad is proud of you." He glanced quickly at Clark, then back to Wade. "Go ahead then. Tell us what happened. Show us exactly where you found the bobber."

Wade went down the bank again. He crouched and leaned out toward the weedy water. "Right over there some place, I think."

Clark pressed against the culvert's edge. He didn't know if Wade was telling the truth or if he was confused. His foot brushed the orange and it rolled over once.

"I'll bet you showed the bobber to Yukiko," Hawley said. "She must have been right there by you."

"No," Wade said. He pointed at Hawley. "She was up there, where you are."

Doyle folded his arms and seemed to be studying the boy. Cooper smirked.

Hawley snapped his fingers. "I got it. You found the bobber and you came up to show Yukiko. Then you bumped her—accidentally."

Clark held his breath.

Wade shook his head. "I was down here. She was up there standing in the rain."

"A bobber like that's a real find, I'll bet. Maybe she came down to see it closer. Did she come down and stand by you?" Hawley kept asking the questions.

Wade shook his head. "She wanted to, but it was too slick. Her boots slide in the mud."

"Did you help her? Grab her hand? Pull her down?"

"No. She was too high up. I wanted to see what else I could find and she'd just get in the way."

"So how did Yukiko get in the water?"

Wade shrugged. "She fell, I guess. I heard the splash."

"You didn't go up there?"

"No." He pointed again to where Hawley was standing, about seven feet above him. "She was up there. She fell."

Clark exhaled.

"I want you to show me what happened." Hawley slid down the bank, getting his trousers muddy. "Shit," he said.

Doyle shifted so he was as close as he could stand while still remaining on the culvert.

"You say that she fell," Hawley said. "But look, the water's not deep. Especially for a big boy like you. Did you jump in and try to grab her?"

"No," Wade said.

"I'll bet it doesn't come up to your stomach out there," Hawley said.

"It was scary," Wade said. "I couldn't even see the bottom."

Clark knew Wade wasn't afraid of water. He'd run so far into the ocean that Clark had to go after him.

"Did she try to get to shore? Did you try to help her?" Hawley stretched his arm over the water. "Maybe you touched her."

"She made a bad sound," Wade said. "I got scared."

"You should have run for an adult, kid." Cooper went down the bank, too, and then Clark followed. Only Doyle remained above.

"Did she yell for help?" Cooper asked.

"She made a bad sound," Wade said again. "Her arms moved a little but she didn't go anywhere."

"Why didn't you get an adult?" Cooper asked. "Run for your dad?"

"He was gone. And Grandma said she wanted to take a nap. She was real tired."

Clark squeezed his eyes shut, hoping this would all go away.

"Okay, Wade, let's just go through this one step at a time." Hawley brushed some mud off his pants. "You're being very helpful now, Wade. Thank you. Can you tell me what you did next?"

"I found a stick," Wade said. "I stuck it out but she couldn't grab it."

Clark opened his eyes. He remembered the stick Wade used to hack at the bushes when he was trying to flush the rabbit. He didn't know whether he should mention it now or not.

"A stick's a good idea," Doyle said, and they all turned to look at him. "You guys should know that. If somebody's in the water and you're afraid to go near them, you put out a limb or something. Even in swimming pools, the lifeguards have those shepherd's hooks."

Cooper and Hawley looked at each other. "I don't see big sticks around here," Hawley said. "Were you making up the stick, Wade?"

He shook his head. "They told us about sticks in school."

"I saw him with a stick," Clark said. "He was chasing rabbits."

"Forget the stick," Cooper said. "Forget the damn stick."

"Let's get back to Yukiko a minute," Hawley said. "What happened next, Wade?"

"She stopped moving, and I felt real bad." He took a twig and starting marking in the mud. He drew a couple of designs. One resembled a fish. "Then a whale came and tried to push her onto the shore." He shrugged. "But she sank. The whale didn't have arms so it couldn't lift her."

Clark snorted and felt his whole body surge. He felt like laughing in the cops' faces. *You figure it out, bright boys,* he thought. A whale! That about took the fucking cake. He wanted to shriek. It was perfect.

Cooper made a disgusted noise and kicked at the weeds along the water's edge.

Hawley tried to continue. "How big was the whale, Wade? Usually whales aren't in rivers. They need big water, like the ocean."

"It wasn't too big," Wade said. "But it was a whale all right. It even spouted."

Clark was surprised the boy knew the word.

Hawley seemed to be studying the mud on his shoes and pants. "I'm wondering what color it was. Blue? Gray?"

"I think it was black and white," Wade said.

"He's from Alaska," Clark said. "He's seen lots of orcas." He didn't want to use the word "killer."

"Black and white," Hawley said without inflection. "Black and white."

Doyle cleared his throat. "Why don't you gentlemen come back up here?"

"Why not," Hawley said, and they all climbed back up.

"I need to talk with the officers a minute," Doyle said. "Mr. Woods, you wait here."

"I got to sit down a minute," Clark said. Suddenly his legs wouldn't hold him and he sat on the top of the culvert, feeling the dry grass under his palms.

Wade squinted at the river. "No whales today," he announced. "Maybe an otter."

Clark tousled the boy's hair. "Whales and otters, huh?" He didn't know how much was real, how much was imagined, dreamed, talked about in class, read in books. "I saw that stick, Wade. You were chasing rabbits with it. Did you really see Yukiko fall and hold it out?"

Wade shook his head. "Not that stick. I had a bigger stick," he said. "I don't know what happened to it."

When the three men walked back, Hawley had his blazer and sunglasses on. Clark couldn't see his expression. "I guess that's going to do it for now," Hawley said.

"I feel pulled by my short hairs," Cooper said. "I know the kid's involved."

"Are we finished?" Doyle asked.

Hawley shrugged.

"Wade, go see what your grandma's doing," Doyle said.

"That kid's in Never-Never Land," Cooper said. "We'll run into him again."

When Wade had gone, Doyle told Clark, "The coroner's report came in. She didn't drown. Her larynx spasmed, so she suffocated. That happens sometimes with kids. Not so much with adults. It probably scared Wade to death."

"What?" Clark's mind had stopped at Cooper's last remark.

"Her larynx spasmed, so she didn't drown. She suffocated. Even the ambulance people couldn't help. It takes a tracheotomy. The coroner ruled accidental death."

"I know who caused the accident," Cooper said.

Clark didn't say anything. He knew events were shifting his way. Doyle glanced at his watch. "Well, if we're through, I need to get going."

"No rest for the wicked, huh, Doyle?" Cooper scuffed his left shoe on the dry grass.

Doyle spoke to Hawley. "The college attorneys have talked with the Kagitas. No one's pursuing a lawsuit."

"I got better things to do," Cooper said and walked away.

Hawley seemed reluctant to leave but he thrust out his hand. After hesitating a moment, Clark took it. "My youngest boy's ten, Mr. Woods," Hawley said. "I stayed up half the night praying about this."

"Thanks," Clark said, although he wasn't sure why. Hawley struck him as sincere, the dogged public servant. "What about Wade's school clothes?" he asked. "You guys took his new coat and boots."

"Come by the office tomorrow," Hawley said. "The secretary will get them for you."

Clark watched him go and his attention shifted to the passing cars up on Pelham Avenue. A group of fraternity boys in T-shirts tossed a red Frisbee. Two young women from the riding academy trotted their horses across a far field. Nothing seemed changed, but Clark knew everything had changed, at least for him.

Doyle stood on the culvert studying the backwater. "This is an attractive nuisance," he said. "All kids go to water. If the university wasn't so damn cheap they'd have fenced this whole stretch years ago. Now you can bet they will. It won't take them long, either."

"Those cops asked some pretty leading questions," Clark said. "I expected you to stop them."

"We weren't in court," Doyle said. "Let them satisfy their curiosity. No one's taking a retarded nine-year-old to court anyway. That's not how you run for office in Amherst." He stepped away from the culvert's edge. "The coroner's ruling and the fact the Kagitas aren't suing the school gets everybody off the hook."

"Except the parents," Clark said.

Doyle nodded. "A fence will cost the school twenty thousand or so. A lawsuit over an attractive nuisance—who knows. But it's not the Japanese way to sue. Money can't replace a child." He shook his head. "No sense blaming another kid either." He glanced at his watch. "I got to run, too. Come by the office sometime and let me know how Wade is getting along."

"So the cops are satisfied and everybody's happy," Clark said. He was being ironic, but he wanted Doyle to say something more, something reassuring.

"The case is closed," the lawyer said. "The mystery will never be resolved."

．　．　．

After Doyle left, Clark remained on the culvert, but he was careful not to bump the orange or upset the rice bowl. High-pitched yelps came from the far field, and he knew the boys had some kind of chase going. His mother limped out of the apartment and headed in their direction.

The breeze rustled the curtains at the Kagita's apartment. Grace had told Clark she had seen them carrying out suitcases, that they'd moved to Northampton.

He looked off toward the dark Berkshires, then quickly down at the water, an action he repeated three times. In spite of the murk, the slight chop, he could see the slim reeds underwater, the grasses undulating in the current. Here and there individual stones protruded from mud. Near Traverse City, he had walked the rocky beaches of Lake Michigan, picking out semi-precious Petoskey stones close to shore. He remembered spotting their lime-gray geometric patterns with Jimmy Olson and loading the trunk of the Swede's big-finned Continental with bushels of the stones. Summers, Jimmy drove to Arizona or New Mexico and cast the lake stones far out in the desert. "Let the fucking geologists figure out the mystery," he had said.

Clark's eyes were excellent then, when he moonlighted summers by scuba diving for the sheriff's marine patrol. Once he picked out a drowned man sitting in a deck chair, thirty-five murky feet below the surface of Grand Traverse Bay. Clark had located him when no one else in the boat could—had seen his watermelon-striped shorts even at that depth. "Shit. I didn't miss her," Clark said. "I know I didn't."

When he had scanned the pond the morning after Yukiko's death, he had spotted one of her tiny green rain boots six feet out from shore. Probably it came off as she struggled. After that morning, it was gone and he assumed the Kagitas had taken it. Or maybe the police.

A screen door slammed and Russell Lemke hurried off, briefcase in hand. His stringy-haired wife remained behind the door. Clark didn't see Louis and guessed they were keeping him inside until things settled. He moved closer to the edge, peering into the water directly below the culvert's opening. Had Yukiko really fallen from the top? If so, Wade wasn't within shouting distance because Clark had him in check all evening after returning from Dummerston.

Cautiously, he made his way down the bank and stood again at the water's edge. They had all trampled the mud that afternoon, but he made out his own shoeprints easily enough. Red Wings. About three feet of water marked the deepest point in front of the culvert's lip. He wondered about the bad noise Wade said he heard. A dream maybe or the boy's wild imagination. He'd better check with his mother to see what she was allowing Wade to watch on television.

The sun hovered above the Berkshires, and the bright chop on the water squinted Clark's eyes. Wavelets lapped against the culvert's dark lip, the rusty screen mesh that prevented anyone from entering. Suddenly, in that late angle of light, Clark noticed a striking dark brown color—not gray cement or dark orange rust—but the distinct brown of wood. Stepping closer to the culvert, he saw a long stick half buried in the muck behind the screen. An opening at chest level made it seem the screen had been partially torn away from the culvert.

Clark couldn't reach the dark stick, but after a quick search in the weeds, he found a ruler-length piece of wood and nudged the stick toward him until he could grasp it. After pulling it out, he glanced around, but no one had witnessed his action.

The stick was muddy and stout, about five feet in length. It resembled a crooked walking stick but uncarved, unfinished. He didn't know if this was the stick Wade had described or not, but the heft in his hands made him unsettled. A weapon.

"Damn it." Clark was surprised the trained cops hadn't spotted the stick, but it wasn't really visible, until the light slanted into the culvert. "No big deal. Every kid plays with sticks," he muttered. "Put that down. You'll poke out your eye." Growing up, he'd heard cautions a thousand times.

Clark tapped the stick against his free palm. Hard. Even as he had wanted a reassuring answer from Doyle, he wanted this stick to tell its story and decided to hang on to it awhile.

Almost a silly thought, he remembered Charlton Heston as Moses in *The Ten Commandments* throwing his staff onto Pharaoh's floor, the stick turning into a serpent and swallowing Pharaoh's magician's serpent. Then Moses had stirred the Nile with his staff, turning the water into blood.

Clark knelt and washed the mud from the stick, using his fingers underwater to wipe off the ooze. He stood, studying the pool. The water hadn't turned to blood, but the reflected sunset over the Berkshires glowed crimson and glorious.

8

Northampton, 1977

Clark didn't carry an umbrella because the men in the Oregon ranch country where he grew up let the water run off their Cenex caps and Carhartt jackets. If a deluge came, they waited in their barns and pick-ups, smoking cigarettes, drinking coffee from Stanley thermoses and listening to the farm reports from the country stations in Redmond and Prineville. Even when Clark worked as a longshoreman in Ketchikan, where it rained almost two hundred days a year, he refused to carry an umbrella. A Helly Hansen raincoat and a Filson mackinaw kept him dry and warm, even in winter. Sugar and the other longshoremen made fun of the tourists in their bright yellow and green raincoats, their over-sized golf umbrellas.

"Pussies!" Sugar spat. "Rich pussies."

The Japanese officers from the lumber ships carried umbrellas around town, however, and no one bad-mouthed them, because the longshoremen liked the Japanese lumber ships. The winches ran smoothly; broken ladder rungs were replaced; none of the officers drank on the job. Occasionally, half a dozen Japanese officers wearing suits and carrying umbrellas would approach Clark or one of the other college kids longshoring and ask them where to find the "pleasure girls." The colorful old red-light district on Crook Street had been swept clean in the fifties, so Clark would direct them to the waterfront bars. If they wanted Asian women, which they seldom did, they could try the Chinese bars.

To Clark's surprise, the UMass Amherst students wore colorful hooded rain slickers that reminded him of the tourists' garb in Alaska. A few carried large blue and white umbrellas that said "UMass" or sported their fraternity affiliation.

Black umbrellas meant a foreign student, and when Clark spotted one approaching, he'd check quickly to see if it belonged to Mr. Kagita. When he had a chance, Clark briskly walked to the other side of the street. Sometimes they'd pass and say hello. Any encounter other than a brief one was too painful for both of them.

One cold, wet Tuesday in mid-December, Clark mailed some Christmas cards at the student union, then waited in the lobby. He wore his mackinaw, virgin wool that shed a lot of water and kept him warm. He was dreaming of Florida, and when he turned to the person next to him, he was startled to recognize Mr. Kagita. His former neighbor wore a yellow shirt and flat blue tie, and the same thin blue jacket he had worn in the fall. His black wing tips were soaked.

"Hello, Mr. Kagita." Clark's voice seemed strange and formal. "How are you doing with your studies?"

Kagita nodded and bowed slightly. "Good to see you, Mr. Woods. Studies very hard for me now. Difficult to concentrate, and electrical engineering require hard courses."

Clark felt his neck and face turning warm. "Yes, I'm sure it is hard."

"Seems like I study too much but learn little."

"And how is your wife? Does she like Northampton?"

Kagita paused, then said, "She went back to Japan, Mr. Woods. I will go to see her in January."

"You won't be home for Christmas then?" As soon as he spoke, he felt silly for not remembering the Kagitas were Buddhist.

"I'll go to Boston for holiday. My cousin lives there." Tilting his head toward Clark, he added, "And you, Mr. Woods?"

"I'm thinking of taking Wade to Florida after Christmas." Clark pretended to shiver. "Is it this cold in Japan? Look at that mess." Outside the rain had turned to driving sleet. Students were running faster, ducking into buildings to avoid the stinging blast.

"Yes, but only in some places like Hokkaidō, the northern island.

Beautiful towns but too much snow." He tried a quick smile. "And how is your boy, Wade? Okay in school?"

"Wade is fine, thank you. He played an Indian chief in the Thanksgiving skit. Corn Planter, who saved the Puritans the first couple of winters." Clark knew Mr. Kagita probably had no idea what he was talking about. "I'm buying him a digital watch for Christmas. You know, he can't tell time off a regular watch. He's what they call Learning Disabled."

"I hope he will be good student." Mr. Kagita zipped his jacket and opened his umbrella. "Pretty soon, my bus."

For a crazy moment Clark wanted to tell him to stop, that opening an umbrella inside was bad luck.

"Hey, Mr. Woods. Have a great vacation!" Two coeds passed by in matching yellow rain slickers and blue boots. Alpha Phi girls, both were marketing majors from north of Boston. Leah Gallagher, the prettier of the two, never wore a bra in class, and distracted some of the boys by wearing tight sweaters. Clark, too.

"How are your finals going?" he asked. "Straight A's this term?"

"I'm getting a B in statistics," Leah said. "Shirley's got straight A's, though. She's a digit-head."

Shirley laughed and replied, "Just because I'm not running off skiing every weekend."

"You only go around once," Leah said.

After a few more pleasantries, they were off, laughing and chatting about the five-week interim.

Clark envied their carefree spirit. *I'll go to Florida and get some sun,* he thought. *It's been one hell of a fall.*

"So young and happy." Mr. Kagita had a faraway look.

"Yes," Clark said. Life didn't seem hard for people like Leah, and he felt like choking but swallowed and said, "Please tell your wife I'm thinking of her every day."

Kagita smiled. "I will speak with her this weekend. And I hope you and your mother and the boy Wade have a very happy Christmas. And you get a trip to Florida." His brow furrowed. "Oranges and alligators, I think. I studied the states before I came to America."

Clark laughed. "Oranges and alligators. You got it right."

The small man's face grew serious and he reached out, touching the sleeve of Clark's jacket with his fingers. "I want Wade to be good citizen, Mr. Woods. Please, you help him grow up be good citizen."

Clark was surprised at the request. "Yes, a good citizen. I want that, too." He felt Kagita's profound sadness and had a wild urge to grab his arm and take him out drinking.

Kagita's eyes glistened with longing. "A good citizen."

Clark took the man's small hand in both of his. "I promise I'll do all I can. Thank you."

Kagita smiled. "No. Thank you, Mr. Woods."

A bus stopped in front of the building. Kagita gestured toward the bus and said, "Northampton. Good holiday, Mr. Woods." He opened the door with his free hand and went outside. The wind caught his open umbrella and for a moment, Clark feared that it might collapse, but Kagita tilted it to deflect the wind and stepped quickly toward the bus.

As he climbed the steps, he stopped briefly and waved back at Clark. Then he took a seat, facing forward, sitting with his back stiff.

The bus pulled away and Clark watched until it was out of sight. "I promise I will," he said.

Sleet snicked against the glass, and Clark decided to have a beer and sandwich at the Blue Wall before going back to Puffton. He felt humbled by Kagita's dignity.

Hollow-stomached more with sadness than hunger, he scooted his tray along the sandwich bar's chrome rails.

Ahead, a graduate student haggled with the woman worker about his food. "Can't you put more chicken salad on this? It's kind of skimpy." He had the kind of whining voice Clark resented.

"We give one scoop of chicken salad per sandwich," the woman said. Her gray hair was covered by a net and she wore a hearing aid. On the front of her white uniform was a button featuring a grinning grandchild.

"You're going to have a lot left over," the student said. "What with vacation coming. And that was a small scoop." He spread a little with his plastic knife. "See, it barely covers the bread."

She seemed perplexed. "I've got another customer waiting."

"Just another scoop."

Clark scooted his tray sharply, bumping the other tray so hard the student's beer slogged onto the sandwich and soaked the napkin.

"Hey, watch it! What the hell!"

He was going to say something else, but Clark grabbed his wrist, squeezing and twisting until the boy winced with pain. "Get going. You're holding up the line." He felt an urge to punch the boy in his whining mouth but held on to his wrist until it passed.

As he let go, the kid moved quickly down the counter and paid the black woman at the cash register. "Did you see that? He's crazy. I'm going to report him." The black woman didn't reply but handed him the change.

"I'd like a twelve-ounce draft and a Reuben, please," Clark said, his voice softened. "Is that your granddaughter's picture there?"

"Yes it is." She broke into a smile. "And I'm going to Lowell this Christmas to see her. She's in second grade already. They grow up so fast."

"I know you'll have a good time," Clark said. "She's a real cutie."

· · ·

After leaving the Blue Wall, Clark didn't feel like driving up to Puffton Village where he'd have to deal with Grace's relentless good cheer. Tuesdays a Big Brother met Wade after school, and today the volunteer was taking him to see a Disney movie at the mall. Clark decided to drive the ten miles to Natalie's Northampton apartment. He avoided the quaint shops on Main Street. He liked the small Western towns he had grown up in, with their wide streets and their sense of impermanence, as though they could be blown across the high desert like tumbleweeds. Towns with names like Fossil and Spray, where there were general stores and western shops. *Stores for real people doing real work,* Clark thought. And for a moment he felt a wave of homesickness. *If only I'd never left. If I could just disappear into the eastern Oregon landscape. Sit at the Blue and White Café in Baker and drink coffee with the men in stained caps. It makes as much sense as this.*

Natalie lived in a small apartment near Joe's Café, in one of the few sections of town that was still old working class. Two houses down was a dime-sized Mom and Pop grocery store called Poleto's. There wasn't much in the store—a few shelves lined with dusty cans and a mostly empty freezer. But Clark and Natalie liked to walk there and talk to Mr. Poleto, a small round man with a bald head, who had once thwarted a robber by striking him on the chin with a can of tuna. A yellowed clipping hanging from the cash register described the incident.

Poleto's sister Rose sat on a high stool by the door reading the paper through Coke-bottle lenses, or just waiting for the next customer to come in, her plump legs dangling, pale, wispy hair framing her face. She never talked, but Poleto himself could be expansive. He wanted to hear about Oregon, a place which clearly seemed like the other side of the world to him.

The Poletos sold the *Sunday Times* and Clark was bemused that most copies were reserved for individuals. Poleto scribbled "Miller," "Stein," "Cavendar," "Pellerito" over the masthead. It surprised him how people in New England worshiped the *Times* and spent every Sunday poring over it. In Portland you couldn't even buy a copy until two or three in the afternoon, and then you had to go to a bookstore downtown by the base of the Morrison Street Bridge. The adult materials were in back; the papers in front.

The Sunday Times *was no big deal,* Clark thought. The sports pages were all about third-tier football teams from Rutgers, Holy Cross, and Princeton. Graduate school in Kansas had taught Clark the excitement of Big Eight play. Nebraska and Oklahoma or Kansas and Kansas State were big-time rivalries featuring the country's top players. When he worked the Great Lakes, he followed Michigan, Ohio State, and Wisconsin. None of the New York teams ever played in major bowls.

Natalie had never been to a football game, even though Clark knew Tubby Raymond ran a pretty decent program at Delaware. Clark had been amazed by this discovery. "Well," she told him, "at least I appreciate the ambience. I remember the sound of the university band practicing their marches. And Newark High was undefeated for years. After games, kids would ride down Main Street yelling and blowing their horns. Understand, my parents were from Kiev, and I spoke Russian until the first grade. Football wasn't exactly top on their list. Those immigrants, they always want their children to do 'practical' things," she laughed. "Like classical piano and ballet. And, of course, get an education."

On this one point, at least, Clark knew they were alike. Grace had always pushed education—the working-class boy's way up; the immigrant girl's way to make roots in a new world.

"Besides, I did play field hockey," Natalie added. "Third string. Girls didn't even have basketball teams in Delaware when I was in school."

Clark had lettered in basketball, baseball, and cross-country, and he didn't consider field hockey a real sport. But he kept quiet.

Natalie's green Volkswagen Beetle, now a snow-covered hump, was in the lot. Clark stepped out of the pickup and stood a few moments watching the small birds flutter from birch to birch along the treeline that separated her yard from the neighbor's. Gray with yellow heads. *What are they?* he thought. At home he knew all the birds. Meadowlarks with their sweet, melancholy songs, scolding magpies, raucous blue jays. Maybe someday he would show them to Natalie. For now, he'd ask about these at the hardware store. Buy a couple of bird feeders. *The long, snowy winters must take a toll,* he thought. *Tough on everyone.*

The porch was old, with worn planks of wood, the only part of the apartment the landlord hadn't fixed. Natalie opened the door before Clark knocked. "I didn't know you were coming." She smiled and tried to smooth her curly hair down with her hands. "I would've cleaned the place up some."

"I was in the neighborhood." Clark stomped the snow from his boots. "Did I scare off your other suitors?"

"Well, Ralph got out the window just before you came."

"I can beat his time. I'll bet the wimp doesn't even have a pickup." Clark removed his boots at the doorway and hung up the red-and-black mackinaw. He brushed a mantle of snow from his shoulders. "Snowing hard here. Sleet in Amherst."

"What were you looking at?" she asked, closing the door behind him.

Clark was startled. He didn't know she'd been watching him.

"Birds," he said. "Little gray ones with yellow heads. I don't know what they are." He glanced at the papers on the table. "You studying?"

"Getting ready for ESL exams." She moved to the refrigerator. "Want a drink? Beer, wine, cranberry juice?"

"I'd go for a beer."

"I'm going to miss my class next semester," she said. "Those foreign students, they really want to learn. In the regular classes, seems like all the kids know they're going to work for Dad's company in Chicopee or wherever, so why do they need an education?"

Natalie handed him a beer and sat down. "Something's on your mind. You didn't come here to talk about my classes."

Clark paused, staring at the wall behind her. A stained-glass icon of Madonna and Child hung in the kitchen window. Dark-complected, the figures seemed Greek or Italian. The Child in the picture raised two fingers in a blessing. Natalie turned around in her chair, following his gaze.

"Byzantine," she said. "My mother has those icons all around the house. When she grew up, the Communists tried to wipe out religion, but it just went underground. Still she knew how to pray."

Clark thought of all the praying he'd done since fall.

"I just ran into Mr. Kagita at the student union. His wife has gone back to Japan." Clark held his beer without sipping it. "He seems lost."

"Well, you're going to run into him. The campus isn't that big."

"You know, I had this wild urge to put him in the truck and go get drunk."

Natalie smiled and shook her head. "Probably a good thing you didn't. I can just see the headline now, 'Graduate student from the West arrested in kidnapping of Japanese resident.'"

They both laughed then sat for a moment in silence. Outside, the clean white expanse of yard was framed in new, wood-stained windows. "You know," Clark said, "I stopped by their place one time, here in Northampton. I found their apartment and finally got up the nerve to knock. Mr. Kagita opened the door. His eyes flickered for a second when he realized who it was, but he said, 'Please come in, Mr. Woods.' That apartment was so tiny, if I stretched out my arms, I could practically touch the walls.

"Mrs. Kagita and two other people were sitting on flat pillows eating dinner. There were plates of steamed vegetables, rice, some kind of meat." Clark spread his hands. "Imagine this table with all that food and five people, too. The room seemed that small. I didn't know where to stand or sit. All of a sudden I just felt like one gigantic fool, and I thought I was going to suffocate. But it was too late to turn around."

"What happened?"

"Mr. Kagita offered me food, and I think I said no, but I took a glass of plum wine. I remembered how you told me if Russians gave you vodka you had to drink it or they'd take offense, and I figured maybe the Japanese were like that, too." Clark smiled. "Same as in eastern Oregon. You don't ever want to turn down a cowboy offering you a drink.

"Anyway, then I squatted down in the corner, babbling about their new apartment, making small talk about Northampton. The other couple didn't speak English, so the Kagitas translated. Who knows what they said. Mrs. Kagita stared silently at me. She was always sort of worn-looking, but now she looked hollow-eyed."

"Why did you go there?" Natalie asked, tracing lines in the condensation on her glass.

"Moral support. Guilt."

"What guilt? You didn't do anything."

Clark shook his head. "You know, Mr. Kagita just kept looking at me with his head tilted sideways, like this." Clark leaned his head to one side. "Like a child expecting an answer. I sure don't have any."

"Maybe God has answers but we don't." Natalie sipped her cranberry juice. "When my brother was sick his friends stopped coming over. I couldn't understand it then. And I still don't forgive it. But now, I think it's as simple as this: people are afraid to face death, either by spending time with someone who's lost a loved one, or visiting a person who's dying. They look into those faces and see themselves, the ones they love. And they keep making excuses without even knowing why. 'Oh, I had to work,' or 'We were moving,' or 'I had exams.' They're afraid."

"I was afraid, too."

Natalie leaned forward and took Clark's hand in hers. "At least you had the guts to go and face the Kagitas."

Clark gripped her hand. "Mr. Kagita wasn't even angry today. If only he'd been angry, that might have been easier. No, he was pleasant, gracious. We made small talk about vacation, his studies. Then he did a remarkable thing." Clark took a swig of beer. "He asked me to raise

Wade to be a good citizen." Struggling to control his voice, Clark said, "I promised him I would. What else could I do?"

"Listen," Natalie said. "I don't exactly get this whole thing. Why would the cops assume that Wade had somehow intentionally killed the little girl?" Natalie shuddered as she said the words. "It's a dangerous place, there, for a child. I've worked with kids and I know that with a two-year-old you have to watch them every second. A marshland, pools of standing water. . . . All you have to do is take your eyes off them for an instant and"—she snapped her fingers in the air—"just like that, tragedy. No, there's no reason to think Wade would . . . what? Intentionally shove the girl into the water and watch her drown?" Natalie leaned back and stared at the ceiling, thinking it through. "He might have pushed her, sure. Kids push each other all the time when they play. And Wade doesn't seem to have the ability to understand what his own actions might cause, that's true. But deliberately try to hurt her?

"Listen"—she took Clark's hand—"you know I think he's a tough kid to have around and I'm not a blind supporter of his behavior. But if I'm any judge of people, I can say this. *Wade is not cruel. He wouldn't set out to harm someone.* And given how easy it was, anyway, for a child that age to have an accident with no one watching her, well, I think the police, frankly, needed someone to blame and Wade was the obvious choice. And poor Mrs. Kagita, God bless her, she couldn't live with the idea that the baby had come to harm on her watch. Who could blame her?"

Clark sipped his beer and let Natalie's words settle in his mind.

"But look, Clark," she added, and squeezed his hand tighter. "There is one thing. I don't believe this boy capable of murder, you know that. But what troubles me is there's no rhyme or reason to his behavior. He operates on some inner direction that we just don't understand. Even assuming he didn't do anything to the girl, which I do, if he knew she was in trouble, wouldn't he call a grown-up to help? Seems like a normal kid would."

"Don't you see? He never was around the culvert after she fell in." Clark could hear his voice rising. He closed his eyes and thought back, replaying that night in his mind. "When I saw Mrs. Kagita holding the pink raincoat and looking for Yukiko, I checked that very spot myself.

I swear she wasn't there." He spread his hands. "Nothing." He paused. "After that, Wade was with me. So he couldn't possibly have done anything to her, or even seen her in the water."

Clark didn't mention the sturdy stick he'd found later jammed behind the wire mesh. He had put the stick behind his pickup seat, hoping someday it might help him understand more about the accident, although he remained convinced that Wade's story about reaching for Yukiko with the stick was only part of his imagination.

"Well," Natalie said. "That's about as much as we'll ever know. As the lawyer said, this mystery will never be solved."

Outside the snow had started coming down again. Suddenly Clark was cold, and the beer tasted bitter. He set the bottle on the table. "Natalie," he said, and it came out more urgent than he intended. "Is it okay if I stay tonight?"

"Sure." She studied his face. "But what about Wade?"

. . .

Clark kept a small room in Amherst, a mile from Puffton Village, where he studied and usually slept on a sofa. He spent most evenings eating with Grace and Wade. He would listen to them tell about their day and take care of business that couldn't wait until the weekend—like talking to Wade's teacher or making a run to the pharmacy for Grace.

The study room was crowded with belongings he had brought from Oregon, much to Natalie's amusement.

"What?" she had said. "Did you really think you would need those old cowboy boots and spurs or fishing poles and shotguns in Amherst, Massachusetts? Home of Emily Dickinson and Robert Frost. Poor Miss Dickinson would roll over if she saw a firearm."

"I only brought the essentials. Anyway," Clark teased, "that's the thing about the poor. We don't have much so we cling all the harder to what we got. Something you wouldn't know about." Clark was surprised how easy it was with her. After all, they'd only known each other a few months.

He first noticed Natalie at a Northampton bookstore reading. She was tan and dressed in that casual understated way that he knew must have cost a lot. Clark didn't know the details, whether her earrings were real pearls or what kind of sweater she was wearing, but he figured he knew as much as he needed to. *Trouble,* he thought. *Rich girl from the East. Doesn't know much about life. I'd be a fool to get involved.*

And she wasn't interested either. "I came here to get away from complications," she told him. "A serious relationship is the last thing I need."

Clark was driving past the library one day in a rainstorm when he saw Natalie, drenched and shivering, standing out front. Water dripped from her hair; she seemed lost and small. *I better just drive on by,* he thought. *She'll find the bus or something eventually. Oh hell.* And he found himself pulling the truck up and offering her a ride. Natalie got in the passenger side. She picked up an old, waterlogged sock from the floor and held it, dangling from her fingers.

"Yeah," Clark said. "You should've seen the faces of the hitchhikers I picked up when they saw that." Natalie had laughed.

As he came to know Natalie, Clark saw how wrong he had been. She was all contradictions: a doctor's daughter, yes, but one whose parents had scrounged garbage from the streets of New York when they first arrived as political refugees from Kiev. Comfortable, but brought up in a house in Delaware that was flanked by a 7-Eleven and a Friendly's ice cream shop. Sheltered, yet a young woman who had watched her brother die after a long battle with multiple sclerosis. Natalie was shy but startlingly blunt at times, especially compared with the women Clark had been brought up with, who prized niceness above all. Just when Clark thought he had her pegged, he would be proven wrong.

"You know," Natalie had said. "I feel good with you. You make me laugh. Seems odd, but I feel like I've always known you."

.   .   .

Now she repeated, "What about Wade?"

"I'll call my mom," Clark said. "Tell her it's too slick to drive."

"Hi, son," Grace said when he called. "We expected you home an hour ago."

"I'm staying put until the storm clears. Don't want an accident."

"Well, little boy will be disappointed." Grace paused. "And do you know what? That Big Brother let him down. Instead of taking him to the movie like he promised, he brought him right home and just threw a few snowballs with him. Can you imagine?"

"It's finals week, Mom. The kid probably had to study."

"Well, a promise is a promise. At least it was in my day."

"The movie's on another week. I'll take him."

"Before you go, son, I just have to tell you what that little blister did when I wasn't looking. He took the kitchen broom and went out to the parking lot to sweep snow off the cars. Wasn't that sweet? He thought of it all by himself. One man gave him fifty cents. And he was so tickled."

"Sounds good, Mom. Is he around?"

"He's outside making a snowman. He's rolled a ball the size of a garage. I don't know how he'll ever lift another ball on top." She laughed. "He's going by with the broom again. Right outside my window. He's intent on his project. Listen, I need you to bring another broom when you come home. A real broom. I don't like those plastic ones. You know I can't sweep the kitchen floor with an outside broom that's been over all those filthy cars."

"All right, I've got a real broom top on my shopping list. Now why don't you put Wade on for a minute, if you can drag him in out of the snow."

Grace set down the phone and he waited while she went to the door and called out, "Wade, honey, your dad wants to talk to you."

"Is he coming home for supper?" Wade asked, slurring his *r* at the end of "supper" as he always did.

"No, honey, he's not." There was a rustling and stomping of boots, and Clark knew Grace was stretching the receiver to the door.

"Hi, Dad. You should see all the cars I cleaned. The dump truck came by and piled up all the snow on the side of the road and I jumped in it. And it wasn't even a pile, Dad, it was a mountain."

"That's great, guy. Grandma told me all about it. Now I won't be home tonight because of the storm, but I'll see you first thing tomorrow morning."

"Are you at Natalie's house?" Wade asked. Then, without missing a beat, "Are you guys married?"

"Yes, I'm at her house. No, we're not married. You know that."

"Well, are you going to get married?"

"I don't know, Wade. Now look, I've got to get going."

"Are you sleeping together?"

"Maybe. Now listen . . ." On the other end of the line Clark heard loud, slurpy kissing noises.

"Oh, sweetie . . . I love you . . . sweetie."

"That'll be enough. Put your grandma back on."

"But, Dad . . ."

"Honey?" Grace said. "What on earth was that all about?"

"Nothing, Mom. I've got to go."

"Well, all right, son. But don't forget the broom when you come. That little blister. They broke the mold when they made him." Clark heard a click. Grace always hung up without saying good-bye.

.   .   .

There was no door to the small bedroom, so Clark watched from the sofa as Natalie took off her jeans and laid them neatly on a chair, instead of throwing them on the floor as he would have. She was slender and small-breasted, like a dancer, though she claimed to be too big for ballet. One of the first things he'd noticed were her hands. They were graceful, with long fingers, yet wide and strong. "Like my mother's and grandma's," she said. "I come from a long line of strong women." Her dark hair framed her face in a casual way, and her cheekbones were high and prominent. "My Mongol ancestors," she explained. Sometimes Natalie's dark eyes had a faraway look, and then Clark would want to reach into her, touch her and bring her back to him. He wondered who she was thinking of and he was jealous.

Natalie always seemed to worry about her looks. "Do I look okay?" she'd ask. "Does this dress make me look fat?" To Clark, she was beautiful, all the more because she wore no makeup. He would watch as she splashed some water on her hair and ran her hands through it. With other women he'd grown used to seeing a jumble of curlers, makeup, sprays, and even wigs. "You know," he said with surprise the first morning they awoke together, "you look just as beautiful in the morning."

She had been puzzled. "What on earth did you expect to wake up to?"

Now Clark wanted to say how she should never worry about her looks, because she didn't realize her own beauty. He wanted the right words, the ones that would make her believe him.

When Clark leaned over and buried his face in her neck, he caught the warm scent of flowers on her skin. On the little bureau by the bed were several bottles of cologne with French names like *"Fleurs de Rocaille"* or *"L'Air du Temps."* The amber liquid gleamed in the lamplight. Clark was fascinated; Payette's perfumes had been heavy and sensual. Grace was adamant about scents—she wouldn't even use perfumed soap or scented laundry detergent.

Now Clark watched Natalie undressing, her arms and legs still showing a summer tan, wearing loose underpants, so different from the sexy thongs Payette wore. "Freedom of movement," she had explained. "I don't like clothes that bind me." *Being with Natalie was a constant surprise,* Clark thought. *A new discovery at every turn.*

Clark lifted her gray cashmere sweater and it was as soft as anything he'd felt. She gently took off his glasses and set them on the bureau. She kissed him and he breathed in her scent. *Natalie,* he thought. He touched her hair. The reflection from the mirror threw a circle of light on the wall. Outside, the snow continued to fall; it muffled all sound so that for one moment in time everything else melted away—Payette and Grace. Wade.

In that moment, warm inside the cocoon of Natalie's space, surrounded by snow, Clark could imagine it was only the two of them, holding each other. Together in a circle of light.

9

Florida, Delaware, 1978

Wade's head stuck out the pickup window and he panted like a dog, the wind winnowing his fine brown hair. His thin left hand held the orange-and-white U-Haul cap from Oregon he'd worn during the cold Massachusetts snows. Now and again, he'd hold the cap out the window, laughing when the air filled it like a stubby wind sock. A bird dog, Wade tipped back his head and sniffed the air. "Smells good, Dad. What is it?"

"Warmth," Clark said. "Green plants. Maybe orange groves." He felt better after two weeks in Florida. Stronger. More prepared. He remembered his Boy Scout motto, "Be prepared," although nothing had prepared him for Amherst in October.

"It smells sweet," Wade said, "like the river where Uncle Roy took us fishing."

"The Deschutes," Clark said. "Those were mock oranges. They smell sweet, but there's no fruit."

"Mock," Wade said, testing the word. "What does it mean?"

"Pretend, I guess. Not real."

"They put an orange out for that little girl," Wade said. "No one ate it."

Clark squeezed his eyes shut a moment, remembering the orange, rice bowl, and chrysanthemum on the brown sere grass above the culvert.

Wade took out his leather billfold with the jumping horse and removed a photograph. "Mom sure is beautiful," he said. "I wish she still lived with us."

"She's studying hard in college," Clark said. "Right now she needs to be alone."

"But we'll see Natalie soon, right?"

"Tomorrow night," Clark said. "If the weather holds."

The boy suddenly smirked. "Kissy. Kissy." He made obscene smacking noises. "Oh my baby, I love you so much!"

"Stop that!" Clark struck the pickup seat beside the boy's shoulder. "You're being silly."

Wade slammed his back against the pickup seat and pouted. His head drooped. He looked guilty, Clark thought. Dark and guilty. The puzzled frown came over his forehead. Without that frown, Wade seemed almost normal, except for his speech. An incomplete palate, the doctors at the Crippled Children's Hospital had said. It might change with maturity.

They rode in silence for a while, until Wade pointed and yelled, "Fruit!" Wooden crates were tilted to display large oranges. Pyramids of oranges covered flat, weather-beaten tables. A scrawled sign read JUICE 25¢ A GLASS.

"I'm thirsty," Wade said and Clark pulled into the dusty driveway.

The orange grower saw the pickup and climbed off his tractor. As he approached, he reminded Clark of his uncle Roy when he still had the filbert orchard in the Willamette Valley. The farmer took off his work gloves and stuck them in his back pocket. His hands were pale, and dusty creases seamed his eyes.

The farmer gave the truck a quick once-over: sleeping bags and camping gear, snow tires, faded turquoise paint sandblasted from the desert winds. "I'm sorry, mister, but we don't need any help right now." He noticed Wade gulping down a paper cup full of juice. "No charge for the boy's drink."

Clark smiled. He had come to appreciate unexpected generosity. "We're not looking for work," he said. "We came south to get out of the damn snow."

"Or-e-gon," the farmer said looking at the license plates. "Where exactly is that? Close to Colorado?"

"Farther west," Clark said. "Above California."

"Hell," the farmer said. "My brother shipped out from San Diego. What do you grow out there?"

"Wheat and cattle in my part of the state, apples in Hood River, cherries in The Dalles, peppermint." Clark thought of the old lumbering Fox peppermint chopper that had nearly killed him at fifteen.

"When I saw that pickup I figured you for a man that knew crops. I'm a Chevy man myself. Can't stand a Ford. Rough riding son of a gun. You know what F-O-R-D stands for? Fix or Repair Daily." He laughed, showing a set of almost perfectly white dentures against the field-tanned face. "I took you to be wanting work. Lots of folks stop by. I didn't mean any offense."

"None taken," Clark said. He felt comfortable with the man, at ease with anybody who worked with his hands. He remembered how his uncle Roy had been after he sold off the filbert orchard. He started selling Chevys. He needed something to do with his hands—smoke a cigarette or drink too much coffee. "It was all that coffee triggered off my prostrate acting up," Roy said, always adding the extra *r*.

"Pretty good-looking oranges," Clark said. "Maybe I'll send some North."

The man brightened. "No better oranges grown under the sun, mister." He turned on a garden hose and filled a galvanized bucket. "You watch." He dropped three oranges in the bucket and they sank to the bottom. "Don't you see?"

Clark shook his head. He didn't know what to expect.

"Indian River oranges," the man said proudly. "Got more sugar content than any other variety. 'Floaters.' That's your common orange. Buy an orange in most states, they float. But Indian Rivers—can't sink 'em with buckshot."

While Clark filled out mailing forms for friends in Oregon and Michigan, Wade inspected the tractor and disc.

"He's got the curiosities," the man said.

"Hey, get off there!" Clark yelled and Wade climbed on the seat and started to work the levers.

"Can't hurt nothing without the key," the man said. "All kids like to fiddle with equipment. Monkey hands. You should see my grandson.

Rides up there on my lap like he runs the outfit. His mom and dad split up and now she works in Knoxville." He lowered his voice. "I was wondering if that boy has a little Spanish in him."

"Native Alaskan," Clark said. "Tlingit from up in Angoor."

"No kidding." The farmer shook his head. "We got Seminoles down here. Damnedest Indians you ever saw. Crazy about wrestling gators. Me—I don't want to be five miles from a gator. One old bull got my best coon hound. Snapped him up like a biscuit." He spat on the ground.

"You should see them damn Indians wrestle those old gators. Some say it's a phoney-baloney tourist show, but them gators are real enough. So are those Indians—fearless. Fearless the way they plunge into the water and grab them gators. You bet them old bulls try to thresh down and drown them Indian boys, but after they're under a while they find their feet and come up again. Twist that gator's neck like a wrung chicken."

He peered at the mail order forms. "That's about sixty-two dollars. Includes UPS."

Clark wrote out the check and the man tucked it into the front pocket of his Bilt-To-Work shirt. He put a dozen extra oranges in a paper bag. "Take these for the road. You and the boy."

"Thanks," Clark said, even though he wouldn't eat any. He squinted at the sun. "I better get it down the road."

"Climb off there, son. Your dad's fixin' to go."

When they were in the pickup, the farmer slapped the driver's door with his palm. "Travel safe now. Stop by if you're back this way."

"Thanks," Clark said. "You travel safe, too."

He laughed. "Where'm I supposed to go? I already live in fuckin' Florida."

As they headed north, Clark studied the brown paper bag between him and Wade. He hadn't touched an orange since October.

* * *

On Assateague Island, a small herd of ponies huddled under a gnarled pine tree, backs to the drifting snow. Clark counted eleven but Wade said twelve.

"I don't know," Clark said. "Difficult to tell from here." They looked miserable in the sleet, their manes shagged with ice.

"I like the one with the brown spots," Wade said. "I want a pony like him."

They stopped at the visitors' center along the ocean but it was closed. In spite of the snow, Clark could see out quite a long ways. A couple of boats hung near the horizon but he couldn't tell at this distance if they were fishing boats or freighters. He pointed them out to Wade.

The boy chased after some skittering sandpipers. Then he stopped and studied the ocean for a long time.

"See any ponies swimming to shore?"

Wade pointed near the boats. "A whale," he said.

"A whale?" Clark was suddenly curious. "I don't think so, Wade."

"Look. Right there."

Clark tried sighting along the boy's arm and pointed finger but all he saw were waves and the lights of the boats. "I don't see it."

"You need better eyes, Dad." Wade lowered his arm. "Now it's gone." He threw some rocks out into the ocean and gathered up a few shells, slipping them in his pocket.

"We need to get going," Clark said. "Natalie expects us tonight."

Wade unzipped his coat. He was wearing the sweater Natalie had given him for Christmas—red with bright snowflakes. It had come from a place called Strawbridge and Clothier. Clark didn't know anything about the store but told Wade, "She'll be glad you're wearing it."

When they got in the truck, Clark turned so they were facing the ocean. "Did you really see a whale, Wade?"

He nodded. "Way out there—by the boats. I hope they don't hurt it."

"I wanted to ask you something, Wade." Clark chose his words carefully. "Do you remember little Yukiko, that Japanese girl who drowned last fall, just before Halloween?"

Wade nodded. "I remember."

"You told the policemen you saw a whale then, too. Is that right?"

Wade lowered his head, half closing his eyes. "Yes."

"Was this whale like that whale?"

The boy didn't answer for a minute. "This whale was different," he said.

"Bigger? Smaller?"

Wade shook his head. "This whale was singing. It was singing high like a little girl."

．　．　．

Clark pulled off the freeway at the Newark/Elkton exit, slowly because it was snowing hard. A couple of times, he had stopped so Wade could help him load rocks in the pickup's bed to keep it from losing traction. In Massachusetts, snowplows cleared the roads quickly, but here the snow turned to slush, then froze again overnight. The sign said Delaware was to the left; Maryland to the right. It seemed strange to Clark. He'd never expected to be in either one of those states, much less visiting a woman here. "I always planned to marry a woman with a ranch in eastern Oregon," he told Natalie. "Ride around on my horse surveying my land and telling the boys what to do."

"Right," she'd said. "As handy as you are. And anyway, you hate horses."

"That's true," he'd replied. "But ranchers don't use horses much anymore. My friend Danny Freeman out in Bend rides around on a three-wheeler. I'll take you there. When you see the mountains and that certain slant of light you get in the high desert, you'll never want to leave."

"I know, I know. It's God's country."

"Damn right. Sunny central Oregon. Sunshine three hundred and sixty-three days out of the year."

．　．　．

Clark took the left fork. The truck stop on I-95 was open, so he had a wake-up cup of coffee and slicked back Wade's hair. Grim-faced truckers sat at the counter eyeballing the storm and telling one another it was bad heading in any direction. Back on the road, he watched for the 7-Eleven sign—Natalie had told him that her parents' house was right next door. As Clark drove slowly up Elkton Road, he spotted the red and green sign ahead, and a haze of neon from the Friendly's ice cream store across the street. It took him a minute to make out the house, which was half-hidden in an oasis of trees and bamboo behind a fence. Through the branches, Clark saw the soft glow of light in the windows.

"Here we are, guy," Clark said. "Now you be on your best behavior." Wade flipped the door latch a few times but didn't reply.

.   .   .

Clark was glad to be in the Kravtchenko's warm kitchen in front of a spread of sweet salami, roast chicken, and good bread on the table—all Amish products from Booth's Corner in Pennsylvania, Natalie told him. Her parents, Anna and Peter, had taken Wade upstairs to get a bath started. Clark thought of helping, but he was hungry and anyway it was a relief to have someone else watch Wade for a while. *You can only be alone with him for so long,* he thought.

Natalie poured Metaxa, a Greek brandy, into silver shot glasses, and they sipped it. Clark ran his hand along the wooden surface of the table.

"Nice."

"Worn smooth by all the people who've had meals here. The kitchen is the center of activity in this house. Seems like one meal just blends into another." She laughed. "And the discussions can get pretty heated. My sister Katya claims to be a socialist. Imagine the irony of that. Your family loses everything, barely escapes the Communists with their lives, and you become a socialist. Only in America. Anyway, Alex, my younger brother, is a dyed-in-the-wool capitalist."

"A Republican?"

"Who knows? He was profiled in the *News Journal* for being one of only two members of Delaware's Bull Moose party. He got mileage out of quoting Teddy Roosevelt. He and Katya are both talkers, but Alex has a short fuse. Once he and my old boyfriend came to blows over the movie director Ingmar Bergman—whether he was a genius or a quack. They pulled each other by the hair, which was long back in the sixties."

"Families," Clark said. "I missed the last Woods family reunion and brawl because I got to Ruby late and they fought early. Nothing to do with politics or art, though. They fight over women and pickups. Two days drinking and fighting, one day sobering up and letting the bruises heal."

"Well, for heaven's sake, don't tell my mother," Natalie said. "She already thinks Oregon is some godforsaken no-man's-land where Indians wander around in pelts and cowboys have shoot-outs."

"How do you know she's not right?"

Natalie shrugged. "I can only hope."

Clark glanced around the room. The wallpaper was covered with framed photos—of Natalie, her brothers and sister, her niece and nephew, and dogs. Some of the photos were taken in other countries—Katya and her family in Central America, Natalie and Steve in France. Clark didn't own a passport.

Numerous certificates and plaques commemorated Peter's medical career, including one that said, "To Dr. Peter Kravtchenko, for his work in developing trauma medicine in Maryland."

"Why Maryland?" Clark said. "Aren't we in Delaware?"

"That's an interesting question," Natalie replied. "They came here as refugees from the Soviet Union in the fifties during the height of the McCarthy era. Pop was already an experienced physician and Mom was a working chemist. They had two small kids, Katya and Steven, my mother's two elderly parents, and exactly thirty-two dollars in their pockets. I was born a year after they arrived here—the first native-born American. Mom and Pop signed papers stating that if they weren't self-supporting within six months, they'd be deported. If that happened, they would have been killed by Stalin's KGB or sent to labor camps.

"People around here thought coming from the U.S.S.R. made you a Communist. Well, if Pop had been a Communist, he surely wouldn't have left his homeland and risked his family's lives to come here. But he was turned down everywhere for work—as a doctor, anyway. They first worked on the estate of a wealthy Long Island eye surgeon, as a caretaker and a maid. Mom scrubbed toilets and Pop pulled poison ivy on the grounds. To this day he has a deadly allergy to poison ivy. But the doctor was a practical man. He didn't have to hire regular domestic help because he sponsored immigrants, mostly displaced professional people, who were desperate to get to America."

"Cheap labor."

"Right. Especially since his workers couldn't complain. Where else could they go? If they went back, they'd be killed. Here at least no one was dragging them away to jail at night in the Chorni Voron."

"What's that?" Clark asked.

"Black Raven. That's what they called the long, black sedan that came for people at night. It had no windows, and only slits for air. Once you left in the Chorni Voron, chances were you'd never see home again."

Clark shook his head.

"Maryland was the one state that gave him a chance. He hung out his shingle, literally, on Main Street, and became such a successful doctor people lined up for hours to see him. Later they moved here to Delaware because the schools were better. By then Pop could have worked anywhere he wanted, but he stayed loyal to Maryland."

Natalie sipped her Metaxa. "You know, it sounds corny in our cynical day and age, but they really were grateful to be here at all. There's a good reason so many people come to America. It's life or death for them, or worse."

.   .   .

One photo on the wall held Clark's attention—a handsome young man stood with his hands in his pockets, an orchard behind him. His eyes seemed distant, his direct gaze fixed on some far-off point, visible only to him.

"Steven," Natalie said. "He and I were the quiet ones. My brother got sick at twenty-one, died at twenty-eight, right in the Maryland hospital where Pop works. But he only went there the last two days. The rest of the time he was here at home and my mother took care of him. One of my most enduring memories is of my mother holding him in her arms, when he was already pretty much wasted away. This guy who was once nearly six feet tall, and strong. And there's my mom, small but fierce, cradling him.

"Sorry." Natalie wiped her eyes with a paper napkin. "Oh well. You might as well know who I am."

"I know a lot already." He took her hand across the table.

Natalie shook her head. "There's an old Russian saying, 'You have to eat a pound of salt with a person before you know them.' It takes a while to eat a pound of salt."

"I like things salty," Clark said. He studied the photo. "Where was the picture taken?"

"Next door." Natalie turned around in her chair and gestured to the windows in the next room. The 7-Eleven sign across the way glowed red through Anna's white curtains. "Used to be a big old Delaware house with a porch, and an apple orchard out back. My grandparents rented the top floor, until my grandfather died. Then my grandma lived with us."

Outside, Clark heard tires screech as cars spun their wheels trying to get out of the icy parking lot.

"Everything's developed so fast, here. Farms gone, beautiful old houses demolished, new four-lane highways where the small quiet roads were. Everything changed except this place. My parents have hung on, tending their garden, like Voltaire. I don't think they'll ever leave."

Clark tried to imagine living in the same house for thirty years. Grace, as a low-level government secretary, had been forced to move from one small Western town to another. They had never lived in one place more than two years.

Suddenly Clark thought of Wade and the bath. "It's too quiet," he said, but just then Anna and Peter came downstairs. To his relief, they looked calm.

"He's having good time with all the tub toys," Anna said. "Some of them are thirty years old. From numerous children and grandchildren. Will he be all right alone?" she asked.

"I'll keep checking on him, Mom," Natalie said.

Peter was shorter than Clark, fit and energetic. And Anna was much as Natalie had described her—high cheekbones, lively dark eyes that could turn from laughter to a kind of fierceness. Both spoke accented English. Anna brought more plates and they sat down to eat. After they were settled, Peter made a toast in Russian. *"Dai Bozhe, na tot god tozhe."*

"But he doesn't understand," Anna said, and translated slowly, thinking of the right words. "Give us God for next year, the same again. And I always add to it 'not worse, anyway. Maybe even better.'" They clinked glasses.

"I'll go for that," Clark said.

· · ·

"The coyote you have out West," Peter said, "very smart animal."

Clark paused, taken aback for a moment. "Yes, smart," he agreed.

"Coyotes are everywhere out West. Lots of places in the East, too. Well, maybe not in Delaware."

Peter nodded. "Here mostly foxes. Natalie tells me your father traps them."

"That's true." Clark nodded. "Coyotes kill lots of sheep, so the ranchers hire him. Sometimes they'll lure a dog away from the house and kill it."

An odd topic, Clark thought. He himself had never trapped anything. And Grace would have been mortified if she'd heard the drift of this conversation. She preferred to say that Emmett was a security guard, which was true, in a way. He had worked as a guard at the Umatilla Army Depot in eastern Oregon for a year.

"What does he do with them?" Anna asked.

"He gets a bounty. About fifty dollars a head. My father traps in tiny places like Diamond and Harper, way out in the high desert and timber. He runs a trap line along a game trail and baits the trap with a couple dead rabbits. He has a coyote call that sounds like a wounded rabbit. If they come, he shoots them."

"In Russia, wolf hunters were very respected." Peter finished his Metaxa. "It takes lot of skill to trap them. Your father must be smart man."

Suddenly, Clark realized that Peter had looked up information on coyotes because he wanted to show an interest in Clark's family. He smiled, imagining what Grace would think about all this. "He is smart, I guess, but he's not rich. The Woods don't come from old New England money."

Anna paused as she spread butter on her bread and peered at Clark over her glasses. "Neither do we, if you didn't notice."

Clark nodded, pleased that Natalie's family seemed to accept him as he was.

They heard thumping from upstairs, and Clark started to rise, but Anna said, "I go check."

As soon as she left the room, Peter disappeared abruptly into his study. "Something I want you see."

"Uh-oh," Natalie said, "now you're in for it." A minute later, he returned with a photograph album.

"He doesn't want to see that, Pop," Natalie said, but Peter seemed not to hear her. Natalie rolled her eyes. "Hearing problem."

When he opened the book, Clark expected to see baby pictures of Natalie on the bearskin rug or on a towel at the beach. He had to stifle a gasp. The first page showed several Polaroids of a woman with her nose split open. Cartilage showed through and one lip was peeled back, exposing teeth. "What is this?"

"Woman kicked by a horse," Peter said. "Fox hunting on the DuPont estate. Look," he added, turning the page eagerly, "what you think of my work?"

On the next page, Clark saw the woman sewn up, but her face was swollen and marred by black stitches. In successive photos, as the healing progressed, she appeared better and finally almost normal. "Pretty good."

"Pretty good?" Pop repeated. "Beautiful job! *Legeartis!*"

"Latin for 'a work of art,'" Natalie translated. Sitting at the other side of the table, she made no attempt to look.

Other pages showed maulings by dogs, motorcycle accidents, one man whose arm and side had been maimed by an outboard motor's propeller. "No shortage of idiots," Peter said. "Labor Day and Fourth of July are bad. They go to Chesapeake or Susquehanna, drink too much. Somebody drowns."

"Same thing in Oregon," Clark said. "But it's the Deschutes or the Sandy."

With a flourish that indicated the finale, Peter set an X ray on the table. "Oh, Pop," Natalie said and shrugged her shoulders, resigned.

Peter ignored her. "What you think of this?"

Clark examined the X ray a long time. He recognized the hips and pelvic area because he had seen his own crushed pelvis after the accident with the mint chopper. His looked like a saltine cracker smashed by a rolling pin. This X ray, however, had a long cylindrical object that narrowed at the neck.

"Looks like a bottle," he said. "A pop bottle."

"Soda," Natalie said. "You're in the East."

"You're right," Peter said with glee, snapping his fingers. "A gentleman came into the emergency room hunched over like hell and walking funny. He wouldn't see nurse and he wouldn't sit down. Upon examination, I discovered he had inserted a glass bottle into his rectum and couldn't get it out." Peter shook his head. "Not so easy for me to get it out either. The rectum contracts. Finally, I took forceps and put rubber tips on them. Guess what? I delivered perfectly healthy twelve-ounce bottle of RC Cola. I tell you I delivered a lot of babies, but that was my first bottle."

Natalie shook her head.

"Why would anybody put bottle in rectum?" Peter asked. "If you know answer to that, you're a smart man."

"I don't know," Clark said. "I really don't."

Peter paused for emphasis. "I had old professor of surgery in Kiev who said, 'When you're dead, it's for a long time. But being stupid, that's forever.'"

Just then, Anna came back with Wade. He had his pajamas on, and his hair slicked back.

"My God, Peter, what are you doing? Put that book away!"

He grinned at Clark. "Talking to young man about medicine."

"Give me that." Anna snatched the photo album and X ray.

"Can I see? Can I see, Dad?"

"This is not for little boys." Anna put the album high on a shelf. "You shouldn't look at things like this."

"But . . ."

"Wade, no," Clark said.

"See what trouble you cause?" Anna said to Peter.

"I was just showing him my work, Matsya."

"It's okay, Mom," Natalie laughed. "You have to admit the man loves his job."

"Maybe too much." Anna shook her head, but she was smiling. "This Westerner will think we are all crazy in the East."

"That's okay. You haven't seen my family. They're a little different." Clark liked the Kravtchenkos. He felt comfortable. They were charac-ters, but then he was used to characters. He hadn't ever gone with a woman from a recent immigrant family. In his part of the West, immi-grants were from the Eastern states and had settled the ranches near Two Rivers a century or so before.

Peter gestured to Wade. "Let's go. I show you blocks. And Lincoln Logs. They were Stevie's."

．　．　．

That night, Clark and Natalie watched TV in the living room and Wade stacked wooden blocks into a tower. Peter had given up trying to read to him and had gone to bed with Anna. Every so often, Wade spun in circles on the floor. *Well,* Clark figured, *at least this way I know where he is.*

"Seems like he ought to be tired by now," Natalie observed. "But he's more keyed up than ever."

"I'll try to get him to bed soon."

A picture window opened onto Elkton Road, with an elegant old lamp placed in front of it. The dangling prisms sent light scattering around the room. Outside a snow-covered evergreen tree partially obscured the sign: FRIENDLY'S ICE CREAM—21 DELECTABLE FLAVORS.

Suddenly there was a crash. "Hoo-whee . . . Dukes of Hazzawd!" Wade yelled, kicking the tower he had built. Blocks scattered across the floor.

"Wade!" Clark grabbed him by the arm. "Anna and Peter are asleep and I told you to be quiet."

"But did you see that tower, Dad? It was just like TV, wasn't it, Dad?" He wriggled away and kicked the remains of the structure with one foot. Blocks flew, hitting the table with the lamp. "Just look at that baby go!"

"I said stop." Clark tightened his grip. "Pick this mess up, *now*."

But Wade's attention was already on something else. He had run to the window. "Ice cream!" he yelled. "Can we get ice cream, Dad?"

Clark sighed. He was getting tired and his head hurt. "Pick up the blocks and if you promise to go straight to bed when we get back, we'll go to Friendly's."

"Oh boy!" Wade threw some blocks into the box and ran to get his coat.

"That was quick. Amazing how a kid who can't read a word knows exactly what the sign across the street says."

"It's cold and late." Natalie walked over to the window. "You think this is a good idea?"

"Bribery. Maybe we can get some peace and quiet." He shook his head. "What would the counselors say? So much for Dr. Feingold."

"Who's that?"

"One of the experts they're always quoting at school. If you just cut out sugar, everything will be peachy. Wade will stop climbing the walls. He'll read and write. Hell, maybe he'll even become an honor student."

Natalie touched his arm. "You sound kind of bitter."

"Just disgusted, I guess. Every so-called expert has the answer, but I'll bet not one of them has actually lived with a kid like Wade. Day in and day out. The experts come into your life for a month or two, tell you what to do, then they're gone. And you're still stuck with the same problems. Here's one thing I've figured out." He paused and said slowly, "No one knows anything."

Wade burst into the room. "Let's go. I'm ready. Let's go."

Clark put his arm around Natalie. "Enough of that. Let's get ice cream. What's your favorite kind? Mocha chip? Rum raisin?"

"Just vanilla," Natalie said. "I guess I've got no imagination."

Clark gripped Wade as they crossed the four-lane road. Traffic was light because of the storm, but he knew cars couldn't stop on the ice if the boy jumped in front of them. At the other side, Wade raced ahead into Friendly's, then ran back again.

"Good news, Dad!" he shouted.

"What's that?"

"They take credit cards!"

"We don't need a credit card. I've got money," Clark said, glancing at Natalie.

"Oh." Wade looked confused.

"Credit cards?" Natalie raised her brows.

"Okay, so sometimes I've got a temporary cash flow problem."

Inside, Wade jumped on one of the counter stools and began swiveling. Chunks of boot snow fell onto the linoleum and melted into tiny puddles. As he spun around, he threw back his head and laughed.

"Is he all right doing that?" Natalie asked.

"Let him be." Clark directed her to one of the plastic booths and picked up the laminated menu. "Slow night and they've got three paying customers."

The waitress was a college-age girl. Her hair was limp and she was wearing an apron that seemed to have several flavors of ice cream wiped onto it. A button pinned to her chest read, "If I don't smile, you get a free drink!"

"I want a banana split." The stool made a grinding sound as Wade turned another revolution.

"Say please, and when you're through, go wash those grimy hands," Clark told him.

"A banana split, please."

"What flavors of ice cream?" The waitress got out her pencil. "And what kind of toppings? Cherry on top? You want whipped cream?"

Wade dropped his chin and stared at her openmouthed.

"The works," Clark said. "Give him the works."

The waitress wrote it down. "Okay, what'll you have, then?"

"Hot tea," Natalie said.

"Coffee," Clark said. "How's the scrapple? Is it made around here?"

She looked puzzled. "It's not on the menu. Anyway, I don't even know what scrapple is, exactly. I'm from New Jersey."

"It's some part of the pig, I think." Clark set the menu back. "I read somewhere that the women in Philadelphia made it for Washington's troops that bitter winter at Valley Forge. Pig parts, cornmeal, lots of seasoning." He shrugged. "I'll try some sausage."

"Fine," the waitress said, and left after giving Clark a bemused look.

Clark saw that Natalie was laughing behind her hand. "What's so funny?"

"Most kids around here probably think that meat comes wrapped in cellophane—they're all from the suburbs and haven't seen a farm in their whole lives." Natalie grinned. "That waitress was called in to work during a storm, probably missing a good party somewhere, and you harass her about the local culture. Scrapple at Valley Forge? The tourist bureau must've come up with that one. Believe me," she chuckled, "no one from around here ever asks what scrapple is actually made of."

"Okay, okay. Make fun of the bumpkin."

Wade had gone to the bathroom and for a moment it was quiet. Clark took Natalie's hand. "Feels good just to be alone with you for a minute. It's been awhile."

"True."

They sat in silence lulled by the occasional cars as they made their way down the road, snow chains chunk, chunk, chunking. Across the street, only the porch light shone at the Kravtchenko's house. Clark imagined Natalie opening the gates in the morning to walk to school, when the highway was just a quiet back road.

"Clark."

He was startled.

"Don't you think we should check on Wade? It's been awhile since he went to the bathroom."

"Maybe he's been kidnapped." Clark tried striking a hopeful tone, but she looked worried. "Okay, I'll take a look."

He walked down the narrow hallway. As he approached the bathroom, he heard running water. Water was pooled outside the men's room door. "Shit." He tried the door, but it was locked. "Wade, open up. What's going on?"

Wade didn't answer, but the puddle grew and the water still ran.

"Wade, open up right now!" Clark hit the door, twice, flat-palmed. When he heard the bolt slide he pushed the door open. The sink overflowed with gushing water and the bathroom floor was completely covered.

Wade bent over the sink, turning the cold water faucet. His face was confused but determined. "It doesn't shut off."

Clark pushed him aside and turned the faucet, first one way, then the other. The threads were stripped and the water still gushed. Water soaked his shoes and the front of his pants where he leaned against the sink. He jerked open the cabinet doors beneath the sink. Water had soaked the extra rolls of toilet paper, commercial cleanser, a black plumber's friend. Locating the shut-off valve, he stopped the water. "Jesus, Wade. What the hell did you do?"

Wade's lips twisted. "Nothing. The faucet didn't work."

"You were messing with it, weren't you?"

"*No!*"

"Why didn't you come get me, then? Why didn't you call me right away?" He grabbed the back of Wade's neck and squeezed. "Just look at this mess." Clark turned Wade's head right and left so the boy could see all the water. The rest room's cloth towel hung off its roller. A few feet lay on the floor, completely soaked. He figured Wade had twisted it off himself because he could never keep his hands off anything mechanical.

Clark pushed Wade outside, then let go of his neck. The boy clumped down the corridor, shoulders hunched, tracking muddy footprints. Clark closed the bathroom door and followed, leaving tracks larger than Wade's. The boy sat at the counter, eating the banana split fast, afraid someone would take it away.

"What on earth?" Natalie asked. "What happened to your pants?"

Clark's sausage steamed on his side of the table, but he had lost his appetite. "You don't want to know," he said in a lowered voice. "There's been a slight flood. I've got to get the waitress."

Natalie's eyes narrowed and her mouth thinned. "I hope Wade didn't make too big a mess," she said. "My parents live just across the street and get ice cream here all the time. Everybody knows my father."

"Sorry," Clark said. *Everybody knows Wade pretty fast, too,* he thought. *And the boy takes some getting used to.*

The waitress took the news without comment, as though nothing this group did would surprise her. Wade still hunched over the ice cream, most of which was gone. "I don't like pineapple," he said to no one in particular. The waitress glared at him as she went to get the mop.

Outside, Wade dashed across the now deserted street. He pushed open the gate, jumped on and rode it, swinging in a wide arc.

"Stop it. You'll break the hinges!" Clark started to jog toward him, but the boy leaped from the gate and ran around to the side door of the house. Natalie paused in the front yard by the evergreen. A dusting of snow fell from its branches onto her hair and jacket.

"Do you suppose he stripped that faucet on purpose?" she said.

"I don't think so." Clark suddenly felt very tired. "I guess the truth is, though, I don't know. I really don't know."

"Why didn't he say anything?"

"He's always afraid he's going to get in trouble."

Natalie was silent for a moment, but still made no move to go into the house. "I wonder if that's what happened with the little Japanese girl. Maybe he saw something or did something but never told."

Clark's neck tensed and he rolled his head to ease the strain. After turning it back and forth a few times, he said, "Did you mention that accident to your parents?"

"No. I wouldn't know how to explain it." She paused. "I did talk to my mom about you and Wade, though."

Clark tried to sound casual. "What did she say? Some Russian version of 'Get out while the gettin's good'?"

"She asked me if I loved you."

"And?" He hoped she said yes.

"I said yes. Then she asked me, 'What about Wade?' I said, 'I think we can handle it. If we love each other, we can handle it.'"

"Good." Clark nodded.

"She didn't say anything. But I could tell she was worried." Natalie paused. "Well, I'm cold. I'm going in." She turned and walked away, following the boy's tracks around the house and out of sight.

Clark watched the snow fall through the streetlight haze, transforming the surroundings to a dreamy, surreal texture. Snow similar to this had fallen in Baker, he remembered, right after he and Payette first married. They had left their snug room at the Pony Soldier just off the freeway, and wandered downtown, heads thrown back, wet flakes melting on their faces and tongues. When they reached the city park, three deer had appeared out of the wooded darkness and walked beside them in companionable fashion. A large doe came close enough for him to touch. White flakes mantled her back and covered her long lashes. Steamy puffs emerged from her mouth.

He interpreted the deers' appearance as a blessing on Payette and him, as if venerable, natural spirits guided their journey together. When they reached Main Street and turned toward the Blue and White Café, the deer ran straight down the road, their hard hooves slipping where earlier traffic had slickened the street. Quiet as ghosts, they vanished into whiteness. Clark watched, then turned to find that Payette had moved ahead, disappearing like the deer. That night he hurried, and managed to catch her, but he was uneasy. Even then he sensed there would be a time she would vanish for good.

The lights at the restaurant across the street flicked out and Clark wondered how long he'd been standing there. He could see the waitress in her uniform moving noiselessly behind the big front window, as if in slow motion, pale in the light of the security lamps she had switched on.

Inside the house, everything was quiet. "Natalie?" he called in a hushed voice, to avoid waking her parents. "Wade!" Clark removed his wet boots and shook the snow from his jacket onto the doormat. He realized for the first time that his feet were wet and cold, and his hands had turned red, even with gloves on. He blew on his fingers. A light was left on for him, and when he looked up, he could see two icons high in the corners, looking down at him, gleaming and gold.

Clark started upstairs, the wooden steps squeaking in the silent house. *Damn. I'll wake them all up. Where is Natalie, anyway?*

Then he heard voices. He paused at the bedroom. Her parents had put Natalie in her old room, him and Wade next door. Clark pushed the door open a crack. Natalie sat on the side of Wade's bed, and his dark eyes were vivid, fixed on her. When she saw Clark, she said, "I've got him into bed, but he wanted a story." She pointed to a photo. It showed Steven at the ocean, holding a life ring. "He asked about that picture."

"What happened next?" Wade said impatiently.

"Well, like I said, we swam out into the ocean, Steve and me. The water's warm in summer in the Atlantic, not like in Alaska where it's always so cold."

"You freeze your patooty in Angoon," Wade said.

"I guess. So, we went out through the waves together, diving through some of them and jumping over the others. It was a beautiful day and the sun felt good, the water was warm on our skin. We got way out past the breakers—that's where the waves break on you, where the water is quiet—so far out we could see porpoises swimming ahead of us; and a flock of pelicans over our heads."

"And a whale?" Wade asked.

"I didn't see one that day, but I'll bet there were some out there. Anyway, after a while we decided to swim back in. And that," she paused for effect, "is when the trouble started."

Wade's eyes widened. "What happened?"

"Well, we were both strong swimmers. But a rip tide had come up—that's when the water pulls you straight back out from shore. It pulls so hard you can't swim against it."

"It drags you out into the ocean?" Wade was focused intensely on the story.

"Right. So it caught both of us but Steve was stronger and managed to make it halfway to shore. The waves were breaking on my head. One wave would cover me and then I'd struggle up through the water to try to catch a breath of air before the next one came. I wasn't moving to shore, just trying to keep my head over the surface."

Wade was transfixed. "Did you drown?"

Natalie smiled. "No. But the waves came faster and stronger." She made a wave motion over her head. "Usually there's a break between them so you can get up for air, but I guess a storm was coming because they came one after another, breaking on top of me, and finally I was too tired to swim to the surface anymore."

"What happened then?"

"Well," Natalie said, and Clark saw her look at the window and off into the distance, remembering. "Finally two or three waves covered me without letting me get any air. And then everything seemed to go into slow motion. It probably took only a few seconds altogether, but it seemed like a long time to me. I remember looking around underwater."

Wade sat up in bed. "What did you see?"

"The water was a clear blue-green, and there were little bubbles all around my head. I could see light above me, but couldn't reach it. But what I remember most is the silence. The roar of the ocean, the sound of the birds, the people yelling, it all faded into complete silence. The only sound was a hum in my head, like a song without a tune."

"That was the whale."

Natalie looked at Wade, puzzled, as if she'd just remembered where she was. "No, Wade, I said there was no whale. It was just in my head."

"But that's what he sounds like. A song without a tune."

"Well, okay. Maybe it was a whale. At any rate, just at that moment, someone grabbed my arm and pulled me up. It was Steve. He had gotten close enough to shore for someone to throw him a life ring—that same orange one you see in the picture on the wall—and had come back to save me. Using that ring, he swam, pulling me alongside the shoreline until the current brought us close enough to the beach to walk. He saved my life."

Clark spoke from the doorway. "You still like the ocean after that?"

Natalie turned. "There's nothing like it. That feeling of freedom, swimming in the waves. But I have more respect for her now. The ocean is moody and mysterious; sometimes we just don't understand what she's going to do. So there you have it. That's my story. Did you like it?"

Wade nodded. "But is Steven dead now?"

"Yes, Wade."

"Maybe he's not. Maybe he's still swimming out there in the ocean."

"Maybe." Natalie rose and straightened the covers. "Now good night. It's way past your bedtime." Natalie joined Clark in the hallway, pulling the door shut behind her. "Why don't you sneak in with me, tonight? We're big kids."

But before they had moved, they heard a noise.

"For heaven's sake."

Clark headed for the room but Natalie put her hand on his arm. "Wait."

"He's singing," Clark said.

Carefully, Natalie pushed the door open a crack and they looked in. Wade was lying on his back, singing into the dark. The night light she had left for him cast a small circle on the floor by the bed. It was a high, tuneless song, a jumble of words—a song that seemed to come from some inner place, as when a person awakes from a deep sleep and speaks, but no one else understands.

10

Chicago, 1978

That summer Clark got a grant to study Tlingit culture at the Newberry Library in Chicago. Grace agreed to care for Wade back at Clark's rental house in Two Rivers. He was supposed to use his research to write an article and for teaching, but he had another motive: to see if he could learn anything about Wade's heritage that would help with the problems that never seemed to get any better, and stood between him and Natalie.

By this time, Clark wasn't one for glib answers. An expert who had visited Wade's Amherst school had designed her own independent studies degree at Hampshire College and had become a self-taught authority on Native American issues. A plump, spiky-haired woman in purple pants and Birkenstocks, she told him that all Wade needed was to "get back to his roots," and had him dance and chant. She had played a chanting record and Wade followed her around the room in a circle, but he started going faster and faster, finally overtaking the woman, until he was yelling "Hoo—wee . . . The Dukes!" jumping and making loud car noises.

"Now, Wade," she tried to say, "imagine yourself dancing. . . . Pay attention to the music. . . ."

"Spin out . . . rrrmmmm. . . . Spin out!"

"Stop now," the woman had said in measured tones as Wade raced from one end of the room to another imitating a racing car. Then louder, "Stop. Wade. Now you've got to . . . *stop!*" She ran after him, panting and sweating, but Wade was too fast for her. Clark had to step in and grab the boy's arm firmly as the woman in purple caught her breath, clearly embarrassed that she had raised her voice.

"I don't think you're playing the right music for him," Clark said, trying to keep from laughing. "That's Navajo stuff. His people are Tlingit. They live four thousand miles north of New Mexico." He paused. "Are you from the Southwest?"

She shook her head. "Upstate New York, originally, but I've vacationed in Arizona."

"Well, maybe if you came back with Tlingit songs, he'd go for it." Clark paused. "But I appreciate what you're trying to do."

"Say that word again, and spell it for me, would you?"

"Sure." After he spelled it, Clark added, "They're from Alaska." She seemed puzzled. "I thought the Eskimos lived up there."

After she wrote up her report on Wade, Clark never heard from her again. *Another Indian expert bites the dust,* he thought.

Even though Clark was beyond expecting any easy answers, he thought looking into Wade's culture might help. What could it hurt? No one had any better ideas. Someday Wade might want to see Angoon and his uncle Sampson. Clark had gone back to St. Paul to see the place his relatives had lived before moving to Oregon. Natalie talked about visiting Kiev with her parents.

. . . .

All Tlingit villages belonged to Raven or Eagle *moities* and subdivided into clans: Killer Whale, Bear, Salmon, Beaver, Shark, and others. Seafood was plentiful and the Tlingits had a saying: "When the tide is out, the table is set." Given the abundance, the Tlingits devoted much of their time to legends, ceremonies, and art. Each area had a specialty. Yukatat weavers made valuable Chilkat blankets; Kake boasted famous totems; Angoon artists carved elaborate ceremonial cedar hats displaying clan emblems.

Raven created the Tlingit world and Fog Woman, his wife, brought salmon and beauty to the people. Clark learned that legends about Raven, Eagle, Killer Whale, Bear, and Salmon were told and retold at the winter ceremonies. During the ceremonies, the storytellers wore elaborate costumes and bold transformation masks.

The Tlingit clan protectors and shamans proved powerless against smallpox and tuberculosis so the culture fell into decline after the villages were decimated by disease. People practiced witchcraft and feared land otters, believing their whistling lured away children and weak adults.

Alaskan brown bears frequently roamed through the villages attacking dogs and humans. More bears populated this Alaskan territory than any other place in the world. Rubbing his jaws and cheeks to stay alert, Clark looked around the sterile library. Not a bear in sight. In Chicago, the only Bears played football.

One day during his studies, Clark came across an article about the destruction of the tiny Tlingit village Angoon by the U.S. Navy in 1883. One of the Angoon shamans had been killed when a whaling harpoon gun exploded. At the time, he had been working for the Northwest Whaling company, which hunted gray whales for their valuable oil. According to Tlingit custom, the Tlingits seized the boat the shaman died on. They believed it shouldn't be used for a year, out of respect for the shaman's spirit.

The U.S. Navy, headquartered in Sitka, used that captured boat as an excuse to destroy Angoon and demonstrate to the proud, powerful Tlingits that the U.S. Navy ruled southeast Alaska by gunboat diplomacy. They shelled Angoon, killing many villagers, then sent Marines ashore to burn the village to the ground, steal the traditional artworks, destroy the food stores. The surviving Angoon villagers were left to starve during the long winter.

One small item sparked Clark's interest even further. During the shelling, six children were killed because they were too frightened to run into the woods for safety. They huddled in their clan houses, certain they would be protected by their totem spirits—Dog Salmon, Bear, and Killer Whale. Three of the children belonged to the Killer Whale clan—*"Keet"* in the traditional language.

"Wade's people," Clark muttered. *Probably that's why Wade is fascinated with whales,* he thought. He wondered whether he should take Wade to visit Angoon someday. Maybe not much was left, after the shelling. Payette had said the place was "backward," with no paved roads, few amenities. The article contained a "before" and "after" photograph in grainy black and white. Before showed large clan winter houses, elaborate carved totems, and bold clan emblems. The second photo showed the blackened wood skeletons of clan houses, charred snags where totems once stood.

A third photo captured Clark's attention. For a long time, he stared at the picture of five bedraggled children digging clams on the beach. Although the photo wasn't dated, their ragged clothes and forlorn appearances suggested the bitter winter following Angoon's destruction.

None of the children had coats or boots. Two wore battered hats against the slant of gray rain; the other three's hair lay plastered to their heads. The tallest girl carried a broken shovel; four children dug with sticks. Glancing up from his work, one small dark boy squinted at the camera, his face twisted with fear or pain. Thin arms and legs, a small head.

Exactly like Wade, Clark thought. He closed his eyes but the images of the suffering children remained indelible. He hoped they had made it through the winter. However, logic told him they had starved or died of pneumonia.

He closed the book and stood. Enough of the gloomy library and centuries-old photographs. "What do you want, Kagita?" Clark muttered. "I said I'd take care of him." Outside the Newberry, bright sunlight favored Chicago. Clark began walking toward Wrigley Field. That afternoon, the Cubs played the Cardinals.

* * *

Clark loved Chicago's vitality. He had worked on the Great Lakes ten years before, and remembered that time as carefree and uncomplicated. Also this summer would give him a chance to be on his own for a while, without Wade, and Natalie was coming out later in July.

A friend had arranged accommodations in married student housing at the Seabury Seminary, and Clark kept to himself there, avoiding questions about his marital status. His schedule was to work in the Newberry during the morning, leave for lunch at one, and take the afternoons off. He figured four hours of work in summer made a day. If the Cubs were playing, he went to afternoon games. Otherwise he hung around the parks, bookstores, and coffeehouses. When he returned to Evanston on the El, he jogged around Northwestern's track and sat admiring Lake Michigan and dreaming of the carefree time on the *Hudson* with Captain Warwick. The Captain always tried to be in port when a party was going on—Mackinac Island after the Chicago-Mackinac sailboat race; Appleton, Wisconsin, for the Apple Blossom Festival; Duluth for the Fourth of July.

Clark took long weekends and drove the pickup to Traverse City, Michigan, to visit old friends. He looked up buddies from the lake days, went fishing for walleyes out near Interlochen, and shot clay pigeons with the Captain at the Traverse City Gun Club. He drove back to Chicago hung over and happy, stopping to eat barbecued chicken and ribs at roadside stands near Grand Rapids. For the first time in a long while, Clark relaxed. And though he missed Natalie's company, he almost wished he could stay here, alone, living exactly as he was.

In July, Clark picked Natalie up at Union Station, and they drove along Lake Shore Drive back to the housing complex. A group of students were sitting on the front steps with guitars. Two young mothers chased toddlers on the neatly mowed lawn. Clark and Natalie said a quick hello and tried to brush by inconspicuously, dragging her bag. "They think we're married," Clark warned her. "Although they're not really sure."

"Did you tell them we were?"

"I tried to avoid the subject. But one of those guys is kind of nosy. He asked where the little missus was. Told him you were visiting family and coming in on the train."

"I'll have to hide my ring hand, then," Natalie said. "They probably don't know what to make of us."

"And that's even without Wade in the picture," Clark replied. "Imagine what they'd think if you turned up with him."

"Just like it is now when I go places with him. He'll be ripping up the place, and people will eye us and say, 'Is that your son?' And I say, 'yes,' because he's standing there watching me and somehow 'foster son' sounds like I'm trying to distance myself." Natalie laughed. "Which I am, of course!"

The apartment was as generic as a motel room—colorless carpeting, imitation wood furniture beat up around the legs, a couple of framed paintings of outdoor scenes depicting noplace in particular. The school-year occupant, a second-year seminary student from Indiana, had left one photo—of his wife and small daughter—both of whom looked pleasant and unremarkable.

Natalie was tired after the train ride and slept for a while. Clark watched her, admiring the turn of her cheek, the thick dark hair. In spite of his earlier misgivings, now it was good to have her here and to know that a woman still cared enough for him to travel halfway across the country just to see him.

Later that night, they made love and then sat together on the living room sofa looking out the window facing Lake Michigan. Natalie curled up and rested her head on his shoulder. Ship lights were visible some distance out, heading north, and Clark wondered where they were bound and what cargo they carried: grain, ore, coal. As they watched, sheet lightning built up over the lake and Clark remembered the violence and excitement of the summer storms.

"Amazing," Natalie said. "I've never seen the Great Lakes before."

"So I'm taking you somewhere you've never been?"

Natalie nodded.

"I didn't think that was possible," Clark said half-teasing.

"Oh, it is. And I think this is just the beginning." She turned to him. "We're going to have many adventures. There's a whole world out there for us. Look . . ." She pointed to the window.

"What?"

"It doesn't even look like a lake, does it? The size of those waves— it could easily be the ocean."

"That's true." Clark studied the freighters. "But it's even better up north. Years ago I rented a cabin on Grand Traverse Bay with a big picture window. At night the town lights from Traverse City twinkled across the black water. Magic. Whoever built that place knew what they were doing. The cabin was snug, even when the wind blew off the lake. Life seemed simpler then."

He was tempted to add that the cabin was perfect except it lacked a good woman. Too many women had slept there overnight after wild parties in town or on the beach. Most were vacationing from downstate, trying to escape rust belt cities like Saginaw and Flint. Traverse City beckoned with a good time; Michigan days resembled a long bacchanal for Clark. Port after drunken port on Superior and Michigan, with Captain Warwick buying rounds of Fog Cutters and Pirate's Grog, regaling everyone with tales of the big water.

The Captain always chose ports with summer celebrations that lured partygoers from downstate. "They left the rust belt and the chastity belt down south," he used to say. "Man the torpedoes and full speed ahead, but wear your rubber rain gear. I don't want the ship getting clapped up!"

Now as Clark looked at the distant ship lights, they reminded him of the long drives he'd made at night in the broad expanses of the West. The land would be pitch dark, empty, and then in the distance, he would see the wavering lights from a town. For people who didn't know, the town seemed close and within reach, just a short span farther along the dark road. But Clark knew that was deceptive. The lights were still far off, the comfort and warmth they promised out of reach.

"It's beautiful," Natalie said, gazing out the window.

"It's okay for the Midwest," Clark answered. "But you haven't seen the Pacific." He pulled her closer. "Just wait till I show you Oregon."

*   *   *

A month passed easily and quickly. Natalie seemed content just to spend time with Clark, doing simple things. Some days they explored the city, eating spicy Peruvian, Indian, and African foods that made their eyes water. She marveled at Rush Street, where fancy blondes stepped out of white Mercedes parked right on the sidewalk. "Somebody's got pull," Clark said. "Green grease, Chicago politics." Once Clark took Natalie's picture casually standing next to a silver Jaguar as if it were hers. She wore a slim skirt and heels. Years later, Natalie came across the photo and held it up. "How slender I look. And how young."

A few times Natalie joined him for get-togethers with the other students in the Native American summer program. "I talked with an Indian guy at the party," she told Clark. "Felt kind of like an idiot."

"What for?"

"Well, every time the word for his people came up I said *Native American* because I wasn't sure what was the right thing to say. And it sounded awkward, you know, *Native American* this and *Native American* that—kind of self-conscious. Then he just gives me this smile and starts talking about 'us *Indians!*'"

"No big deal," Clark said. "Real Indians usually call themselves Indians or name their tribes. Muckleshoot. Blackfeet. Sheepeater. Tlingit. If anyone tells you he's Cherokee, watch out. A lot of wanna-bes claim to be Cherokee."

.   .   .

One day Clark announced, "Well, I think you're ready to meet the Captain," and the two of them drove five hours north to Sleder's Bar in Traverse City, Michigan. When Clark took Natalie inside, the Captain sat at one of the old booths, drinking gin and eating navy bean soup, a house standard. Over his booth was a gigantic, sad-eyed moose head. When Clark introduced Natalie, Warwick stood and doffed his black and gold cap with the *Hudson* insignia.

"You heard it sank again?" Warwick asked.

"I heard," Clark said. The first time the *Hudson* sank was fifty yards offshore directly in front of the Grand Traverse Hotel. Faulty maintenance. Someone had left the pitcocks open and the ship took water during the frozen winter, but the lake ice held it up until the spring thaw. Then it rolled unceremoniously on its side, the hull's bottom facing town. Wags from the maritime academy had painted "This Side Down," in bright red letters on the light gray hull for all passersby to see.

"The ship is bitched," Warwick said. "No offense, miss. Excuse my language. I'm not used to being in the company of pretty ladies." He touched the rim of his cap.

Natalie smiled, clearly pleased, and Clark thought the old fart hadn't lost his touch.

"The last few trips out, I wore my life jacket on the bridge," Warwick added. "Didn't give the crew much confidence."

Clark ordered a pitcher of beer, white wine for Natalie. Warwick switched to beer and raised a toast. "To shipmates. Just starting their journey."

"Did you know I'm from Delaware, too?" Warwick asked Natalie.

"No. That's something. Most people have never even heard of Delaware except as a sign on the freeway as they drive to New York or D.C."

"I was born in Lewes. That's *Lew-is* for those among us who are out-of-staters," Warwick said, winking at Natalie. "My father ran the ferry to the Jersey shore. I loved the ocean. In summer, I'd grab my sleeping bag and a coffeepot and hike the beach until I came to Baltimore. Then I'd hang around the ships. When I was sixteen I joined the Merchant Marine."

"Hmmmmm . . ." Natalie was humming softly. "When you mentioned Baltimore, it reminded me of a song. 'Eliza in Baltimore.'"

Warwick grinned and lifted his glass. "Eliza, Eliza, in Baltimore . . ." he sang.

"Eliza, Eliza Jane," Natalie finished. Then they sang together:

There was a girl in Baltimore
Eliza, Eliza Jane.
There was a girl that I adore
Eliza, Eliza Jane.

They ended the song laughing, and when they had quieted down Natalie said, "That was one of my brother Steven's favorites." She paused. "Things have changed a lot since you lived back there. These days even Lewes has fancy little shops downtown. And a museum."

"Not back then." Warwick took a pull on his pipe. "It was just a sleepy southern Delaware port town. Fishing boats, crab pots . . ."

". . . the smell of tar on the pier, the piles of fish, horseshoe crabs, the salt air . . ." Natalie continued.

Warwick glanced at Natalie, surprised. "You know just what I mean."

She smiled. "I've spent lots of great days at the Delaware and Maryland shores. Some of the best, in fact."

Clark could see that Warwick was getting comfortable. They ordered cheeseburgers, and the Captain leaned back in his chair, smoking his brier pipe, and entertained them with stories of the "big water" and mysterious cargoes.

"In India, they tried to smuggle contraband in snakes," he said. "Some guys made a living letting the Anacondas swallow their arms. They might have packets of heroin in their hands or illegal gold. It took the snakes six or eight hours to swallow the arm far enough so they couldn't regurgitate the drugs or gold. Then the smuggler opened his hand, leaving the package deep in the snake's belly. The smuggler's friends helped him pull his arm back out of the snake. But by that time, the digestive juices burned the arm pretty bad. Still, in India, it beat being a beggar."

Although Clark knew he couldn't match the Captain's stories, he chipped in with a couple his father had told him, including spotting Sasquatch.

"I believe it," Warwick said, nodding solemnly. "We haven't found half the creatures in the ocean yet, I'm convinced. No one can explain certain blips on the radar screen. Near New Guinea, I've seen some things that would make the Loch Ness monster look like a teddy bear." He tapped his pipe into the ashtray, refilled the bowl with tobacco, and lit it. When the pipe was drawing well, he tapped his forehead with his thumb. "The sea is like the mind. Mostly uncharted."

After Natalie left for the rest room, Warwick seized Clark's wrist with a gnarled hand. "Don't let her wash away. Marry her and keep her in port."

The Captain's eyes ran salty with drink, and his skin had turned leathery after years of wind and sun. On the streets, his rolling walk and squint-eyed manner suggested just another rummy laker from the bum boats. But Clark had learned from years on the lakes that the Captain proved a fair judge of character and weather.

As they walked away from Sleder's, Natalie said, "The Captain's quite a storyteller. Even better than you."

"More experience," Clark said.

"I don't know about some of that stuff with the Sasquatch and the sea creatures, though. I suppose it would depend on how much whiskey a guy had drunk that night."

"Skeptic," Clark replied. "Well, maybe some of the stories *are* a little embellished now and then. But my father's actually seen Sasquatch."

"If you say so," Natalie said, pulling her light sweater around her shoulders.

As they passed under the lamplight, Natalie said, "I can see why you have such good memories of your time here. It must've been a great adventure—the high seas, pirates, contraband . . ."

"Well, maybe not quite *that* exciting." Clark smiled. "But almost."

"It brings to mind a song I always found haunting."

"You've got lots of songs tonight."

"It must be the Captain. Being around him you want to sing and tell stories. And drink too much." She laughed. "Anyway, the song is about a crippled boy who sits at his window watching the ships on the river. He imagines the adventure of the seas, which he can never experience except in his mind." As they walked down the street she began to sing:

"Out of my window, looking in the night
I can see the barges' flickering light.
Silently flows the water to the sea
And the barges too flow silently.

Barges, I would like to go with you
I would like to sail the ocean blue.
Barges, have you treasures in your hold
Do you fight with pirates brave and bold.

How I would long to sail away with you
I would like to sail the ocean blue.
But I must stay here by my window, dear,
As the barges float away from here."

"I think of that song every time I drive along the rivers back home and the C&D Canal with its huge barges and ships from all over the world."

"Those barges could be on the Columbia River back in Oregon. It's got to be more scenic than some old canal."

Clark put his arm around her waist and turned her toward him. "You're not the only one who can sing. I've got one for you, too," and he sang, off-key, "'Casey would waltz with the strawberry blond, and the band played on. He'd glide 'cross the floor with the girl he adored, and the band played on . . . Whirling and twirling old Casey would whirl, dancing around with his favorite girl . . . Casey would waltz with the strawberry blond and the band . . . played . . . on . . .'" They danced on the empty street in the lamplight, Natalie's step light, Clark trying to avoid her feet, turning and turning.

*   *   *

As they approached Chicago on the drive back, Clark pointed at the glorious sunset. "I never get tired of seeing that," he said. "Even if the great color comes from pollution. In Oregon, the sunsets are one hundred percent natural."

Natalie didn't answer.

"Sleepy?" he said.

"A little. Clark, we need to talk."

"Uh-oh," he said. "Sounds ominous."

"July is almost over."

"I've been thinking about that." His buoyant mood faded. August loomed ahead. He had to go back to Oregon to keep his job while Natalie stayed in Amherst to finish her degree. Then there was his mother, and of course, Wade. They'd been getting long letters from Grace full of the latest news. They all ended with, "Now you two take care of each other," and finally, "Little boy misses you and wants you to come home."

"Next year, everything will change. Maybe we can see each other on vacations. Christmas is only four months away . . ." Her voice trailed off.

"Sure," Clark said, but he wasn't hopeful. *Distance makes the heart go wander.* "Your father's been writing those letters from Delaware. 'When will we hear from the courthouse?'"

"Pop's an Old World kind of guy. And not too tactful, as you know. I think he expects you to make an honest woman of me." She chuckled. "But seriously, I've been thinking. On the train ride out here, I was watching the landscape roll by, relaxing and listening to people around me. An elderly couple sat across the aisle. The man was white-haired, slightly stooped, a little confused—I don't think he was used to traveling. His wife was small, sat straight, real matter-of-fact. No makeup.

"I was being conversational. I said, 'Where're you headed?'

"And he says, 'Lima, Ohio. We're supposed to get there at . . .'

And then he stops and says to his wife, 'Mother, when was that we're supposed to get there?'

" 'Five forty-five in the morning, I believe,' she says. 'We were going to ask my son to pick us up but we hate to do it. He's a dairy farmer, you know.'

"The man says, 'Right, five forty-five.' And he looks over at his wife and rests his hand on hers, in her lap. The way he called her 'mother' and took her hand in his callused one. The look on his face when he turned to her. When I saw the two of them, their shared life so apparent in every word and gesture, well, I knew I wanted that."

Natalie sighed and looked out the window. "All of a sudden, though, it doesn't seem so clear. That's the trouble with moments. You know what they mean but you can't always live up to them."

"Maybe we can."

"I have one word for you."

"What's that?" Clark said, although he knew.

"Wade."

"He'll improve," Clark said hopefully. "He'll mature."

"It's not a question of maturing. He's damaged. Retarded. I don't think he'll ever be able to function like a normal person."

"He's not retarded." Clark felt heat rising in his neck. "He's been evaluated, poked, prodded, and not one of the so-called experts has ever said he was retarded. 'Minimal Brain Dysfunction,' one of them said. But they never said he couldn't learn."

"Empty words," she said coldly. "They have no idea what's wrong with him or even what to do about it. You said so yourself."

"Fine. So what the hell am I supposed to do? Ditch him? Send him into the foster care system where he'll probably end up dead?"

"Well, what am I supposed to do?" Her eyes sparked. "Did you ever think about that?" She continued, her voice flat and controlled. "A kid like Wade will take up our whole lives. Everything will revolve around his problems. Is it fair to ask that of me?"

"I don't know," Clark said. "I think about it all the time."

"If God gives you a child like that, of your own, then you deal with it. But your ex-wife's cousin? Why?"

"You know why, damn it. He needs somebody."

"Look, I don't pretend to be a saint. Life throws enough crap at us, without us taking on more than our share. For six years I watched my brother die. Believe me, there's no romance in taking care of someone who's sick, wounded."

"God!" Clark was almost shouting. "Don't you think I know that? Sometimes, believe me, I just wish he would disappear. I have these awful thoughts, like Wade is riding his bicycle crazy all over the place and maybe this car comes along . . ."

"Don't say it." Her lips thinned.

"Natalie." He stopped in mid-sentence. "Do you want me to give him up?" They were passing an industrial area where smokestacks emitted a foul-looking smear across the sky. Ash fell onto the windshield. Natalie had put her hands to her face and Clark could tell she was crying.

"Damn." Clark hit the dashboard with one hand. "Damn it all to hell."

They rode the rest of the way in silence. When they got to the apartment, a group of students was sitting on the steps singing folk songs and playing guitar. Clark could make out some of the old standbys: "Kumbaya" and "I Gave My Love a Cherry." *Songs for young college kids,* he thought. Simplistic. Overly sentimental.

He left Natalie at the door to the apartment. She was no longer crying, just silent as stone. "I'm going for a walk."

"Fine," she said without turning around.

Clark crossed Lakeshore Drive and walked briskly across Northwestern's campus to the shore of Lake Michigan. Large granite boulders had been placed there as riprap to keep the winter storms from eroding the shoreline. Far out on the lake, sheet lightning streaked the sky along the storm line blowing toward Michigan. Every so often, he smelled cordite on the wind.

He sat on one of the hard wet boulders and stared out at the lake, letting the quiet lap of the water soothe him. He was sick of talk, he decided. Talk never seemed to get them anywhere. After a while he walked back. The guitar players were gone by that time and Natalie was in bed, asleep, or at least pretending to be. He lay awake for a long time, listening to the crying of the baby in the next room, its wails clearly audible through the thin walls, wondering how in the hell people did it. *Maybe I'm not cut out for marriage,* he thought. *I've already failed at it once.*

•   •   •

They got blood tests at a run-down clinic with a cardboard sign tacked to the door stating its hours. A vague, gum-chewing girl in a white lab coat had trouble finding Natalie's veins, and Natalie ended up bruised from her clumsy attempts. "Some way to start a marriage," Natalie joked.

"Look," she said when they had finished filling out their marriage license, and both paused to read it. In the line stating father's name and birthplace, Clark had written "Emmett Newton Woods; Ruby, Oregon." Natalie's read: "Peter Kravtchenko; Kiev, Ukraine."

"What are the odds," Natalie said, "that the two of us would ever meet, much less get married?"

There were mysterious scuff marks all around the bottom half of the courthouse walls. "Probably from all the guys dragged here kicking and screaming," Clark said.

On their wedding day, Clark was in the shower when Natalie yelled to him, "Throw on some clothes. I've been making phone calls. If we get to the Skokie courthouse before noon, we can get married."

Judge Nix performed the ceremony, reading it from his podium in a monotone, peering over his bifocals at Clark and Natalie. It wasn't his usual work—that morning he had sentenced two armed robbers to twenty years in prison. Mr. Reuben Wax had dropped by to report a stolen car, and appeared somewhat perplexed when Clark asked him to serve as witness. Mr. Wax also took their one wedding picture, which turned out blurry because his hand shook. "Still," Clark said, "at least you can tell it's us." They were standing in front of the courthouse, smiling.

That night they ate Chateaubriand at Hi's Steakhouse, then wandered around until they found a jazz club where they listened to Sonny Stitts and Red Holloway. They called Anna and Peter, and Pop said he was glad "to hear from the courthouse." Anna congratulated them, then, with Clark on the line, told him he'd better not do anything to hurt Natalie, because she would be watching. "That sounded like a threat," Clark told Natalie. "I'm sure it was," she said. "I wouldn't cross my mother, personally."

Grace said she was "so glad little boy would have a happy home." And Wade seemed more interested in getting a dog than having a new mother. He asked if Payette was still his mother, too.

"You know, I've got a question for you," Clark said later that night, as they sat next to each other on the sofa, watching the lights out on the lake.

"What?"

"Did we ever resolve anything?"

"No."

"I didn't think so. What made you decide?"

"If you always wait till the perfect time, you'll never do anything," Natalie said. "Besides, I remembered the boots."

"What boots?"

She looked at him. "One day back in Amherst I caught a glimpse of Wade's boot, scuffed and tied up with frayed laces, and his skinny ankle above it, where the pant leg was too short because he grows so fast. And I knew I couldn't hurt him. All the argument in the world could not mean the same to me as the glimpse of that skinny, defenseless ankle and boot. I couldn't get it out of my head."

"He hits me that way, too," Clark said, brushing a strand of hair from her face.

A week after the wedding, they each went their separate ways, back to opposite sides of the country.

11

Two Rivers, Oregon, 1978

Two Rivers Community College boasted a festive atmosphere as Silver Dollar Daze approached. The college had no permanent funding, but had to ask the voters every two years to pass an operating budget. This meant the faculty walked door to door, put up lawn signs, and drove through town with bullhorns. Had Clark understood the institution's precarious financial position, he would never have taken the job. Some voters objected to every part of the college. Auto mechanics didn't like the frivolous courses such as French and Dance. Every time Clark took the truck into Al's Repair Shop, Al complained, "They do weird dancing and foreign language stuff up at the college. We voted for a *technical* college when it started." Nursery owners didn't like the horticultural program because it offered inexpensive flowers at Valentine's Day and Mother's Day. Remarkably, some citizens even objected to the football team because they recruited players from big Portland schools.

Silver Dollar Daze attempted to offset public criticism by demonstrating to the community the large financial impact that the college had. All salaried staff were encouraged to take a healthy portion of their October salary in silver dollars and spread them around the community.

Since this was the end of the Oregon Trail, the hoopla included an ox-drawn prairie schooner carrying thousands of silver dollars from the bank to the college. Community members were invited to a barbecue and bluegrass festival.

In an odd way, the Daze reminded Clark of Payette, because she had always hated the event and resented paying for groceries, gas, clothes, and makeup with the silver dollars. "These weigh a ton," she complained. "I can't carry them in my purse. What if they break my compact?"

When she tried slipping some into her tight jeans, they emphasized her bulges. "I'm not taking these to the grocery." She threw them onto the kitchen table and a few rolled across the floor. A couple went behind the stove and Clark knew they'd be digging them out around the third week of the month, when things got tight. "Anyway, it's like begging for your job or something. I hate it." Her lips thinned. "Don't give me any more of these unless you're taking me to Reno."

No Payette this year, Clark thought, with a wince of regret. He didn't know how Natalie would react to the event, but imagined it was beyond her comprehension, at least for now. How would Mrs. Wohl, her former piano teacher who had taught at Oxford, respond to a month's lessons' worth of silver dollars?

Clark always approached the "paymaster" with some trepidation. Faculty members called Bob Willis "Bushwhack" because he was always trying to screw them in negotiations. "Crooked River" Connie Wagner, the public relations officer, earned her moniker because she never got anything straight. People shuddered to read their interviews in the school newspaper. One time when Clark and his colleagues organized readings about peace, the newspaper announced the series would feature peaches.

In spite of all the boosterism of Silver Dollar Daze, Clark had a lot of anecdotal experience indicating businesspeople really didn't like a floodtide of silver. Grocery and convenience stores, gas stations, fast food places were swamped with silver, far more than their cash registers and counters could hold. In part, he agreed with Payette, but he always participated. Once, when he had raised a question about the silver ploy during a budget campaign, Bushwack and Crooked River had regarded him with disdain.

Bushwack Bob had recruited local farmers to offer hay wagon and Shetland pony rides for community children. The wagon rides circled the campus every twenty minutes and a gray-haired man in a ten-gallon hat served as wagon master. A variety of shaggy Shetlands trudged dutifully in a circle, carrying shouting youngsters on their backs. Clark had a longing to bring Wade for a ride, but he didn't trust the boy to behave, and he didn't want a spectacle in front of his colleagues.

An old woman, much older than Grace, approached the hay wagon. She wore a pink raincoat and her hair was dyed pimento. A big man stuck close to her side, reaching for her hand. His eyes were dull, his clothes clean but out-of-date. Trying to keep up with her, he shambled from side to side in the roly-poly manner of a trained bear on hind legs.

When he saw the horses, he grabbed the old woman's hand and pulled back hard. She strained forward, trying to get him to climb onto the wagon, but he made frightened noises and his eyes grew wide with terror. He blocked the path of half a dozen teens who pushed past him, laughing and poking one another. "Get out of the way, Slowmo," one said, before springing into the wagon.

The old woman dragged the man off toward the bluegrass music. Fascinated, he watched the fiddle players draw bows back and forth across the strings, and when three young women in long dresses and bonnets started dancing, he threw back his head and cried out in a long, eerie squeal. The woman with pimento hair began dancing and, to Clark's amazement, she was pretty good. She clapped her hands and encouraged the big man to dance, but he looked sullen and fell to the ground.

Half an hour later, Clark saw them again eating barbecue at one of the long cafeteria-style tables. Dark red sauce smeared the man's chin and the green bib the woman had put over him to cover his shirt. From time to time, her eyes darted around like a mother bird protecting her young.

As Clark considered the man's bulk and slowness, he was glad for Wade's quick impulsiveness, even though it got him into trouble. Thinking what an odd couple they made, he shook his head, worried what might become of the man when his mother could no longer care for him. "We've all got our own crosses to bear," Grace was fond of saying, and he realized Wade was his. But what would become of Wade if anything happened to Clark? Grace was too old to take him. Would Natalie stand in the gap? Why should she?

Clark put two hundred silver dollars, one quarter of his take-home pay, in a large fishing tackle box and then picked Wade up at the baby-sitter's. When he gave her forty-three silver dollars, she became sullen. "My husband's going to love these," she said.

"Well," he explained. "It's Silver Dollar Daze up at the college. We're just trying to show people that Two Rivers has a big financial effect on the town." He knew his smile seemed pasted on; he felt like an encyclopedia salesman.

"I got to ask you for three more dollars," she said. "Wade blew boogers in a big jar of peanut butter and now the other kids won't eat it."

Clark reached in his pocket for the money. "Sounds just like him," he muttered.

She shrugged and took a puff on her cigarette. "What makes that boy tick? One of the kids said something about goobers and Wade thought it was boogers. That's what they told me anyway. I was gone for a little bit when it happened." She took the three dollars he handed her and stacked them on the counter beside a jam-smeared toaster.

"Get your coat, Wade!" he yelled. The television blared in the other room. The smile again. "Anyway, the election is coming up next week. A special levy for the police, fire department, and college."

"Russell and I never went to college," she said. "He got kicked out of high school."

"A lot of our students did, too," Clark offered. "We've got many alternative programs."

Clark always filled the truck at Cliff's Lightning Gas because Cliff had supported the teachers over the years and even filled their cars during the oil crisis with its long lines, gas rationing, odd-even days. "Far as I'm concerned, teachers *are* emergency workers," Cliff had said when filling Clark's pickup in 1974. "Let them little sons of britches stay home from school four or five days, and you'll have one shitpot full of emergencies."

"We gonna see the pigeons?" Wade kept fooling with the dollars on the dashboard. "And I'm gonna get a candy bar?"

"You betcha," Clark said. He handed Wade two sacks of Franz Bread that he bought for a silver dollar. Wade loved to feed the oily-colored pigeons that hung around the station parking lot eating gravel and the birdfeed Cliff gave them.

Cliff's pigeons created a local controversy. The neighbors complained that the pigeons lowered property values. Roosting pigeons fouled their roofs and shrubbery under the eaves. Two months' worth of Two Rivers Council meetings were dominated by the pigeon wars. Oregon SPCA members came to proclaim pigeon rights and members of the fringe elements dressed in pigeon costumes.

"Only in Oregon," Natalie had said when Clark told her about it on the phone.

"You haven't seen anything yet. The Earth First people dress up like trees out here and the loggers wear chainsaw outfits. Another guy bicycles around wearing a fake salmon on his head."

An Oregon State University County Extension agent recommended coating the rooftops with a chemical compound designed to give pigeons an "itchy hotfoot," but Cliff had filed a protest with the Department of Environmental Quality. Some neighbors invested in pellet guns and bagged a few pigeons a week until the heat of summer. Then while they were on vacation, Cliff threw the pigeons he'd kept in his freezer into their yards. After two weeks passed they were thoroughly decomposed.

"I can't abide people shooting pigeons out of meanness," Cliff told Clark as they watched Wade throw bread to the strutting birds. They surrounded him like a bright, oily pool.

"Let the neighbors move." Cliff squinted through Cigarillo smoke. The pump stopped and he squeezed in another fifty cents' worth. Some slopped onto the pickup's side. "Good thing you're not too worried about that paint job, Teach. When it gets too bad, I got a cousin working at Earl Scheib's. Any car painted for half-price. That includes Clearcote." He checked the register. "Gas is nine bucks."

Clark tried to give him silver dollars, but Cliff whipped two more little cigars out of his railroad shirt pocket and formed a cross. "Get that silver away from me. I'm fed up with the fucking stuff. Just because we're pals doesn't mean I'm taking that shit."

Clark opened his wallet and handed him a ten, then followed him inside. Silver dollars covered the counter, stacked high beside the Quaker State cans, jammed the register.

"Sometimes I regret ever supporting you teachers," Cliff said, tossing Clark a silver dollar. "I'll throw my back out just going to the bank."

• • •

Clark had rented a small yellow house on Meeks Road, five miles from the college. Although the place seemed modest by comparison with the house he had rented with Payette, now he had only one income, and the smaller place was a bargain. Moreover, he saved commuting time and mileage. The house had drawbacks: originally moved from a construction site in Gladstone, the place had been split in half. When hastily reassembled, the bedroom section didn't quite match the rest of the house. Cold drafts and field mice entered the gaps. The garage was similarly detached and always remained open because the large door had been damaged in transit.

Polished hardwood floors in the tiny dining room and front room provided a kind of charm. Both faced south, allowing ample sunlight to enter through the picture windows. The light was important, given western Oregon's rainy, gloomy seasons and the number of handwritten papers Clark had to read and correct.

The large windows enabled Clark to work, yet still keep an eye on Wade as he played outside, racing his bicycle up and down the dead-end road or digging holes and constructing dams in the run-off ditch. Out front, the landlord had planted hay where grass should have been, so he'd have a supply for his horses, and it grew thigh-high. Clark literally had to beat a path to and from the front steps.

Field mice scampered in, and sometimes as Clark sat working, he saw them run across the living room, disappearing into the gap between the wall and floor.

Red and Olga Stroud occupied a ramshackle place directly across Meeks Road. A retired electrician turned farmer, Red raised thirty cattle, rabbits, chickens, and guinea fowl on a sixty-acre parcel. He put bells on the cows. "They just enjoy themselves, running across the field," he told Clark. "I like having them around. I like to walk out and see them." Early every morning, Clark could hear the cowbells in the dawn quiet and he knew that Red was up and about.

Red was fascinated by magnetic fields, dowsing, and metal detecting. He puttered with numerous projects in his lean-to overflowing with circuit boards, defunct appliances, games, all kinds of electronic gadgetry. When Olga got palsy, he tried stringing a copper wire over her bedside.

"Don't know if it did any good," he said. "Olga, she's real religious and she's hoping for a miracle, but I just don't know."

When he learned that Clark had spent time in the East, Red told him stories of his own travels "Back East" in Virginia. "They liked me," he explained, "because I was a Westerner. They'd say, 'He ain't no damn Yankee!' " Clark didn't try to explain that Massachusetts and Virginia were two entirely separate regions.

Red and Olga tolerated Wade and seemed to understand his lapses. "Hell, it ain't your fault," Red would say. "Our adopted boy, he got traits when he got older, that I don't know where they came from. He likes classic music. Now I'm just a workingman, work on the land, and I never cared for that. I tried to go to a concert of his once, but I didn't understand it."

. . .

Grace found Clark's place cozy. "It's so light and lovely." She considered it her home away from home and busied herself two or three days a week with running the vacuum cleaner, washing Wade's clothes, or preparing dinner. "Natalie will just love it. I like a bright place, what with the gloomy weather over here on this side of the mountain. You know, while I was sitting at the picture window reading the paper, I saw six rabbits. And maybe a coyote. I couldn't tell if it was a coyote or a dog, but he had his eye on those rabbits."

Grace had lived most of her life in the small towns of central and eastern Oregon, where the weather was always sunny. Clark knew she had never really felt at home in the rainy western part of the state.

On sunny fall afternoons, Clark frequently came home around four to find his mother sound asleep on the couch, a blanket across her large legs, warm afternoon light slanting through the picture window.

The Oregonian newspaper was scattered all around her, covering half the front room floor. As long as he had known her, Grace read the paper a page at a time, and let the loose sheets drift to the floor, then walked over them, scattering the pieces even further. "I'm retired and don't have to be neat anymore," she said, but in fact she had always been messy.

His mother was getting older, slowing down and sleeping more, Clark realized. At least she was comfortable here. All her life, she had wanted to own a home, but she could never afford a down payment. For a while, she owned a small lot in eastern Oregon and always hoped to build a tidy house there someday, but it was a pipe dream, and she sold the lot after she retired to buy a better used car.

Reluctant to disturb her, he'd drink a Coke and quietly grade papers. Sometimes she woke up startled, uncertain where she was. Then she'd see him and say, "Son, have I been asleep? I just closed my eyes for a minute." She looked around. "Is the little boy home?"

"I'm about to go get him, Mom." Clark checked his watch. "Twenty more minutes of peace."

She'd sit up with some difficulty. "I'd better stir up some dinner. I bought some lovely pork chops at the Grange today. That meat department has an excellent selection, and those butchers are so neat and clean." She'd pause. "Of course, they kid around a little too much and call me 'Darling.' You know I don't go for that kind of cheeky talk."

"Maybe they'll propose, Mom. You might run off to Paris with a cheeky butcher."

"I'm not interested in any of that." On her feet, she shuffled toward the kitchen. "Would rancho pork chops taste good to you, honey?"

"You bet. Now I've got to go get Wade. Prepare yourself for the onslaught of Attila and the Huns."

She'd laugh. "You go on! He is a little dickens, but he's not that bad."

"Talk to his teachers. They've put in for combat pay."

As Clark drove to pick up Wade, he was glad he didn't have to prepare supper. Wade ate a lot and usually Clark got fast food or fixed Hamburger Helper. He just didn't have the time or energy to do better cooking, but he made certain Wade got vitamins and plenty of fruit.

Backing the pickup out of the driveway, he saw his mother's blocky silhouette through the kitchen window. This arrangement was temporary, he thought. Next year, when Natalie moved in, his mother would spend far more time in the basement "mother-in-law" apartment she rented from his uncle Roy and his wife. They had a washer and dryer, so she had given Clark hers "to keep the little boy spic and span." The small pine kitchen table was also on loan because her place didn't have room. *How would Natalie fit into all this?* he wondered.

*   *   *

Observing Wade at school made Clark thankful for his skills. The boy shared a special education class with twenty-six other students, all with distinct difficulties, and Clark was amazed at the energy and care the teachers put into the students. Randy had cerebral palsy and was confined to a wheelchair. The teachers explained that his mind was okay, but he had trouble talking, eating, and gesturing. Wade seemed protective of Randy and was allowed to wheel him around the playground at lunch and recesses. Clark became nervous when Wade made the wheelchair "spin out" or "do wheelies," but Randy was strapped in securely and enjoyed the excitement. Wade also helped Randy eat and get cleaned up after meals. And Wade helped Mr. Grant, the teacher, if Randy needed to use the rest room. The boy was heavy and both had to lift him onto the toilet seat and secure him there. "I'd throw out my back, except for Wade," Grant said.

For good behavior, Wade took a fireman's hat outside. The battery-operated hat had flashing lights and a piercing siren. Wade wore it proudly, chasing around the playground, screaming and yelling, "Fire!" Most of the other students were so intent on their own worlds, they barely noticed.

A few had Down's syndrome or displayed symptoms of autism. A couple of the bigger boys were aggressive and tried to hit weaker students. Kate Davis, the other teacher, informed Clark that Ben, an overweight boy with a perpetually angry expression, had attacked a student in his old school with scissors.

The saddest case, Clark thought, was Cherise, a ten-year-old girl who appeared severely retarded. She spoke only a few words and never followed simple instructions. The teachers spent six months trying to get her to distinguish a circle from a square. They isolated her desk with a cardboard screen, and for half an hour each day, she received intensive one-on-one drills with food reinforcements—M&M's or Cheerios.

The teachers showed her squares and circles in various sizes and colors, encouraged her to identify one from the other. But in six months her ability never improved. Finally the teachers gave up and dismissed the TMR evaluations from other districts. When they dug deeper in the matter, they learned the evaluators had simply listened to Cherise's mother, who told them her daughter knew directions and could count to ten. She refused to accept the fact that her child was severely handicapped.

Clark was thankful Wade made small improvements, unlike Cherise. But he grew impatient with the snail's pace of Wade's learning. He still couldn't read, tell time, make change, or do simple math.

"Don't worry," the teachers assured Clark. "He'll make a breakthrough any day."

Clark hoped it was true, but felt less certain than when Wade first came to live with him. Wade simply didn't do well in school. More than anything else the boy liked being outside. Wade loved riding his bike down Meeks Road with his hair flying in the breeze, a happy grin on his face. He was crazy about "spinning out" from the gravel driveway on the big knobby tires, churning pebbles and skidding to a stop. "Burning rubber," Wade called it. Although he was awkward and uncoordinated, he liked shooting baskets with Clark or Tony, the curly-headed neighbor boy three years younger than Wade's ten. They chased each other, built dams in the roadside ditch to flood the field after a heavy rain, constructed forts in the blackberry thickets and nearby abandoned barns.

Clark enjoyed watching them play together. Chums. Yet even as he did, he realized that in a couple years Tony would outgrow Wade mentally and have other interests. He had seen it happen before. It saddened Clark to think of Wade alone, uncertain and confused.

.   .   .

About a month after they moved in, Red showed up at Clark's door, wearing his Can't Bust 'em Union bib overalls and a red-and-black-checked shirt. "I got steaks on the porch," he said. "Can you and the boy help me get them off?"

A large heifer had wandered through the open gate between the pasture and the yard, then climbed onto Red's dilapidated wooden porch to eat some house plants Olga had set out. The cow had plunged a hoof and leg through the rotten planking, so she was caught. Frenzied eyes rolling, she was bawling, tossing her head from side to side, frothing at the mouth.

"Worked herself up, all right," Clark said.

"That's a mean bull," Wade said.

Red chuckled. "You don't know much about the cow business, boy. This one's a heifer. A she. The little horns don't mean anything. Look for big balls, right back here." He showed Wade the spot.

Olga opened the door. "I want that cow off my porch. She's already eaten some of my best plants."

"We were just getting her off, pumpkin," he said, wiping his nose with the flannel shirt sleeve. He turned to Clark and Wade. "All we can do, I think, is lift and push her back. Front end probably weighs four hundred pounds so don't you greenhorns strain the milk."

Clark didn't like the idea of standing near those tossing horns. He planned on keeping his body low.

"Your dad and I will lift and you push her back hard, Wade," Red told him. "Get down low by the chest so she don't hook you." He grabbed a hatchet from the porch and pounded away some pieces of plank so she could clear. "Come on then, mates."

The three of them got ready. "One, two, three. Bingo!" Red said. Clark lifted as hard as he could, and Red lifted, too. Wade pushed. The cow rose a few inches but shoved her leg back down hard, trying to get footing. After ten seconds, their hands slipped and Red said, "Let her go before we bust our guts."

The cow continued bawling. Red took the hatchet and broke out a larger section of plank. "Don't force it. Get a bigger ax," he said. Sweating from the exertion, Red wiped his forehead. "We might have to shoot her for hamburger."

This time, they lifted harder together and Wade pushed the cow free. She stepped off the porch, walking around to the side of the house as if nothing had happened.

"Well, that like t'did me in. I'm getting too old to be a cow-puncher." Red put his arm around Wade's shoulder. "Let's get Blackie and chase those cows down to the barn."

"How'd it get on the porch, anyway?" Wade had picked up a willow and switched the air in front of him.

Red led him over to the wrought-iron gate. "Somebody must have ran through here and left the gate open."

Wade's head drooped.

"I know how we can solve that problem," Red said. "You help me build a stile this weekend. That way you can climb over the fence any time you want without leaving the gate open."

Clark stood at the closed gate, watching man, boy, and dog drive the cattle into the barn. *Red's plenty country smart,* he thought. Dealing with Wade, you had to be creative, but Red handled that about as smoothly as possible.

Clark wanted to stay behind and take in the scene. Autumn mist gathered on the rich pasture and thicker mist hovered above the hill-side stand of evergreens. The cows headed for the barn, their bells clinking in the dusk. Blackie circled the herd barking and nipping to move them ahead. Red and Wade followed along, scuffing dust.

Clark checked the gate, making certain it was latched. No doubt Wade had left it open, allowing the cows to get out. His thoughts shifted to the playground's gate, but he shook his head and took a deep breath of cool Oregon air. Amherst was three thousand miles and a year away. Although he missed Natalie terribly, he and Wade were off to a fresh start.

Dear Clark,

It's snowing in October. Can you believe it? New England autumns are spectacular, but when they're over—wham! Sometimes I miss Delaware. Autumn isn't as flashy, more of a brown and yellow, but I love the sunlight slanting through the trees and the smell of leaves.

I walked down to Poleto's store, and he asked about you. When I said you were in Oregon, and I was going, too, after I finished this year, he told me, "Yes, you should go West. It's a better place for young people. There's more opportunity." That surprised me, coming from someone who's never left his little store on Market Street in Northampton. But I guess it's true. New England seems kind of sewn up with old boys and their sons.

I'm sorry we sometimes argue on the phone. This separation bit is harder than I thought. The more we're apart, the more doubts I have. When I'm alone with you, I feel like I'm right where I should be. But we'll never be alone, will we? We'll never have that idyllic, prechildren time, the way other people do when they start their marriages.

Anyway, I just got back from a quick trip to Delaware where I saw my old school friend Ginny, the lawyer. She lives in Wilmington now but came to Newark and we went to the Deer Park. You remember, that hundred-year-old bar on Main Street where they said Edgar Allan Poe drank till he passed out? That's the legend, anyway. So Ginny sits on the bar stool opposite me, getting drunk, and she says, *Why do you follow him out to Oregon? Why do you give up everything for a man?* She's angry. She can't understand what we have, together, and that it's something worth preserving.

Pop says to say hello and that he has more pictures to show you, and Mom says I should get out there with you. She doesn't trust men when left to their own devices. Neither do I.

Miss you. Give my best to Grace and give my love to Wade. Does he even remember me?

Love,
Natalie

When Clark got home from teaching, he always hoped for a letter from Natalie. He could read and reread them and he felt closer to her from letters than from their lengthy, awkward phone conversations. In the long pauses, he realized, were her uncertainties, the troubles they couldn't solve even when together, much less when separated by three thousand miles. Of course the letters expressed her doubts, also. But once she came out, he was convinced that their love would keep her here.

One afternoon, he walked down Meeks Road and leaned against Red's gate, studying the cows. The day was pleasant and he closed his eyes, letting the angled sun warm his face. With his eyes closed, he smelled the clover and the sweet grass. Someone was making applesauce. Cowbells tinkled and the wind rustled the remaining leaves. *If I can just get Natalie settled out here, she'll love this countryside,* Clark thought. *And even Wade's not too big a hassle, except on weekends.*

He prayed the Andersons would have moved by the time Natalie arrived. From Red's side of the road, Clark contrasted the shabbiness of his place with the tidy, trim appearance of theirs. Theresa and Richard were healthy, wholesome blonds, high school sweethearts from large farm families, who were building their dream home on fifty acres out past Beaver Creek. When they had Clark over for coffee and Bundt cake, they eagerly showed him the floor plans, including the nursery. Meanwhile, they occupied a shipshape honeymoon cottage next door and apparently lived in relative bliss.

Each drove a new vehicle, financed in part from wedding money. His was a sky blue Jeep Cherokee Chief, loaded with options, and hers was a cherry red Jeep Wrangler. Warm days, she removed the canvas top and drove down the country road, long blond hair flying in the breeze. Behind sunglasses, she looked both beautiful and mysterious.

Clark nursed a jealousy of their comfortable backgrounds, their youth and overwhelming good health. Mornings they jogged in matching canary yellow Nike outfits. Weekends, she exhibited her statuesque figure by wearing tight shorts and small halter tops while planting flowers or trimming the bushes. A good-sized Angora goat followed her everywhere. Angoras had been her 4-H specialty, Clark learned, and she had a trophy case filled with gold cups and blue ribbons. "Angora mohair is the hottest ticket in weaving right now," she explained. "When our new place is finished, I'm going to have ten bucks and thirty ewes. I can dye and sell the mohair for a small fortune."

He tried tempering his jealousy by pretending she was dumb, but she always acted pleasant, bright, and articulate. At Oregon State, she had majored in farm management and business agriculture. "People ought to have better sense than to keep goats," he muttered darkly from time to time. His old high school basketball coach used to say, *"Anybody who has goats never changes their underwear,"* and for some reason that adage stuck with Clark. For the most part, the goat was only a nuisance who butted Clark when his arms were filled with groceries or foraged in the garage for orange rinds and Wade's socks.

Clark checked his watch. *Shit,* he thought, *five-thirty.* He had promised to call Natalie at eight her time, and he had to pick up Wade from day care. Maybe he could make it a short call, but Clark wasn't hopeful.

"Where've you been?" Natalie asked.

Clark could tell by the tone of her voice that it wasn't going to be an upbeat conversation.

"Sorry. I lost track of the time. That three-hour difference. It screws me up."

"Well, as long as there's no other woman," Natalie said. He thought she was teasing, but her voice had an edge. "How's Wade doing?"

"Great. Really great. But listen, I've got to get him at day care. . . ."

"Is he reading yet?"

"Well, not exactly." Clark added quickly, "But he's got good teachers in Oregon City. Young; enthusiastic. They're trying this new DISTAR method with him; sounding out words a little at a time. c-c-c c-c-cat, r-r-r-r-rat. Wade picked 'hat' out of *Curious George* the other day. The man in the yellow hat is one of the characters." Clark found himself grinning with enthusiasm, trying to convince her, then wondered what the hell he was grinning at.

"I know the book," she said. "He might not be reading. Maybe it's just memorization."

"No. This was reading," Clark said, and hoped it was true. "He does have a pretty good memory for some things though. You know what?" he said, changing the subject. "I wish you were out here right now. The weather's great and there's terrific color on the trees. Not like New England, but our autumn sticks around a lot longer. Almost until December."

He paused, but Natalie was silent on the other end.

"We could drive up on Mount Hood and eat pie at this great little restaurant. They've even got gooseberry. Remember how your mom and dad ate gooseberry pie one time and kept talking about what they called gooseberries in Russian?"

He tried the happy tone again. "Wade and I went up last Sunday and drove all around, saw the vine maples. They're crimson. And when you drive across the mountain to the Warm Springs Indian Reservation, there's red and yellow willows all along the river."

He waited for her to say something.

"Are you sure you miss me?" Her tone was subdued. "It sounds like you're pretty busy. I'm not sure I'll fit in."

Clark gripped the phone. He hated these calls, her worries and his attempts at reassurance. Being apart was hell. You never got to say what you wanted at the right time. Their schedules were out of sync. She was still in graduate school while he was caught in the trenches of single parenthood and making a living.

"Hey," he said, "I want you to listen. Of course I miss you."

"What about Wade and your mother? Do they even know I'm not around?"

"Listen. You're just depressed and worried. I love you with all my heart. We're fine when we're together. You said that yourself in a letter—when you're alone with me, you feel like you're in the right place. That's how I feel, too."

"I said *alone* together."

"My mother can watch Wade sometimes. There are summer camps."

"It's never going to be normal for us, is it?"

Clark tried to joke. "I guess this isn't the right moment to go into a philosophical discussion of 'who's to say what's normal.' "

She didn't respond.

"I don't know what to say," he said. The conversation had reached an impasse, as so many of them did. He checked his watch, imagining silver dollars rolling toward the phone company. "I'm going to be late picking up Wade at the child care center. For every late minute, they charge you extra."

"We can't even finish our conversations," she said.

Clark's head buzzed. "I'll call you when I get back. Okay?"

"Maybe I won't be home."

"Well then I'll call you tomorrow. Where are you going, anyway?" He tried to sound casual.

"You'd better go, if that's what you have to do."

"I love you," he said, a little louder into the receiver.

"All right. Good-bye."

.   .   .

After she hung up, he realized the phone was damp because his hands had been sweating. He stared at the receiver, expecting more words somehow; he heard only the monotonous tone. He hung it up quietly but by the time he reached the back door, he was angry and slammed it shut.

He glowered at the pickup's right front tire. Flat. Checking his watch, he found it was five after six. He raced across the road and looked in Red's tumbledown garage. No orange Volkswagen. He dragged the jack and lug wrench from behind the pickup seat and started changing the tire. Two of the nuts were tight with dirt and rust so he sprayed them with WD-40. While he waited for it to penetrate, he called the after-school day care. "Listen, I've got a flat tire, but I'm changing it. I'll be there in fifteen minutes."

The director's voice was cool. "Get here as soon as you can," she said. "Today, Wade's behavior has been terrible. He's made very bad decisions, touching other children in an inappropriate manner, violating their personal space. Anytime I've tried to correct him, he's walked on my words, by shouting and interrupting." She paused. "I'm just not certain we're meeting his needs here."

Clark squeezed the receiver but kept his voice calm. "I'm sorry he made some poor decisions today. You realize much of his behavior comes from cultural differences. The Tlingits don't have the same taboos we do." He waited for her response. Mentioning the cultural differences usually caused Wade's critics to back off, because they were afraid of lawsuits or reprimands. Clark continued. "Today he may have made poor choices, but overall, he's improved one hundred percent."

Give her some of her own psychobabble, Clark thought. "You are not a *bad* person, you just made a *bad* decision." Hell, you could even murder somebody, and it wouldn't be your fault. Just a bad decision.

Over the course of the six years he had taken care of Wade, every school program and day care had run batteries of tests on the boy and called in their own specialists for diagnosis. As far as Clark was concerned, except for RealBird, most were fools. And this director was just the latest in a long string.

No one agreed on anything. Some claimed he was Learning Disabled, while others said Emotionally Handicapped or Minimal Brian Dysfunction. A few said Trainable Mentally Retarded. *It's like having two or three watches,* Clark thought. You never know the time. Moreover, you never knew the *terms,* because they shifted with the vague and random psychological theories.

One Amherst psychologist had hypothesized that Wade had been toilet trained at the wrong time. Retraining him would help him learn, she claimed. Clark expressed serious doubts because Wade was nine then and didn't wet the bed. Nor did he ever have "accidents."

Another expert, fresh from college, believed Wade hadn't crawled and walked in the right sequence, so he spent several sessions crawling with Wade on the floor and making certain he came in contact with children's playthings: plastic blocks, wooden animals, Legos, and finally pull toys. However, Wade insisted on returning to crawling, and the accommodating psychologist complied, joining him in crawling around the play room until Wade slipped into his dog routine and bit the expert on the ankle.

A Two Rivers counselor, who had learned of Wade, drove to McLoughlin School and spent fifteen minutes on Tuesday and Thursday afternoons rolling with the boy on the floor, tickling him, giving him bear hugs. His theory was that Wade had exhibited failure-to-thrive characteristics because he needed touching and affection.

When Clark picked him up those afternoons, Wade was especially wild and Clark was furious when he learned the circumstances why. His teachers had allowed the romps because the counselor indicated that he had Clark's permission. At Two Rivers, Clark burst into his office and threatened him, so the romps stopped.

All the while, Grace insisted that a loving home and nutritious diet would work miracles. Her simple formula was as good as anyone else's, Clark figured.

"You know, honey, when you were born, half of your body was blue," Grace told Clark. "One whole half because of circulation problems. And your head was so misshapen it came to a peak on one side, just like poor Denny Dimwit's in the comic strip." She peered up at him through her trifocals. "The doctor was so apologetic because the delivery was tough and they finally squeezed your head with forceps. That's why it was so out of shape.

"I was knocked out. Don't remember a thing. I told the doctor, 'Don't worry. I'll take him home and love him back to normal.' And that's exactly what I did."

She said the last with a kind of triumphant tone as if to add, "Just look at you now."

"It sure seems it's like that with Wade," Grace said. "Only it's taking a little longer because he's had so many troubles. But with all the love he gets from you and me and Natalie, I just know he'll be fine. He's blooming more every day, just like a little flower in God's flower garden."

.   .   .

Now Clark focused on dealing with this after-school day-care director. "I appreciate all the improvements Wade has made," he told her. "And he's seeing an excellent Indian psychologist, who's helping him overcome cultural differences. Overall, Wade's making fewer bad decisions. Don't you agree?"

After a moment's hesitation, the director cleared her throat. "Well, when you get here, we need to talk about encouraging Wade to make more appropriate decisions."

"I'll be there as soon as I change the tire."

As Clark worked to free the last two nuts, the Anderson's goat came down and began butting his back. Clark slapped it on the nose, but it butted harder, knocking him off balance. He realized the goat was trying to lick the WD-40 on the wheel. He didn't know why goats and deer liked petroleum products.

"Get away, God damn it." He thumped its head with the lug wrench, and the goat retreated a short distance. "All I need now is to be arrested for poisoning a goat." When he pulled off the tire, he could see the nail and realized he probably picked it up on the Mount Hood dirt roads.

He put on the spare and released the jack, letting the pickup back down. To his amazement, the spare was almost flat. He couldn't believe it because he'd checked it at the Grange before they'd gone up on Mount Hood. Then he saw the nozzle cap was missing, and he realized Wade had let the air out.

Furious, he kicked the side of the pickup with his shoe, making a dent. "I have a retarded truck!" He kicked again. "A retarded house." Again. *"A retarded boy."* Once more. "A fucking retarded life."

Four baseball-sized dents on the passenger door's lower panel, just below the ding guard.

Exhausted, Clark sat on the hard cement driveway. Too angry to cry, he kept his eyes closed until he felt the goat bump his back half a dozen times. He picked up the lug wrench, prepared to bash the goat's skull, but instinct checked him, and he threw the wrench as hard as he could into the field grass. The goat shouldered past him and started licking the small patch of WD-40 on the ground. Clark didn't try to stop it. He lay back on the driveway, oblivious to the grime, and lifted his hands toward the sky. "How are you going to screw me next?" he demanded.

Clark was still lying on the ground, almost asleep, when he felt the goat's shadow blocking the weak sun. "You fucking goat. Get out of here." He flung back his arms to strike the goat, but he hit a firm leg, and his hand rested on silk stocking. He smelled perfume, not goat.

"Did Grampy hurt you, Mr. Woods? Can I help you up?"

Clark wished God would strike him with lightning before he could open his eyes. "No, I'm all right." His voice cracked.

Theresa Anderson bent over him, her eyes clouded with concern.

She had the longest lashes, he thought. Were they real? Her skin was so smooth he didn't see a single pore. Up close and the way she was leaning over him, her breasts seemed huge. She slipped strong hands under his shoulders. "Let me help you up. I'm awfully sorry. We've got to stop Grampy from butting people."

She got him to his feet, and he tried brushing himself off. Dirt and WD-40 soiled his clothes and hands. "Your goat's fine. I had a flat tire."

"Do you need a lug wrench? I can slip out of my office clothes and help you change it. I used to help my father change tractor tires out in Estacada, so it's not any trouble."

"Thanks, but I changed it. The spare was flat."

"Don't you just hate that? You have to check these new tires all the time."

Clark nodded. "I checked it last Saturday when Wade and I went to Mount Hood. But I think he let the air out."

She laughed. "I don't doubt it. Anything mechanical, he's got to check it out. He's such a busy beaver."

"That's right. Could I ask you a really big favor? I'm late to pick up Wade at the day care, so could I borrow your Jeep? Just to go and get him?"

"Of course. What are neighbors for? I could take you there, if you'd like."

"I don't want to put you out," he said. Then he thought about the bitchy day-care director, the other stressed-out parents. Why not give them something to jabber about? Show up with a drop-dead blonde in a cherry red Jeep. Make their gossipy day. "Actually, that would be great," he said. "That way, I'll have two free hands to keep Wade from taking apart the Jeep on the way back."

"Oh, he's just rambunctious," she said. "I love children. Richard and I are planning on having four. I can't wait until we're in our new place and get the family started."

She leaned down, running her hand over the baseball-sized dents. "I don't remember seeing these," she said. "They make an odd shape."

"I think it happened in a parking lot," Clark said. "That's all I can figure."

She shook her head. "Bummer!"

12

Two Rivers, 1979

For smelt fishing, Clark wore the Helly Hansen rain jacket he had used to longshore in Alaska. Underneath was a wool Filson vest—rugged and warm—that left his hands free. The vest was new, but the rain jacket was getting a little snug because he had put on weight. He loaded three twelve-foot dip nets from Red's garage plus gum boots and a cheap orange slicker for Wade. It was oversized, so they rolled up the sleeves several turns. Wade kept asking what other equipment to put in the truck.

"With Wade helping, it only takes twice as long," Red joked.

At first Clark doubted that Wade could handle the twelve-foot net, but as the boy was becoming stronger, nothing surprised him anymore. "When our arms give out, Wade will still be fishing, Red. You wait and see."

They threw some Hamms and sodas into one cooler, and Grace came out of Clark's house with sandwiches she had packed for the trip. She wore funny little ankle boots. Clark studied the sandwiches she handed to him. "Boy oh boy," he said. "Black olives. My favorite." Actually, the sandwiches were *her* favorite—canned olives mixed with Philadelphia cream cheese. He couldn't imagine anything more useless on a fishing trip, not like the fistful of Snickers and PayDays he kept in the truck for emergencies. Still, he would eat his mother's olive sandwiches to be polite.

"I'm so sorry Olga can't go," Grace said to Red. "It's just a dirty rotten shame."

"The palsy's gripped her bad today," Red said. "I think the rain makes it worse. She's taken to bed and put on some extra copper bracelets."

"Just look at Wade load that gear," Grace said brightly, cheered at the prospect of an outing. "He loves playing around the water so much. Maybe he could work on a ship. That wouldn't be so bad.

"I love running water," she said. "You men just park where I can see the river. There's something so peaceful about a stream. When I lived up in Baker, I loved to go out to Catherine Creek and listen to the water rush by. And in the spring there were buttercups and lupine." She patted Clark's shoulder. "You always wanted to fish back then, honey. I don't know how many times you brought the catch to show me. Do you remember that piece of clothesline rope you used for a stringer? I'd see all their fishy eyes. It gave me the creeps."

When they were in the pickup, she started talking about smelt. "The heads are the parts I can't stand," she said. "I'll cook up a smelt fry for you men, but you'll have to cut the heads off first. I remember Grandma Spencer and her second husband Farrell snipping the heads off smelt with the scissors. Farrell got bucketfuls of them any time he went, it seems."

"You got to cook 'em with the heads on," Red teased. "Those crunchy heads and tails are the best part. Or, if you don't like them, you bite 'em off and spit in a bucket. Just like biting butts off cigars."

Red knew a dairy farmer on the Lewis River who let them drive past a locked gate and set up their smelt-dipping station where the current edged toward shore. They started a warming fire and spent ten minutes on litter patrol gathering up beer cans, cracker boxes, potato chip bags, then putting them into a burlap sack. Fires glowed on the opposite bank where shadowy fishermen worked their dip nets along the water's edge. The night breeze carried smells of gasoline, wood smoke, and cigars. Overhead, raucous seagulls called and occasionally swooped toward the water, emerging with a wriggling smelt.

Dipping was good, and every sweep of the net yielded nearly a dozen smelt. Soon, Clark's back and shoulders ached from holding the net steady, then sweeping against the current as it caught and held the fish.

At first Wade lost most of his smelt because he tilted the net at the wrong angle, allowing them to escape, but after twenty minutes, he caught on to the technique. Intent on the task, he fished in a robotic manner, dumping dozens of silvery smelt into a large blue cooler.

After an hour, a bone-numbing fog settled in, obscuring the opposite shore. Clark set his net in the grass and joined Red at the fire. The old man offered him a cigar, but he shook his head. Red gestured toward Wade bent almost double as he swept the net.

"Nothing to that boy but asshole and elbows," Red said.

"He's plenty strong though." Clark flexed his shoulders, wincing at the sore muscles.

A long, mournful whistling sound carried on the night wind. The whistling made Clark feel cold and he shivered inside the jacket and vest.

"What's that?" Wade asked, cocking his head to one side.

"Some kind of a night bird," Clark said.

Red flicked his cigar butt into the water and it hissed out. "That's Otter Oscar whistling," Red said. He lowered his voice and leaned toward the sound. "Oscar's ghost, I mean. Hear it getting closer?"

"It's some kind of bird," Clark said.

"A ghost," Red insisted as he lit another cigar. "Meanest damn ghost on the river. When you hear that, Wade, it means someone's drowned and you'd better pack up fast. Oscar's ghost is waiting to grab you and drag you under."

Wade stopped fishing and splashed to shore.

"Sounds like a few drunk fishermen made that ghost story up for a dark night," Clark said.

Red puffed a cigar. "Otter Oscar still haunts these waters. He was a strange old man who trapped otters and muskrats from the swamp. 'Swamp rabbits,' he called them, and once a year, the old geezer had an otter and muskrat feed at Bootleg Landing. He soaked the meat forty-eight hours in salt water so it tasted less gamey. Made a damn fine stew, pretty much like squirrel.

"Oscar whistled all the time he was fishing or trapping. Some claimed he could whistle up game by imitating an otter's call. When the smelt were running thick and the fog hung low on the water, you always knew Oscar's location, just by his whistling." Red peered across the water. "Fog's laying in thick now, don't you see? Yep, Oscar was a strange old coot."

"Lots of people get that way, when they live alone." Clark was thinking about his father.

"Greed was the end of Oscar," Red said. Turning to Wade, he added, "Don't be greedy, boy. See, we just got this little cooler of smelt. A couple gallons maybe. But every spring the smelt ran, Oscar filled his whole pickup bed with smelt. One time he had them two feet deep all wriggling and flopping. Still, he kept netting fish, whistling all the while.

"Then something horrible happened. Willy Chester was dipping close by, and he claimed the water turned silver from all the smelt. And Willy felt this force, stronger than the current as they all surged upstream. Suddenly he heard loud whistling, high and frantic—so shrill Willy dropped his net to cover his ears.

"Those smelt ran at Oscar like a wild silver stallion, hitting his boots, his body, that net he held with his grasping, clawlike hands. And then a big sinkhole started opening up beneath his feet."

Red's voice quavered. "Willy says Oscar stopped whistling, but called out in a dead-hollow voice, 'Help me, boys. Sweet Jesus, something's dragging me plum under.'" Red swept his hand across the water. "Then Oscar was gone, swallowed up by the black water."

Seizing the net, Red stepped into the river and thrust it at arm's length. "The other fishermen poked their nets in the current, trying to feel him, but came back empty."

Wade's eyes gleamed with fear and fascination. "What happened to Oscar?" he asked.

"Nobody knows. We found his net and fishing cap a couple days later. The smelt fishermen built watch fires up and down both sides of the river. Oscar's glasses fell off, so maybe he didn't know which way to swim. But they hoped maybe he'd see the lights.

"It was awful spooky, young fella," Red said. He pulled a smelt out of the cooler. "See, when Oscar opened his mouth to scream, the smelt swam into it and choked off his cries. Like this." Red jammed the smelt into his mouth, then spit it back into the cooler. "Awful."

"That's enough, Red," Clark said. "You'll scare the boy."

Red held out a wriggling smelt to Wade. "What do you think?"

The boy hesitated, but as the smelt approached his mouth, he lunged and snapped, like a dog catching a fly.

Only the tail remained in Red's hand. "Jesus!" He jerked back.

"Spit that out, Wade." Clark was relieved the boy hadn't bitten Red.

"I swallowed it," Wade said. "Any smelts swim into my mouth, I'll bite off their fucking heads." He reached for the smelt cooler, but Clark took his hand. "Wait until they're cooked."

Red slapped his thigh. "Boy's tough as a bad boot. Guess I'm lucky he didn't nip off my finger." He flipped the piece of smelt into the river. "If Otter Oscar's ghost tangles with that boy, I'll wager on the boy."

"Haven't you men caught enough smelt?" Grace called from the pickup. "I don't want to spoil your fun, but I'm going to need a rest room. Anyway, you can't eat too many smelt. They're so oily."

"Hell, they freeze up good," Red said. "Olga seals them in freezer bags. Drags out a mess when things get tight. She'll use a big frying pan, some Crisco and cornmeal. Cook them up right. I bet you can eat two dozen." He tousled Wade's hair.

"Raw," Wade said. "With the heads on."

Red threw a couple pieces of driftwood on the warming fire so it blazed high, sending sparks toward the black sky. "Over here, Oscar!" he called toward the dark water. "Damn your scoured bones! I got me a double-tough boy here that's ready to whip your soggy ass." Red leaned toward the water, listening. "Hear that splash? Oscar's coming. Don't look at his face, boy. The crawdads picked him blind."

Grabbing a driftwood club, Wade peered into the dark. His body shook. "I'm ready, Oscar."

Chuckling, Red searched his bib overalls pocket for another cigar. "Out of smokes. I'm heading to the pickup. You boys best skeedaddle before Oscar sinks a claw into your soft hides."

"Red's full of blarney," Clark said as the old man hobbled toward the truck. He touched Wade's knotted shoulders.

Wade shook his head. "I heard whistling, too. The otters are coming."

"Relax. Red made up that ghost story just to rattle you."

Wade turned toward Clark. In the firelight, his cheeks glistened.

At first Clark thought the sheen was mist, but then he saw tears. Wrapping his arms around the boy, he asked, "What's wrong, fella?"

Wade trembled. "I don't want the otters to steal me, Dad."

Clark drew him close. "Don't worry."

Wade clung to Clark. "Maynard always said the otters would come get me. Drag me under the water." His voice quivered. "They'll change me into an otter like them. With round eyes and a hairy face and a long tail."

Clark patted Wade's back. "I won't let anything happen to you. Anyway, otters don't really steal children. It's just a silly story."

Wade moved his head back and forth. "I know it happens. You go ask Sampson." He dropped the driftwood club and looked up at Clark. "Do you got something metal, Dad? Kids are supposed to hold something metal when otters are around."

Wade seemed so agitated that Clark handed him his pocketknife. "Hang onto this, buddy. Then the otters won't bother you." He gripped Wade's shoulder. "Red was just joshing, trying to get you shook." The boy's shaking lessened. "Maybe we'd better go," Clark said.

"My boots are full of cold water," Wade said.

Clark had an idea to divert Wade's attention. "Sit down. Let's get the water out of your boots." Wade sat down on the sand, back propped against a log. Taking the boot by the toe and heel, Clark lifted Wade's leg fast, so cold water ran down his leg into his crotch.

"God damn it! That's cold!" Wade kicked and twisted his leg so the boot came off.

Clark chuckled, backing away to avoid being kicked. "Did that wake you up?"

Eyes blazing with anger, Wade threw a chunk of driftwood at Clark. "Fuckhead! Don't tease me. Don't laugh at me."

"It's all right," Clark soothed, retrieving Wade's boot. "Cold water won't hurt you. Uncle Roy played the same trick on me when I was your age."

"You're mean." Wade hung his head.

"Well, I made you forget about the otters." Clark sat beside him on the log. "That trick means I love you. We're pals and can kid around. It's like an initiation. Now, you're a genuine smelt catcher. In fact, we can buy you your own net. How does that sound?"

Wade sulked a minute longer, then lifted his head. "All right, I guess."

Clark handed him the boot. "Put that back on and we'll walk to the car."

Wade tugged at the boot, but it was difficult to pull on with the wet sock, and he still clung to the knife, so he could grip the boot firmly with only one hand. "You help me, Dad. My hands are cold."

Clark put the boy's foot in the boot. "Point your toe so I can yank it on."

Wade straightened his foot but the boot slipped off to the side.

Clark tugged a couple of times. "Maybe we'd better carry the boot to the car."

"She had boots on," Wade said. "Do you remember that girl, Dad?"

Clark stopped pulling on the boot. "What girl do you mean, Wade?"

"We were living someplace else. Where was that?"

"Massachusetts," Clark said. "Amherst."

"She was dark," Wade said. "Dark like me."

Clark set down the boot. He knelt beside Wade and studied the boy's face. "Yukiko was Japanese, not Tlingit." He spoke quietly, trying to coax the memory to the surface without disturbing it too much.

"Yukiko. Yukiko." Wade rubbed his eyebrow. "That was the girl's name?"

Clark nodded.

Wade gazed into the dark fog as if imagining that long-ago event. "She liked playing on the swing set. So did I, but we had to find bigger swings. I always wanted you to do the 'underdog.'"

"That's right." Clark smiled, remembering how Wade had chortled when he pushed the boy high, then ducked and ran beneath the swing.

"Underdog!" Excited, he turned to Clark. "Do you think we can find a park near here?"

"It's too late to go to a park. Anyway, we've got lots of smelt to clean." Touching Wade's shoulder, he asked, "Do you remember Yukiko's accident? When she fell into the water?"

"Just like Oscar." Wade smiled. "The smelts ate her up. Smack! Smack!"

Clark gently gripped the shoulder. "No, they didn't. She fell in and drowned. We looked for her that night but couldn't find her. Later the fire trucks and ambulances came. Remember all those flashing lights? The firemen in their yellow coats and black boots?"

Wade shrugged away from Clark's hold and took a couple strides. "I can walk just like the big firemen. She walked funny in her little boots. Yukiko was tiny and clumsy." He lurched and stumbled. "Like that." The boy looked directly at Clark. "She lost one boot and went kerplop. Now the otters got her."

Clark stared at him. Was Wade telling the truth? Closing his eyes, he remembered she wore only one green boot when the firemen pulled her from the water. The other boot had remained submerged in the marsh. "Now listen carefully. Did you see her lose a boot and fall in the water?"

The boy's eyes slitted and his lips twisted before he answered. "She walked funny in two boots. Clumsy Yukiko."

"I believe it," Clark said. "But what about that time she fell? Just that one time? Can you remember? Did she lose a boot and trip?"

"Yukiko's a funny name for a girl." Wade's face seemed troubled as he turned to stare across the water. "Sometimes she fell down just to act silly."

Clark waited for the boy to say more. *If she lost her boot and fell in,* Clark thought, *how did the second boot wind up in the water? Had Wade been there and tossed it in?*

The boy turned back to Clark, face blank. "How many smelts can Red eat?"

"What?" Clark shook cobwebs of doubt from his mind. "I don't know. Thirty."

"I can eat fifty," Wade bragged. "That's more than thirty, right?"

"Come on, Wade. You know it is."

"If I gobble up those smelt, they can't get me like they got Oscar. When the otters come, I'll kill them with this knife." He opened his fist so Clark could see the gleaming metal.

"Keep the blade closed so you don't cut yourself." Clark reached out and tugged the brim of Wade's cap. "I won't let the otters get you."

Wade half-smiled. "Can we go? I'm hungry."

"Do you think you can carry that cooler?"

"Watch me." Slipping the knife into his pocket, Wade lifted the heavy cooler and began hurrying toward the truck. "Clomp! Clomp!" he called over his shoulder. "She sure walked funny, that girl."

Clark paused, studying the fog. Fantasy, ghost stories, otter legends, actual events all jumbled in Wade's mind, obscuring any accuracy.

The fog's moisture beaded Clark's face and he wiped away a wet smear. According to Tlingit legend, when Raven was out fishing and became lost in a deep fog, he drifted for days, unable to find his way back to shore. Then Fog Woman, the beautiful mother of Creek Woman, appeared in Raven's boat and asked him to give her his cedar bark hat. After he did so, she turned the hat upside down and captured all the fog in the hat. With the sky cleared, Raven finally could see to find his way home.

Night after night, Clark prayed that the fog in Wade's mind might clear so that he could understand his bearings. But so far, Fog Woman had kept her distance from the boy's flimsy boat.

13

Two Rivers, 1979

Natalie found a job in Portland, teaching the large influx of refugees who were coming into the area. "I'm comfortable with them," she told Clark. "They remind me of my family." The school was in northeast Portland, a forty-minute drive from Meeks Road and Clark's work at Two Rivers, although, as Natalie said, "It might as well be a thousand miles. It's such a different world." Its location was tough inner-city, although Natalie laughed when anyone commented on the neighborhood.

"Listen, you should see Baltimore, or Philadelphia," she said. "They make this place look like a scene from *Happy Days*. Or try driving through Chester one day like I did when the freeway was under construction and I had to get to the airport. Devastation. Looks like Berlin after the war."

"You're not old enough to have seen that," Clark said, "unless you're lying to me about your age."

"It was 1968. I went to Europe with Steve. In '68, East Berlin still looked like the war was yesterday. Piles of rubble. And the ghettos of some of our cities look the exact same way now."

Natalie taught night classes and though she swore it was safe, Clark still worried. "Not a problem," she said. "We've got a security guard on campus. Well," she said, teasing, "*somewhere* on campus. His name is Willie and I have yet to see him, but the other women say if you really need him you'll probably find him in the cafeteria drinking coffee."

"That's reassuring."

At the end of a term, Natalie's classes would have parties, and Clark came to a few of them. He enjoyed the commotion, the variety of languages, the meals. The students put several tables together and set a buffet, each bringing their native foods—Vietnamese, Cambodian, Russian. Once a couple of Buddhist monks came dressed in orange robes. "Talk about culture clash," Natalie had told him. "One day I touched one of them on the shoulder to have him hand out some papers, and the whole class started giggling. He just gave me this odd look. Turns out a woman is never supposed to touch a monk!"

At the parties, women usually presented Natalie with special foods as gifts to take home.

"Look," Natalie said. "You'll never eat anything so exquisite in any restaurant. This chicken is kept in its whole shape, but every single bone has been removed. The Vietnamese lady made it for me, but my grandmother used to make the same thing for a special occasion. I have no idea how it's done."

Clark was happy hanging around the buffet table, smiling at people. "I can't tell any of my stories," he said. "They don't understand me." One time he noticed a group of Vietnamese women whispering and pointing at him, then talking to Natalie. "What was that all about?" he asked.

"They asked if we had children. And I said we had Wade, but none of our own. Well, that was too much for them to comprehend. They just looked completely puzzled and said"—Natalie held both hands palms-up and shrugged in imitation—"'If no baby, then why husband?'"

"I guess that shows where I stand in the scheme of things."

"I could've told them I'm pregnant," Natalie laughed, "and that you're earning your keep."

"They'll know soon enough." He wondered if the students could tell. She wasn't showing yet, but she seemed even prettier to him.

"True. But I'm afraid of talking about it too soon. I don't want to jinx anything."

Clark watched Natalie moving easily among the students, some of them her grandparents' age. Nights, she made the drive back to Meeks Road in a Honda she had obtained by trading the VW Bug. "I like the contrast," she told Clark. "I drive out of the city, then suddenly I get here and it's still; quiet."

After they managed to get Wade to bed, they would sit in the tiny kitchen, unwinding from the day. "You see," she explained one late night as Clark fixed tea, "you come here as a foreigner, not speaking the language, dressed funny, and it doesn't matter who you really are or what you did before. Now you're a refugee. My grandma spoke only a few words of English. Grandpa never spoke any. I know how they must've seemed to others, and I know who they were before.

"To Dr. Howard on Long Island and his wife, Mom and Pop were dirt-poor foreigners who couldn't drive a car or even speak the language."

"Your parents don't seem to hold a grudge against them," Clark said.

"No. They just figured the Howards were ignorant and didn't know any better." She smiled. "The Howards didn't realize that while they may have looked down on my parents, the feeling was completely mutual."

Natalie removed her tea bag. "I can only imagine the history behind some of those foreign faces in my class. And I know the importance of language. I spoke only Russian for the first few years of my life."

"How did you learn English, then?"

"Our neighbor, Bea Schwartz. She was a great cook and she always treated me to Mandelbrot and other Jewish goodies. They say I would hang out with her, stuffing myself and learning to speak English. Of course, she herself was only a generation further from being a refugee than I was." Natalie laughed.

"All these foreigners. I couldn't have found a nice ranch girl from, say, Pendleton."

"I'll ignore that. Seriously, I know just how it'll be for these people I'm teaching. Even if they learn to speak flawless English, it will never be as comfortable, and comforting, to them as their native tongue. Look"—she took a sip of tea—"I don't even speak Russian well anymore, but I feel awkward talking to Mom and Pop in English. The native language is the one for family, for arguing, laughing, talking about private things. It's *home.* So we're always caught between two worlds, in a way. You are, too, Clark. That's probably why we get along."

Natalie went to the window and peered out. "There's one thing I can't get used to in the country."

"What's that?" Clark walked over and put his arm around her.

"It's so dark." She shivered. "If I go outside and put my hand in front of my face I don't see it."

"I thought you were going to say, 'the smell of the paper mill.'"

Downtown Two Rivers had an operating mill, and though they usually bypassed the center of the city on the way to Meeks Road, Clark had taken Natalie there to show her around.

"You better get a look at an old mill town while it's still there," he told her. "What with all the layoffs." The city was located on the banks of the Willamette River, and dams created churning whitewater. The mill was at the end of Main Street and billowed clouds of steam into the air day and night. They had even ridden the elevator, which the Chamber of Commerce billed as "The World's Tallest Outside Municipal Free Elevator."

"It's not really all that bad a smell. Can't compare to the chicken processing plants in southern Delaware," Natalie said. "But you know how you associate scents with certain times of your life? Well, I imagine years from now every time I smell a paper mill it'll remind me of this time on Meeks Road."

.   .   .

Weekends, when Clark and Natalie could get away from grading papers and preparing lessons, they went for drives. Sometimes Grace would watch Wade and they went for longer trips, crossing Mount Hood and the Cascade Range to the high desert country of central Oregon.

"As soon as I get over the mountain I feel relief; this sense of freedom," Clark said. "Leaving the city lights behind."

"I see what you mean. It's a different world, isn't it? Miles of sagebrush and juniper, the dry landscape." They passed the ghost town of Shaniko, where snow blanketing the ground glowed almost blue at dusk. Suddenly, as they were passing ranch land, four cowboys on horses galloped out of the distance in a spray of snow, decked out in hats, boots, and spurs, horses' manes flying. They grinned and waved at the pickup. "My God," Natalie said, "it's just like the movies."

"Now you're really seeing the West."

As they drove miles through the dry country, Natalie became silent. "Well, what do you think?"

"I was just thinking it's beautiful, but so different from what I know. No tall trees. Great stretches of empty land between the towns. I wonder, will I ever get used to this country?"

"Just wait," Clark said. "You've barely seen anything yet."

They headed further into eastern Oregon, along the winding road shadowing the John Day river, through the cathedral-like rock formations of the fossil beds. "It's remote out here," Natalie said. "There's a sense of danger about this country that you don't get back East. If you got a flat tire or got lost out here, you really could die. There's a certain wildness."

"Don't worry, you're in good hands. I'm an expert guide. But I know what you mean. I missed that when I was in New England. Too tidy. Too safe."

After dark, Clark pulled to the side of the road and turned off the headlights. "Step out. I promised I'd show you things you'd never seen before, and that's what I plan to do." He came around to her side and helped her out of the truck. The snow crunched under her boots.

"Now look up."

Natalie gasped. The sky was ablaze with stars.

"Out here in the clear air, away from city lights, that's the only way to see the night sky."

"I've never seen so many stars in my life. Not even in a planetarium."

Clark stared up at the stars, bright pinpoints of light; the milky galaxies. And he thought of the baby, a new life. "Thank you," he whispered.

But driving to John Day for a motel room, Clark felt a gnawing fear, as he had since realizing Natalie was pregnant. There'd been Payette's abortion. The drowning of the Japanese girl. Somehow he hadn't been smart or strong enough to prevent either. Clark wanted this child more than anything he'd ever wanted before.

The wind picked up and blew drifts of snow across their path. In the sweep of headlights, the road seemed to disappear, appear, then disappear again.

. . .

Saturday and Sunday evenings, Clark and Natalie jogged to the end of Meeks Road. Sometimes Wade followed on his bike, but usually after doing a few wheelies and looking for mud to race through, he lost interest and rode back ahead of them.

They passed Red's cows, a small herd of Angus and Herefords. Often Wade helped Red drive some of the cows and weaker calves into the barn at night. Coyotes lurked in the undeveloped sections of woods and thickets. Wade was all business following Red's directions, switching the reluctant beasts with a stout willow cut from the fence line swale. Red's cow dog Blackie ran among the cattle separating those bound for the barn. Red claimed Blackie was part Australian shepherd, but Clark was skeptical. "Mostly mutt, half mongrel," he told Natalie.

Wade always had trouble with a small, twisted Black Angus Red called "Willie Shoemaker." Its spine was bent because the mother ate wild parsnip while it was in the womb. "That'll cripple a calf, like as not," Red said. "Poor thing can hardly walk. After Willie was first born, we bottle-fed him because he couldn't stand to reach the tits."

When Clark and Natalie reached the end of the road, they stopped to admire the view of the Willamette River, the forested hills on the far bank. An old filbert orchard stretched to their left. No one harvested the filberts anymore or tended the orchard, which was yellow with field grass, green with Russian thistle.

One weekend a blue-and-white sign appeared:

FIVE- AND TEN-ACRE VIEW SITES.
HILLTOP REALTY 655-8479

"That doesn't look good. Pretty soon all this country will be just a bedroom community for the city," Clark said.

They were resting on an old cedar log. "Should we buy land out here before it's developed? Run a few cattle like Red and Olga?" He knew buying land was a dream. With both their salaries they were just squeaking by. Even the modest house they rented would be beyond their means with the added value of five acres. Once Red and Olga were gone, Clark knew, their ramshackle place would be torn down to make way for something much grander.

"You know we can't possibly afford it," Natalie said. "Besides, we're not cut out for this place, in the long run. I don't want to drive miles to get everywhere, and I like the feel of the city. And you hate fixing things. What do you know about taking care of animals? I can just see you up at four A.M. feeding the cows. No, what you really want is to ride around inspecting things and telling the workers what to do." She tipped a pretend cap. "Good job, fellas. Carry on." Natalie took a deep breath of cool evening air. "It *is* beautiful, though."

Leaves crinkled in the orchard. Skittering. More crinkling and skittering. "Pheasants," Clark announced before he'd actually spotted them. "By that vine maple." He pointed. "Right near the hedgerow."

"I see them," she whispered.

Two colorful China roosters ran through the orchard. Their large yellow feet made the dry leaves hiss. The pheasants disappeared into the blackberries, but not before the sun caught the deep red and greens of their heads, the burnished copper feathers of their breasts, the long arrogant tails.

"Let's just take our time and walk back," Clark said.

"You'll do anything to get out of exercise."

The sun had set but a crimson glow remained on the water. Wind rustled the high pines, and the wind shift blew the paper mill smell in another direction so it was hardly noticeable. Venus hung in the west; a few stars glimmered faintly in the dusk.

"That's the old Kepler place." Clark pointed to a dark house with a falling-down barn. "They lived there over sixty years. Then Mr. Kepler fell out of the hayloft while he was pitching down feed for the cattle. Two weeks later, she had a stroke.

"I came down after the funeral. One of their boys worked with me at the college. Inside, the linoleum was worn through to wood. Saggy furniture. The pattern on the countertop was completely worn away, except for a few little yellow flowers." He put his arm around her waist. "Do you think people will come by and remark on 'the old Woods place' someday when we're older?"

"They do now." Natalie laughed. "They say, 'What a claptrap. Can you believe anyone actually lives there?'"

"Hey, we're livin' on love."

"And your ex-wife's zebra-striped couch with the big rip."

"Come to think of it, that would make a good country music song." Clark sang, "Livin' on love, and your ex-wife's couch. . . ."

Natalie stopped. "Is that coming from our place?"

"What?" Clark said, but then he heard it, too. Loud music carried along the quiet road.

As they rounded the bend, Clark saw the yellow house too bright against the dark background of fields and trees. Every light was switched on. It seemed odd. "Well, now we know Wade's hit puberty," he said loudly. "He's got the stereo cranked up." At least the honeymoon couple's house was dark and both vehicles were gone.

"My God."

Clark heard Natalie's sudden sharp intake of breath. They both stood as if frozen. Through the open garage door they saw Wade's wiry figure silhouetted against bright light. Music blared from his tape recorder. Wade was gripping Red's dog, Blackie, forcing her to the floor with both his hands around her neck. He was so intent, he didn't notice Clark and Natalie in the driveway.

"What is he doing? Stop! Wade, stop!" Natalie yelled but he couldn't hear her over the music. They both broke into a run.

"Wade!" Clark got to him first and grabbed his shoulders. Startled, Wade jumped up, releasing Blackie. She scampered across the road to Red's.

"Wade!" Clark said. "What the hell were you doing?"

The boy jerked out of Clark's grip and backed against the wall, staring at the cement floor. His lower lip hung out.

"You were hurting the dog," Clark said. "You were hurting Blackie."

When Wade looked up, his face was full of confusion and anger. "I wasn't doing anything bad. I was playing Elvis for Blackie and she wouldn't listen. She kept trying to run away. I put her by the tape recorder so she could hear the music. I wasn't doing anything bad."

"Dammit, Wade, *can't you see you were hurting the dog?*" Clark felt the heat rising in his neck.

"I didn't want to hurt her. I didn't want to hurt Blackie, Dad. I didn't do anything. I swear." Tears rolled down the boy's face and his upper lip glistened with mucous. "I just wanted her to listen to the music."

"God damn it . . ." Clark stepped toward him, but Natalie grabbed Clark's arm.

"Look, Wade," she said. "You better go in."

"I didn't do it, Mom." Wade wiped his sleeve across his face, snuffling.

"We'll sort this out later. Go inside and get a Kleenex."

Wade slunk into the house.

When he was out of sight, Natalie turned to Clark. "He was trying to strangle the dog."

Clark didn't answer.

"Wasn't he?"

"It looked that way, didn't it?"

"I don't know." She shook her head. "His explanation makes sense, in his own weird way of thinking. But it sure looked like he was hurting Blackie. Did we overreact?"

"I honest to God can't tell."

In the glare of the garage light, her face was drained of color. "Clark, what do we do? How can we even explain this sort of thing to anyone?"

They stared at each other. Finally, Natalie said, "I'm tired. And we're not getting anywhere just standing here. Let's go in." She picked up the tape recorder.

* * *

The house settled into an uneasy silence. Clark heard the water running and knew Natalie was soaking in the tub. Wade was lying on his bed.

Just before ten, as Clark was preparing his lecture for Monday morning, he heard a car honking outside. For a moment he thought it was teenagers driving by, but the honking continued, insistent.

Natalie called from the bedroom. "Can you see what that's about? I've got my nightgown on. Maybe somebody's having car trouble." Clark peered out the living room window, but it was too dark to see. "We need a porch light," he muttered.

He got a flashlight out of his dresser. If he kept the light in the kitchen or garage, Wade would use up the batteries. When he went outside, he recognized his mother's car near the end of the muddy driveway. Wade's bike had been knocked over by the front bumper. His mother had the passenger door open and was bending across the front seat. She backed away, holding a large flat box in her hands. She tried closing the heavy door with her rear end, but it only swung partway. Then she saw Clark.

"Honey, can you close that door? I didn't get it quite shut with my bum. I'm so glad you brought the light. It's *dark* out here." She took small steps toward the house, avoiding the muddy potholes.

"Mom, what are you up to?"

"I've got a treat," she said. "I can't wait to show you."

Natalie opened the door as they approached, and Clark saw her eyebrows go up.

"It was Mom out there honking."

"Natalie, I'm just dying to have you try these desserts," she said. "Is the little boy still up? I brought him one, too." She handed the box to Natalie. "I'm dying to have you see these. I hope they didn't get too messed up in the box." Her voice was too loud and Clark knew she was excited.

"Wade's in bed," Natalie said, taking the box and going into the kitchen.

"Son, can you get me a chair?" Grace said. "I'm going to slip off these rainboots so I don't track mud across Natalie's nice floor. I just love hardwood floors. I wish I still had those braided rugs Grandma Spencer made. They'd be perfect in here. Of course I don't know if Natalie would want those family rugs. Everyone has their own tastes."

"They were nice all right," Clark said. "Why are you out so late?"

"Come into the kitchen so I can show you. I know my voice carries, and I don't want to wake little boy."

Natalie was sitting at the table, the box in front of her unopened.

"Aren't you dying to see what's inside? I know I couldn't wait. Maybe that's why you stay so slim." Grace's fingers plucked at the Scotch tape sealing the box but she didn't get it loose. Clark ran his thumbnail along the edge and opened the box. Inside were four elaborate desserts.

"I feel just like the Queen of Sheba," Grace said. "Marge Maw read about this place in Sellwood that has these marvelous desserts. The pastry chef was from Austria and went to all these fancy chef schools in Europe. I had the itchy foot so I decided to drive into town and try them. I ate two there and brought these to share with you. Honey, could you get us some forks and plates?" she asked Natalie. "Just look. Those are fresh raspberries on that chocolate cake. Fresh this time of year! Imagine! They get them from Brazil or somewhere."

Natalie put two forks and plates on the table. "Would you like some tea, Grace?"

"That would be perfect. With cream and sugar, please. Two teaspoons. You kids know me. I can't wait to eat dessert. This one's called Death by Chocolate. You try some, Natalie." She cut a big hunk and held it out on the fork.

Natalie turned on the gas and set the teapot on the ring. "I don't really care for any right now."

"You better try some. *The Oregonian* called Papa Haydn's the best place in Portland for dessert." She was still holding out the fork.

"I just can't eat sweets this late at night."

"I can eat chocolate anytime," Grace said. "My stomach's made of cast iron." She put the chocolate in her own mouth. "As good as it gets," she said. "Oh darn me, I got some crumbs on the floor." She took a napkin and tried stooping over to get the crumbs but she couldn't bend that far. "I get so mad. I'm always dribbling things all over the place. I think I've got dropsy. That's what Grandma Spencer always used to say."

The teapot whistled.

"Gas scares me," Grace said. "When it comes to gas, I'm an old scaredy cat. I guess it doesn't bother you any, but I remember the Peterson boys back in The Dalles. Roger and Terry. Somehow, the pilot light went out. There was a big explosion. Killed them both. I thought it was a bomb going off or a disaster at the flour mill—maybe a dust explosion in the grain elevator. But it was the Petersons' place all right. Just two blocks from where we lived." She took a bite of bread pudding. "You should have seen how stuff was scattered around—books and pictures and clothes. A man's coat was draped over the power line for weeks. My father took me by there and said, 'Don't ever mess with gas.' Of course, we had an electric stove and heat. They say gas is cheaper but then the Columbia River had all those dams so you could buy electricity for a song. In those days."

"Well, now gas is cheaper," Clark said.

"Maybe so. Things have changed since my time. I don't understand all I hear about." Grace frowned, then brightened. "I bought your favorite, son. Apple pie."

Natalie's mouth had formed a thin line. "He's been putting on weight."

"Clark can't help it," Grace said. "It's in the genes." She patted Clark's stomach. "I'm glad he's a little bit stout. That's what they always said about his uncle Roy and his grandpa. They had a little tummy. Clark used to be so skinny when he started grade school in Pendleton his pants just hung. I worried about him all the time. He had to wear suspenders because he didn't have any hips. He was skinny as a traveling minister."

"Something's happened," Clark said, trying to lighten the mood.

Natalie poured water into a mug.

"Don't you have a real teacup?" Grace asked. "I'd prefer that, if you don't mind. I don't know what it is exactly, but tea just tastes better out of a real teacup. And I want my tea to taste delicious with these wonderful desserts. Natalie, you better try one, honey."

"No. Thank you."

"I can eat dessert any time," Grace said. "Any time at all. I don't have a delicate stomach." She sipped her tea and her eyes widened. "Just look who's here! Well, my sleepy bear. Come and give Grandma a big kiss. Goodness. What happened to your pajama top?"

Wade stood in the door. His eyes squinted so much they were almost shut. He was naked above the waist.

"What's that?" he asked, pointing to the leftover desserts.

"Grandma brought some desserts," Grace said. "Wade, you have to bring Mom and Daddy to this restaurant. They even had a carved wooden horse from an old carousel there. It was mighty fancy, I can tell you that. Have some cake, little boy. Look, this one is triple chocolate cheesecake with raspberry sauce."

"It's late for him . . ." Natalie said.

"You better listen to your mother." Grace gave him some cake. "Just a couple of bites and then skeedaddle along to bed."

Wade ate the larger portions of two desserts. "Don't they ever feed you?" Grace asked. "Well, just wait until your new little sister or brother comes. You'll get to feed the baby. Won't that be fun?"

Wade stared at her, sullen.

"He'd better get to bed," Natalie said. "School tomorrow." From behind Grace's back she mouthed something and nodded toward the door.

"I don't want to rush anybody off," Clark said. "But I've got to finish my lecture for tomorrow. Eight in the morning. I've got to be bright-eyed and bushy-tailed."

"I know, son. I know about work." Grace rested her hand on his arm. "I did it for thirty-five years." She looked puzzled a minute. "You've got class tomorrow?"

He nodded.

"What day is this? I thought it was Saturday."

"It's Sunday."

"Are you sure?"

"I know when I have to go to work," he said. "Wade's got to get up, too. Anyway, you were reading the Sunday paper about Papa Haydn's."

She seemed convinced. "That's right. I was. Sometimes I buy the Sunday paper on Saturday, the early edition. Maybe that's what goofed me up."

Clark heard the toilet flush and the bathroom door open.

"Is the bathroom all clear?" Grace called. "If it is, I'll just use it and then head out." She shook her head. "Sunday. Places used to be closed on Sunday."

Clark sat in the kitchen alone for five minutes and sampled the desserts.

When Grace returned from the bathroom, she asked, "Son, could you back the car out into the road? I can't see very well at night to back up, and if I turn my head too far, I get a kink in my neck. The last time I had one, it took a week to go away."

Clark put on his jacket and went outside. As he backed his

mother's car out, he thought of older women alone. Back in Traverse City, he had helped his landlady back her car out through the snowdrifts on Peninsula Drive every winter. After each new snowstorm the plows piled up large drifts of snow that he had to shovel through. He didn't mind, and in exchange, she didn't acknowledge his occasional drunkenness, the young women who sometimes stayed over at his cabin. She didn't press him too hard. In the spring, when she trimmed her bushes, he was happy to haul the trimmings to the dump, and when she fell on the ice and sprained her ankle, he took her English spaniel Penny for walks.

His mother also needed someone, he figured, and when he married Natalie, the balance shifted. He wasn't around to carry Grace's groceries, run errands. But Natalie didn't like these unannounced visits. Clark almost dreaded going back in the house.

His mother left her seat belt unfastened. She had had a breast with cancer removed years before and she said it hurt her to fasten a seatbelt.

"Good night, son," she said, giving him a big hug. "Natalie seemed kind of quiet tonight, didn't she?"

"I think she's tired of the rain," he said.

"That's what I loved about working in Bend," she said. "All that clear blue sky."

"Drive carefully," he said.

"Well, I'll catch you a little farther down the crick," she said.

Clark watched her pull away. Before going in, he checked the sky. It was drizzling, that constant, soft rain that seemed to last all winter. Still, he could see the outline of the moon over West Linn. Lights were on in Red's toolshed, and he knew Red was tinkering with some old machine part, "fixing it up."

* * *

The light went off in the bedroom. He was glad Natalie was turning in; otherwise they'd argue—one of those arguments that never resolved anything because they weren't really angry with each other. They were caught, he knew, in a situation neither knew how to handle. But knowing that didn't stop them blaming each other.

Looking at the darkened garage, he remembered the scene with

Blackie and it gave him a sick feeling. Now that Wade was growing into puberty, Clark wondered, was his confusion turning to anger?

That night, Clark lay awake replaying the scene with Blackie over and over again in his mind, and listening to the crickets, until the windows lightened with dawn and he heard Red's cows in the field, their bells clinking.

. . .

Clark waited for Dr. Shockley in a small office adjoining the examining room. Wade was in the waiting room outside because the doctor wanted to talk privately. "If he takes anything apart out there, I sure hope insurance covers it," Clark muttered to himself.

The visit was Natalie's idea. She had done research and discovered that Dr. Shockley was one of the best neurologists in Portland, specializing in children. Clark tried telling her he'd already covered every angle but Natalie just said, "Maybe there's something we've missed. There must be something."

"All right," Clark told her, just to soothe her feelings. However, he was convinced the doctors couldn't solve Wade's problems. He and Natalie had to deal with his unpredictable behavior themselves.

. . .

Doctor Shockley came in and set up the X ray.

"Did you find anything?" Clark asked him.

"Yes and no. Whatever's wrong is inside his brain, but you can't see it. You could set his brain and yours side by side on this table and the two would look pretty similar. However, in his case, the electrical connections keep misfiring somewhere in the synapses. We don't know exactly why."

"What can I do?" Clark asked.

"That's the hell of it," Shockley said. "I can't tell you much." He ticked off the program on his fingers. "Good nutrition, a stable home life, clear sets of boundaries. I guess he's already on Ritalin. One indication is how far he's come since you first got him. What would you say about that?"

"Lots of improvement. Night and day, really. But he still can't read or tell time. And sometimes his behavior is bizarre."

Shockley patted Clark on the back. "Well, you've done a heroic job. Just keep hoping for more improvement." His expression became troubled. "And be ready for setbacks."

Clark paused. "How do you mean?"

"All these situations are different. He may not improve at the rate you want him to. Or he may show a skill one day, but lose it the next. Like recognizing words or telling time."

"That's right," Clark said. "He'll be going along great, making progress. There'll be a stretch where we think he's passed another hurdle, and wham!" Clark hit the table with his palm. "Then he'll do something really stupid, and any progress flies out the window."

Shockley nodded. "We can only hope that with each setback, he still retains some of the progress he's made. A 'two steps forward, one step back' situation. I wish I could tell you more. Just don't get too frustrated."

Clark shrugged. "I'm beyond frustrated."

*   *   *

Later that day when they were alone, Natalie asked Clark, "What did the doctor say? Did he find anything?"

"He said there's nothing wrong with Wade that we can see."

Natalie looked incredulous. "What?"

After Clark had explained, Natalie said, "You know, that reminds me of the time I was working a summer job at a school for kids with problems. There was a four-year-old boy named Tim who wouldn't speak. Not a sound."

"Wouldn't or couldn't?"

"Wouldn't. When he was two, someone rammed a spoon down his throat and he hadn't uttered a sound since then; not a word or a cry, nothing. He was examined by a slew of specialists, went through all these tests, but no one could find anything physically wrong with the boy. His vocal cords were fine. In that sense, he was like Wade. Nothing wrong *that anyone could see.* Yet the damage was done, obviously."

"So what happened?"

"I don't know how it all ended. Tim grew attached to me; he started to brighten whenever he saw me. And I liked him, too—he had lively eyes and a sweet face. But I went back to college that fall." Natalie shook her head. "And in the busy rush, summer sort of receded from my mind. I wrote once to see how Tim was doing, and they said he acted sad, as if he missed me. But after that, I lost track of him. I always felt bad about that. Funny, the irony. Now here I am, dealing with Wade. You don't think the cosmos is getting back at me, do you?" She smiled, but Clark could see she was troubled.

He pulled her close. "It doesn't work that way."

"And we'll figure all this out, won't we?"

"Absolutely," Clark said.

14

Glenwood, 1980

Clark pretended to be a bear. He shook the huckleberry bushes and roared. "Run. There's a bear!" Rattling the bushes harder, he cried, "A big bear's attacking me! Grab a stick. Help, Wade!"

Nonchalant, Wade stuffed huckleberries into his mouth, staining his lips and teeth dark blue. Squinting at the bucket, he said, "I picked more than you, Dad."

Deflated, Clark emerged from hiding in the bushes. "Whew! That bear almost got me. Thanks for all the help."

"Come on, Dad." Wade grinned. "I've been living with you five years, right?"

"Six." Clark sat on a stump.

"All that time, we never seen one bear."

"But we *could* see a bear today!" Clark was hopeful. "Bears like huckleberries."

"Angoon had giant bears." Wade picked a couple of green stems out of the bucket. "I remember when Maynard smacked a bear right in the kisser with a big stick. That old bear was coming into the kitchen after smelling the bacon frying."

"Good thing we're not packing bacon way up here," Clark said. He didn't know if Wade actually remembered seeing bears in Angoon or made it up from watching television. Before he got so involved with the *Dukes of Hazzard* or monster truck shows, Wade had enjoyed watching *Gentle Ben.*

"Maynard was my real dad, huh? And now you're my dad and Mom's my mom."

Clark nodded. "When your father died, I wanted to be your dad. And when I married Natalie, she became your mom."

Wade's brow furrowed. "And when baby Helen's born, you'll still be my dad, and her dad too."

"That's right."

Wade frowned. "But you'll be her *real* dad." He put more berries in his mouth and chewed slowly, waiting for Clark's answer.

"I'm your *real* dad, too." Clark didn't like the term "real." "You were born to Maynard and Amber, but they couldn't take care of you. In some ways, the people who take care of you every day are the real moms and dads."

With a stick, Wade drew lines in the dusty trail. His lips moved while he counted silently. "Six," he said. "How long is a year?"

Clark knew if he said three hundred and sixty-five days, Wade wouldn't understand. "Think of it like this. From one Christmas all the way to the next. That's one year. Or from one birthday to the next. That's a year. Last year, you were eleven. This year, you're twelve.

"Here's another thing. You've been with me six years, but you were only with Maynard and Amber for five." Five seemed generous to Clark, given all the times Wade had been bounced between Alaskan foster homes.

Wade checked his fingers. "Six is more." He drew another line. "Do people still have birthdays when they're dead?"

Clark considered before answering. Two ants were crawling up his ankle, and he brushed them off. "I guess they do. Sure, if people remember them. What were you thinking about?"

Wade drew more lines but these zigzagged. "A while back Mom was crying, and when I asked her why, she said it was her brother's birthday. I never cry on Maynard's birthday, though, because I don't even know when it is."

"I guess if it's important, I can find out. Your uncle Sampson should know."

Wade nodded. "Okay." He squinted at the berries. "Mom's going to make us a big old huckleberry pie soon. She should come hiking with us."

"Next time." Natalie had stayed behind at the Flying L because she was seven months pregnant and didn't feel like climbing the steep trail to Goat Rocks lookout. The lookout tower was gone, but the concrete supports remained, and the high ridge commanded a spectacular view of Mount Adams, Mount St. Helens, and Mount Rainier further north. The Goat Rocks Wilderness Area stretched away in the slant of hazy afternoon light, and clouds dappled the dark forested foothills and green meadows of the Trout Lake Valley. The White Salmon River cut through gray basalt and surged toward the Columbia, thirty miles south.

"You ever seen a real bear up here?" Wade asked. Along the trail, they'd seen piles of fresh scat, dark with huckleberries.

"You can never tell," Clark said. "Bears are full of surprises."

"If I had a gun, I'd shoot the bear," Wade said. "Then I'd cut off his head and wear the teeth. The claws, too."

Clark shook his head. Wade's people had worn bear masks and some of the shamans wore bear claw necklaces, but he doubted if Wade had seen any ceremonies. "You better leave the bears alone."

"Now I see one, but he's a long way off."

"Where?" Clark thought the boy was joshing but he sighted along Wade's outstretched arm and pointing finger. All he could see was the jagged backside of Mount St. Helens, blown to pieces after the eruption. He wondered if the abundant huckleberries this year were due to the blanket of ash that drifted east after the eruption.

"When Mom has the baby she better not leave it in the woods," Wade said.

"Don't worry, she won't."

"If I don't protect the baby, the bears will smack her up."

Clark kept squinting. "I don't see any bears. You were joshing."

"Bad eyes."

As Clark studied the jagged, reshapen structure of Mount St. Helens, he thought about the Bear Boy legend. According to that story, a boy and his sisters were playing in the woods when, without warning, the boy transformed into a bear and began chasing the sisters for real, meaning to kill them. The sisters climbed onto a large tree stump for safety, and the stump grew and grew into a tall mountain while the angry bear clawed and ripped at its side, tearing out deep gashes. The sisters were taken into the sky for safety and became the stars of the Big Dipper, while the boy became Ursa Major.

From time to time, a bear boy wandered into Tlingit fish camps from the dense wilderness. It ate with the people, listened to campfire stories, and went to sleep under their crest blankets. But by morning it was gone. Later, the people could never agree if the dark, speechless child was a boy or a bear cub.

Clark had been interested in the legend because so much was left unexplained. Why did the boy suddenly become the bear that threatened the sisters? Were the sisters missed by their family? Could the bear transform back into the boy? He studied Wade's shaggy hair on the way down. Much about his boy couldn't be explained either.

Natalie's face seemed less strained when they got back to the Flying L. "I took a long bath," she said. "The phone didn't ring once."

They both laughed because the Flying L had no phones. It was a place to rest. Natalie's name had gotten on some list and the home phone kept ringing with offers for baby clothes, cosmetics, toys, mood relaxing tapes.

Wade stuck his head in the door. "Prince wants to go on a walk," he said. "I'm going to take him on the loop, okay? Don't you think Prince looks just like a brown bear?" Wade petted the chocolate lab.

"Stick right on the trail," Clark said. "Follow the blue arrows. And don't pick any of the trilliums." Darvel, owner of the place, had marked all the wildflower clusters with thin poles. At various times during the summer, they had wildflower groups up for hikes and nature lectures.

"Do you think he'll be all right?" she asked.

"If he's not, Search and Rescue will have to come out."

"You're not funny," she said.

*   *   *

That evening, Clark sat in one of the Adirondack chairs by the main lodge and watched the sunset over Mount Adams. A cloud shaped like a flying saucer sat on the peak, turning from gold, to rose, to dark violet. Down at the pond, he could hear Wade shouting and Prince splashing after a thrown stick.

A large woman in white pants, a fuschia blouse, and a floppy straw hat came across the lawn toward him. She stopped next to the chair, taking one deep breath, then letting out a sigh. "You're with that boy, aren't you? The thin child down at the pond?"

Clark half nodded. "I'm his foster father. He's a Tlingit boy from Alaska."

"Foster," she repeated, lisping. "I don't usually peek over other people's fences. I stick to my own backyard."

He half-turned, facing her. Several rosy patches dotted her face and neck. "That's probably a good practice."

She took a handkerchief from her pocket and dabbed at her cheeks and forehead. "I just had to tell you about the boy. What I saw him doing this afternoon."

"Is that right?" Clark was on his guard. For some reason, perhaps because Wade was brown, complete strangers felt entitled to comment on his behavior. And if he acted unruly in a group of boys, he was often singled out.

"I was hiking back in the woods, looking at the flowers. Then I heard a strange noise, like whimpering almost, and when I looked harder . . ." She swatted at a mosquito. "This is really difficult for me to say." Her voice trailed.

"What?"

"The dog and the boy were behind a log. At first I thought he was just petting the dog. One hand was there on the dog's stomach." She glanced around but no one was close enough to eavesdrop. "It wasn't natural."

"Not natural?" Clark pretended that he didn't understand.

"Not appropriate. The boy was touching himself privately. I thought you should know, perhaps get some counseling for him. Maybe they do things differently in his culture."

"So he was masturbating?" Clark asked. "Is that what you're saying?"

She nodded and avoided Clark's eyes. "You can get him help. There are lots of resources."

"Thanks for telling me," Clark said. *You old busybody,* he thought. *Weren't your ancestors at the witch trials?* he was tempted to ask. Since Wade had hit puberty, he had a lot of different behaviors. As the woman walked away, Clark studied her ample rear, a yellow moss smudge on the back of the white pants. *Hogs fighting under a sheet,* he thought. His hunch was she hadn't been touched in quite a while.

* * *

That night Natalie spooned some of the huckleberries and sugar on Tillamook Ice Cream. "Mount Adams huckleberries," Clark said. "You can't get berries like these in the East."

"We had some nice blueberries up in Maine," Natalie said. "Remember those muffins we ate in Kennebunkport?"

Clark shook his head. "I was too busy with the lobsters."

"I remember those," Wade said. "Like big crawdads. They had rubber bands around their claws."

Clark studied Wade a minute. Odd, the things the boy remembered. Usually, by afternoon, he couldn't remember what he ate for breakfast, but then he'd dredge up some long-forgotten occasion.

"You should have seen Dad pretending to be a bear." Wade shambled around the room, swinging his arms and shoulders, bearlike. He coughed and snuffled.

"You had me fooled." Natalie smiled at Wade. "You sound just like a bear." Then she winced and touched her belly. "That was a strong one."

"Maybe she'll be a soccer player," Clark said.

Wade squinted at Natalie's belly. "Can my little sister taste the huckleberries?"

"I'm sure she can," Natalie said.

Wade leaned closer. "I chased off the bears and picked them just for you, Helen. Now eat up." His expression clouded. "You're my baby sister and I want you to listen to me. Stop hurting Mom."

Natalie didn't miss the edge in his voice. "She didn't hurt me. All babies kick."

"Stop it, sister!" Wade's mouth twisted.

"All right. Time for a bath." Clark wanted to break things up before Natalie got in a mood.

After he ran the water, Clark took a beer out of the refrigerator. He didn't supervise Wade's baths anymore, figuring the boy needed some privacy. Hair now sprouted from Wade's groin and under his arms. A faint mustache appeared on his upper lip. After school, he smelled sour, and he had grown moodier—sullen at times, belligerent at others. "The hormones are kicking in," RealBird had said. "He's going to be more of a challenge."

"I don't know how much more of this fun I can take," Clark had cracked.

Now, opening the cabin's back door, he let in the night breeze, enjoying the scent of wood smoke and pine needles.

Squeals and loud splashing came from the bathroom. More high-pitched squeals.

"Clark. Get Wade to settle down. I'm trying to sleep."

Clark tapped on the door and it swung open. Wade had his finger in his nose. He flicked a booger into the water. "Booger burgers, snotty snot." He giggled. "Patootey."

"Did you and Prince have a good walk in the woods?"

"Dog slobber tastes like pennies. Old pissy pennies." Squinting his eyes, he stuck out his tongue and licked his arms. "Germy pissy pennies."

Clark took his shoulder. "Dogs are clean. They say dogs' mouths are cleaner than people's."

"Rotten wormy penny dog slobber." Wade quieted as Clark gripped his shoulder tighter.

"Ow! Owee!" The boy took a breath, shaking his head and opening his eyes wide. "Do dogs have snot, Dad?"

Clark released the grip. "I don't think so. Maybe in the winter if they catch a cold." He knelt beside the tub. "It's time to quiet down. I mean it."

Picking huckleberries and walking with the dog had overstimulated the boy. Clark wished he had an "off" button.

"Mom and the baby are trying to sleep."

Wade scissor-kicked at the water. "No, they're not. The baby's wide awake and kicking. I felt her. Mom says the baby's in a sack of water, like a cushion."

"That's right. That's how babies are protected until they get bigger."

"How can she breathe, if she's in a sack of water?"

Clark thought a minute before he answered. "Mom and the baby are connected by a hose. Mom's breathing for her. Later on, after Helen's born, she'll breathe by herself and they'll cut the hose."

Wade touched his penis. "Nobody's cutting my hose. That would hurt like hell!"

Clark laughed. "Wrong hose, buddy. Look. See your belly button? That's the old part of the hose, where you were connected to your mother. She breathed for you when you were a baby in her sack of water. Grace breathed for me." He pulled up his T-shirt. Here's my belly button."

Wade jabbed a finger at his own belly button. "My mother loved me." He sounded uncertain. He twisted around, so he could see Clark. "Right?"

"Yes." He reached for Wade's shoulder, but the boy dipped that side. "She breathed for you a long time." *But she didn't love you enough to stop drinking,* he added silently.

"I don't know where she is, so I can't thank her."

"Don't worry, buddy. I think she knows. Right now she's sick."

"I want to talk with her." Wade began soaping his belly and chest. "She's been really sick a long time or she'd call me."

* * *

The next afternoon, Clark and Wade rode battered Flying L Schwinns north toward the Yakima Indian Reservation, stopping two miles from the ranch to watch eight mule deer, all does and fawns, grazing in an alfalfa field. Mount Adams formed a glistening white backdrop.

Clark took two cool Pepsis from his backpack, tossing one to the boy, who tapped the can's top to keep soda from fizzing out. They sipped their drinks and watched the deer. Wade sighted along his arm. "Bang, bang. Venison stew."

"You should wait for a buck," Clark said.

A yellow Dodge power wagon approached, stirring up dust on the graveled road. The driver slowed to a stop and lifted a sunburned arm in a half wave. He wore a faded straw cowboy hat, a green pearl-buttoned short-sleeved shirt. Nodding toward the browsing deer, he said, "Come October, they'll be long gone."

"You said it." Clark studied the orange-and-black magnetic sign on the driver's door:

KLICKITAT COUNTY SEARCH AND RESCUE

"You fellas seen a little girl anywhere?" the driver asked. "We got one missing."

"We haven't seen anybody," Clark said. "What does she look like?"

"Five years old. Plump. Curly brown hair. Jeans and a blue sweat-shirt. Name's Tessie Baxter. Her mom says she took off last night, or maybe early this morning. The mother's kind of casual."

"Where does she live?" Wade became alert. "I want to see what's going on."

The man rubbed his jaw. "We're headquartered at the Spar Tree Café back in town. Tessie lives just across the street."

"You got any dogs?" Clark asked.

"Not yet. But they're bringing some in from Stevenson any time now."

"We'll get Prince!" Wade almost shouted. "He can track her."

Smiling, the driver said, "You must be staying at the Flying L. Everybody in this country knows Prince."

Wade raced ahead, stopping every so often to signal for Clark to hurry. A trail of dust marked the boy's bicycle path. Clark had his doubts about joining the search. Wade was unpredictable, and he didn't want to leave Natalie alone. Still, it wouldn't hurt to see if the searchers needed help. No harm in being a good neighbor.

Battered pickups, green U.S. Forest Service vehicles, and tan sher-iff's cars crowded the Spar Tree's parking lot. Across the street, a horse trailer blocked the post office, and Clark realized a mounted sheriff's patrol was joining the search. Two dozen people milled in front of the restaurant. Half wore orange caps and vests that said "Search and Rescue."

Two lanky rangers and a short, middle-aged woman studied a map spread across a picnic table. The woman was giving orders, and after a couple minutes, Clark realized she was the sheriff.

"Look at all the local people," Clark told Wade. "We'll just get in the way."

"Dang. I wish I had one of those hats!" Wade released the bike's kickstand and climbed off his bike. "Where's the sheriff?" he asked one of the rangers. "My dad and I want to help find Therese."

"Tess." The sheriff stretched her mouth in what passed for a smile, but her flat eyes suggested she didn't want amateurs. "Do you know Tess from school?"

Wade shook his head. "Do you got any bloodhounds? The man told us there'd be dogs."

Clark explained to the sheriff about seeing the pickup driver and wanting to help. She seemed disinterested. After giving their bikes a glance, she said, "Maybe you two should search the Flying L. Tess could have strayed over there, I guess." She lowered her voice as a bedraggled woman in a bathrobe came onto the porch of a small blue house across the way. "Tess is a little off. She had a real high fever when she was two."

"I want to ride in a big old truck with flashers," Wade told Clark, causing one of the rangers to snicker.

Clark handed the boy a dollar. "Step inside and get a soda."

Wade pocketed the dollar. "Do you think I could go in a truck?"

Clark shook his head. "We need to ride these bikes back. Anyway, you wanted to get Prince."

The bathrobed woman glanced around and shuffled toward them. Her eyes were sunken and dark. "Any word?"

"Not yet, Mattie," the sheriff said. "Just wait inside your house by the phone. We got dogs coming, so find us something Tess wore recently."

Mattie shook her head. "She's got on her jeans and blue sweatshirt. Tennis shoes. She hasn't worn her church dress since Sunday."

"Get a sock or some soiled underwear. They give the dogs a strong scent," the sheriff said.

The woman wandered back into the house, muttering.

Turning to Clark, the sheriff said, "She's mighty worked up."

"I'd be worried if Wade ran off."

"Kids are a concern," she said. "Is he a Yakima Indian?"

"No. He's a Tlingit from Alaska. Wade's my foster son."

"Clink it?" She thinned her lips. "Looks almost Asian, doesn't he, what with those narrow eyes." She brushed her hand across the map. "Half this county's Yakima now, the way they keep spilling off the rez. The crime rate's shooting straight up."

· · ·

"I'm going to get Prince and go look for her," Wade insisted when they were back at the Flying L. "Maybe she thinks she's in trouble so she's hiding."

"You'd better stick close to the cabin," Clark said. He thought searching the heavily hiked loop trail around the ranch was useless. "Anyway, the sheriff has it covered. You saw all the people searching."

"Why haven't they found her yet then?"

Clark studied the boy's face. He wasn't being lippy; the question was genuine. "I don't know. Maybe they'll find her with the horse patrol or the dogs."

Wade didn't answer for a moment. Then his voice sounded far away. "They never found that one little girl soon enough. Right?"

"What girl?" Clark pretended to be casual.

"Grandma lived with us then but Mom didn't. The policemen came. They were huge."

"You were smaller then," Clark said, but they had seemed huge to him, too. He remembered how they filled up the tiny Amherst apartment.

"I could have helped them find her, before it was too late."

Clark carefully asked, "Did you know where she was, Wade?"

Wade squinted. "I know where she played. That's where they found her."

Clark couldn't read the boy's eyes. "Her mother kept her in the playground. She didn't let her play near the water."

"If she got out, she did. If someone left the gate open, she liked playing near the water."

"Did you leave the gate open, Wade? That was a long time ago and no one will blame you."

"Heck, no!" Wade shook his head. "Other kids might have, but I was careful. Anyway, I was little then."

Clark figured that, somehow, learning about this missing girl had sparked Wade's memory of Yukiko, but Clark couldn't guarantee the accuracy of that memory. The boy's imagination was too vivid. Still, he was curious what other details Wade might recall. Perhaps he'd mention the stick. "You were small, so the adults overlooked what a big help you could have been. All we know is someone left the gate open."

"Not me," Wade insisted. "I knew they wanted it closed tight." He held up his hand, closing his fist. "Maybe they should get a fence to keep Tessie in."

"That might help."

Wade started toward the lodge. "I'm getting Prince right now. If we find her, Tessie's mother will be happy. Come on, Dad. Let's get started!"

Clark stood. "I guess there's no stopping us."

*   *   *

Two horses blocked the loop trail just past the abandoned landing strip Darvel's father's Hollywood buddies had used when they flew into the Flying L. The riders were a man and a woman with loden green jackets and striped whipcord trousers that marked them as deputies.

Wade reached out to pet one of the horses but it whinnied and shied. "Stay back, son," the man said. "A big snake just spooked Revolver. Mind that dog, too. He doesn't favor dogs."

The man's bulk and dark mustache reminded Clark of Furman. The second rider, a lean blond woman with a prematurely lined face, wore mirrored sunglasses. "We're looking for a little town girl that's gone missing. Tessie Baxter. Five years old. Jeans and a blue sweatshirt. Shoulder-length curly hair. Have you seen her?"

Clark shook his head. "We're looking, too. We were riding bikes after lunch and stopped in town when we saw the searchers. The sheriff said she might be around here."

"Could be. Could be anywhere," the man said.

When he straightened in his stirrups, Clark noticed the exotic light brown cowboy boots he wore. "Once they found Tessie hiding under a bed in the bunkhouse," the deputy said. "Another time, she was halfway to Trout Lake." Tapping the side of his head, he added, "Slow."

"Prince will find her," Wade said. "He knows every hiding place around here."

"She might come to a dog, all right," the woman said. "Children like dogs."

No one said anything for a minute and Clark felt uncomfortable with the lapse. Far away past Mount Adams, thunder rolled.

"Fancy boots," Wade said, pointing to the deputy's feet. "Can you run fast in those?"

"I can fly." He cracked a smile. "They're ostrich skin. Soft as a baby's rump."

"Ostrich?" Wade was perplexed. "What's that?"

"A big bird," Clark told him. He wondered if the deputy knew ostriches couldn't fly.

Wade peered at the boots. "Tessie was wearing plain old brown cowboy boots. And a brown sweatshirt with a jumping horse. That's how we'll find her. Look for little cowboy boot tracks."

All three adults stared at Wade.

What the hell! Clark thought. He started to speak, but his mouth tasted like brass.

"Tessie had on tennis shoes," the woman said. "That's what I thought."

"Me, too," the other deputy said. Dismounting, he stepped closer to Wade, studying him. "What makes you think she was wearing cowboy boots and a brown sweatshirt? Have you seen her?"

Clark moved closer to the boy, afraid the large deputy's closeness might influence him.

"No." Wade's lips twisted and he shook his head. "But we're going to find her."

"Listen, why did you say she was wearing cowboy boots?" the woman asked.

Wade shrugged. "When I go someplace, I wear cowboy boots."

"That's right." Clark finally found his voice. "He got new boots for his birthday. Black Justins. He wants to take them everywhere."

The woman studied Wade's dirty tennis shoes, then focused on Clark. "He's not wearing them now."

"They're back at the cabin. He put tennis shoes on this morning when we played softball. After lunch, we went bicycle riding. That's when we saw the searchers and talked to the sheriff. I was surprised you had a woman sheriff out here, not surprised, really, but interested." Clark realized he was talking too much. "She might have mentioned the boots."

"That woman will be out on her big butt, after next election," the man said.

His partner shot him a dirty look, then turned her attention back to Clark and Wade. She dismounted, offering Wade the reins. "Hold Goldenrod for me, please. What's your name?"

"Wade," he answered, looking down. His response was barely audible.

"My name's Corporal Williams," the woman said, smiling to show small even teeth. "Tess's mom's going to be very happy when she gets home safely." She paused. "I sure hope Tess didn't get lost out in the woods somehow. I wouldn't want her to get hurt."

"Maybe a snake bit her," Wade said. "If I see a big old rattler, I'll kill it and put the rattles on my hatband."

The two police officers studied the boy. Williams asked him several questions without getting satisfactory answers.

"We got to find her before the otters do," he said at one point.

Jesus Christ, Clark thought. *Jesus H for Helluva Mess Christ.*

He scarcely remembered walking fifty yards back up the trail with the woman, but he heard more thunder and caught snapshot glimpses of Canadian jays darting from tree to tree. The air became thick and oppressive. Gulping shallow breaths, he felt the flush rising in his neck.

Williams took a notebook and pen out of her green jacket pocket. "I didn't want to say anything in front of your boy," she explained. "But he's a little different, isn't he?"

"He's my foster son, actually," Clark said. "He has some learning problems."

She wrote a note. "Can you be more specific about his problems, sir?" She paused. "You seem nervous. We're asking a lot of people if they've seen anything. This is just routine."

"Right." He thought of all the people who went to the doctor for a routine checkup and wound up terminal.

"Does Wade get along with other children, fight in school?"

"No," Clark said. "He's got an active imagination, and he makes things up. That's about it."

"But not all the time?"

"No, not all the time. But like seeing the girl. Or the otters. That's just an old tribal legend about otters stealing children."

"Kind of primitive," she observed. Tapping the pen against the pad, she asked, "How can you tell the difference? What's made up, what's real?"

"After a while you learn," Clark said. "Sometimes he makes things up, especially when he's trying to help."

"Give me a rundown of his morning, would you?" she said.

"Sure," Clark said. "Wade and I were playing softball early, about eight. We ate breakfast. After lunch, we rode bikes."

She wrote it down slowly, printing block letters.

"What about between ten and twelve? Were you or your wife with the boy?"

"Not the whole time," Clark said. "But most of it. For a while, he tried catching box turtles at the pond." *How long had Wade been gone?* he wondered.

"And last night?"

Clark shrugged. "Most of the time he was with me." *Except when he was on the loop trail with Prince.* "We spent the afternoon hiking Goat Rocks."

Nothing had happened. He was convinced. The sun became a little warm and he felt lightheaded so he moved under the shade of a lodge-pole. *They were at the Flying L to relax and nothing had happened.*

She stepped closer and flipped to a new page. "Any chance *you* saw the girl, Mr. Woods?"

Clark resented the question and nearly blurted "Absolutely not!" But he decided that was too strong. "I haven't seen her," he said evenly. "A couple of the other guests at the Flying L have children here with them, but no one who resembles the little girl."

"You're convinced he made up the cowboy boots?"

"That's right. Like I said, he got a new pair for his last birthday."

"You also said you were a teacher. I'm just curious. Do you work with little children?"

"No." *The blond bitch,* he thought. She was fishing and not very subtly. "I teach at Two Rivers Community College. The average student is twenty-six years old. As a matter of fact, one of our biggest programs is law enforcement. Maybe you took a program like that at Treaty Oaks or Clark."

Her mouth thinned. "I had to learn on the job," she said. "A classroom's not the real world."

He resented her earlier insinuations and had no intention of agreeing with her, so he stayed quiet.

"We might need to stop by and talk with your wife a second. Does she know you're out looking for Tessie?"

Clark nodded. "We're staying at the Rose Cabin. Come by any time."

She closed the notebook. "We appreciate your cooperation." Her voice sounded like a telephone operator's.

On the short walk back, her demeanor appeared to soften. "My cousin Jean has an eight-year-old niece. She's got trouble in school, too. 'Learning Disabled,' they call it." The deputy sighed. "Sometimes, she's all right, but others she acts strange. One day, she's going to break her mother's heart."

* * *

Leaving the loop trail, Clark and Wade cut across the old weedy airstrip back toward the cabins. The boy had wanted to continue, but Clark felt exhausted after the encounter. Anyway, the deputies had gone over that section of the trail.

"She might be hiding from the horses," Wade pointed out.

"Then I don't think she'd come out for us," Clark said.

When they reached the lodge, Darvel was hitting a softball to a couple of kids. Prince and Wade ran off to join them and Clark sat on a stump to clear his mind. A squirrel scolded from a tall pine; a couple of others scampered onto the porch looking for crumbs near the outside table. The ominous clouds had cleared from near the summit of Mount Adams, so maybe it wasn't going to rain after all. A shaft of sunlight struck his resting place, and Clark felt his shoulders relaxing with the warmth. He closed his eyes, a prayer on his lips. *Let them find the little girl unharmed. Or if she is harmed, miles from the Flying L.*

． ． ．

"Are you okay?" Natalie nudged Clark's knee with hers under the picnic table.

"Never better." Shifting his attention toward her, he smiled. "What a view!" Their table had a spectacular vista of Mount Adams and the Goat Rocks Wilderness Area. "After you have the baby, we'll hike up Bird Creek Meadows and see the wildflowers."

"You seem preoccupied. You haven't eaten all your dinner."

He studied the half-eaten barbecued chicken, potato salad, baked beans. "Maybe I'm just relaxing." Three hours had passed since the time he and Wade had left the officers along the trail. If they were going to rattle Natalie, he wanted them to get it over with. Instead, they were probably drinking coffee and eating doughnuts.

"You're breathing funny."

He swelled his chest. "Clean mountain air. All this physical activity."

"I don't like fat men. You need to get back in shape."

"Not fat. I'm substantial."

Shouts followed by barking came from the pond.

"Wade's up to something. Don't you think you'd better check on him?"

Clark nibbled the chicken. "He's just down at the pond trying to catch a turtle." He knew he'd have to go check soon. Once she started worrying, Natalie fretted until it was easier to do what she wanted rather than listen to her constant anxiety.

Instead of enjoying her own meal, Natalie kept her head tilted—listening to the barks, yelps, shouts, and splashes. Finally, she stood, struggling to clear her pregnant belly from between the picnic bench and tabletop. "Somebody better check to see what's going on."

Reluctantly, Clark set down the chicken and stood. "I'll go. You're pregnant."

Her face showed annoyance. "I'm glad you noticed." She didn't sit down. "I'm walking back to the cabin. I've got to pee again."

Large yellow-winged grasshoppers whirred out of tall field grass as Clark cut across the meadow to the pond. Dozens of colorful butterflies zigzagged in the late afternoon light, and he remembered that several rare species populated the Glenwood area. Sometimes the Flying L had special weekend seminars led by butterfly experts. As he approached the pond, Clark heard cackling red-wing blackbirds in the tules, and he started when a pheasant exploded from the meadow's edge.

Wade's raucous laughter rose from the pond. Prince barked. A stick splashed followed by a larger splash, more barking, somewhat stifled. "Bring it here, boy! That's it! Bring it here." More wild laughter.

Clark started onto the wooden dock and saw Wade knee-deep in the pond as the boy poked at the water with a long stick. Due to the angle of the sun, Clark couldn't see Wade clearly until he closed the distance. "My God! Look at you!"

Wade's entire body was covered with mud, long slimy strands of pond weed, gunk from the pond bottom, gelatinous strings of frog eggs.

He wiped mud and gunk away from his eyes and shook his head to clear his ears. "I fell in the pond, Dad. It was an accident."

"Don't give me that shit!" As Clark stepped closer, he turned his head. The boy reeked of decay, fetid pond water, chlorophyll.

Wade drooped his glistening head and slumped his shoulders.

"You're a terrible mess. Your mother's going to kill us both." Clark regretted not checking on Wade and Prince sooner. He hated it when Natalie was right. He looked around the pond but didn't see the dog. "Where's Prince?"

Wade's eyes squinted. "He went home, Dad. Prince got tired and went home."

"I heard him," Clark said.

"I fooled you, huh, Dad?" Twisting his mouth and sticking out his neck, he imitated the dog's high yelps.

Clark stood, amazed at the accuracy of the barking. Still, something strange in the pitch had attracted Natalie's notice.

Wade came out of the water. His shirt and shoes lay on the bank. When the boy picked them up, Clark said, "Don't put those on until you shower. Just take the loop trail back and hope Mom doesn't catch you. You look like Swamp Thing."

As Wade climbed the pond bank, he dropped a brown sock behind him.

"Wade, you lost a sock." Clark wondered how many socks the boy had lost over the years. At least a hundred.

Wade paused. "No, I got two. See?" He tilted his tennis shoes so Clark could see the two socks stuffed inside. Then he shuffled away.

"Don't litter." But Wade didn't turn. Clark picked up the sock and studied it with curiosity. Each end had a hole. *Not a sock. A piece of brown sleeve,* he thought. He dropped the cloth scrap and stepped back quickly as if it were a snake. *A brown sleeve!*

As soon as Wade was out of sight, Clark grabbed the long stick. Rolling up his pants legs, he waded out in the soft mud and warm water. Broken bottles or rusty cans might cut his feet, so he left his tennis shoes on. For five minutes, he poked and prodded without feeling anything but weeds and mud. Two box turtles eyed him from a safe distance, and a green dragonfly skimmed the pond's surface. *Nothing.*

Semi-relieved, he paused, catching his breath. After studying Wade's tracks on the shoreline, he shifted a little to the left. Again, he prodded the bottom. *Still nothing.* Then he felt something soft and heavy, and his heart fell. *Maybe a tire,* he hoped, poking again. It yielded to the stick's tip. Not a tire. Panting heavily, he considered stepping deeper into the mucky pond and submerging himself to grab . . . *No.*

He cut another stick and waded back out. The sun had settled behind Mount Adams, and the night wind was cool but Clark sweated. As he labored, chicken and barbecue rose in his throat, a terrible choking gorge.

Images flashed through his mind: horses in the woods, mirrored sunglasses, the fat woman's unpleasant pink mouth when she said "unnatural," the mother's distraught expression, the pink raincoat, the green boot, the stick behind the pickup seat. He fought back those images and thought of Wade running hard that morning—joyfully chasing the long white arc of the softball across the green meadow.

Now straining to see in the muddy water, Clark caught a glimpse of a drifting leg—thin and dark brown.

"Jesus Christ, no!" he said, half prayer, half curse of disbelief. Plunging his arms into the water, he felt the coarse texture of cloth. He seized a brown shoulder with his left hand, grabbed the leg with his right, and gave a tremendous sobbing heave toward the shore. The leg pulled away in his hand like an overcooked drumstick, and he stumbled backward, rolling over and vomiting chicken and barbecue onto the mud.

After wiping his mouth and nose with the back of his free hand and wrist, he stared until his heart quit racing and his head cleared. He gripped a thick, crooked, black root. Before him lay a muddy burlap sack. Sizing it up quickly, he was convinced the sack was too small to hold a torso, arms, and legs. His laugh was bitter but relieved.

Coming to his feet, he swayed unsteadily. Taking out his pocketknife, he approached the bag. "You filthy landlubber. I'll run this clear through your stinking yellow gizzard. Slicing the bag's rope tie, he lifted the heavy sack. Small rocks poured out, mud, the skeletons, skulls, and fur of three small cats.

Rocks, mud, bones, and fur made an oozing pile at his feet. The whole fetid mess stunk, but he didn't throw up again. "Sorry, fellas," he told the cat skulls. "I was looking for Jimmy Hoffa."

Clark trudged up the muddy bank, following the trail as it looped through the woods. If he reached the cabin before Natalie, perhaps he could clean up and avoid too many questions. Away from the pond, he smelled mock orange and wood smoke on the night breeze. Venus twinkled over Mount Adams and north, beyond the Yakima Indian Reservation, the sky cast a greenish glow. Aurora borealis.

The cold night breeze hit him and his teeth chattered. Wild with relief, he began singing. "MANY BRAVE HEARTS ARE ASLEEP IN THE DEEP, SO BEWARE . . . BEWARE."

The deep notes came out in an animal's ferocious growl.

*　*　*

Three women gathered in the hot tub under the stars. Two lit cigarettes, and the smoke drifted in Clark's direction on the night wind.

Clean, dry, and warmed by two cups of rum and tea, Clark wore his swimsuit under his jeans and carried a towel, but he stopped beyond the circle of light, knowing he wouldn't join the women. Even at this distance, he saw the thick fleshy neck and buoyed bosom of the gossip. As she slid deeper into the tub with a squeal of delight, he considered all the water she displaced.

Archimedes. Ponder this.

Clark felt lighthearted. Not only the rum. Darvel had stopped by before ten to inform him they had found Tessie hiding in the old boarded-up Glenwood grade school. She was terrified but all right— physically safe if not mentally sound.

Wade had made up the details about the boots and brown sweat-shirt. His imagination was even wilder than Clark's. Clark shook his head, relieved but also angry at the deputies and at his own inability to help Wade more.

Tilting his head far back, he saw the Big Dipper, then remembered the Bear Boy legend, how the wild boy transformed into a snarling bear that attacked his sisters in the wood.

Myths are for primitive people, Clark thought, now convinced Wade wouldn't hurt their daughter in any way. Fuck the experts and behavior predictors. They might as well read bird entrails and babble in the wilderness, tapping at the earth with walking sticks. He and Natalie would know how to take care of Helen, mold the little group into a family. As for Wade, well, he'd kept the boy going for all those years now.

Before entering the cabin, he stopped at the pickup and grabbed the old stick he'd found in the culvert from behind the seat. It felt light. All the moisture had dried out over the years.

Bending his knees, he broke the stick into two pieces, then four. "Kindling." He opened the woodstove door and peered into the fire. "Speak now or forever hold your peace," he told the broken pieces, then shoved the mute wood into the glowing tongues of fire.

15

Portland, 1980

Standing alone outside the Portland Greyhound Terminal, Emmett looked as sturdy as a wind-gnarled juniper. Beside him were a small suitcase, shopping bag, and tightly rolled sleeping bag.

Clark noticed his father's new Western clothes. Stiff Levi's, polished dark brown boots, a leather vest over a denim shirt. Clark honked. Emmett peered at the Honda a moment, then waved.

A group of winos shared a bottle in a doorway. Hustlers and whores passed on the street, but no one acknowledged Emmett. He seemed to create his own space and stand comfortably in it, just as if he'd brought a section of Ruby with him.

"Kind of rough out there," Clark said, opening the passenger door. "Hop in before you get mugged."

Emmett threw his suitcase and bedroll in back, but hung on to the sack. "Thanks for coming to get me." He put out his hand and they shook awkwardly. "You put on some weight," his father said. "Must be city living."

"We didn't expect you," Clark said. "Your call sort of caught us by surprise." He was concerned about the sleeping bag. Maybe Emmett was planning on staying with them awhile. Grace said it used to embarrass her the way Emmett just showed up places at mealtimes.

"You quit buying American, huh?" Emmett asked, referring to the Honda. "Your uncle Wesley plugged a couple Japs on Iwo Jima, but they make good cars."

Clark didn't say anything for a minute. Then he asked, "What happened to Wesley, anyway?" No one had mentioned that Woods before.

Emmett rubbed his eyebrow. "He got plugged himself, standing out in front of the Elkhorn. While he was in the service, his wife took up fancy with a rancher from Long Creek. That rancher shot Wesley to keep her from running back to him." Emmett paused. "We almost named you Wesley, but your mother thought him getting shot meant bad luck."

"I'm glad someone was looking out for me," Clark said, although he didn't intend it as a slight to his father. He changed the subject. "Great little car. Quick steering. Thirty-six miles a gallon."

"We don't see many Hondas in Ruby," Emmett said. "The nearest place you can get one fixed is Boise. Furman says they're hard to work on. He can fix any Chev or Ford. Some Dodges. In Ruby you got to have some practical skills to survive."

"That's true here, too," Clark said. "If you don't pay attention, a bus will run you over." He still wondered about his father's plans. "You got personal business in town? Going up to the Vets' Hospital for tests or anything?"

"I'm tough as an old badger." Emmett rolled down the window halfway. "Getting stuffy. No, I'm here mainly to see my granddaughter. Furman fired off two boys."

"You'll love Helen," Clark said. Now he wondered whether sending Emmett a note announcing her birth was a good idea. "And Natalie's looking forward to meeting you."

Emmett studied the people on the street. "What part of town do you live in anyway? I see a lot of coloreds outside."

Clark had figured his father would find their mixed neighborhood strange. They had purchased a modest but solid home in Northeast Portland, which reminded Natalie of Eastern neighborhoods and of the house she grew up in. "It may not have five acres," she said, "but at least the walls meet the floor and field mice don't chase across the living room."

And they hoped Wade wouldn't be quite so conspicuous with the variety of people living there.

After sizing up the house, Emmett turned to study the street. "Trolley cars used to run right through here," he said. "That's why the street's so wide. My cousins Ernest and Charlie lived farther out, almost to the river. They worked at the shipyards building liberty ships." He reached into the car, taking out the shopping bag and suitcase. "Charlie shipped out with me. Ernest had a defective heart. The Army wouldn't take him."

"I never thought about you being in Portland," Clark said.

"Well, I'm no city boy. But I can find my way around in one."

"Right." Clark glanced at the gear in his father's hand, the sleeping bag in the backseat. Was he planning to stay? Did he think they had an extra bunk? Could he find his way back home?

Natalie greeted them at the door. She regarded Emmett with curiosity. Ever since Helen had been born eight months ago, she had wanted to meet him.

"I don't see why," Clark had said. "He was never any part of my life."

"But his genes are. Whether you like it or not, he *is* part of it now you have a child of your own. Besides, people understand themselves better when they know their own past."

"I understand myself just fine. I understand I have no burning desire to see him."

They had made no move to visit Emmett in Ruby, but Clark sent him a birthday announcement. Even so, his call from the bus depot surprised them.

Now Natalie said, "We're having chicken. You're welcome to eat with us. It'll be done soon."

"Sure smells good," Emmett said.

"Clark, take his coat. Why don't you put it in the closet?"

"I think I'll hang on to it a minute." Emmett sat in a chair by the fireplace. "My bones are cracking. Bus was kind of cold."

"You came a long way," Natalie said.

He unbuttoned the coat. "I wanted to see my granddaughter. She was born on my birthday." He got a sly expression. "Did you remember that, Clark?"

"That's an amazing coincidence." Natalie looked at Clark, expecting him to respond.

What a cosmic joke, Clark thought. *I don't even meet the old man until I'm fifteen, hardly ever see him since then, and Helen's born on his birthday.* "Quite a surprise." He tried smiling. "The digit heads at Two Rivers say if thirty-two people are in a room, two will have the same birthday." He spread his hands. "Laws of probability."

"When I'm ninety, she'll be thirty," Emmett said. "I done the figuring."

"Helen's taking her nap," Natalie said. "She'll be up pretty soon."

"What about the boy, Wayne? You still got him?"

"Sure. We still have Wade," Clark said. "Right now he's at Outdoor School with his class. They're gone for four days."

"He was a spark in dry grass," Emmett said. "I thought maybe he went back with his mother now that you're remarried."

"She wasn't his mother," Clark said.

"He didn't look much like Payette," Emmett said. "She was a stunner."

Clark glanced at Natalie and got a couple beers from the refrigerator. "Care for a drink?"

"I don't mind." Emmett looked at Helen's most recent picture. "She's got my eyes and nose." He touched his forefinger to his nose. "I'm the only Woods without a honker. Clark, he's really blessed."

"Clark's and mine are more classic noses," Natalie said. "Greek or Italian."

Clark handed Emmett a beer and the old man lifted the bottle toward Helen's photo. "To those just starting at the trailhead. Over the lips and past the gums. Look out belly, here she comes." He tilted his head back and drank; his Adam's apple bobbed four times.

When his beer was half gone, Emmett pulled a small brown blanket out of the shopping bag. Rough-textured, the blanket showed two rips patched over with similar material. On one side was a dark brown leaping horse.

He handed the blanket to Natalie. "Kind of beat up, but that's good wool. My mother, Wilma, made it."

Natalie smoothed the material with her hands. "Thank you." She held the blanket high, showing off the horse. It resembled the Army surplus clothes hippies had worn during and after the sixties. Clark wondered if it had covered him when he was a baby. Had the old man taken it when he ran off?

Opening the suitcase, Emmett gave Natalie a large flat package with a ribbon around it. The package said "Emporium John Day, Oregon." She opened it, revealing a bright pink dress with an enormous bow in front, an equally garish bonnet. A smaller package held a pair of tiny pink cowboy boots.

"This is nice. Really." Natalie studied the dress with a perfectly straight face. "Helen's a little small for it now."

"We were thinking she'd grow into it by Easter. Furman helped pick it out," Emmett said.

*   *   *

"For once it's not raining," Natalie said. "Show your dad the backyard."

"You've got more than a single lot here," Emmett said when they were outside.

"It's a lot and a half," Clark said. "The guy we bought it from used to raise chrysanthemums in the side yard. He took the best ones and entered them in shows. Always won several prizes."

Emmett studied the flower bed with the dead stalks and rotten blooms. "It takes all kinds."

"I like that big maple." Clark pointed to the enormous tree at the back of the lot growing just this side of his neighbor's tall laurel hedge. "The leaves turn gold and crimson in the fall. Last year, we took a bunch of pictures when we bagged leaves."

Emmett's face was bemused. "Out our way, they just blow into the next county, unless the sagebrush stops them."

Clark pointed to a huge rhododendron. "The blooms on that are terrific. When we go in, I'll show you pictures of Natalie I took there last spring."

Emmett glanced away from the rhododendron and concentrated on the maple. A portion of the trunk had a large crack about two inches deep. He dug his thumb into the crack and pulled out a wriggling grub. "Bark beetles start working a crack like that, pretty soon you'll have to take her down. Five, maybe six good cords. Should keep you warm a couple winters."

The maple was one of Clark's favorite things about the house. In the summer, he sat under it and watched the squirrels scold the blue-jays, chasing them from branch to branch. "I don't want to lose that maple," he said. "It gives us privacy and keeps the neighbors from looking in the upstairs window. Maybe I better call a tree surgeon."

"Suit yourself, but when maples get old, they start cracking like bad ice. Call Furman. He'll help you buck it. Just got himself a Stihl chain saw with a twenty-six-inch bar. Sucker's longer than a horse pecker."

"I'll keep Furman in mind," Clark said. Glancing toward the house, he saw Natalie waving them in. "Helen's awake."

Helen sat in her chair wearing lime green bib overalls with a bright orange ladybug decal, a white shirt, and tiny red tennis shoes. Natalie had pulled her straight brown hair up in a topknot.

Emmett bent over, grinning when he saw her. "She's too pretty to throw back. Hi, Helen. Hi, little girl." He held out his hand so Helen could take his finger. "Stout. Got a grip like a blacksmith."

Natalie smiled. "She's got your eyes and nose, Emmett. I wondered where those gray-green eyes came from."

He nodded. "She looks exactly like my sister Clarissy did when she was a baby. Spittin' image."

As he studied Helen's features, she reached a plump hand toward his face and grabbed his taped glasses.

"You got my cheaters," he said. "She's quick as a coyote." He tickled her beneath her chin, trying to distract her so he could take back his glasses, but she gripped them firmly.

"Here, Helen." Natalie handed her a teething biscuit and gave the glasses back to Emmett. "She's getting hungry. And the chicken's done. Let's eat."

Emmett studied his callused hands. "Maybe I'd better wash up. Where's the facilities?"

"You show him, Clark."

Clark led him to the bottom of the stairs. "Straight up, turn left."

While he was upstairs, Natalie said, "Emmett's quite a good-looking guy. I can see where your mom might've fallen for him. Especially when he was in uniform. My mother always said never marry a man in a uniform." She chuckled. "I wish I had a picture of him out in our little city yard in that cowboy outfit. I was just hoping he didn't make any remarks about the neighborhood."

"He said it wasn't Ruby."

She pulled the chicken out of the oven. "He had brand-new clothes on. Did you notice that, Clark? He dressed up to meet his grand-daughter."

"Sweet."

Natalie looked at him. "You're in a bad mood. Anyway, speaking of your mom, I sure hope she doesn't show up right about now."

"That would just about top off the day."

"Is he planning on spending the night?"

"We can spring for a motel," Clark said.

Clark spent most of the dinner feeding Helen with a little silver baby spoon that had been his and that Grace had saved for her grand-child. The baby seemed distracted and kept knocking away the spoon, smearing apricots and carrots around the tray and on her overalls. Emmett ate with hearty appetite, complimenting Natalie's cooking and telling stories.

"Mostly I eat venison. You know, I'm leaving my deer rifle to Clark." Emmett paused.

"That's great," Natalie said. "I'm sure he'll be happy to have it. Won't you, Clark?"

"Right," Clark said. He reached under the counter for the Virginia Gentleman bourbon. "Cowboy coffee, Emmett?"

He shoved his cup toward Clark. "Two splashes." After a sip, he said, "I didn't want to sour anybody's appetite while chicken was on the plate, but I used to make a little weekend money shooting rabbits to feed Felton Warnick's chickens.

"Chickens will eat about anything, including other chickens. They're cannibals and carnivores. I wouldn't want to die in a chicken coop." He set down his coffee cup and pointed to Helen. "That ex-pression looks exactly like Clarissy."

Emmett continued. "Sometimes, if the flies blew those dead rab-bits with maggots, the chickens got the limber neck."

"What's the limber neck?" Natalie asked.

"Don't know exactly," he said. "Something they get from fly-blown rabbits. You know how a chicken puts down its beak to drink, but it has to lift it up high to swallow." He demonstrated by tilting his head forward, then stretching his neck out and tilting his head back. "When limber neck hits them, their head droops way down. They can't lift it to swallow. After a while, they die of thirst. Some get so thirsty, they just put their heads underwater and drown. When that happened, old man Warnick would be mad as Scotch."

"You're quite a storyteller," Natalie said. "I can see where Clark gets it. Now you'll have to excuse me. Time to change the baby."

"Well, there's a mystery cleared up," Emmett said. "I thought maybe you bought this place downwind from the stockyards."

Clark and Emmett moved to the front room and Emmett studied pictures of Wade and Helen hanging on the wall. One picture showed Wade wearing a surgical mask because he had the flu when she came home from the hospital. In the picture, his mouth was covered but his brow showed confusion. His eyes seemed angry and uncertain. Clark didn't like the picture but Grace had it framed for Wade's birthday and they hung it to please her. "Look how little boy is holding his precious sister," she said. "They're both so sweet I could eat them up."

Grace appeared only once because she never liked the way she looked. Her photo albums were loaded with pictures where she'd cut out her own head. "My legs are like barrels," she said. "When I look in the mirror now, I see Aunt Maud."

"Why don't you leave your face and cut out your body, then?" Clark had teased.

In the front room photo, Grace held Helen on her lap. Her face appeared radiant as she admired her grandchild.

"Grace wintered pretty good all these years," Emmett said.

"She got by." *No thanks to you.*

.   .   .

Natalie tiptoed down the steps. "I can't believe it, but she's knocked out."

"Oh no, we'll be up all night," Clark said.

"At least Wade's not home," Natalie said.

"Has he calmed down any?" Emmett asked.

"He's settled down some." Clark took a gulp of coffee. "When we dropped him off at Outdoor School, he was calm at first. Wade hangs back ten minutes or so, sizing up things before he turns on the juice. We tried explaining to the counselors but they thought we were just anxious parents. 'Stop hovering,' they said. 'He'll be *just fine.*' We could see them smirking at each other.

"Okeydokey, you bright boys, I thought. On the way back we stopped at Tad's for chicken and dumplings. By the time we got home, they'd called every emergency number we'd left."

"The phone was ringing off the hook before we got in the front door," Natalie added.

"But give them credit," Clark said. "They brought out two more counselors and are keeping him on a day-to-day basis. Whoever they have deserves combat pay."

"Next summer, you better ship him out with Furman," Emmett said. "He should learn to split wood, build fence, and trap coyotes."

"We'll think about it," Clark said, wondering if they'd get desperate enough to give Furman a try.

*   *   *

Emmett stood by the fireplace. "Did Clark tell you I was in the war over there?" he asked.

"Yes, he did," Natalie said. "The Battle of the Bulge. Clark said you saw some hard fighting."

"Not too bad," Emmett said. "A couple days, we had to fire some shots at the Germans. When I could, I killed deer for camp meat. After all those C-rations, venison tasted swell."

Upstairs, the baby cried. They waited to see if Helen calmed down, but she started squalling.

"I'll go this time," Clark said. He warmed a bottle for her.

Helen was hanging onto the crib's slats, her cheeks wet with tears. When she saw Clark, she lifted up her tiny arms to him.

"Hello, pumpkin." He picked her up and held her against him. Her warm breath smelled like apricots. "Daddy's girl."

After a minute, she started squirming, so he sat in his grandfather's old rocking chair. Holding her on his knees, he gave her a few bounces.

"Pony girl, pony girl, won't you be my pony girl? Here we go, here we go, over fields of snow." He kept his voice low so Emmett wouldn't hear.

As he sang, tapping his feet, she smiled and her round cheeks almost met her forehead; her happy eyes closed to slits. "Squarehead," he said. On the "giddyups" and "whoas!" he raised her up above his head and she chortled.

"Time to settle down now." He held her and rocked, feeding her the bottle, and imagining how his grandfather had held him in the chair. "He thought you were your uncle Roy all over again," Grace had told him. "He even called you Roy half the time. And when he got older and forgetful, he couldn't tell which pictures were you growing up and which were Roy's."

Clark smoothed Helen's hair with his free hand and gently touched her silky eyebrows with his forefinger. "Nobody's going to get your pictures mixed up with mine. You're a beauty." Maybe her eyes did resemble Emmett's, for now. But eyes changed. *A miracle,* he thought. He felt that she was on loan to him and Natalie, somehow, and one day they'd be called to account. "Look at this angel I've given you," he imagined the Big Fellow saying. "How well did you take care of her?"

Clark didn't feel the same about Wade. He loved him, but not as much as he loved Helen. He couldn't. Clark had tried loving the boy completely, but a cold stone pebble remained buried in his heart.

After the bottle was empty and Helen was almost asleep, Clark held her on his shoulder until she gave a tiny burp. The hair at the back of her head felt smooth as goosedown, and now her breath smelled of sweet milk.

He laid her down in the crib as gently as if she were a hollow, painted egg. Illumination from the street lamp outside entered the window, and the swaying tree branches cast flickering patterns across her smooth white forehead and curved cheek, the sweet bow of her mouth. Leaning over, he kissed her on the forehead.

A car passed and he could tell from the sounds its tires made, rain was falling. A world existed out there, but it didn't concern him. The only world he cared about was in this room and downstairs talking with his father. And Wade, maybe Wade. He wondered if they shouldn't modify that sign at the children's hospital. WHEN YOU HAVE A CHILD, YOU HAVE A UNIVERSE.

· · ·

Downstairs, Emmett had on his coat. The suitcase and folded sack were by the door.

"Emmett needs a ride to the bus depot," Natalie said. "Are you sure you don't want to stay the night?"

"My cousin Charlie's expecting me," Emmett said. "The last bus to Salem leaves at ten-thirty."

Clark checked his watch. Plenty of time.

"Thanks for the good dinner," Emmett said. "I was glad to meet you and Helen." He shook Natalie's hand.

On the way to the bus depot, both men stayed quiet until they passed the Union Station. Then Clark said, "You didn't mention shooting the Germans."

Emmett squinted at him behind the taped glasses. "Women don't go much for that shooting talk. Anyway, I didn't want her to hold it against me, what with her folks being from over there and all."

"They were *fighting* the Germans," Clark said. "She's Russian."

"All those foreigners get mixed up," Emmett said. "After every battle, they redraw the boundaries. Half the time, you didn't know who you was shooting. It's not like over here, where things are settled."

Emmett cleared his throat. "Anyway, I had something else to tell you."

"What's that?"

"When I learned Helen was born on my birthday, I figured maybe that was some kind of sign."

Clark hoped Emmett wasn't going to start in on astrology or other mumbo-jumbo. "A sign?"

"I know I wasn't a prize-winning father, but that's blood under the bridge."

Not to me it isn't, Clark thought.

Emmett licked his lips. "That boy's trouble brewing, Clark. You'd better keep a close watch on him, what with the baby and all."

"Trouble brewing," Clark repeated slowly, resenting Emmett's warning.

The old man shifted his eyes toward Clark. "I saw something wild flicker behind his eyes that time you and Payette came by. Furman noticed it, too."

Clark bristled. "Something wild? Jesus, Emmett! What are you talking about?"

"You're like Grace," Emmett said. "Just see what you want. When I got a coyote or a lynx trapped, I always check their eyes. Most will hunker and slink away as far as the chain allows. But a few will go for your throat. Their eyes give them away."

Clark didn't reply. As far as he was concerned, the old man hadn't earned the right to offer any family advice.

At the bus station, Clark stayed in the car while Emmett unloaded his gear on the sidewalk. Leaning across the passenger seat, Emmett offered his hand and they shook briefly.

"I hope this one sticks," Emmett said. "Come see us in Ruby. Bring the little lady and my granddaughter."

Fat chance, Clark thought, but he nodded.

Emmett rapped the car door with his fist. "Don't forget to keep an eye on Wade."

"Sure thing," Clark said through gritted teeth. As Emmett headed toward the revolving door, Clark abruptly drove away from the curb. *No looking back,* he vowed.

He knew that Natalie would want to talk about the visit, how Clark thought it went, what it all meant. She didn't understand that Emmett's trip didn't amount to anything but a visit and a cockeyed warning.

You couldn't relate to Emmett, Clark thought grimly, unless maybe you were a dog or a coyote. He had tried a couple times. Once, when his aunt Clarissy told him that his father was visiting relatives down near Salem, Clark had driven to the place. For three hours he hung around making small talk with the relatives, while Emmett watched FBI reruns on television. A couple of times his father had wandered into the kitchen for more beer and pretzels. "That Efram Zimbalist, Jr., can sure act," he said.

"That's all there is to him," Clark had tried telling Natalie once, but she didn't understand. Emmett was a guy who just bagged out on life. Whether or not he experienced shell shock, Clark didn't know. For a while he had swallowed his mother's story that Emmett skipped out because of the killing and battle fatigue. No. Clark suspected he skipped because he didn't want any responsibility. It was easier than sticking around.

Thinking of Helen asleep in her room, Clark muttered, "God, don't ever let me skip." When he drove across the Steel Bridge, Clark glanced back and saw a dark bus pulling away from the depot, heading south on glistening, rain-slicked pavement.

16

Portland, 1981

For Helen's birthday, Grace was bringing her traditional birthday lamb cake, the one she always made from scratch for Clark's birthday and Wade's. She had an aluminum mold and decorated the chocolate cake with white three-minute frosting and coconut, to resemble the wool. She placed a yellow ribbon around the cake's neck since that was her favorite color.

"It's a tradition for all my wonderful kids," she insisted when Natalie suggested they buy a bakery cake. "No sawdust-tasting bakery cake. It wouldn't be a proper birthday without my lamb cake."

At Wade's last birthday, she was frustrated because the lamb's head fell off in spite of all the skewers and toothpicks she used to hold the cake together. "I had to bake it three times," she complained. "For some reason, it just kept falling apart."

Wade wore a new dark blue cowboy shirt with pearl buttons and a pair of gray cords. Because his arms were so long, his wrists jutted out of his shirtsleeves. His thick hair had been cut and washed.

"You help Grandma bring in the cake when she comes, okay, partner?" Clark said.

"I want to eat lamby's head again," Wade said. "Eat lamby's head all up. Bite out lamby's raisin eyes."

"That's enough silly talk. You're too old for that. Anyway, Helen gets to eat the head this time," Clark said. "Get out the plates and hats, okay? They're in the cupboard under the sink."

"When do you think your mother's going to get here?" Natalie asked every five minutes that Grace was overdue.

"She's moving slowly with her arthritis," Clark said. "It takes her a while."

"She'll be late to her own funeral," Natalie said. "I wish she hadn't insisted on making that cake." Natalie tried to reach Grace on the phone, but there was no answer. Frequently, Grace didn't hear the phone because she refused to wear a hearing aid.

"I hear as good as I ever did," she said. "Even in high school I was deaf in my right ear."

When Grace was over forty minutes late, Natalie was about to drive to the bakery to pick up a cake. "I'll just get any damn cake they have and let them write Helen's name on it."

They were upstairs when the doorbell rang six or seven times. "Get the door, Wade. Let Grandma in." He heard Wade run and open the door.

"Happy birthday to baby! Happy birthday to baby . . ." Grace's loud voice carried up the stairs.

"Damn," Clark said. He didn't want his mother to wake Helen. As he raced down the stairs, he caught a glimpse of Wade running toward the backyard holding two sparklers, trailing a shower of sparks. "What the hell is going on?"

Grace stood on the front porch, singing and waving two more lighted sparklers like batons. Her face was flushed and her eyes glittered with enthusiasm. "There you are, son! Where's my baby? Where's that birthday girl?"

She was wearing a green Nancy Frock and three cotton sweaters, blue, white, and black. Only the blue one—the first she had put on—was buttoned. Black tennis shoes and ankle socks covered her feet. "What happened to little boy?" She peered through the screen door. "He was here a minute ago to greet me and he looked so handsome with his haircut and shirt."

"Put those sparklers down and come in," Clark said.

"Honey, you better get a pop bottle or a coffee can, something to put these in." They had quit sparkling and the wires glowed red. "One time in The Dalles, your uncle Roy set the neighbor's lawn on fire. It was all cheat grass, but they called the fire department anyway. Your grandfather was furious at Roy. The neighborhood smelled like burned grass all summer."

"Just toss them beside the camellia bush," Clark said. "This is Portland. Wet as a soggy dishrag."

"Not today. It's stopped raining for my baby's birthday." She studied the sky. A few patches of blue shone through. She wouldn't put down the sparklers until Clark took them from her and tossed them beside the bush.

"I wish you wouldn't do that. You don't want to burn the place down."

"Maybe I do," Clark said. "Burn the bastard down, collect the insurance and head for the wild territory."

"You go on," she said. Her face brightened even more. "I hear the baby and Natalie upstairs. Listen to Helen babble." She stepped inside. "Hold on, sweetheart. I'm coming. Grandma's coming to her baby girl."

"Go on," he said. "I'm going to see about Wade."

She shoved a package toward Clark. "I got a gift for Wade, too," she said. "That's what Dr. Spock said to do so he doesn't get jealous."

Clark carried a coffee can to the backyard. Wade held the glowing sparklers. "Put those in the can and help bring in the cake."

"When will it be *my* birthday?" Wade asked.

"July. That's four more months." Clark wasn't sure when Wade's birthday actually was because the documents from Alaska had different dates or no dates at all. Payette had said it was in July so he picked the fifteenth, right in the middle of the month.

.   .   .

The Polaroid showed Helen beaming with her dark brown hair pulled into a topknot secured by a red ribbon. Clark held her under a banner strung across the kitchen. HAPPY BIRTHDAY ONE-YEAR-OLD. The lamb cake was on the table in front of them, the yellow ribbon around its neck.

Wade's left hand rested on the shoulder of Clark's green shirt. His right just touched Helen's white dress, as if helping to hold her, but she was secure in Clark's arms. The dress was pulled up in front, revealing a strip of belly, the large white diaper.

Natalie had taken the picture because Grace claimed she couldn't hold the camera right. "My hands tremble too much. Now that I'm old, I'm falling apart. That's the fringe benefit."

Clark took numerous photos with his camera, but Grace couldn't wait until they were developed. "I want to see this little happy family, right now," she said.

She wouldn't allow her own picture to be taken. "My nose is too sharp," she said. "And I don't like the way Eloise chopped my hair this time. I look just like a bag lady. 'Tennis Shoe Grace.' That's what they'll call me. My legs are all swollen up like I don't even have ankles. I look just like Aunt Maud. She wrecked her legs changing sheets and cooking meals for those roomers that worked on the dam so many years. That poor woman worked herself to death."

Clark insisted on taking a couple of photos of Grace with Helen and Wade. "You were here on her first birthday," he said. "She'll want to see these pictures." In the photos, Grace's head tilted to the side, perhaps from her difficulty in hearing. Clark imagined her wanting to cut off her head before mounting the photos in her book.

She drank two cups of tea, then walked heavily upstairs to the bathroom. "You know your handrail is loose," she said. "I'm not bellyaching, but I thought you should know. You don't want anybody getting hurt."

"Don't lean on it so hard," Clark said. "It's not heavy-duty."

"Now you be careful what you say, Mr. Smarty Pants."

"You're putting on a little weight yourself, Clark," Natalie said. "If you want to know the truth."

"Spare me the truth," Clark said.

* * *

When the sun came out, they took the party outside. After the cake and ice cream Wade took out a wet washcloth and began wiping off Helen's hands and face. She made her fists into tiny balls, and he had to pry open her fingers to get at all the sticky frosting in the crease of her palms. "Look how messy you are, baby," he said. "You made all that work for Mom. Messy, messy baby," he scolded.

She thumped one tiny hand against her hat, then pointed to the sparklers in the bucket. "Hot. Hot."

The hat slipped down the back of her head, almost to her neck. As Wade tried to adjust it, the rubber band broke, snapping Helen under the chin. Her eyes squinted with hurt and surprise and her mouth flew open in a squall of rage.

"Jesus, Wade," Natalie said. "What have you done?"

"It broke," Wade said, holding the hat. "The rubber band broke."

She snatched it from him, examining the band. "You've got to be more careful, Wade. She's just a baby."

Back from the bathroom, Grace hovered near the baby. "Ohhh. My little pumpkin. Your brother wouldn't hurt you, darling." As she leaned over, Helen's gaze went from her grandmother's round face to the birthday hat she wore on her head.

"Owee! Owee!" she said, pointing at the hat. She cried louder and kicked at the high chair tray with her patent leather black shoes.

Wade took off his own hat and held it toward Helen. "Here, baby sister. You can take my hat."

Howling, she kicked the high chair and pounded on the aluminum tray with her fists.

Wade turned sullen. "Dumb baby."

"Just leave her alone, buddy," Clark said.

"Go in the house and watch TV for a while," Natalie said.

"I didn't do anything," Wade said. His mouth twisted in an unpleasant expression.

"Go on in, buddy," Clark said. "Helen's tired. Too much excitement."

"A little trouble in paradise," Grace said heartily. "That's all. It wasn't little boy's fault. He was just helping her out." She took a bite of cake. "All afternoon, both of my grandchildren have been good as gold."

· · ·

Natalie took Helen out of the high chair and carried her inside. Her back was stiff and she took quick firm steps. Helen had closed her eyes but was still crying.

Clark gathered up the paper plates and a few large pieces of cake that had fallen on the grass and put them in the garbage.

"That little stinky is so cute when she cries," Grace said. "All babies are cute, but she's special. Even when she cries, you can't help but love her. She's such a little dickens."

Clark turned on the hose, running some water into the bucket, even though he was certain all the sparklers were out.

"Shall we get little boy out here and light these last three sparklers?" Grace asked. "I don't want them to go to waste. If they get too old, they break and don't light well. No one likes stale sparklers."

Clark's jaw tightened. "We better let things settle down. I'm checking on things in the house."

"All right, son. I'll just say good-bye to little boy and then drive home. Tell Natalie it was a wonderful party. Here, I'll leave half the Polaroids with you. She's such a beautiful baby." Grace reached up to kiss him, and he bent over so she could reach his cheek. She was getting terribly gray, he realized. Hardly any blond left now at all. Behind her glasses, her eyes filled with tears and she blew her nose. "I'm getting just like my mother," she said. "Mother always teared up at every party, and I used to wonder what on earth her problem was. Well, I'll see you a little farther down the crick."

Wade had the television on too loud, and Clark was surprised Natalie hadn't shouted for him to hold it down. Upstairs, their bedroom door was closed. He tiptoed into the baby's room. She was asleep, her face red, her small topknot lying against the baby elephant pattern sheets. Lying flat on the bed, she held one arm in the air, as if reaching toward heaven. Clark didn't know why she did that. He loved it, and yet it bothered him.

When he'd first come to Two Rivers, he saw a physician who overprescribed and overcharged. In the waiting room there was a book about children. One story dealt with a very sick little boy they told to put his arm in the air for Jesus. By morning the boy had died—but his arm was held stiff reaching for heaven. Clark thought it was a bad story to have in the doctor's office. He watched Helen sleeping for twenty minutes, not quite ready to go in to see Natalie. When he was ready, he gently lowered the baby's arm.

"Is your mother gone?" Natalie asked, putting down a magazine.

"She's gone. She just stopped downstairs to see Wade." The party hat was on the bed and Clark picked it up by the broken rubber band.

"Whoever heard of bringing sparklers to a birthday party? You can't let a one-year-old hold sparklers."

"Well, you can't choose your relations. And you have to admit, sparklers are festive."

Natalie closed her eyes and leaned back against the pillow. "I've had about all the fun I can take today. Why don't you handle dinner."

• • •

Helen sat in her playpen as Wade raced through the house with her teddy bear. A birthday hat was perched on its head. Each time he ran through the kitchen, Helen started fussing and yelling "Owee, owee," pointing at the hat with a plump finger.

"Would you do something about that noise?" Natalie yelled from upstairs. "I've got a headache and I'm trying to rest."

"Teddy wants a party! Teddy wants a party!"

Clark seized Wade's arm the next time he ran into the kitchen. "No more partying. It's time to calm down, Wade."

Wade's eyes turned to slits and his lower lip hung out. "Teddy's having a birthday party."

"All right, but it's over. Put the hat up for now. Helen's getting upset." As Clark tried to take the hat off Teddy, Wade twisted away from him. "I can do it myself!"

"Fine. Take the hat downstairs or up into your room. Tomorrow, you can play with it again."

"I never get to have fun," Wade said as he sulked away.

"Wash your hands," Clark told him. "We're going to eat." It sounded like a threat.

Clark got a knife and cut some small pieces of chicken for the baby. It was a little dry so he cut the pieces fine because he didn't want her to choke. He also poured a little milk in the mashed potatoes. When the food was ready, he got Helen from the playpen and set her in the high chair.

Wade came up from the basement. "No more party," he said. "Teddy is sleeping." He gave the baby a sidelong glance.

"Foo, foo, foo," she chortled and slapped her tray.

"Quiet, Helen," Wade said. "Teddy is asleep." He put his fingers to his lips.

Clark gave him a wing and a thigh. "I have good teeth," Wade said, taking a big bite. "She just has tiny teeth, so her food has to be all chopped up."

"That's right. She's only got four teeth and they're not very big." Clark gave her a spoonful of mashed potatoes, another of applesauce.

"I'm going to save some of this chicken for Blackie," Wade said. "We haven't seen Red and Blackie in a while, Dad. When can we go see them?"

"Maybe this weekend, but you can't give chicken bones to a dog. Chicken bones are too small and brittle. They'll splinter and choke the dog."

"I can eat chicken," Wade said. "I'm not a baby."

"Well, you don't eat the bones," Clark said. "That's where the trouble starts."

Wade studied Helen a minute. "If she had a drumstick, wouldn't her tiny teeth take tiny bites? That should be okay, right?"

"That's good thinking," Clark said. "Different teeth do different jobs. She can rip off little pieces with those front teeth, but she doesn't have back teeth to chew."

Wade put his face close to Helen. "You don't have back teeth to chew," he said in his imitation of talking-to-a-baby talk. "No chewy chewy. Not yet. But when her get bigger her can have a drumstick. Yes her can."

Clark put on tea water. He went to the stairs. "Do you want some tea?" he called up. "We miss your company."

After a moment, she answered. "I'll be there in a few minutes."

He sat down and fed Helen a few more bites. Wade had taken the other leg and thigh. When he ate, pieces of chicken were visible in his mouth.

"Close your mouth, Wade."

The doorbell rang. Clark went to answer it. He'd been meaning to put up a NO SOLICITING sign, but never got around to it. Now, each time the doorbell interrupted, he regretted it.

A grade-schooler was selling candy to sponsor a trip to Ashland to see the plays. "It's our fifth-grade-class field trip," she said. "We're going to see *All's Well That Ends Well* and *Julius Caesar* along with *Charley's Aunt.*"

"What kind you got there?"

She looked in her big shopping bag. "Mint, peanut butter, plain chocolate. They're really good."

The teakettle began to whistle. "Wade, take that off, would you?" Clark yelled. "Don't burn yourself." Turning back to the girl, he said, "I'll take one of each."

"That's six dollars," she said, handing him the three bars.

Opening his wallet, he gave her a five and a one. "How many have you sold anyway?" He felt a flush of generosity realizing his own daughter would be selling candy for field trips before he turned around.

"This is six so far, right in this block!" She stuffed the money into a child-sized black purse. "Thank you for supporting Irvington fifth-graders," she said.

As Clark closed the door, he realized the teakettle was shrieking. "Wade, pull that off, damn it!"

Steam rose from the kettle, and the window near the stove was running with sweat. Clark started for the kettle but saw Helen leaning over the high chair's tray. Her face was purplish and her fists clenched. She was choking. The teakettle shrieked louder.

He grabbed her shoulder, straightening her in the chair, and thrust his finger into her mouth. He felt the scrape of sharp teeth, the small hard gums, the soft sides of the cheeks, and—in the back of her mouth—hunks of food. Frantic, he pulled a couple of small gobs out, but she was a darker purple. He released the tray and jerked her out of the chair, tilting her forward until she was almost upside down. He slapped her twice on the back and another wad of food came out. She began squealing, and Clark carried her high over his shoulder, patting her back. "It's all right, Helen, it's all right."

Moving toward the stove, he set the kettle on a cool burner. For the first time since coming from the front door, he noticed Wade sitting and eating applesauce. He was staring at the table.

"What the hell is going on!" Natalie came into the room. "Give her to me." She grabbed Helen from Clark. "Tell me. What is going on?"

"She was choking," Clark said.

"Oh my God! Weren't you watching her? What's wrong with you?"

He held up his hand. "I just answered the door for a second. A girl from Irvington was selling candy."

Natalie's glare was fierce. "You can't leave her alone like that. Don't you have any sense?"

Clark gripped Wade's shoulder, squeezing until the boy twisted his face and gritted his teeth. "Why weren't you watching your sister? She was choking."

"I didn't do anything," Wade said. "Stop squeezing my shoulder. I didn't do anything."

"Your sister was choking," Clark said. "You come get me next time, damn it. Or I'll whip you good."

"I didn't do anything," Wade said.

Clark cuffed him. He was almost ready to hit him again when Natalie grabbed his arm.

"Are you crazy? Don't go taking it out on Wade. You're the adult here. You're the one responsible!"

Wade used the distraction to duck out of the room. Clark heard his shoes clomping down the basement steps.

Natalie still glowered at him. "If I leave you alone for ten minutes, all hell breaks loose. This is Helen's first birthday, and it's been nothing but one big strain, if you want to know the truth." She sat in the chair, shoulders slumped. "I wish my parents could have been here," she said. "I feel all alone out here. I'm responsible for everyone."

Clark tried to put his arm around her, but she stiffened her shoulders. "I don't want to be held right now. I want some relief. Can't you see that?" Moist-eyed, she looked up at him.

"I'm sorry," he said. "I shouldn't have left Helen. I screwed up."

"Wasn't Wade sitting right here? Why didn't he do something?"

"She choked. I don't think she made any noise. Wade was lost in his thoughts."

"A boy his age should notice his sister choking," she said. "That's not normal. I mean, you're the one responsible, but it's still not normal."

"I guess not." Clark didn't want to get into it with her again.

"I'm going to bed," she said. "I'm exhausted and I've got to teach tomorrow. Do you think you're capable of putting away the food and wiping the table?"

"My duty as I see it," he said to her back.

He put the leftovers in the refrigerator, then got a sponge to wipe off the table. Wade had left a few hunks of thigh around. He tossed them into the garbage can and got a paper towel to clean up the wad Helen had spit out. Clark was about to throw it away when a dark, stringy piece separated from the wad. He stared at the meat in his hand. With a sinking heart, he knew he had not left a piece that large.

17

Portland, 1981

Clark and Natalie had always been hard-pressed for child care but now faced the added problem of finding care for both Wade and Helen. Grace had been an occasional safety valve, but as she grew older, Clark realized that his mother wasn't able to watch both children. He and Natalie asked everyone with children how they managed. Frequently, the answer would come: "Oh, you know, we got lucky. There's this wonderful woman down the block." However, Clark and Natalie couldn't find anybody who approached wonderful. The expression "wonderful woman down the block" became a running joke between them. "WWDTB," they would mouth to each other, with a knowing smile.

Natalie read books and articles on finding child care. She prepared a detailed list of questions for the sitters. What was their philosophy on discipline? How about diet? Did they have special skills they could share with the child? Later, weary from the experience, Clark and Natalie agreed the list might have been more useful if it included questions like, "When were you last arrested and what were the charges?" Or, "Have you been clean since you kicked your drug addiction?"

For daytime, Natalie tried calling the Senior Center and found a warm, grandmotherly woman to watch Helen part-time while she went to work and Wade was at school. But when the woman explained to Natalie that people were breaking into her apartment every night and stealing her pants and underwear, and she was down to one pair, Natalie decided to let her go, making up some excuse.

"Who on earth would want her pants, anyway?" Natalie told Clark. "They're bright green and polyester."

"Elitist," Clark teased. "Not all of us grew up shopping at John Wanamaker."

"That woman must be hallucinating."

They tried day-care centers. At one highly recommended center, Natalie watched as a toddler wandered out the gates to the street while the rest of the group sat in a circle singing "Baby Beluga." Natalie waited until she realized no one was aware of the child, then snatched her and brought her back to the group, leaving immediately after.

"My God," Natalie would say. "Is it just us? Are we incredibly bad at this?"

"I guess we're just inferior people," Clark said, ironically.

Wade, of course, was another story entirely. Clark had known for years that no one wanted to watch him, unless they were desperate for money. Now it wasn't possible to get a sitter over for both him and Helen. Most baby-sitters for Helen were girls of Wade's own age, and he always acted strange around them.

"Look here," Natalie said. "We've taken this on and we're saving the state over a thousand dollars a month, since he would've been institutionalized if not for us. The state must have a way to help us; give us a break now and then." So she called and made appointments to talk with caseworkers. Clark knew her reasoning was logical. He also knew that logic had nothing to do with it, but figured she might as well try. Maybe she'd get lucky.

"Respite care," Natalie told Clark. "That's what they call it. See, you're just too cynical. The resources are there, all it takes is some research." They had to make an appointment for care several weeks ahead of time, which was tricky to arrange, but by this time they were getting desperate for some help. But the respite center was for children who were severely handicapped or seriously disturbed, like the boy who wore a football helmet and kept slamming into the other kids yelling, "Touchdown! Touchdown!" At home, Wade imitated the boy, banging his teddy bear so hard against the wall he knocked off the pictures.

"There's no place for a kid like Wade," Natalie said after the respite care attempt. "He's not really that handicapped; he can walk and talk. But he's not normal either."

Another failed try, Clark thought, but didn't say anything. He didn't want to discourage Natalie any more than necessary because he always worried she might take Helen and leave.

In lighter moments, Natalie would joke, "At least I've met some interesting people." Wade got along with eccentrics and people who were down on their luck, and Penny was one of those. Her boyfriend Deke was an Elvis impersonator; she lived with him and her three teenage children in a big, run-down house. Deke had a shrine to Elvis in the basement, complete with special red lighting that gave it an eerie glow, and Wade was beside himself with excitement. Elvis was his favorite and Clark figured the boy considered an impersonator about as good as spending time with the King himself.

Clark and Natalie found themselves in a tiny tract home outside of Portland to see one of Deke's performances. A small stage had been set up in the living room and everyone crowded around it. Wade hung on the sidelines, awestruck, mouthing the words and swiveling. Penny wore a fluffy dress and a flower in her hair. She beamed as Deke/Elvis pulled her onstage next to him and announced, "She's going with me— all the way to the top!"

Penny's son wanted to learn French, and Natalie taught him a few phrases, which, to her surprise, he picked up easily. "He has a real knack for languages," she told Clark. But their informal lessons ended abruptly, along with the baby-sitting arrangement, when Penny decided to marry Deke and move to Vegas, taking the teenagers. "That kid's so bright," Natalie said. "Now he'll never have a chance."

"Maybe he can do Buddy Holly," Clark said.

Years later, a letter came from Penny. She had returned to Portland and was selling a secret Mesopotamian potion out of her home. Discovered five thousand years ago and used by all the great kings and queens, the potion guaranteed eternal youth. The letter made no mention of her husband or children.

Clark found the next sitters through a church referral—Doreen was the Sunday child-care provider. Her house had a heavy smell of old cooking grease and cigarette smoke; she and her boyfriend Otto were chain smokers. Doreen was thin and gray, older than her years, and had a constant cough. Otto was wiry and wore oversized jeans rolled up over scuffed black cowboy boots with silver heel taps. He had a large Honda motorcycle parked outside and walked stiffly because he'd had four vertebrae fused. Once he told Clark, "When I wake up, I'm always thankful if something hurts. Otherwise, I died in the night." They had a dog, Sarge, a German shepherd, and Wade spent most of his after-school hours playing with it until Clark came home.

When Otto got tuberculosis, Clark had to take Wade to county health care each week for a checkup. Clark, Natalie, and Helen all went in for a checkup, too.

"Nobody gets TB any more except for winos," Clark complained.

*   *   *

In the fall, Natalie went to Delaware for her father's heart valve operation and took Helen. Clark was exhausted trying to hold everything together, especially after night classes. Driving to pick up Wade, he was almost asleep at the wheel and hoped that Doreen and Otto weren't too liquored up. They'd want him to have a social drink, and he'd have to stick around for at least two.

As he pulled up to their house, Clark noticed one of the front room windows had been broken and boarded up with plywood. *I hope Wade didn't do that,* he thought. Muddy broom marks indicated someone had swept up glass outside. Probably Otto or one of his pals threw a chair, Clark figured.

When he knocked on the door, Doreen and Otto shouted, "Come in!" in unison. As soon as he stepped in, he recognized the atmosphere of a bad bar. Otto and Doreen squinted at him while Wade sat in a chair across the room, his head drooping to his chest. Sarge wore a large bandage on his back thigh and leg. A white plastic ring circled his neck, keeping him from reaching back with his teeth and pulling at the bandage.

"What happened?" Clark asked.

"We had a hell of a scare," Doreen said. "We're still mighty shook."

"Your boy scared the living be-Jesus out of us today," Otto added.

"What happened? Did Wade break the window?"

"Hell, no," Otto said. "Sarge jumped through it after Wade stabbed him."

Clark was incredulous. He couldn't believe Wade had stabbed the dog. The boy adored Sarge. Doreen had given him duties of feeding and watering the dog. Sometimes he ran through the cemetery behind her house with the big shepherd in pursuit.

"Are you sure Wade stabbed the dog?" In a way, Clark felt silly asking the question.

Doreen nodded. "With my best kitchen knife." The shadows around her eyes made them appear bruised.

"We're damn sure." Otto's voice boomed out, then seemed to crack under its own force. "What we're not sure about is how to pay the vet's bill. A hunnert and thirty-five dollars to stitch Sarge up and pump enough doggy blood in him to keep him alive." He seemed about to rise from his chair, but then sank back. "Damn dog only cost her forty dollars to start with."

"He's my boy's dog," Doreen said.

"Kid's run off to California anyway," Otto said. "He doesn't give a shit about that mutt."

Clark turned to Wade. "Why did you stab Sarge?"

The boy stared at the floor, shoulders slumped. His mouth dropped open and some saliva bubbled inside his lip.

Clark touched his shoulder and tried to make Wade look up, but he wouldn't. "Go ahead, Wade. You're not going to get in any more trouble. Just tell me."

Wade shrugged but didn't speak. Clark couldn't tell what the shrug meant. "Where's the knife?" he asked the boy.

"The police took it with them," Doreen said.

"The police came here for a dog?" Clark asked.

She nodded. "At first we thought the worst. Wade got himself kidnapped or killed, just 'cause we had car trouble and got home late. Seeing the trail of blood and window all smashed to hell . . ."

"Window's going to be a shitload of trouble," Otto interrupted. "It's not a regular-size fit or nothing."

She lit a cigarette. "Anyway, the police followed the trail of blood outside and found Sarge lying under a big old rhododendron a couple of houses away. They called animal control and rushed him to Dove Lewis. That's an emergency place for dogs and cats. When Wade saw all the police cars and emergency vehicles he came slinking back. Curious, I guess." She shook her head. "I can't tell you how glad I was to see him alive. I couldn't imagine what I was going to tell you about the boy—if anything bad had happened. I was fixing up a story in my mind."

"The cops finally got the truth out of him," Otto said. "At first he lied like a bad rug."

"Did they?" Clark remembered the police in Amherst.

"Damn straight," Otto said, becoming more upset. He turned to Wade. "Don't you have any sense, boy? Sarge is your pal. God damn it! Is that how you treat a pal?" When he tried lighting a cigarette, his hands shook.

Both Otto and Doreen needed to be appeased, Clark thought. He would listen to their concerns, offer to pay for the vet and the window. If the cops called or Children's Services came to visit, he could handle them.

"Maybe it'd be a good idea if you made up with Sarge a little," Clark told Wade. "Get back together."

Wade scooted closer to the dog. At first, Sarge whined and tried crawling away, but Doreen took his collar, holding him tight.

"Good dog, Sarge," Wade said. "Good doggie."

The voice didn't sound like Wade's, Clark thought. A thin pretend voice, it resembled the tone Wade used when talking to Helen, if he was trying to imitate Natalie or Grace. Clark found the voice both unnatural and disturbing.

"I'm sorry you got hurt, Sarge," Wade said. "Maybe you'll feel better tomorrow. I've got to go home and sleep beddy bye tonight. Tomorrow, I'll be back and we can play."

"Get your coat and we'll head out," Clark said.

Sarge whined softly and laid his head on his extended front legs.

Clark stared at the large bandage covering his back thigh and leg. Dried blood still matted the fur around the hip and down the leg.

"I'll come back in with a check," he told Doreen. "One thirty-five to Dove Lewis Hospital and another fifty for you. That should get the window started and buy you a new knife."

"You can just make it all out to me," Doreen said. "I'll settle up with everybody."

"Sure," Clark said. "Whatever works."

*   *   *

Wade didn't say anything on the drive home. He just kept fastening and unfastening the seat belt until Clark told him to stop. Two blocks before their house, Clark stopped at the Plaid Pantry for a 7UP and some Unisom tablets. He doubted he'd be able to sleep, but maybe if he took four. He bought the boy a root beer and a package of Starbursts. The individually wrapped candies kept Wade's hands busy for a while.

Clark smiled quickly when he checked the time. Almost twelve. At least the crazy woman from Medford wouldn't call him tonight, he figured. She had read in *The Oregonian* that he was having a book published and she began calling on Wednesday nights at eleven, when the rates dropped. At first he had tried to be helpful and generous, sharing a little of his good mood with her, but now he had grown tired of her ceaseless questions about writing and publishing. Somewhere, in a writing magazine, she had read that a best-seller should appeal to various groups. As a result she was concocting a story about professional golfers who were also gourmet cooks. They visited various golf courses around the country and whipped up their special recipes to the delight of the locals. As she explained it, the book would appeal to people who enjoyed golf, cooking, and those who lived near the various courses she described.

Clark tried to be encouraging. It was nutty enough to work. Then she brought up the idea of murdering them off, one by one, sort of a *Ten Little Indians.* All of this had gotten to be too much at eleven at night when he was exhausted, so he got a little grim satisfaction in knowing he'd missed her call tonight. Small compensation.

Wade put his pajamas on backward, but Clark let it go. He just wanted to get to bed. Kneeling beside Wade's bed, he said a prayer with him and asked God to watch over Natalie and Helen. Then he added Sarge. When he had finished he asked Wade, "How did Sarge get stabbed? I wasn't quite sure."

Wade sighed but didn't answer.

"Just start at the beginning," Clark said. "Start with getting off the school bus."

Wade took a deep breath. "I got off the bus, and I rang the bell. Sarge was barking and barking inside the house, but I yelled for him to be quiet and he stopped. He knows my voice. He's a good dog."

"Then what happened?"

"I know where Doreen keeps the key, so I got it from under the rock. But no one was home and I got scared. I tried to watch television awhile, but then I heard something down in the cellar, so I went down to look."

"Did you take the knife?"

Wade nodded. "I snuck down quiet and Sarge came, too. When I got to the bottom of the steps, I heard something moving over by the furnace. Sarge heard it because he barked and his hair stood up on his back. He growled real deep and ran over there. That's when I saw the monster—like a big otter. They fought—all this barking and growling and whistling. The big otter came right at me, trying to get up the steps. When it clawed at me, I tried to defend myself." He paused. "I was scared, Dad. Where was Doreen and Otto?"

"Their car broke down, Wade. They got there, but not until the trouble happened."

Wade clenched and unclenched his fists. "They shouldn't have left me alone like that."

Clark ran his hand through the boy's hair. He was sweating and his head was damp. "Sometimes people get delayed. You have to handle yourself."

"Sarge was trying to protect me," Wade said. "He charged in there growling and snapping. Like this!" He shook from side to side and snapped at the air.

"Calm down, Wade. Take it easy." Clark gripped the boy's shoulders, pushing him back onto the bed. "Now listen, I want you to think hard about this. Did you get confused? Maybe you thought Sarge was the otter monster. You were scared and it was dark down there. Maybe Sarge came out."

Wade shook his head so violently that Clark could hear his teeth click. "There was an otter monster! It had huge brown eyes and a hairy face. I saw it! Sarge saw it. He hurt Sarge. He bit him and clawed him and Sarge was bleeding. There was blood everywhere. He might have killed Sarge but I was yelling and crying and he came after me, so I stabbed him." He paused. "Maybe I saved Sarge."

"All right," Clark said. "Let's talk about this tomorrow." *None of this made sense,* he thought. "You can try talking with Dr. RealBird and telling her about it. She likes dogs. I think she has a dachshund."

"What's that?"

"A wiener dog."

Wade laughed in a strange way. "Wiener peener." He brought his hands close together. "A wiener dog wouldn't attack that otter monster like Sarge. He'd just get eaten up."

"Maybe you're right. Well, let's get some shut-eye."

"I'm scared, Dad. Can you leave the light on?"

"I'll tell you what. I'll leave the bathroom light on. It's not too bright, but that should help."

*   *   *

Clark read the precautions on the Unisom bottle, then took three, washing them down with the 7UP. No, he didn't have high blood pressure or glaucoma or an enlarged prostate. He didn't even know what malady to call this.

Tomorrow he would call in sick. Heartsick. For a long time he'd felt obligated to trudge in and fake it, but not now. Some of his colleagues acted as if the students lived for their classes, but he suspected most students were more than active enough with their work, families, sports. They enjoyed nothing more than a snow day, and a canceled class gave them at least a sliver of freedom.

He'd call RealBird's office and tell her he had an emergency. *They should have emergency psych wards for people like me tonight,* he thought. Probably they did, but he didn't know exactly how they worked. Billboards were up indicating people took better care of their pets than they did their children. In Wade's case at least, that had once been true.

Clark pushed the heavy bureau against his bedroom door. Tomorrow he'd go to the hardware store and get a bolt to install so Wade couldn't open it. Until tonight he had doubted Wade would hurt him. At the same time, he couldn't figure any reason the boy would stab the dog. That was the most disturbing thing about Wade. You believed you were getting somewhere, had made a breakthrough or at least were approaching one. Then he'd do something so bizarre, you couldn't imagine it.

Before turning off the light, Clark picked up the heavy flashlight by his bed, holding it like a club. "It's come to this," he muttered grimly.

Clark didn't know how long he'd been asleep when he heard the dresser move. "Hey," he said. He felt groggy and grabbed the flashlight. "What is it?"

"Dad, there's something wrong with the door. It's stuck." Wade pushed the door open about six inches so the bathroom light shone through. He was silhouetted against the light. "I can't get in."

"Wait a minute." The dresser blocked the light switch. Clark turned on the flashlight.

"Dad, what's in front of your door? Is something wrong? Are you okay?"

Wade held something in his hand. Clark shook his head trying to clear the fuzziness. It was a phone.

"Someone wants to talk with you," Wade said. "The phone rang and rang. I thought maybe it was Mom."

"Give it here and go back to bed." Clark took the phone as Wade handed it through the opening.

"I thought maybe it was Mom."

"Hello," Clark said.

"Mr. Woods. I hope I'm not disturbing you." The Medford woman sounded fully awake and cheerful. "I was working on this one section and realized I had a couple questions, so I thought I'd ask your advice. One of my golfers has been in a car wreck and has to wear a prosthesis, an artificial leg. It's a left leg in my book. Well, one of my friends informed me there actually is a professional golfer with an artificial foot, but she couldn't remember if it was right or left." The woman paused. "I was worried that I could be sued for copying the real golfer. Do you think that's likely?"

Clark didn't answer.

"Mr. Woods? Are you there? I tried calling earlier, but there was no answer. After that, I was working so hard, time just slipped by. Usually you're home by eleven. Where have you been anyway?"

18

Portland, Eugene, 1981

Clark wasn't prepared for failure. He had grown up in the West with tales of legendary self-made men. At college in the sixties, he was excited by the spirit of the times. He had marched for civil rights and seen blacks register to vote. At first he was ambivalent about the Vietnam War, supporting it for three years, then changing his mind after hearing Dick Gregory speak out against it. Years later, at a college reunion, one of his classmates, an artist, brought a flag she had created for the event. It was blue and maize, the school colors, with a bold "1967," but she had singed the borders and burned holes in the flag to represent the tumultuous times. Later, when Clark saw the class reunion photo, his classmates lined the steps of Memorial Hall with the tattered flag flying above them. A sign of victory after a battle. *Or maybe,* he thought, *it's just a statement that most of us are still here.* After the important social changes those times had produced, Clark had been convinced he could save one small boy's life.

However, Wade's stabbing the dog had toppled that belief. Clark had called RealBird the next morning, desperate for help, but had to wait for two days until she returned from a conference. Although he knew he couldn't handle things anymore, he still worried over what friends and colleagues might say. Giving up Wade was like admitting "I tried for eight years and it didn't work."

Sitting in RealBird's waiting room, Clark studied the pictures of giraffes, whales, and wolves. Her walls held no happy-face sayings, offered no platitudes. *Thank God for that,* he thought. Clark had grown to distrust fine words and tidy slogans.

When the office door opened, the Taylors came out with their son Jerry. Clark had seen them two or three times before and realized the boy was a menace. His hooded eyes were red-rimmed and malevolent. Wade had never seemed like that to Clark, but now he wondered how he appeared to other people.

"You by yourself today?" RealBird gestured toward a chair and Clark sat.

Clark nodded. "Natalie's father just had an operation and she's back in Delaware."

"It never rains, but what it pours," she said.

"Then I must be soaked." He paused, not knowing where to start.

She took off her glasses and studied him with her dark wide-set eyes. Her eyebrows seemed thicker without the glasses and her face more compassionate, less studious. Clark noticed she looked tired.

He didn't know how to start. "Should I lie on the couch while you take a few notes?" he joked.

"You've been watching too many old psychiatrist movies. These days we sit around on pillows." She paused and locked eyes with Clark until he turned away. "I think I can tell you what you're going to say, Mr. Woods. You are scared to death after the dog stabbing. You have a small child of your own and you can't understand Wade's behavior, because it's completely unpredictable. You're afraid he might hurt your daughter, intentionally or unintentionally. And in the end, what difference does it make? If he means it or not?"

Clark was surprised that she had guessed so well. "Go on."

"You're torn and feeling guilty, as if you've failed. Your marriage is strained to the breaking point, and everyone you talk to says, 'Love is all he needs. A stable home is all he needs.'" RealBird stood and faced the windows. *"Love will conquer all."*

"Understand this." Her words were deliberate. "You have done all you can for Wade. You have a right to a life, to a family." She took a breath. "We live in a society that gives lip service to children, 'Children are our future,' that sort of thing. But in reality, children are the most neglected and abused group in the country. People pay more attention to animals than to children. I've seen child-care situations that make some dog and cat kennels look like palaces."

She spoke intensely and seemed to have forgotten that Clark was in the room. "The medical and psychological communities have labels to plaster on kids like Wade: Emotionally Handicapped, MBD, schizophrenic. Now they're talking about Fetal Alcohol Syndrome, where the mother's constant drinking has affected the fetus. No doubt Wade suffers from that condition. But all the labels can be an evasion; a catch-all for things we can't explain. Think about it." She shook her head. "A child whose mother was a down-and-out drunk, or who was addicted to cocaine, a child who, in the first years of life, had bar food and orange soda for nutrition . . . a child who was beaten or otherwise abused—or all of the above. That child will be damaged in ways we are only just beginning to understand." She turned toward Clark. "And I see more of those kids every single year."

"I keep thinking," Clark said, "if only we could find some other place for him, at least for a while, some normal family. But most normal people won't take a kid like Wade."

"No." RealBird's voice softened. "That's just not true. Normal people do take on kids like Wade. But they have no help. The problems become overwhelming, and everyone tosses platitudes and slogans at them. That makes them feel even more alone and desperate. They think everyone else is doing fine while they're failing."

"Sounds like you speak from experience."

She pointed to snapshots of children on her wall. "That's my role in life. Each one of these kids in a way, is mine. Look, I'll tell you this because I feel you'll understand." She said, "I have my own *Weyekin*. My guardian spirit which led me to this work. Trouble is, the work just seems to get harder and harder. Wave after wave of kids. Fewer resources."

She rubbed her eyes. "I ask for guidance. I even talk to my Lutheran grandfather, God rest his soul. The way I figure it, the odds are so stacked against me I might as well cover all the bases. It's like that island in the Columbia River, Memaloose. No whites are buried there, except for one guy, Victor Trevitt. He said when it came to salvation, he'd take his chances with the Indians."

Clark smiled but when he put his hand to his face he was crying.

"Here." RealBird reached into her desk and pulled out a box of tissues. "Your mascara's going to run."

He choked a laugh. "I should have put on waterproof this morning." He blew his nose. "It's a damn hard decision."

"Of course it is." Her hand rested on the tissue box. "Nothing's easy when it comes to children like Wade. Even if you get things settled temporarily, when they hit adolescence and the hormones kick in . . . you're off to the races again."

"I got to tell you a story," Clark said. Just hearing her put a voice to his troubles made him feel lighter, somehow. "Seeing that Kleenex box reminds me that when I was teaching at Wisconsin State, some of my students would come in and cry about their papers. It was deer season and Kleenex made red tissues in those days just for the deer hunters."

"Why?"

"Well, they claimed that sometimes a hunter would pull out a white tissue and get shot at by another hunter who thought that was a deer's tail flaring. So some marketing genius came up with red ones."

"I'll see if I can find some," she said. "Look. You and I are both trying to do the same thing, in a way. And sometimes it seems like we're standing on an island waving at the ships that pass by, but nobody notices."

Clark was startled at how well she understood. "So, what now? What do I do?"

"After a very serious event like the dog stabbing, I usually recommend a cooling-down period. You haven't been taking him back to the care providers, right?"

Clark nodded. "I'm using up my personal business leave at the college. But I'm running short."

"We'll find an alternate shelter for him," she said.

"Okay, but what does that mean?"

"Place Wade in another home for a while, until the dust settles." She watched his face. "I know, you're thinking, 'Where?'"

Clark shook his head. "You got that right."

"I have to give you the options. Have you thought about returning him to his tribe?"

"Not really. That's where the trouble started. Anyway, if he was in Southeast Alaska, I'd hardly ever see him."

"You could give him back to the state."

"He's already been in dozens of different foster homes. That doesn't inspire confidence."

"My thought, too. So I'll give you this one. It's not conventional, but we're talking survival, here. Wade's, and yours."

"Okay."

"There's a family in Eugene that takes on damaged kids. Dan and Cathy Stanley. I've worked with some of them. Handicapped, retarded. A few are autistic. Some are just plain thrown away. Disposed of like trash." She took a deep breath. "The Stanleys are real good people, and it seems to work. I can't tell you why. But it's better than anything else I've seen."

"That sounds good," Clark said, his hopes rising. "But what if they don't want him?"

"Well, why don't you take Wade down there and see the people?"

"How many kids do they have anyway?"

"Twenty-seven at last count."

"Oh my God," Clark muttered, but he figured this was his last hope. He'd try. There surely wasn't much to lose.

RealBird looked at her watch. "I'm sorry to rush you, but I've got more coming."

Clark rose. "Thank you." But as he headed for the door, she stopped him.

"I've got one more thing to say. Wouldn't go over well at the psychologists' convention, but I trust you. Here goes." She paused, considering her words. "Remember when I asked you about the boy's people? I wondered if they were Raven."

Clark nodded. "Angoon's a Raven village. He belongs to the Killer Whale clan."

"Now I'm not here to give you a bunch of New Age mumbo-jumbo. That's for old hippies and people from California. I'm past believing in miracles, but the boy is Tlingit. He has relatives, even a guardian spirit. If I were you, I'd keep that open as a possibility."

"Okay," Clark said. "I will."

As he left RealBird's office, Clark felt a glimmer of hope, the first in months.

•   •   •

The Stanleys lived in a large, ramshackle former Methodist church on Eugene's south side. Just the seventeen bikes in front suggested an unusual household. Two large Ford vans, the fifteen-seaters that colleges used for wrestling and tennis teams, were parked in front. These had rusty wheel wells and numerous Bondo patches.

Four teenage boys unloaded boxes of groceries, flats of tomatoes and sacks of oranges from the newer van. A motley group: two were tall boys of indeterminate race who seemed to be following the instructions of a muscular red-haired boy and a lean Asian wearing a Grateful Dead T-shirt.

Clark stood by the driver's door a minute, trying to determine whether to lock the truck.

"You're not a cop," the Asian boy said. "Are you with CSD or a reporter?"

Clark thought of the old TV show *What's My Line?*

"I'll bet he's a minister," the red-haired boy said. "He's here to save my soul, but I'm already hitched to the Marines. In three weeks I'm heading off to boot camp. Are you a minister?"

"Not even close." Clark decided to leave the pickup doors unlocked, the windows down. He figured these kids could break into the truck in about ten seconds anyway. "I'm looking for Cathy Stanley. Or Dan."

"Check inside," one of the tall boys said. He squinted at Clark. "You planning to stay for dinner?"

He smiled. "Sure, if I'm invited."

"You got to be a minister," the Asian boy said. "No one else stays for dinner."

"Maybe I'm an inspector from the Health Department." Clark could see he'd caught the lippy boy off-guard with that one and he headed toward the house.

PLEASE KNOCK. THIS IS OUR HOME. The sign on the door had bright irregular letters, the kind made by grade-schoolers.

Clark knocked, but he could hear a ruckus inside. Loud voices, shouts, disco music, someone trying to play the piano. He knocked louder but no one answered. Finally, he opened the door.

The hallway was lined with more bikes, worn tennis shoes, and two dozen coats hanging from pegs and hooks. Underwear and socks covered a cafeteria-sized table. He had never seen so many socks—hundreds in different sizes and colors. He smelled soap and Clorox, heard the washing machine switch cycles and the whir of a dryer.

A small girl, about five, with frizzy black hair peeked from around a corner, then raced away. "Mama, somebody's here! A big man."

"I'm in the kitchen. Tell him to come in," a pleasant voice called above the din. "You kids need to wash your hands for supper. Mark, go upstairs to see if anybody's studying, which I seriously doubt."

Clark smelled frying onions and hamburger, warm cornmeal, sweaty shoes, diapers, baby lotion. When he stepped around the corner, he saw three young girls setting two long church tables for supper. Another two helped a woman cooking in the kitchen by filling pitchers with milk and Kool-Aid.

The woman seemed about Clark's age, with round, pleasant features, short blond hair, large blue eyes, and a smear of taco sauce along one cheek. She wore low-cut Converse tennis shoes, jeans, and a Garfield T-shirt. "Mandy, set another place for this man. Who are you anyway?"

"I'm the man who came to dinner," he said.

"I saw the movie," she said. "Monte Wooley. I loved it. I don't have much free time for movies now," she said. "I'm what you might call a full-time mother. So who are you really? Children's Services? A school counselor? I don't want any more troubles today."

"Clark Woods. Dr. RealBird called you about me and my boy Wade."

She put down the spatula, wiped her hands on a dingy towel, then offered her hand. "Cathy Stanley. I thought you weren't coming until the weekend. That's what Dr. RealBird said. Not that it makes much difference, except Dan, my husband, is working swing shift this week at the plywood mill. What you see is what you get around here. But on Sundays, we have roast chicken and Dan is home all day."

"Tacos sound good," he said.

"Better wash your hands in the kitchen sink. If you wait for the bathroom, you'll have cold food."

He crossed over to the sink, smiling at the two girls. They nodded but didn't smile back. One seemed Hispanic, the other Indian, but he wasn't sure. He used a chunk of yellow bar soap to wash.

All the people at the table held hands and prayed. A couple of kids snickered, and Cathy cleared her throat. Then the three girls in the kitchen served the food. Clark counted heads twice to make certain he had the right number. Nineteen counting Cathy and himself. Wednesday night, he thought. The church youth groups always met on Wednesdays when he was growing up.

"I notice a few children are missing," he said to Cathy. "Are they at church?"

One of the girls serving dinner laughed and put her hand over her mouth.

"Della, you mind your manners," Cathy said. "No, they're at Teen-Anon, and drug rehab. A couple are doing community service because they broke a store window downtown last month. If the newspapers try to do another human interest story on us, this is a bad week."

"I see," Clark said. *Nothing's perfect.*

Clark tried guessing the ages of the children at the table. Five were younger than Wade. Three about the same age. The rest were older.

Cathy introduced them so fast he couldn't remember their names. He smiled and nodded at each. One of the girls who appeared to be about sixteen had a baby on her knee.

"This is our little granddaughter, Lateisha," Cathy said. "She's just three months."

"She's a pretty girl," Clark said. "Lots of dark hair." He smiled at the mother and wondered if the father was one of the young men at the table or someone outside the household. Several of the other girls took turns holding the baby, or playing with her fingers.

"Lateisha's pretty spoiled," Cathy said. "But as you can see, she gets lots of love."

"She's in the catbird seat," Clark said. *Lateisha was off to a better start than Wade got,* he figured.

* * *

"So tell me about Wade," Cathy said. "No secrets. You've seen us. Do you think Wade will be happy here? We're a little different than the normal foster family."

They were sitting in the big bedroom downstairs, which had once been a Sunday School classroom. Bible verses and pictures still covered the walls.

"Well, Wade's kind of different, too," Clark said. "Of course, he'll need to adjust some." No secrets? Clark was desperate, but didn't want to say so. How much had RealBird told Cathy? He wondered if he should hold anything back. Cathy probably knew most of Wade's story already, but Clark started with the easy part. Wade was in sixth grade although he was almost fourteen. He didn't read or write much more than his name, address, a few animal names, boys' first names if they didn't have silent letters. He didn't tell time. He didn't understand consequences. He was getting more cooperative in school and tried to help with simple tasks around the house, but got distracted after a few minutes. People liked Wade because he seemed happy most of the time and interested in cars, animals, mechanical projects.

He told her about Wade's early years—how the boy was found frozen in his own urine; how his hands had been burned when one of his mother's boyfriends held them to a hot plate. Then Clark listed the bizarre behaviors. Wade soiled his pants, crashed toys into things, pretended to be a dog. He'd stabbed Sarge. Clark told her he was afraid Wade might hurt someone with his erratic behavior, but he didn't think the boy was malevolent.

While he talked, he studied Cathy Stanley. She was listening carefully, nodding now and again, her face impassive. So far as he could tell, there was no sense of alarm. He debated with himself whether or not to tell Cathy about Yukiko. Finally, Clark took a deep breath and explained the incident. When he was finished, he waited, thinking, *Well, at least I gave this place a shot.*

"Good heavens! That's awful. But it sounds like a tragic accident," Cathy said. "As you might imagine, I've seen just about everything, and the police show up here at least twice a week to check up on somebody."

Clark was relieved that she didn't seem more shocked.

"Here's a real important issue for me," she said. "Does he start fires? Living in this old tinderbox church with all these children, some in wheelchairs, that's what worries me most."

"No," Clark said. "He's never started a fire."

"Good. Now you need to know some things. I hope you're not squeamish."

"Cast-iron stomach," Clark said.

"I'll start with the easy stuff. Some of the older boys have been in jail and we have one girl who was a prostitute in Thailand. When she first arrived, that's how she tried to get the boys' attention. And she did. She was older, twenty-two, but looked fourteen, and the orphanage had lied about her age so she could be adopted."

She rubbed the back of her neck and rolled her shoulders. "We've had a lot of challenges over the years. Once in a while, we'll get an adolescent who tries to rape the younger children or the pets. When that happens, we take drastic steps—restraining, hospitalization, pacifying drugs. We don't tolerate one child hurting another."

"Wade's not like that, but he is very interested in sex. He makes silly jokes and talks about titties, that sort of thing."

She nodded. "Hormone overdrive." Looking at Clark, she said, "Now I don't want to shock you, but usually we tell the adolescent boys that masturbating is okay. It eases the sexual tensions around here somewhat. Right now we've got eight boys past puberty and they're wired. So are you okay with that?"

He was surprised by her candor, but decided the Stanleys were survivors. Given all the kids, they had to be. "I'm okay."

"Good," she said. "We try to have the preteen boys in bed by ten, the older ones by eleven. With homework and chores, that's tough. On Fridays, everyone gets an extra hour. School holidays, same thing. I tell you, every day I pray for patience."

"I'll bet those are long prayers."

Cathy laughed. "Do you want to see one of the boys' bedrooms?"

"Sure."

She took him up the stairs and through a labyrinth of partitioned rooms that reminded him of Whitman College student apartments—gerrymandered in odd ways so the landlords could squeeze in more "study rooms." He doubted if this place could pass fire codes and guessed some of the inspectors had winked. Most of the bedrooms had radios, a rack for clothes, a couple of Spartan single beds, pictures of teen heroes, rock bands. All smelled like sweat, tennis shoes, and sour towels. The older boys' rooms reeked of cheap cologne.

When the door opened, Clark recognized the Asian boy from outside. He was wearing running shoes and a pair of maroon Nike shorts with a yellow T-shirt.

"Jake, you remember Mr. Woods? His boy Wade might be coming to stay with us for a while. Since Tim's leaving for the Marines, I thought we might put him in here."

Jake shrugged. "Okay, I guess."

"Jake's on the high school track team," Cathy said. "He's the best freshman they have in the eight-hundred meter."

Clark studied the boy. More muscular than Wade. About the same height. "I used to run the half-mile," Clark said. "That was twenty years and forty pounds ago."

"What was your best time?" Jake asked.

Clark paused. "Well, remember, I went to a small high school. My best time was two twenty-seven."

"Not bad. Did you run in college?" Jake asked.

Clark shook his head. "I was too slow. The Seattle and Portland kids were a lot faster. So were the runners from California. I just couldn't keep up with them." He paused. "So what's your best time, Jake?"

"No offense," he said. "But it's two-nineteen."

Clark shook his head and whistled. "You must be a greyhound."

"After I finish high school, I'm going to Lane Community College, then the University of Oregon. I want to run like Steve Prefontaine." He nodded at the runner's poster on his wall.

"Jake's from Vietnam," Cathy said as they walked back down the hall. "His father was a GI. I think he'll be good for Wade. All A's and B's."

Clark was encouraged. Maybe with someone closer to his own age, Wade would make some of those breakthroughs the experts kept promising. "So you're willing to give him a try?" he asked Cathy.

"Bring him down," she said. "We'll see how it works." She held out her hand and Clark shook it.

"Sounds like a plan," he said. "How much do you charge?"

She smiled and seemed amused. "Dan and I believe this is what God wants us to do. It's our life's work."

Clark took a breath. "I can appreciate that," he said. "But the state helps me with Wade. He gets an SSI check."

"We can accept a donation," she said.

As he drove back to Portland, Clark considered how to explain the Stanleys to Natalie and Grace, and decided he really couldn't. *You just have to see it for yourself,* he thought. Like RealBird said, it shouldn't work but it does.

He wondered how Wade would react. At least he'd like the tools scattered around the backyard, the older boys fixing up cars, the constant commotion. With a sudden stab of pain, Clark thought, *Maybe my expectations have been too high. It's tough for the kid to be wrong so much of the time and not understand why. Wade was spontaneous and jumped without looking, often landing in trouble.*

He remembered Wade in the pool at his first swimming lesson. The line of kids hanging onto the wall kicking out their legs, an overwhelming white spray and rush of water. Wade stared in amazement a moment, and then suddenly leaped from the deck into the water, gliding under the surface, then emerging, his body sleek and wet. Kids' voices cheered in the cavernous pool room, flashes of color from bright swimsuits, red kickboards. Sheer joy.

As the swimming instructor pulled Wade out by his arm, Clark saw the look on his face—a sly grin. Jake and the other kids might be good companions, Clark decided.

Night had fallen when Clark left the Stanleys. Had he stayed that long? On the drive north, the truck's headlights swept patches of fog and darkness. Clark switched them to low. Staring ahead into the night, he remembered his promise to Mr. Kagita—that he would raise Wade to be a good citizen. *You had to be young to make that kind of promise,* Clark thought.

.   .   .

Nothing seemed right to Clark until Natalie stepped off the plane, holding Helen in one arm and dragging the carry-on bag in the other. Just seeing them gave Clark strength. He hadn't been sure Natalie would come back after the news about Wade and the dog. *Why should she leave the comfort and security of her parents' house to come back to this mess?* he thought.

The day after her arrival, they drove to Eugene, leaving Wade with Grace. On the way down Clark filled her in on the details. "I tried convincing myself he didn't stab the dog," Clark said. "They're all looney over there at Doreen's. Anything can happen. I mean, who even gets tuberculosis like Otto did anymore? But like I told you, when I got home and shoved the dresser in front of my door, I knew things were beyond my control."

She nodded and touched his knee. "It's time, Clark. It's been time for a while."

They took the Stanleys out to dinner and recounted Wade's whole story again. Cathy and Dan listened carefully, occasionally asking questions. When they were finished, Cathy looked straight across the table at them and said, "All right, I have one more question to ask you, and it's the most important one. Are you sure? Is this what you really want, deep in your hearts?"

Clark said, "We're sure."

*   *   *

At home in Portland, Clark put Helen and Wade to bed, then joined Natalie at the kitchen table. Shadows rimmed her eyes. He imagined her flying seven hours across the country in darkness with the baby, into an uncertain future. Would he be that brave?

"Jet lag?" he asked.

"A little."

"Shot of Metaxa?"

"Sure."

He poured the brandy into two small silver shot glasses that she had brought from Delaware. Clark raised his in a toast. "To us. To the Stanleys. And Wade." They took a sip.

"If this were vodka and my grandma were here she'd chug it in one gulp, then slam her glass down and go 'Aahhh . . .'" Natalie smiled. "Her cheeks would get red. And she had these laughing gray-green eyes."

"Like Helen's."

"And like Emmett's. Who knows what's in our kids and where it comes from? Are those Kiev eyes, or Ruby eyes? It's all a mystery, and we just have to do our best as things come."

Natalie stood and walked over to the window. A small icon hung on the wall near it. "A replica," she had told Clark. "I never had any formal religious education. But the image of Mother and Child. It's so basic to life. So essential."

When Clark joined her, he saw that a couple of small maple limbs had fallen near the sandbox they had built for Helen. Her plastic push-trike and some rubber balls were scattered around the yard. A fine, rainy mist hung in the glow of the backyard floodlight.

"I had this dream after he stabbed the dog," Clark said. "Wade and I are in the pickup driving down a foggy road. The fog gets thicker and thicker. I can barely see but I think I'm getting somewhere. Then the road just flat out stops. Fog starts coming in the window like the killer fog in one of those old B-movies. I reach over to grab Wade, but the door's open and he's gone. Something keeps me from going out into the night, but I'm not really scared. I'm sort of peaceful.

"Wade and I used to travel on weekends, maybe fish or do a little hiking, then we'd have dinner someplace. He'd be tired coming back home and he'd nap with my coat bunched against the pickup door. I'd make sure the door was locked, his seat belt fastened.

"Sometimes I'd stop for coffee to go, leaving the door open when I got out so as not to wake him by slamming it. On the way home, the coffee tasted good, and Wade was quiet, a pretty good companion. I'd turn on a country western station—keeping it low. Then I'd contemplate the future. I truly believed we were going somewhere, getting closer to something important."

She turned from the window and faced him.

"I've hit a dead end," he said. "I knew that when I slid the dresser in front of my door."

Natalie touched his arm. "Let it go. Let someone else try."

.   .   .

That night Clark was jolted awake from a deep sleep. He thought he heard someone crying and ran to Helen's room, but she was sleeping. Then he went to Wade's room. The boy was silent.

Clark leaned against the wall, his heart pounding. Natalie had left the window open a crack as she always did, for fresh air, and he could smell industrial odors carried on the wind. The pungent, burnt smell reminded him of the paper mill.

He remembered driving into Two Rivers at night with Natalie—the flag above the elevator half-visible, disappearing into fog. And suddenly, ahead of them, the paper mill coming into view, an eerie orange.

Clark imagined the mill. Somewhere within that smoke and haze, he knew, people were working, even in the darkest hours of night. As he closed his eyes, the workers transformed into Grace, Natalie, even tiny Helen. Anna cradling Natalie's dying brother in her arms. Clark was there, and Wade. He saw their forms wavering in the intense heat amid the towers, and the brilliant smoke rising into the night as if it were all part of some vast explosion. *Incredible that we survive,* Clark thought. *Impossible.*

Clark heard singing: a thin, high voice like Wade used to have when he was younger. A jumble of words that seemed to make no sense. He went back to Wade's room, but the boy was asleep. A ray of light from the street slanted across his face. His brows were drawn into the perpetual frown he wore, as if trying to figure out a problem too difficult for him. In the dim light, Clark saw that his face was no longer that of a small child, but of a young man.

Let it go. He repeated Natalie's words to himself. *Give it over to someone else now. It's time.*

19

Eugene, 1983–1985

More than two years had passed since Clark and Natalie had driven Wade down to the Stanleys'. Clark had intended to visit Wade once a week, and he nearly kept that schedule for the first three months, missing only two weeks. But the pace got to him. Even when he drove fast to Eugene and back, the entire process, including visits with the Stanleys, taking Wade to a movie and a meal, shooting hoops and playing catch, took about eight hours. Enough to make an additional workday—one squeezed into midweek or the weekend.

Wade talked about girlfriends, but at first Clark and Natalie didn't believe they existed. After all, they reasoned, what girls would be interested in him, immature as he was? But Cathy Stanley backed up his story. "You'd be surprised," she told Clark. "When he fixes himself up, he looks pretty good." And it was true. Wade was growing tall and filling out, although he was still lean. He had the faint beginnings of a mustache. In jeans and one of the western-style shirts Clark bought him, with his hair combed and teeth brushed, a person could almost think he was completely normal. *At least,* Clark thought, *if you didn't look too closely.* Even in the best times, Wade's face always remained slightly off-kilter.

The idea that Wade could become a father at some point was a sobering thought. Cathy taught the kids about birth control, but, as she pointed out, "I can't make them use it." Clark talked to him, too. He wished that Wade was growing mentally as fast as he was physically. Mostly, though, he prayed that whatever Wade was doing, he wouldn't get a girl pregnant.

Sometimes Natalie and Helen came down, but between Helen's ear infections and Natalie's job, those visits became fewer and fewer as time went on. Problems at work were weighing heavily on her mind, she told Clark. Many of her ESL students were illiterate, even in their own languages, yet standards were tightening. She was being forced to fail them. "And if I do that, they lose the small grants they have for school," Natalie said. "What will happen to them? These people work all day and sometimes nights; they have families. How will they live with no education or skills?"

Grace was popular at the Stanleys'. Every time Wade had a birthday, or on other holidays, she would ride down with Clark bearing enough small gifts for all the kids, party favors, and cake, and generally stirring up excitement. "They all know Grandma Grace," Cathy said, laughing. "Even the littlest ones."

As time passed, Clark would sometimes substitute a phone call for visiting. Wade was still enthusiastic about the *Dukes of Hazzard,* the General Lee, and Elvis. He and some of the older boys were fixing up a Toyota pickup they had salvaged after a wreck, and Wade reminded Clark that he'd be old enough to drive soon. Clark didn't have the heart to tell him the truth: the chances of Wade ever getting a driver's license were remote. He'd never pass a test.

Still he was fascinated by cars. One Saturday night, Clark received a call from an angry man in Eugene. "Are you the father of Wade White Fish?"

"I used to be his *foster* father, but not now," Clark said. "Who is this?"

"Corporal Schell of campus security at the University of Oregon. We caught Wade directing traffic at Autzen stadium for the Oregon-Washington game. Now we've got twenty-seven cars bogged down in a pasture."

Clark had to laugh at Schell's exasperation. Later he learned that Wade had put on a blue janitor's uniform and signaled the cars with a flashlight.

"It's serious, Mr. Woods. We can't get a tow truck down there—too muddy. One already sank up to its axles."

"Use some horses, then," Clark said. "Or call Oregon State and tell them you need someone who can drive a tractor."

Clark always laughed when he told that story about Wade, but it cost him over six hundred dollars in tow fees to keep the university from pressing charges against the boy.

*   *   *

At other times, Wade seemed subdued. Trouble with schoolwork, time-outs, conflicts with other kids. "I want to come home, Dad. When can I come?"

The words sliced Clark's heart and he stalled, making up excuses.

Wade did come for visits, though. Clark took him out to see Red Stroud and round up the cows, and to visit Tony. He bought Wade new running shoes, so he could "run like Jake," but he lacked the coordination.

Helen was always excited to see him. But while Wade was in the house, Clark and Natalie monitored his every move. "It's like you keep a floor plan in your head," Natalie said. "You're always aware of his whereabouts at any given moment. And of where Helen is, too."

In the second year at the Stanleys', there were rumblings of trouble. Wade would take off for days at a time. Usually Cathy Stanley knew where he was—he stayed in the area, sometimes with a girlfriend. But once she called Clark to ask if he had seen Wade. He'd been gone a week.

"No," Clark said, troubled by his disappearance.

That night Wade called collect. "Where are you?" Clark asked. "Everyone's worried."

"Dad, can you get me? I'm in Portland."

"Is there someone who can read the street sign for you and tell me where you are?"

He was on Burnside, the skid row of Portland. Wade claimed he'd lived there two months. They brought him back to the house, fed him and washed his clothes, which smelled so bad Natalie wore rubber gloves to handle them. Then he slept. The next day, Clark put him on the bus and told him he needed to get back to the Stanleys' and to school. Wade mugged at the window as the bus pulled away.

Cathy Stanley called with the news. "Jake waited over an hour for him at the bus station, but Wade never showed." Several weeks passed before he surfaced again.

"You have a collect call from an Oregon State Correctional Facility," the automated woman's voice said. "The call is from"—beep—"Wade" —beep. "If you wish to accept the call, press star one now; if you wish to refuse the call, press two."

"Damn," Clark said as he pressed star one. "Hello. Hey, Wade, I'm here." The line sounded blank. "Wade, I'm here."

"We are connecting your call now," the voice said.

"Hey, Wade. I'm here," Clark shouted.

"Hi, Dad. This is Wade." His voice sounded subdued. Music and loud voices crowded the background.

"Speak louder. Where are you, Wade?"

"They put me in jail," he said.

"What happened?" Clark wasn't entirely surprised. Maybe Wade had stolen something. He was glad Natalie was out shopping and couldn't hear the conversation.

"Can you come down and get me out?"

"Where are you? What did you do?"

"Nothing," he said, his voice dropping.

"Listen. Ask one of the other guys where you are." Clark reached for a pencil.

"I'm in the county jail. Blane County."

"Lane County. It's Lane." Clark wrote the word down, an action that was more automatic than purposeful. "That's right there in Eugene. Tell me what you did."

Wade whispered into the receiver. "They say I stole a car, but I just drove it around a little. Then I left it in the Albertson's lot."

A car! Clark had thought maybe a jacket or some tools.

"How did you steal it in the first place?"

"Somebody left their keys in it at the 7-Eleven. That's a stupid thing to do, right?"

"You can't go driving around, Wade. You don't even have a license." Clark closed his eyes, thankful Wade hadn't run over somebody.

"I spun out, Dad, like the Duke Boys. That car screamed across the parking lot!"

"Have you called the Stanleys?"

"I'm pissed off at them. No one accepted my charge. Maybe you better call them, Dad. Somebody should come get me out."

"I'll see about that." He didn't know how getting a kid out of jail worked but figured Cathy did.

"Dad, somebody else wants to use the phone, so I gotta go. Hey, Dad? I love you."

As soon as he hung up the phone, Clark called information and got the number for the Lane County jail. They confirmed that Wade was indeed in jail for grand theft auto, but refused to discuss any specifics. Clark wasn't able to get in touch with Cathy Stanley until later that afternoon. She seemed to take the news in stride and he realized, for her, jailings were fairly routine.

"I told you that several of the older boys had been in jail. I think Wade's gotten a little carried away trying to outdo them. But I don't want to get him out yet. We believe that if one of the kids here gets in trouble with the law, they need to take the consequences."

"Well, theoretically, I agree with that, I guess," Clark said. "But I'm not certain Wade understands the link between his actions and the consequences."

"Jail's not the worst thing," Cathy said. "It gives him a chance to realize his actions *do* have consequences. Maybe he'll learn not to steal cars. I'm afraid he might hit another car or a child on a bicycle. Wade can get pretty wild."

Cathy sounded as if she knew what she was doing. "Well, I thought about that, too," Clark said. "If he ran over somebody, that would be horrible."

"That's the point. The situation could be a lot worse. A few weeks in jail and most of the kids straighten up." She paused and talked with someone in the background. "If you want, I'll give you the number of the public defender's office."

"Shoot."

.   .   .

Later that day, Clark talked with April Hedin in the public defender's office. "I wouldn't get too upset," she assured Clark. "This is your boy's first offense and so many cars get stolen around here, the judge is likely to be pretty lenient. A fine, a few months probation. As long as he didn't hurt anyone or smash up the car."

Clark tapped the pencil on the desk. "Well, they wouldn't say much at the sheriff's office. I don't like the idea he's in jail. He can be influenced pretty easily."

"You don't need to worry about Wade being in with the general population. There's a special wing for juvenile offenders. Lots of penny-ante drug dealers, but that's about it.

"It would be helpful if you could tell me a little about Wade, his background, where he grew up—that sort of thing. Sometimes it helps when we can present the judge with a pretty complete file. First of all, how exactly are you related to Wade?"

Clark spent half an hour going over the details with April. Several times she had to stop him and ask for clarification. "So he's not a blood relative to you? He's your ex-wife's cousin from Alaska? He was in how many different foster homes before you got him? Different schools say Emotionally Handicapped? Trainable Mentally Retarded? Learning Disabled? A Challenged Learner?"

When he told her about the episode of Wade parking the cars at Autzen Stadium, she laughed. "That's sort of a local legend around here already, but I had no idea he was the kid. At least it's not on his county record. The university has its own way of handling things. If he goes there, they'll probably make him pay a huge fine in order to graduate."

Not much chance, Clark thought.

"One more question. Is the tribe involved in his support at all? Does he get a per capita check or have close contact with his relatives?"

"No," Clark said. "Wait. Maybe a check. When my ex-wife and I first got him, she looked into that. The tribe has a little timber money and that's going into an account for when he's eighteen. She thought it was better to get SSI money from Oregon and save tribal money for later. Job training or something."

"That's not really my department," she said. "But no one from Alaska is actively involved in his welfare or support at this time?"

"No."

As Hedin had predicted, the judge was lenient the first time, and Wade got released after a hearing. Hedin made a strong case for "diminished capacity" or "dimcap," arguing that Wade didn't fully realize the consequences of his actions.

However, the pattern continued. Over the next eighteen months, Wade stole more than a dozen cars, joy riding a few blocks or miles, then trudging back to the Stanleys when he was out of gas money. He was locked up seven times for car theft and criminal mischief. Every three or four months, Clark received calls from the public defender's office. Each time, one of Hedin's new assistants asked, "Can you fill us in a little on Wade's background? Some of his files seem to be missing."

Christ, they're as bad as the public schools, he thought. Angry though he was, Clark was so worried about Wade hurting someone with his reckless driving, he felt relief when he knew Wade was locked up. However, Natalie was afraid that he'd get out and drive north with a couple other inmates intending to rob or harm the family.

"Wade's not like that at all," Clark would say, flaring.

Then she'd glare at him. "Face the facts. Wade's changed. You don't have any idea what he's like or who influences him now."

Clark would make plans to visit Wade once a week, whenever he was in jail. Ironically, he was seeing Wade more often now than when he first went to live with the Stanleys.

The newest PD's assistant assigned to work with Wade brought up old questions and new. "Mr. Woods," she said. "I've got Wade's file here. It takes up half a drawer, but there are just a couple questions I need to ask."

Clark braced for the entire background routine. "Shoot."

"Has Wade ever been diagnosed with schizophrenia?"

Clark laughed. "No. Somehow they missed that one. Add it to the list."

Her tone became a little edgy. "The county psychiatrist says Wade hears voices and seems remote, lost in his own world. I just wondered if he had a history of that?"

"Wade tells a good story," Clark said. "Don't you think the other inmates informed him that's a good way to get out? He's got some street sense."

"Do you think another evaluation is in order?"

"You bet. Start with the psychiatrist."

* * *

Clark passed the front of the Eugene Hilton and turned right on Olive Street. After parking in a well-lighted place across from the post office, he walked into the new Lane County Correctional Facility. With its pleasant brick facade, beautiful landscaping, and downtown location, the jail resembled a utilities building.

Inside, Clark stopped to give Ricketts, the deputy on duty, the thirty dollars so Wade had commissary money.

"How was the drive down today, Mr. Woods?" Ricketts handed him a receipt for the money.

"Not bad. No field burning. No fog. Just all those trucks." The drive at night back to Portland was always worse. He didn't leave Eugene until around ten so he arrived home shortly after midnight. That allowed him ten minutes for a truck-stop coffee in Woodburn. "How goes it with you, Officer Ricketts?"

"Same old, same old," he said. "But next week I'm going down to Coos Bay to see my son. We're going to duck hunt a little."

"What are you shooting?"

"I got a Mossburg 12-gauge that shoots three-inch magnums. Kicks like a mule but it can drop a goose at sixty yards."

"That's a cannon!" Clark signed in at the desk, gave Ricketts his driver's license for positive ID, then surrendered his keys and pocketknife, anything metal. Since he talked with Wade on a telephone, each person on different sides of bulletproof glass, he couldn't imagine how the jailors thought he could sneak in a weapon or drugs.

Clark sat on one of the orange plastic chairs until seven-thirty, the time they moved Wade from the holding cells. Usually, Wade was a little slower than the other prisoners and arrived during the second or third fifteen-minute session of the visitor's hour.

Without being obvious, Clark studied the other visitors. Most wore clothes from K-Mart or Penney's but a few were more upscale. Meier and Frank, Nordstrom. Many reminded him of Two Rivers students.

Certainly no one looked like the relatives of big-time criminals.

Most were visiting deadbeat dads, car thieves, chronic drunks, drug users. A few who looked like Dead Heads fell into the last category. Part of Eugene was lost in the sixties, as evident by the number of watery, red-eyed visitors whose clothes smelled of hemp.

A different group were women cuddling small, slicked-up children, waiting to see Daddy or Grandpa. Some wore too much makeup, clothes that were too bright, high heels.

Clark always dressed the same for these occasions: worn clean Levi's, flannel shirt, scuffed work shoes. He didn't want inmates or their visitors spotting him as a mark, someone to tap for protection money if they threatened Wade with any violence.

Clark hated the bright orange jumpsuit Wade had to wear. The color made him look sick and sallow. When the guards first directed him to the phones, Wade looked downcast, but he brightened when he saw Clark and gave him a little half-wave. They sat on black plastic stools, the bulletproof glass in between, and both picked up the phones. "Hey, Dad. How did the truck run coming down?"

"Good," Clark said. "You're not going to have one of your buddies steal it, are you?"

"No way!" Wade grimaced. "I warned them nobody touches my dad's truck. It's a Ford, isn't it? A big, green Ford."

"A Chev, Wade. Don't you remember? We bought it from Uncle Roy and he sells Chevys."

"What's the license plate number?"

Clark made one up, even though he doubted Wade could remember the numbers. Some of the jail's trustees worked at the Department of Motor Vehicles, and he didn't want them accessing information with his license plate or Social Security number.

"M-C-L-eight-seven-oh." Wade repeated, closing his eyes. "They won't go bothering it, Dad. They're my buddies. They listen to what I tell them."

"That's good. I'd hate to walk home. So how's it going?"

"Not so good. I was running and I tripped down the steps and hurt my knee. They put ice on it and everything. Took me to the hospital for X rays. You should have seen the nurses, Dad. Man oh man! One even gave me her phone number. She thought I was federal."

"What about the knee? Is it okay?"

"Just a little water on the kneecap. I'm tough, Dad."

"Okay. Well, be careful. Don't go running around in there. What's 'federal' mean, anyway?"

Wade smiled. "Big time. Bad ass. Like in federal jails. The guys call me that because I've been in here so much."

Clark shook his head. "Listen. I left money for you at the commissary. It should buy one candy bar, one soda, and a bag of chips every day until I get back. Three things." He held up three fingers. "Only three a day."

Wade grabbed his throat, making a choking sound. "The food is terrible in here, Dad. Makes me burp and fart like an old grampy." He giggled. "Fart and fart and stink up my cell. Burns off the paint. I got to take Rolaids to sleep."

"Maybe you shouldn't steal any more cars. That way you wouldn't have to eat jail food. I think a Big Mac would taste better."

"Big Mac attack!" Wade started clowning, rocking back and forth on the stool, opening his mouth and snapping it closed. "I got a Big Mac attack."

Clark rapped on the glass with his free hand. "Hey, buddy. A Mac Attack won't do you much good in here. When you get out, if you promise not to steal more cars, I'll buy you a hundred Big Macs."

"People shouldn't leave their keys in the car." Wade's face grew puzzled. "Why do they leave them in the cars, Dad? It's not really stealing, is it? I'm just driving them around." Before Clark could answer, he rushed on. "When am I getting out? I want to ride my bike over to the hospital and see those nurses."

Clark rapped the glass again. "Now pay attention, Wade. You've got four more months left in here." He held up four fingers. "Four more months."

Wade's face grew puzzled. "How long is four months? That's about a year?"

"No. Did you get that Elvis calendar I sent you? It's four pages under his pictures. Four pictures. Start with *Blue Hawaii*. That's this month. Then *Flaming Star* . . ."

"They wouldn't let me keep the calendar." Wade lowered his head, dejected. "I liked those Elvis pictures, though. When I get out, they'll give it back."

"Shit. I'll talk to Ricketts about it." Clark knew Wade would just get confused about the months and days without a calendar. With the calendar, it wasn't easy. "Hey, you remember that good-looking red shirt with the pineapple design Elvis wore in *Blue Hawaii*? And all those pretty girls in bikinis who came to see him play guitar on the beach. If you quit stealing cars, I'll take you to Hawaii. We can buy fancy pineapple shirts just like Elvis. And you can try surfing in that sparkling blue water."

"That's a promise, huh, Dad?"

"You bet."

Wade half closed his eyes and tried crooning into the mouthpiece. "I'll have a blue, blue Christmas without you. A blue, blue Christmas without you."

The fat inmate next to him shot the boy a dirty look and said something offensive.

Wade started on "Blue Suede Shoes."

Clark remembered junior high school dances in Prineville, the pretty girls swirling in taffeta skirts, smelling like lipstick and perfume. He and Darrell Maxwell went to Portland and bought blue suede shoes in the Lloyd Center. They attended the dances wearing silver-threaded shirts, black tapered jeans, silver belts, skinny as a shoelace. When they were hoeing mint and bucking bales, summer jobs to earn money for school clothes, life had seemed simple. Win the basketball games; kiss the girls; go to college. Clark never imagined he'd be visiting his boy in jail.

"You ain't nothing but a hound dog, just crying all the time!" Wade was loud enough to disturb the other conversations, so the guard came over, gripped his shoulder, and told him to knock off the singing. Wade started to rise, ready to replace the receiver and return to his cell.

Clark rapped the window and looked at the clock. He held up three fingers to the guard and pointed at the clock.

"Cool it," Clark told Wade. "I didn't drive two hours down here to get cheated out of three minutes."

"Did you leave money for me, Dad?"

"Yes. You can buy three treats a day. Four on Saturday and Sunday."

"Three and four." Wade nodded. "I got it, Dad. I ran out of money last week."

Time was up and the guard took Wade's phone. "I love you, boy," Clark said, uncertain Wade heard, but he could read his lips.

Clark gave him a thumbs-up and Wade returned it. As Clark was hanging up his receiver, a slim man of about thirty slid onto the stool across from him and gestured that he wanted to talk.

"You must be Mr. Woods." He smiled showing capped teeth. Veins bulged on his thin wrists and his biceps had blue and red panthers. "Wade thinks a lot of you."

Clark was on his guard. "Not enough to quit stealing cars."

The man grinned. "Just a little joy riding. Remember when we were that age? Driving all over town looking for pussy and beer? That's no biggie. I got my first juvie bust for stealing a '56 BelAir." He smiled at the memory. "It was cherry."

He placed his right hand against the glass, as if to shake. "Terry Knorr. Inside, they call me 'Kitty' because of these tattoos." He indicated the panthers. "I just want to let you know, I'm watching out for Wade, him being a juvie and all. When we have rec time, I keep track of him, just like a big brother or something."

"Thanks. I appreciate that."

"I share my coffee with him. If the deps aren't looking, we'll sneak him a cigarette." Knorr spread his hands. "Smoking calms my nerves.

"Anyway, I just thought I'd say hello." He squinted at Clark. "Wade said you wrote a book. Man, you should write my life's story. They got me on a bogus armed robbery rap. Now they want to ship me out to Salem to do a dime." He shook his head. "Ten years. That's hard time." He brightened a little. "Hey, maybe I'll get off and enroll at Two Rivers. You can help me ghost write the book."

The jailor stepped behind Knorr and placed a hand on his shoulder.

"Man, Last Dance already." He winked and gave Clark a grin. "Just when we were getting acquainted."

"Thanks for helping Wade," Clark said, wondering if Knorr really was any help inside.

"No biggie. No biggie at all. But when I'm gone, someone else needs to watch out for that squirrely kid."

Clark hung up the phone. It was almost eight-thirty and most of the visitors had left. He picked up his driver's license from Ricketts. "Thanks," he said. "Hey, I got a question for you. I sent my boy Wade an Elvis calendar. He's crazy about Elvis. Anyway, Wade says they wouldn't let him keep it in the cell. They showed him the pictures and then took it away. What gives?"

"They can't keep that stuff that's sent in," Ricketts said. "Not even letters. We read them the letters. See, people might put LSD on the stamps or something. Maybe they soak some of the pages so the inmates suck them."

"You think I'm going to soak an Elvis calendar with LSD?"

"Not you, but somebody. It may sound crazy, but I've seen some things. We've got druggie Grandmas running loose out there."

"I believe it." Clark's tone softened. "This is Eugene, right?"

"I live in Springfield," Ricketts said. "Eugene is too screwball weird."

*　　*　　*

Clark didn't arrive home until almost one. He had eaten dinner in Eugene, then lingered at the Woodburn truck stop having a second cup of coffee and a piece of cherry pie. The conversation with Knorr worried him. Was the guy going to try something? Maybe a shakedown? Or did he just want to write his life story? Clark decided not to tell Natalie about Knorr.

She was awake when he went upstairs. "You're late."

"It was foggy. I had to go slow. And I stopped for coffee." He got undressed quickly and slipped into bed.

"Do you think it's a good idea driving down there so much? You're always wiped out the next day for work. And Helen really missed you tonight."

"It's not my favorite pastime. Turn off the light, would you? I'm whipped."

"Do you think Wade hates us for sending him away? Do you think he hates Helen?"

I can't deal with all her questions, Clark thought. *Just let me sleep, for Christ's sake.*

"No, of course not," he said. "He always asks about you and Helen." Clark figured a lie was easier than trying to explain why Wade didn't ask about them.

"I worry that he's going to show up here and do us some harm. What if he blames us? What if he tries to hurt us or hurt Helen?"

"Wade's not like that."

"Then why did he stab the dog? Remember Karen Fredericks's aunt and uncle in Detroit? They took in a foster boy and raised him for six years. One day years later they pulled into their driveway and when they stepped out of the car, he shot them to death. He'd been hiding in the bushes."

"He's not Wade. Wade's okay." Clark knew he wasn't convincing her; his words sounded flat and repetitive even to him. He got up and went downstairs, hoping she wouldn't follow.

Clark sat in the dark kitchen, sipping Metaxa and staring out the window at the tall fir trees half a block away. He pretended the trees were high in the Wallowa mountains where his uncle Roy kept an elk camp. Now he knew why men went up there—not to hunt, that was the excuse—but to find some peace. At camp, the wind swayed the tall evergreens and the campfires crackled, sending sparks into the night sky. No counselors, no evaluations, no jails. No worries about Wade. No nagging questions. Clark doubted that he'd ever get a week of peace to restore his soul.

. . .

"What the hell happened, Wade?" Clark was alarmed at the boy's appearance. He had a deep bruise, plum-colored, around his left eye and a bandage covering a row of stitches on his chin. He walked with a hitch as if his side hurt.

Wade's eyes were downcast and his lower lip hung out. "I got in a fight, but it wasn't my fault. Two guys beat me up playing basketball. They knocked me down and kicked me, pushed my head into the concrete." He rubbed his chin. "Nine stitches, the doctor said."

"Where were the goddamn guards?"

Wade shrugged. "Who knows. I guess they were having a smoke. A bunch of guys crowded around yelling, but no one helped me."

"I thought Knorr was watching out for you."

Wade shrugged. "He got sent to Salem."

"I'll talk to somebody, Wade. You shouldn't get picked on in there." He was angry Ricketts was away. "Did the doctor give you some Rolaids or something to help with your stomach?"

Wade nodded. "The food's lousy," he said. "They say the cook jacks off in the soup." He made a little giggle. "Soupy-soup, tastes like poop." He grinned, but then winced in pain and clamped his mouth shut. "My chinny-chin hurts."

"I know the food isn't very good, but I'm sure the cook doesn't do that."

"Dad, Jake was in here. He's running five miles every day. I got to get out and start training, but I can't even go to the rec yard."

"Why not?"

"They wrote me up for fighting, but it wasn't my fault. Those other guys started it. When I missed an easy shot, they called me a spastic Indian. What's spastic, anyway? Then they called me a retard."

Wade's face grew long. "Listen, Dad. I don't want to be in here anymore. I'm afraid of getting beat up again. Please help me. I don't want to live with the Stanleys either. I want to come back to live with you and Mom. *Please.* I can help you take care of Helen and I promise to do more chores. Mow the grass, take out the garbage, anything you need." He paused. "At the Stanleys', I carry groceries and stack wood. I'm a big help. You ask Cathy."

Clark felt as if he'd been clubbed. He couldn't speak.

Wade paused, then shook the black receiver. "Can you hear me, Dad?"

The guard stood behind Wade and tapped his shoulder.

"Dad, can you hear me?"

Wade's desperate voice sounded as if it were coming across the ocean. "I hear you," Clark said. "Hang tough, buddy. We'll figure out something."

Wade hung up the receiver and slowly shuffled through the green door. He paused once, looking back over his shoulder, and Clark saw in his eyes the fear of a lost child.

Other conversations hummed around him, but Clark remained on the hard black stool. He felt like a diver trapped on the ocean floor. No air. The helmet filling with water.

* * * *

April Hedin took a sip from her water bottle. She seemed confused by the strategy Clark, RealBird, and Cathy Stanley had offered. "If he's out on bail but doesn't show up for trial, the judge will issue a bench warrant for his arrest," Hedin said.

"He'll be in Angoon visiting his uncle," Clark said.

"An extended visit," RealBird added.

Clark was certain that the details could be arranged—no problem. The most difficult part for him had been calling Payette and asking for advice. She had been helpful, suggesting that Wade go back to Angoon where there were practically no roads or cars, and where his uncle Sampson Frank could try raising him. She'd made a couple of calls on Wade's behalf.

"But I can't get him released to your custody, since you're no longer his guardian," Hedin told Clark.

"I'm just putting up the bail," Clark said. "Release him to the Stanleys if you want."

"You realize you'll forfeit the bail?"

Clark shrugged. "If it helps Wade . . ."

"Look. It's fairly simple," RealBird said. "I've talked with Larry Squamish up in Juneau; he's also the one Wade's cousin, Mr. Woods's former wife, contacted, and Mr. Squamish will do the necessary paperwork to have Wade become a ward of his tribe and his uncle, Sampson Frank. It's according to tribal custom. When a boy becomes a teenager, the maternal uncle is responsible for his upbringing, especially if the father is killed. Frank is taking on that responsibility."

Hedin sipped some more water, then took off her reading glasses and massaged the bridge of her nose. "How can we shift guardianship when there's all this car theft business and a court date?"

"The tribe will sign guardian papers. Oregon's not going to fight Alaska and the tribe for this kid," Clark said. "If it went to the Supreme Court, the tribe would win."

RealBird leaned toward her. "The Tlingit have their own way of doing things. Remember when those two Tlingit boys in Juneau got in trouble for stealing cars and vandalism? The state of Alaska gave custody to the tribe and they banished them to an island instead of prison. That was their traditional way, not prison."

Hedin leaned back in her chair. "I sort of remember. How did it turn out?"

"One made it. One went to prison." RealBird tapped her chair's arm. "That's a lot better rate than our prison system."

Clark sensed Hedin was leaning toward their plan. "See, Angoon is a little village on an island," Clark said. "Only a couple miles of roads. No point in stealing a car. It's isolated, and right now Wade's uncle Sampson needs help. He's carving totem poles for a ceremony and his hands are crippled with arthritis. So Wade can keep out of trouble by helping him."

Hedin turned toward Cathy Stanley. "You think this is a good idea?"

Cathy nodded. "We've been praying hard about it. I think this is the answer. Every time he gets home from jail, we keep a close eye on him, but eventually he has to have some freedom. After all, he's sixteen and all those hormones are kicking in. So he rides around on his bike, and when he sees the chance to take a car, he does. Every police officer in Eugene knows Wade and his bike. If they find that bike abandoned anywhere near the location of a stolen car, their radar locks on Wade. And usually, they're right." She paused. "Over the years we've had a lot of Indian children in our care. Many of them eventually go home."

Hedin opened the thick green file on her desk. "Seventeen cars. Minor damage to six, major to three. The boy's a menace. Damn lucky he hasn't run over somebody."

Clark tugged at his tie. He had dressed up for the meeting. "I'll tell you the truth. I was so afraid he might run over somebody, I've been kind of glad to have him in jail. That keeps people safe on the street. But after this beating . . . I'm really worried for Wade."

Hedin snapped the folder shut. "I'll tell you what worries me. All the politicians keep pushing 'Tough on Crime' bills and we keep building prison after prison. If Oregon voters adopt a three strikes and you're out law, Wade might be locked up for life. The judge won't have any leeway."

"At least Wade might have a chance in Alaska," Clark said, praying under his breath.

Hedin tapped at Wade's file. "If he stayed here, we could get him into a program. We have several for young offenders."

"Most programs are full," RealBird said. "What's the waiting time?"

"A year, maybe six months if we move him ahead on the list."

"Listen, no offense," Clark said, "but he's been in programs all his life. This is how it turned out. I don't want to see him programmed all the way to the state pen."

Hedin turned to RealBird. "What's your take on all this, Doctor?"

"I think Mr. Woods is right. The recalcitrant rate for juveniles is alarming. With Indians, over seventy percent who enter juvenile programs wind up in prison." She paused. "Clearly, something's not working. If he goes to Alaska, who knows? I've seen some miracles, real turnarounds. And even if it fails, God forbid, at least we tried."

Hedin folded her hands. "Okay. I'm not entirely convinced, but I've got you people to share the blame. Anyway, I was looking around for another job. Maybe a quiet bed-and-breakfast on the coast." She shook her head. "I must be nuts for listening to your plan."

Clark was relieved. "We're consultants. Everyone's a consultant these days."

"I thought we were enablers," RealBird said.

"Make sure the bail check doesn't bounce," Hedin told him.

Clark handed it to her. "Good as gold." *A down payment on a new truck,* he thought. *Right out the window.*

She wrote Clark a receipt and slipped the check in Wade's file. "You can pick Wade up Thursday at eleven. Whatever you do, don't let him steal another car."

"Short leash," Clark said. He thought of the projects. Crate up Wade's bike, pack his clothes, guitar, Elvis memorabilia. Say good-bye to Natalie and Helen. Stop by to see if Red Stroud and Tony were around.

"Angoon," he kept saying on the drive to Portland. "Angoon." A mantra, a prayer.

20

Angoon, 1987

Clark strained to see Angoon through the small plane's rain-streaked window, but all he saw below were clouds, misty gray-green islands, and the rough waters of Chatham Strait. The plane bounced around in the air currents, making him queasy. Leaving Sitka, the ride had been exciting. Coming over Baranof Island, Clark had seen three mountain goats in the high alpine meadows. Brilliant yellow flowers covered the mountain slopes. However, as the weather became gloomy closer to Angoon, Clark began to feel uneasy about the journey. How would Wade respond toward him after two years' separation? How much would the young man be changed?

What Clark knew of Angoon's history slipped through his mind like phantoms. Old myths and superstitions that held the same credibility as recorded history. Distrust of outsiders, witchcraft, warfare and slave raids, the naval bombardment.

He didn't know what sort of greeting he'd get. Wade and Sampson had invited him to attend a celebration honoring Angoon's survival over one hundred years after the Navy had tried to destroy the village. For the occasion, Sampson and the other carvers had created six totems dedicated to the clan houses that the Navy shelled. Wade had helped with the rough physical labor.

For two years, Clark had postponed visiting Wade in Angoon, but now he felt compelled to see him. Phone calls on Christmas and the boy's birthdays, letters a schoolteacher wrote for Wade, and half a dozen Polaroids had presented only the sketchiest view of Wade's life in southeast Alaska.

Whatever he found in Angoon, Clark knew that he was powerless to change it now or to offer Wade anything but encouragement. Without Payette, he could never wrest the boy from the Tlingits, nor could he take him back to Natalie and Helen.

During the two years Wade had been north, Clark concentrated on memories and photos of him as a child: Wade riding his bike, swimming, fishing, running with Tony through the fields. He knew he had saved his marriage by sending Wade to Angoon, yet guilt dogged him. People judged him a failure, he figured. Even Grace, though delighted with her granddaughter, remained silent whenever the subject of Angoon came up. And Clark believed he saw accusation in her eyes.

"If someone hasn't done this every day over the years, they can't know what it's like from the inside," Natalie had said. "They don't have the right to play judge."

He knew Natalie was right, in a way. Still, Clark blamed himself. Failures haunted him: Payette, her miscarriage or abortion; Yukiko, Clark's broken promise to Kagita; Wade shipped off to Angoon. Staring at the clouds outside the plane's window, Clark recalled the sign at the Crippled Children's Hospital. SAVE A CHILD AND YOU SAVE A UNIVERSE. *I've left more wreckage than an earthquake,* Clark thought. *I had Wade for many years and what universe did I save?*

. . .

Angoon had no restaurant, coffee shop, or motel. Sampson told Clark that he could bunk and eat in the clan house, but he didn't know what that meant. RealBird had called the nurse's aide at Angoon's small health clinic in case Clark needed another contact.

He chuckled as he remembered that before Natalie's mother had gone up to Vermont for a weaving class, she bought toothpaste and soap, tea and coffee. She wasn't sure if you could buy those things in Vermont. Now in one of his packs, he carried cheese, salami, apples, and Snickers bars.

"Big doings in Angoon," Buddy, the pilot, said. "Some kind of mucky-muck tribal celebration. I've flown a few people over, but most came by ferry. I can't get all their costumes and drums on the plane."

"They're celebrating over one hundred years after the Navy bombed them," Clark told him. He wondered what the Tlingits had thought when they saw the Revenue cutter *Service* steam in close to shore. The only raiders they'd experienced previously were the Haida from down south, paddling in forty-foot dugout war canoes. Although the two tribes had brutal hand-to-hand combats over territory and slaves, the ferocious Tlingit warriors usually repelled the Haida attackers. However, the U.S. Navy's gunships sitting offshore and shelling the helpless villagers was another type of warfare altogether. "The Navy almost wiped them out," Clark told Buddy. "It's been a long struggle back."

"Yeah, this is a hard-luck place," Buddy said. "No jobs, no paved roads, bears marauding through town. Witchcraft and booze. I wouldn't want to live here."

They hit an air pocket, and Clark winced.

Buddy asked, "How's the stomach?"

"Not bad," Clark said. "I used to work the Great Lakes. Big winter storms."

"I hear you." Buddy grinned. "One morning I had five passengers from a bed-and-breakfast in Sitka. They'd eaten salmon omelets. When they started puking, the whole inside of this plane smelled like bad fish. If you want a sick bag, it's right in front of you."

"I'm okay." Clark swallowed hard.

Buddy tapped Clark's shoulder and pointed below. "Danger Point. Then Angoon."

Through a stretch of fogless sky, Clark saw the tall blue water tower, clumps of mustard-yellow houses huddled on the hillsides, older corrugated-roof houses stretched along the rocky shore. Muddy dirt roads, half a dozen kids on bikes, a dozen dogs, two moving vehicles. Although the village clung tenaciously to the rocky spit, it seemed fragile and temporary, as if one good wave would wash it to oblivion.

The houses gave way to forest and a rough dirt road ending at a small ferry terminal. Across a narrow channel lay Killisnoo Island. The Tlingit word meant "fortress of the bears" because of all the roaming grizzlies. At the turn of the nineteenth century, Killisnoo had been the largest settlement in Alaska, with a thriving whale hunting station and a rendering plant to make oil from the whales and herring. Before petroleum was discovered, whale oil was important for lamps. Now Killisnoo was abandoned, except for a small fishermen's lodge where Wade worked part-time, cleaning fish for the doctors and dentists from the Lower Forty-eight.

Buddy banked the plane and descended to a clear bay halfway between the town and the small ferry terminal. "Next stop Angoon," he said. "If you lived here, you'd be home."

As they taxied the pontoon plane toward the shore, Clark saw two figures standing on the dock, one taller than the other. The taller one seemed to be waving at the plane.

Wade, Clark thought, catching his breath.

"Someone you know?" Buddy asked.

"Maybe," Clark said, his throat tight. *God, I hope so.*

* * *

Clark hadn't known how he would feel when he met Wade again, and now he stood gripping his gear in both hands, unsure about the young man before him. Wade loomed taller than Sampson and his shoulders had broadened. His hair was almost shoulder-length, and he sported a wispy goatee and mustache. He grinned, showing a broken tooth.

"Dad!"

As soon as Clark heard Wade's voice, years fell away, and he dropped the gear and grabbed him in a bear hug, biting his lip to hold back the tears. "You're grown up, fella."

"Taller than you, Dad."

Clark noticed he slurred the *r*'s just as he had done since Clark had first known him. Somehow that was reassuring—a reminder of their shared past. Clark stepped back and gave Wade a long look. "What happened to that tooth?"

"He got in a fight," Sampson said. "Good to see you." He reached out his hand and they shook lightly, the Tlingit way. "Nothing too bad. The new kid always has to prove himself."

"I know about that," Clark said, remembering the challenges he had faced as his mother moved from one hardscrabble town to another.

"I whipped 'em good, Dad. You should've seen me. There were three, and one guy was like seven feet tall, and I thumped 'em . . ."

"Not that tall," Sampson said. "Well, maybe six and a half feet. I think there were two, not three." He winked at Clark. "Fish stories. Anyway, let's get your gear put up and we'll show you around."

●   ●   ●

"Okay, let me get your picture." Clark aimed the camera's viewfinder at Wade and Sampson as they stood next to the Raven totem on a knoll overlooking Angoon. Clark knew that Raven had created the Tlingit land, water, and fish. All villages belonged to Raven or Eagle. Raven men married Eagle women and vice versa, so the villages shared close ties. Angoon was a Raven village populated equally by both clans. Along with other carvers, Wade and Sampson had created the Raven, one of six totems to be dedicated at the ceremony. Five stood on the knoll, but the sixth was missing.

Compared with the elaborate Sitka totems which featured intricate, decorated figures carved the entire length of the cedar pole, Angoon's totems seemed small and stark. *Like the town itself,* Clark thought. *No boatloads of Japanese tourists would stop here to take pictures. This is no tourist destination.* Here, a single crest figure topped each pole.

Wade squinted at the camera, the corners of his mouth drawn down as if he were trying not to smile. The shutter snapped. "Got it," Clark said. At least it would be an improvement over some of the old photos. Before he left for the trip, Clark had looked for some pictures to bring, and found one from Helen's first birthday party. Natalie stood at the kitchen table grinning and holding up Helen. Wade hung at her side, his stare angry and sullen. The baby twisted away from the camera, reaching her hand out to touch Wade. *My God,* Clark had thought, startled. *We never saw that anger in his face. Or the baby reaching out to him. The camera had captured a moment outside of us, outside of our lives.* He stuffed the photo back into the box and left it in Portland.

●   ●   ●

"This is Raven." Wade thumped the yellow cedar pole with an air of authority. Clearly, he enjoyed showing Clark around. "That one's

Eagle. It's got a crooked beak." A look of confusion passed across his face and he called to Sampson, "Doesn't the Eagle one got a crooked beak?"

"Yeah, Wade. The Raven's got a straight one."

"Right." Wade repeated solemnly. "The Raven's got a straight one. The Beaver and the Bear got big teeth and ears."

"Where's the Killer Whale?" Clark asked.

"Along the waterfront by the new clan houses," Sampson told him. "We'll take you down there."

From the knoll, Clark could see most of the village. Tall crimson fireweed filled vacant lots, nearly obscuring the junked cars and boats. Pink, purple, and green bicycles decorated the front lawns of mustard-yellow BIA houses. The deep blue water in Chatham Strait sparkled in the sunlight. *This is a beautiful landscape,* he thought.

"See those trailers down there?" Sampson pointed to a huddle of tiny silver trailers behind the school.

"Classrooms?"

"Nah. The white teachers stay there packed in like herring. No one lasts more than a couple years up here. Too isolated. Too rainy. Pays good, though. If you want a job, I'm on the school board."

"Thanks, but no thanks." The idea of spending ten rainy months in this remote place, cramped in a trailer, confounded him. Even worse, he wondered how many of the students would be damaged like Wade. "Maybe if I were younger," he said. "Anyway, my wife thinks Portland's remote enough. She's from the East Coast."

Sampson nodded. "We get teachers from there, too. They come out of those fancy schools back East and travel all this way to help us. Only trouble is, we're doing okay without their help. They think we've got some big Tlingit secret about life." He shrugged. "Most leave by February."

. . .

As they got into Sampson's Jeep Cherokee, Wade climbed behind the wheel.

"So you're driving legal now?" Clark asked.

Wade grinned. "I don't got a license, but out here no one cares. Anyway, the policeman is Sampson's cousin. I get to drive the old people to the Senior Center for lunch and over to the clinic for their blood pressure checks."

"I hope you don't drive like the Dukes."

"No way. I can't spin out or the old women cuss me good."

Clark wondered about Wade's reliability. He still couldn't tell time. Sampson had stuck strips of duct tape on the Jeep's dashboard. Each strip indicated the positions of the clock hands, showing Wade when to run errands. But it wasn't Clark's place to question anymore. He had lost that right when he gave up Wade.

As they drove through town, Clark saw kids passing cigarettes. Several houses had signs: KEEP KIDS OFF DRUGS. Scribbled in crayon, other signs read: KEEP MOM AND DAD OFF DRUGS. *In the land of the blind . . .* Clark thought. *Maybe up here Wade was one of the more reliable ones.*

After driving downhill to the waterfront street, they passed a Presbyterian church and a blue house with a crude sign featuring a pencil-outlined popsicle and the faded wording:

CHERRY POPSICLES—50¢—BIGGER
AND EVEN BETTER THIS YEAR.

"See that?" Sampson asked, and when Clark nodded, he added, "Popsicle Clan. A good-looking girl lived there, but last summer Wade pestered her so much she took off to Sitka."

"I did not. She went to live with her aunt." Wade frowned.

"Relax. I'm teasing." Sampson put his hand on Wade's shoulder.

For a moment Clark felt a twinge of jealousy at their easy familiarity. *Much like I used to have with him,* Clark thought, but he said, "What about the signs that say 'Keep Mom and Dad Off Drugs'?"

"Whiskey Clan. Cocaine Clan." Sampson shook his head. "We got problems. A school board member was bootlegging whiskey and selling it to the high school students. Eighty dollars a bottle. They could buy good stuff off the ferries for sixty, but by midweek, some of them get desperate."

"Where are the real clan houses?" Clark asked.

"You're looking at them." Sampson indicated the houses they were driving past. "All along the waterfront."

Clark was surprised because the new clan houses lacked crests and were indistinguishable from the other places in Angoon. The exception was one small white house with a double Killer Whale emblem facing the water.

Wade stopped the Jeep and pointed at the Killer Whale pole in front of the house. "There's the totem."

"This isn't as big as the totems up the hill," Clark said. He figured it was less than ten feet tall.

"The Killer Whale is so powerful, it doesn't need to be big," Sampson said. "It protects the village, so we put it down close to the water, in a place of high honor. When we have the ceremony tomorrow, maybe killer whales will come. They're out around Sitka, but usually a couple pods hang out in Chatham Strait, too. We haven't seen any so far this season. Guess they're waiting to hear me drum and sing."

"You guys did a great job with the totems," Clark said as he studied the impassive carved face of the Killer Whale. He remembered reading the story of Angoon's shelling at the Newberry Library—how the six children had huddled in the clan houses, scared and certain they would be protected by their totem spirits, but had burned to death. *The totems had failed them,* Clark thought. *Would they watch over Wade now?*

Clark could hear one of Grace's favorite expressions: "Well, I don't understand all I know about." And he remembered Natalie's words back in her Northampton apartment. *We don't have all the answers,* she had said after his chance meeting with Mr. Kagita. *Maybe God does.*

We all look to our own faith, our own totem spirits, Clark thought.

He knew Wade didn't really understand much about the carvings, but it didn't matter because now the boy was part of something; he was helping rebuild a ravaged past.

* * *

"My cousin Boots Charley is a powerful spiritual leader," Sampson told Clark. "Visitors always want to learn about Tlingit spirit paths. Lots of anthropologists traveled way out here just to study us. During winter dances you couldn't throw a salmon over your shoulder without smacking a professor puffing on a pipe and taking notes."

Clark studied Sampson, but the old man's sober expression didn't change. Wade concentrated on driving, lifting one finger from the wheel if they saw a young woman.

"They wrote down what we ate, what we wore, how we sang," Sampson continued. "Tape recorders, video cameras—all that stuff. Mention witchcraft and they went crazy. Anything primitive, they got into whole hog. Right down to the cloven hooves." Sampson touched Clark's shoulder. "You interested in all that hocus-pocus?"

"A little, I suppose." Clark wondered how much Sampson was leading him on.

"Boots is your man. He and my dad were responsible for a boat-load of Ph.D.s. But we haven't seen those professor types lately. I guess their grants ran out."

Wade braked abruptly in front of a tidy yellow house perched above the bay.

"Jesus, Wade!" Sampson said as he pitched forward. "Take it easy."

"Brakes are good, tires are fair," Wade cracked.

A huge satellite dish and three flamingos served as lawn ornaments.

*   *   *

Clark studied the shaman's gear hanging on Boots's front room wall: a sealskin drum with a weasel emblem; Killer Whale dancing sticks; a moose-hide apron decorated with puffin beaks and bear claws. Boots's Navy pictures showed him standing beside a destroyer escort and holding hands with a beautiful dark woman in tribal costume. The profusion of tropical flowers in one picture indicated a climate far from Angoon.

Boots reclined on a green La-Z-Boy drinking a cup of tea and watching television. He still wore plaid pajamas although it was close to suppertime. According to Sampson, Boots had a neurological disorder that Indian Health doctors failed to diagnose. His limbs had withered, and he trembled even as he sat. Although now Boots appeared frail, his broad shoulders and wide wrists indicated a once-powerful physique.

Oral Roberts appeared jaundiced on the large television. He seemed to shout his predicament because Boots had the volume cranked so high. God had instructed Oral to raise fifteen million or He planned to call him "home to glory" early. While faithful contributors had sent in most of the amount required, Satan had prevented Oral from receiving the rest.

As Oral lamented his unfinished earthly business and exhorted the viewers to send in the seven million, tears streamed down his cheeks. Clark wondered if he actually believed his own spiel.

"I like Billy Graham better," Boots finally said, turning down the volume so Clark could hear. "To me, Billy makes a lot more sense. And he's not putting his hand in your pocket. Don't you think Billy is more sincere?"

After a moment's hesitation, Clark said, "I guess if I had to choose one, my vote would go to Billy."

"That settles it." Boots tried snapping his fingers, but his crippled hands prevented them from making a sound. "I'll have to tell Sampson we agree." Boots sipped his tea. "He's so stubborn, he claims they're all hucksters, but he's hooked on pro wrestling. How phony is that? Any time Gorgeous George comes on, Sampson's glued to the spot. I can't watch my shows."

Clark smiled. "You guys sound like typical relatives."

"Quarreling all the time. Everyone in Angoon used to argue outside in the streets. People yelled, dogs howled, bears coughed. That was fun. But now that we got TV, everyone stays inside to quarrel." He spread his hands. "Bad for gossip."

Clark nodded. "In a town like this, rumors must race like wildfire."

"Faster. So much rain up here, wildfire's kind of slow." He smiled.

Clark nodded. "Thinking about gossip, I heard people still practice witchcraft out here. Any truth to it?"

Boots handed Clark his teacup. "If I'm going to talk about witches, I need to wet my whistle. Check the cupboard above the sink for a bottle. No ice, no water. Pour a splash for yourself."

Clark rinsed out Boots's cup and found a Seagram's 7 bottle. Filling two cups half full, he returned to see that Boots had shifted to his wheelchair and moved underneath the shaman's gear.

After taking a drink, Boots said, "This shaman stuff belonged to White Weasel, one of the most powerful old village shamans. He was my mother's great-uncle, so the trappings passed down to me. All his other stuff got stolen, sold to museum people.

"Way out here, witchcraft hurts us, drives us apart, causes lots of trouble. Anyplace that's real isolated, where people have carried grudges, there's witchcraft." He took a drink. "People turn jealous and want an advantage, so they use witches to make other people real sick. They send a mouse helper to collect people's food drippings or fingernails." He held up his hands so Clark could see neatly trimmed nails. "I burn all my nail clippings. Hair trimmings, too."

Clark stared at the large cross Boots wore around his neck. He was surprised to find himself wondering about the possibility of Boots being witched.

"'Dirty stuff' is what the witches call those drippings and fingernails. They take all that dirty stuff and wrap it in straws to make a little doll, then bury it in the ground with a corpse. Sometimes they put that doll in the mouth of a dead dog, and sink it upside down in a pond. After a doll is placed, the witched person starts getting sick. If the dirty stuff was hair, he might get terrible headaches. Saliva and food mean their throats and tongues swell up so they can't talk right or quit breathing. Toenails and fingernails cause crippling arthritis of the hands and feet. Witchery is horrible to see."

"What about Wade's mother, Amber?" Clark asked. "Do you think she carried on any witchcraft?"

"If you don't have Jesus, then Satan gets a strong foothold." Boots fingered the large cross. "Jesus keeps the devil at a distance. Sampson talks about land otters stealing people away. Others talk about witches. But it's all inspired by Satan wrecking lives." He shook his head. "Amber, she was a hard case, right from the get-go. A sniffer straight out of grade school—glue, antifreeze, Lysol, Hair-Net. When she got old enough to go to Juneau she added drinking to sniffing."

"That's tough," Clark said.

"I know about the hard cases," Boots said. "How do you think I got tagged with this name?"

"I figured you liked boots, maybe." Where Clark grew up, most of the Indians wore black cowboy boots.

"I liked boot *polish*," the old man said. "Sniffing the fumes, drinking the liquid, eating the paste. In the Navy, I'd smear black parade gloss on white bread like peanut butter. A Shinola sandwich. Kiwi and carrot sticks. Anything for a kick!"

Clark tried to imagine devouring shoe polish. Just the thought made his tongue thick.

Closing his eyes, Boots said, "Even now, I can remember the jolt." Touching two fingers to his forehead, he added, "It's burned deep in my skull, so now I lean on Jesus. Without Him, I can stumble, fall, and crawl." Opening his eyes, he fixed Clark with his gaze. "I know these young people's fiery demons."

"What about the cure?" Clark asked.

Boots shifted in his wheelchair, leaning back a little so he could touch the moose-hide apron on the wall. "In the old days, we had shamans to fight witches. But when the diseases came and the villagers were dying, the shamans seemed powerless, so people lost faith."

"Once it was different. My great-great-uncle White Weasel came from a little settlement over on Killisnoo. When the witching got bad, they sent for White Weasel. I saw him once, and he scared me to death. Shamans never cut their hair, and White Weasel's hung in eight long braids, some dragging on the ground." Boots ran his twisted hand across the apron. "That moose-hide outfit has over a hundred bear claws and those puffin beaks clacked as he danced. He carried a dance stick with three land otter heads. Somehow their eyes stayed big and sleepy soft even after they were dead. They should have looked like dull buttons, but they didn't. People turned their faces away from that stick, so they wouldn't get transformed into otters.

"White Weasel never missed finding a witch, sniffing her out. One time an old woman named Betsy Tall Bear called for the shaman because her son and daughter-in-law, her husband and brother were all suffering from witchcraft. Before Betsy even knew he showed up, White Weasel trapped a mouse inside her house. She was off at her fish shed. That night, when all the family had gathered, including some village elders, White Weasel took that mouse and put it inside a human skull, covered with wire mesh so the mouse couldn't get away. He'd dance a little, shaking the puffin beaks and pointing that dance stick at people so they got nervous. Using his foot as he danced, he slid that skull closer to the fire. Pretty soon old Betsy, who called him about the witch, she started talking faster and faster as the mouse raced around inside the skull, afraid of the flames.

"White Weasel, he'd chant some more and nudge that skull closer to the fire with his dance stick. When the skull got real hot, that old woman started sweating nervously and moving around the clan house just like that mouse was running around the skull. When he put the mouse right by the fire, so it was getting singed good, she started screaming and slapping her face, then shrieking like crazy. That cunning old shaman knew he had her then. Betsy was the witch herself, and had summoned him just to throw off suspicion. He made her remove the dolls from all the people she'd been witching on.

"White Weasel took her way up on the hill to the graveyard and told her to get those witching dolls from the corpses. She made herself tiny, mouse-sized, and scurried down into a hole beside the grave, just a little round hole big enough for a mouse or snake. Sure enough, in a few minutes, she came up with a little doll, maybe three inches long. When she came back up she was naked because she had to shed all her clothes to fit into that hole. In the moonlight, her skin was black and peeling from being scorched by the fire.

"She removed three dolls that same way. But one was left.

"'Climb up that pole,' he told her, pointing to a tall cedar for one of the dead elders. And she did it, sticking to the pole by her tongue. That's how witches can climb, even without their hands. Just their tongues and feet pushing them up.

"'You're still a witch,' he accused, because she had climbed that pole. 'Go get that dead puppy with the doll,' White Weasel commanded. Then he showed her a glass of rainwater that he'd taken from one of his own footprints, so he knew it was clean. But Betsy was afraid the water came from the pond where she'd sunk the dead puppy. If she drank that water, she'd die in slow agony, so she gave up and took White Weasel to the pond out behind her fish drying shed. There she lifted up the rope with the dead puppy and rock weight. And that doll in its rotting mouth. She kept jabbering and slapping herself, but White Weasel knew she would stop when the dolls were cleaned.

"He carried all four dolls to the ocean and threw them into the clean salt water. After he chanted over her, the witch spirit left. And the people started to get better."

"Why did she witch her own family?" Clark asked.

Boots smiled. "Envy. Jealousy. Hate. Greed. All the deadly sins."

The old man scooted his chair over toward electronic recording equipment on the other wall. "I don't want you getting nightmares about all that witch stuff. What if I sing a song for you?"

"I'd like that." By this time, Clark realized it wouldn't be an old Tlingit canoe chant accompanied by the sealskin drum, and it wasn't. Boots switched on the complicated stereo system, added a tape of religious music, then sang "God's Precious Love."

Although Boots's voice now trembled, Clark could discern its richness. The old man's singing was so sincere Clark felt embarrassed. "Very nice," he said when the last note died. "You sure have a good voice."

Boots smiled. "We had a great choir at Mount Edgecoomb school, and I also sang in the ship's choir." He nodded toward the Navy photos on the wall. "See that beautiful woman. A princess from the Philippines. She loved my voice. We almost got married, but she couldn't leave her people."

Holding up his withered arms, he gave a rueful smile. "Body's no good anymore, but I still got my voice. Later on, the devil might get that, too." He tried smiling. "At least Jesus has my soul."

"Well, you sounded *great*." Clark put enthusiasm in his voice. "Who sang that song, anyway? Tennessee Ernie Ford?"

"Nope. It was Jimmy Swaggert, Jerry Lee Lewis's cousin. Both those boys could belt a tune." As Boots lifted himself from the wheelchair back into the La-Z-Boy, pain scoured his face. "I feel sorry for Jimmy. Hanging out with prostitutes cost him a good testimony."

Outside, a horn signaled the Jeep's return. Clark stood and shook the old man's twisted hand. "Thanks for talking to me."

"Come back again." Boots covered his knees with a shawl.

Clark paused on the porch. Was an enemy witching the old man? More likely, the shoe polish had damaged his nerves. He saw the satellite dish shining white in the slanted light and smiled at the way Sampson had tricked him with that "spiritual talk."

. . .

At Sampson's suggestion, Wade and Clark went on an evening "bear tour" while he fixed dinner. All the foliage had been scraped off the seven-acre dump site. Garbage, used appliances, old tires, camping trailers littered the landscape. When Wade drove the Jeep close to a smoldering garbage pit, Clark spotted two good-sized bears lumbering amid the garbage. A third bear sat on the far hill pawing the remains out of large commodity food cans. One of the closer bears nosed around a leaky auto battery.

"You want me to take your picture?" Wade asked.

"Why not?" Ragged spectacles in a roadside attraction, the bears looked sorry-assed. But Clark realized this bear tour was small-town entertainment.

"I need to get them closer." Wade stepped out of the Jeep and walked to the edge of the pit. One of the bears lifted its head and swayed from side to side, getting a better look at Wade. "Come on, big babies," Wade said. He threw half a candy bar into the ravine so it landed downslope, about thirty feet from the rig. Two of the bears ambled up the hill to eat the bar, but the third kept its distance.

"Usually the bears want a dollar, but since you're my guest, it's free."

Clark laughed. "Pretty good. Who says that?"

"Old Sampson. I stole it from him. Stand over there by the edge."

Clark got out, leaving the passenger door wide open. He was wary of turning his back on the bears. They could move pretty fast uphill. He calculated the distance to the open door.

"All right. Get ready." Wade focused the camera. "Kuush, watle, Kwatoon," he said. "That's bear talk."

Clark heard the bears shuffling below him and he turned to look over his shoulder. The closest two bears stood on their hind legs, swaying back and forth like shabby, happy drunks.

"Look at me!" Wade snapped the shutter as Clark turned to face him. "Good picture!"

The young man tossed them the other half of the candy bar.

"What did you tell them?" Clark asked.

Wade put the camera back in the Jeep. "Stand up straight. Hold in your stomach for the picture. Say 'Berries.'"

Clark rubbed his own stomach. "I should have remembered to suck mine in. Bears make me a little nervous."

Wade nodded. "When you're out fishing and covered with salmon slime, that's when you don't want their old cranky uncles to come crashing through the brush after you. No time for pictures then."

* * *

Before returning to the clan house, Wade drove Clark to the ferry dock at the end of the two-mile dirt road. Across the channel, Clark saw a few fishing boats at the lodge.

"If I stay up here, I want to be a guide," Wade said. "I'm learning to work the marine radio. Sometimes now I go along as bait-boy."

"How do you like that?"

"Pretty good," Wade said. "I get big tips. People like catching the salmon and I'm the best netter they've got. I can tell which way that salmon's going to run, just by watching his tail."

"That must come in pretty handy," Clark said.

"No one likes losing fish," Wade said. "I don't like the gut bucket, though. We cut up pinks and fish heads and all that stinky stuff for those old halibut. Man, those suckers are three hundred feet down there sometimes. No wonder they're so flat. And they got screwy eyes. You got to pull and pull on a halibut pole. Keep on reeling." He made the motion of pulling in a big fish. "A big halibut is like lifting a barn door off the bottom of the ocean."

"Who told you that?"

"Gary Cuomo. An old guide who used to be a New York cop. When I told him how many cars I stole, he laughed and said I could make a good living back in New York."

Wade turned serious. "But I don't want to spend any more time in jail," he said. "I like being outside. I don't even mind the rain. This is a bad place to steal cars. You can't go anywhere. Into town, then back out to the ferry—just two and a half miles." Wade pointed one direction, then the other. "And when you run out of gas, that's it—only one station, so if you try to buy gas, you get caught."

Clark nodded. At least sending Wade to Angoon had stopped him from stealing cars.

"You know what people steal up here?" Wade asked. "Just things they can eat or drink. Sometimes they steal salmon drying in the smokehouse." Wade shook his head. "Not me. Sampson said I can't steal or drink if I want to help him. You remember when I was living down in Eugene? Sometimes I'd wait outside the 7-Eleven and get one of the college students to buy me some Annie Green Springs. I'd drink it all up and then go steal a car."

"I remember," Clark said. "I wore out the truck driving back and forth to see you."

.   .   .

The inside of the clan house closely resembled the inside of other houses. Clark had expected columns carved with clan emblems, large screens decorated with red-and-black animal designs, sealskin drums, and cedar dancing sticks. Instead, stuffed chairs and a wobbly lamp occupied the front room. Deer and moose horns hung over the fireplace. The kitchen had a Mr. Coffee, toaster, and a small avocado-colored refrigerator with matching stove. An old chest freezer hummed on the back porch.

Clark, Sampson, and Wade sat around a homemade kitchen table drinking Raven's Brew coffee from Sitka, and waiting for a frozen pizza to cook.

"You should think about staying up here," Sampson told him. "A couple of the schoolteachers are worth eyeballing. The rain drove their husbands off, so now they got the heebeejeebies waiting for a man."

"Can't a shaman cure that?" Clark kidded.

"Not the heebeejeebies. We're too isolated, but things have picked up in the village. We got the totems now. We're supposed to get paved roads in a couple years. A little store with videos. That's progress—we're not going backward."

Clark nodded.

Sampson sniffed the air. "Well, that pizza smells good for frozen. I miss the food in Sitka, but I can't stand to be around when those tourist ships come in. Some days they dump four or five thousand people in town. You can't even buy a cup of coffee without tripping over three blue-haired, retired schoolteachers."

"I know," Clark said. "I had to fight my way into the Back Door for a cup of coffee."

"I'm glad I'm over here now. Maybe I'll go back to Sitka in January when it's quiet. Last year, all the summer women tourists were wearing orange clothes. I thought the town was being chomped up by lady-bugs." He paused. "You know where they got the best pizza?"

Clark tried to think of cities the old man might have visited. "Seattle?"

"Chicago, man. Chicago. That's where they have the best pizza. Deep dish."

"What were you doing in Chicago?"

"What does any Tlingit do in Chicago? Eat pizza, watch the Cubs, and chase women." He grinned. "The best pizza and women. But the Cubs were always struggling. I was just nineteen and taking fire fight-ing training at the Great Lakes Naval Training Center."

"How long were you there?"

"Six months. You know the code talkers the army had in the Sec-ond World War. Well, the Navy was trying to get some Tlingits to try that stuff, too, but they could never round up enough guys at once. I served in Korea."

"I'm just curious. Why did you go in the Navy? After all, they de-stroyed Angoon."

"Two reasons. The first was to get out of here, see the world. Like I said, I was nineteen and full of vinegar. And I figured if I served with distinction, I could get the Navy to apologize for destroying our village. I wrote a couple letters to the Secretary of the Navy, but nothing hap-pened."

＊　　＊　　＊

As they ate pizza, a shrill whistling came from the beach. *Night birds or the wind,* Clark thought, and went on eating, but Sampson cocked his head, listening. After a minute, he stood, took a pair of pliers from the drawer, and went outside.

"What's up?" Clark asked.

Wade chewed with his mouth open, revealing chunks of pineapple and pizza crust. A sly look came over his face and he tapped the side of his head with a forefinger. "He's got land otters on the brain."

Sampson came back inside and returned the pliers to the drawer. "*Kooshdaakáa,* you know about them?" Without waiting for Clark to answer, he continued. "That young Kanosh girl got depressed last weekend after her boyfriend took off for the Army. She swallowed two bottles of Tylenol. Now her kidneys are shot. The *Kooshdaakáa* plan to drag her away soon."

Clark nodded, remembering how Wade used to fear otters.

"Land otters steal people, mostly women and children," Sampson said. "They drag them way down into their dens and change them to land otters, too. You never see those people again. Well, maybe you'll catch a glimpse of them at night or somewhere way back in the woods. Once I saw a couple up by the cemetery. By that time, they were partially covered with fur and they had those dark, dark animal eyes the land otter has. You can't look in those eyes or they'll take you away."

"Can you get those stolen children back?" Clark asked. He thought of the legendary Stick Indians on Mount Hood and Mount Adams, how they lured children away from the huckleberry fields.

Sampson nodded. "Shamans used to have the power. Now we teach the kids to dirty their pants. Land otters don't like bad smells so sometimes they let the kids go. Metal confuses land otters, too. You saw me grab those pliers. Whenever kids go out into the woods, they need to carry nails, a pocketful of pennies."

"A pistol will chase them off," Wade said. "I'm too old to mess my pants."

Sampson gave him a look. "You'll shoot off your leg."

Noticing Sampson was angry at Wade's comment, Clark asked, "Why do they want the children anyway?"

"I think they're lonely. That's what my father told me. A long time ago, we trapped so many land otters for their pelts, hardly any were left. So they snatch children to rebuild their families."

Clark was skeptical, but he understood the reasoning. Losing a child was too hard to accept.

"I can tell what you're thinking," Sampson said. *"Just superstition."* He gestured toward Wade. "That's what the young people think."

Wade turned sullen. "I didn't say anything." Grabbing the last piece of pizza, he pushed back from the table. "I'm going outside. If I see any *Kooshdaakáa,* I'll let you know."

"We've still got land otters dragging away our people," Sampson insisted. "Now we call them alcohol and drugs, depression and suicide. When I go and warn the school kids about the land otters today, they snicker and jab each other in the ribs. 'Old man with crazy talk,' they say.

"But I tell them, 'Think about your moms and dads drinking, your big brothers killing themselves, your sisters running off to Ketchikan and Anchorage, living on Skid Road down in Seattle." He studied Clark's face. "You seen those signs the kids put up on their houses?"

Clark nodded. "They made me wonder if you've heard anything about Wade's mother?"

Sampson shrugged. "Still in Anchorage, I guess."

"What about Wade?" Clark asked. "I always worry about him."

"Me, too. I'm hoping the otters don't want him because he's so darned ornery."

"Knock on wood," Clark said. Then he added, "I see how it works. The land otters are a good metaphor for drugs and alcohol."

The old man shook his head. "Sometimes there are real land otters."

*   *   *

After Sampson had finished his coffee, he told Clark he was going on a walk.

In a few minutes, Wade came back in. "Sampson's hurrying off to Elsie's," he explained. "I don't know how he can sleep with that old woman. She's all wrinkled up."

"You're young, Wade," Clark said. "When you're old, you'll be glad to sleep with an old woman, too. She'll keep your feet warm."

Wade made a sour face, then said, "Sampson's kind of crazy. You know what he did?"

Clark shrugged. "You got me."

"Look at this." Wade took Clark onto the back porch and opened the freezer lid. Clark saw packages of venison in brown butcher paper, salmon fillets frozen in cutaway gallon milk jugs, frozen peas and carrots. Wade rummaged around, pushing some of the packages aside. Then he lifted a large plastic bag out of the freezer. "Here."

Clark took the bag. Moss, he guessed, brushing away the freezer ice so he could get a better view of the gray objects inside. He studied the contents. Gray with bright orange sections, a color similar to salmon yarn. Then he read "Wigwam" on an inner band. "Socks," he said. "What the hell are these wool socks doing in the freezer?"

"Sampson's afraid they'll quit making his favorite socks so he went over to Russell's in Sitka and bought two dozen pair. Then he froze them so the moths and mice couldn't get them. He says these will last him until he dies. He wants to die with warm feet. Is that crazy or what?"

Clark shook his head. "I don't know. In eastern Oregon, they used to say cowboys wanted to die with their boots on. Maybe it's the same thing." He thought a minute. "With all those socks, you could start a Wigwam clan."

Wade frowned. "You're just like Sampson. You old guys think you're funny."

.   .   .

Sampson and Wade put their carving tools into a large cedar bag with a black raven design. As the five Tlingit singers began beating their drums and chanting the honor song, the carvers began a dance, circling the five totems, pausing only to take out the tools and lift them high, to thank the wood for letting them carve. "In some ways, I feel bad about cutting down the old cedars," Sampson had told Clark. "So it's important to honor that tree, show respect. Up here, it takes a tree five or six hundred years to grow big enough to make a good totem."

Hundreds of Tlingits from Angoon, Kake, Yukatat, and Matlakatla formed a large circle around the five poles. They wore colorful button blankets and tunics, crest hats with Raven, Eagle, Dog Salmon, Beaver, and Bear designs. Many of the crests reflected the clan houses that had been destroyed in the shelling of Angoon.

Wade wore a red button tunic with a black Killer Whale design on the back, two Ravens on the front. A Killer Whale design decorated his wooden headdress with three dangling ermine skins. As Clark watched him dance, he was surprised at Wade's grace. The boy seemed exactly in the right place, where he ought to be, in a way that he never had before. Clark was reminded of Natalie's words: "When you grow up first generation in America, you dress like an American and learn to speak the slang, fix your hair to look like everyone else's. And you fit in, more or less. But when you put on the dress of your native country, whether it's the turban, or the Greek shawl, or the dashiki, you become transformed and look natural, exactly right, as if that was meant for you."

Watching Wade now, Clark thought, *That goes for him, too.* After all his years with Wade, he had become wary of the glib answer; the easy solution. He had no belief in the magic of going back to Wade's roots, as some of the experts had suggested. *Now,* he thought, *in a deeper sense, maybe it's working.*

Clark knew that he himself had returned to Ruby for a reason. And Natalie pored over old letters and whatever mementos her family could salvage, running her hands over photographs as if by touching them she could reach into her family's own turbulent history. "The past is always at your elbow," she told Clark. "Waiting for your attention like a child that won't leave you alone. Watchful, persistent, fixing you with dark eyes."

When the singers finished the first song, Sampson and Wade laid down their tools. As the singers started up again, all the Tlingits circled the poles, celebrating the occasion.

Clark shielded his eyes from the low sun and scanned the waters of Chatham Strait for the killer whales Sampson had told him about. No sign of them—the waters were calm. *Unlikely,* he thought, *even in this wild land where much of the sea and wilderness are undisturbed.*

He turned back to the ceremony, the blur of color, the five totems on the knoll. In the slant of afternoon sunlight, it seemed to Clark their faces were almost alive, staring out at the water, keeping silent watch over the history of their people.

*   *   *

The Potlatch feast took place in the grade school gymnasium and cafeteria because Angoon had no tribal center, and the Senior Center was too small to hold the feast and dancing.

Salmon, halibut, coffee, bread, cedar, fish eggs, and other smells filled the rooms and Clark realized he was hungry. No one would eat for a while, he figured. If celebrations here were anything similar to the festivals along the Columbia, a lot of singing and speech making would precede the feast.

He searched the crowded gymnasium for Payette, both hoping and fearing he'd see her. The heavy cedar hats and the bright dancing tunics partially concealed identities, but he was certain he'd recognize her. *She should be here,* he thought. *After all, these were her people, and Wade was her cousin.*

Her friends at Two Rivers always managed to buttonhole him and report how well she was doing, the frequent trips she made to New York and Europe representing Northwest Coast artists. Well, he'd tell her. He was getting by.

A couple of times he recognized women from Maynard's funeral and his heart skipped a small beat thinking she might be sitting close to them, but she wasn't. Somehow he was both relieved and disappointed.

Entering the gymnasium from the cafeteria, Angoon dancers circled the hardwood floor, pausing to hold both hands out and rub them briskly. This was the Warming of Hands greeting dance in honor of the Angoon guests. In the old days, the hosts would build warming fires for their guests, as a sign that they were welcome to participate in the festivities. Even now, Sampson had explained, it was important to show respect for the guests and, in turn, for the guests to honor their hosts. The Warming of Hands dance made everyone feel relaxed and welcome.

Because the Dog Salmon was the most important food for Angoon village, the Dog Salmon dance came next. Two dancers with blue tunics and Dog Salmon crest designs emerged from the cafeteria dancing backward, holding a sheet-sized, blue-green piece of material that concealed the third dancer. They stayed at one end of the gym so none of the spectators on the varnished bleachers could see the Salmon dancer.

By pulling the sea-green cloth back and forth in rhythm with the drumbeats and chanting, the two exposed dancers simulated the rolling ocean waves. As the drumming reached a crescendo, the huge red Salmon mask appeared above the cloth, and the onlookers gasped at the dramatic appearance of the powerful mask. Fiery red, the mask had round black eyes and a gaping mouth filled with sharp white teeth. Long cedar bark strips hanging from the huge mask swung dramatically as the dancer swayed back and forth behind the rippling blue-green sea.

Three frightened young children began to cry. When comforting failed to silence them, two mothers carried them outside.

The dancing lasted almost an hour as the various crests were honored. Dancers from the Eagle village of Kake performed the Raven dance to honor their hosts. When the Raven dancer emerged from behind the dancing cloth, he moved from side to side, tilting his head in an exact imitation of a perching raven's intense movements and penetrating eyes. As the drumbeats continued, the dancer clacked the long wooden beak, making raucous chatter like the Ravens.

Finally, the drumming and singing reached a crescendo. The dancer pulled a cord and the Raven mask flew open from the center, revealing a smaller Eagle mask inside. Everyone murmured at the beauty of the second mask; the transformation revealed the closeness of the two clans.

The final dance was unlike anything Clark had witnessed before. The chanting shifted to a sad, haunting tone and the drumbeats slowed. An elderly man, stiff with arthritis, and supported by two canes, moved toward the center of the gym floor. His dancing was not dramatic or fluid, but stately. Even though his crippled condition limited his movements, Clark felt the power and dignity of this old man, whose hair was white as ermine. The Ravens on his faded-green tunic were outlined in coppers, the shoulder crest in abalone. Instead of a carved Bear or Dog Salmon hat, he wore a black-and-white Navy admiral's cap. When he reached the center of the room, the drumming stopped and Sampson picked up the microphone. He touched his right hand to his chest, signaling he was speaking from his heart.

"Over a hundred years ago, the United States Navy came to destroy our village. Our brother Keechklain, a shaman and village leader, died in that whaling boat when a harpoon gun exploded. Out of respect for our dead brother, it is our way to leave that boat on the beach for a year.

"But the whaling people were greedy and did not honor Keechklain. Every day, his widow and children saw that boat go out to hunt more whales, and every day their grief became stronger. So six young men from our village seized that boat. They told the whaling company they could have it back only if they showed respect by giving that widow and her children ninety blankets."

Here, the audience murmured and some touched their hands to their chests, indicating Sampson told the truth.

"That company went to the Navy in Sitka and told them the Raven people at Angoon had pirated their boat. Then the Navy anchored its gunboats offshore and demanded four hundred blankets from the village. Most of the able-bodied men and women were off at summer fish camps, getting more salmon for winter. Only the children and old people and the sick stayed behind in the village.

"By the next day, the village could produce only ninety-four blankets. So to subdue our people, the Navy gunboats began shelling the village. First, they destroyed our canoes, so we couldn't travel or gather food. Next, they blew up the storehouses where we kept our salmon and meat, the dried berries and roots to feed ourselves and our children through the long, cold winter. When the storehouses were all shelled and burning, the Navy started firing at the clan houses along the waterfront. The big shells from the gunboats destroyed the houses, the totems, the crest screens, all our people's heritage. Women and children ran along the shore to escape the shells and burning buildings. They were mowed down by a Gatling gun. Sailors broke out rifles from the ships' munitions and fired at the people running on the shore. They killed seven old people and wounded many more.

"Some young children were too afraid to run, so they hid in their clan houses where they thought they were safe. Six of those children were burned up in the fires. Three in the Killer Whale house, two in the Dog Salmon. One in Bear."

Clark heard a low moaning coming from the spectators.

"When all the clan houses were burning, the Marines landed and stole whatever treasures were left—the ancient ceremonial masks, the dancing sticks, the screens, tunics, Chilkat blankets. Anything they could carry. The rest they piled on the hungry fires."

Sampson remained quiet a moment, letting the people remember the destruction.

Clark felt the heat rise to his face as he imagined the offshore gunboats firing round after round into the helpless village, the children dying in the clan houses. Surveying the onlookers, he realized most of the spectators were old or very young. The bleachers held only a few teens and young adults, including Wade.

"Now a hundred years have gone by since the Navy destroyed our village," Sampson continued. "Because of that destruction, many Angoon people died in winter. They starved without their food supplies; they grew weak from the cold, the long dark days, the rain and snow. No one knows the death count.

"You see old Wendell standing there. In 1957, he was a younger man and went to the U.S. Navy in Washington, D.C., seeking an apology for our village. Three days, the Secretary of the Navy kept him away from his office. Finally, he sent out a lieutenant with that hat as a souvenir. But he refused to see Wendell or apologize for the Navy's action."

Sampson tapped the mike to make sure it was still on. "When a country is young, just like when a man is young, he might be making some mistakes. When he gets older, and a little ermine starts coming into his hair, maybe his eyes don't see well, but his mind sees clear. That man should admit the mistakes he made when he was young and say he's sorry. If he's an honest man, he should apologize to the people he's hurt. For a hundred years, we've been waiting for the Navy to admit their mistake and apologize. Right now, we are giving them that chance again."

Sampson lowered the mike and the drummers struck their drums five times. The spectators quieted and Wendell stood, leaning onto both canes, trembling slightly. Clark could tell it took determination for the shaky old man to continue standing. However, he knew there would be no apology tonight, that the silence was a ritual. He checked his watch. Five minutes passed but seemed far longer.

Other massacres flashed through his mind: Wounded Knee, the Bear Paws, Sand Creek. Angoon was a slaughter that Hollywood hadn't found, that history ignored. "This has puzzled me my whole life," Payette had once told him. "What does history remember? Which massacres and wars are part of our memory, and which long forgotten?"

The drums beat five times again. Wendell turned slowly, limping off the hardwood floor. Two other old men helped him into a chair. He removed the hat and held it on his lap.

.   .   .

After eating, Clark walked outside to get some air. A driftwood fire blazed on the beach in front of the clan houses. Five teens, three boys and two girls, hunched on logs, grinning and passing around a couple of bottles. Clark stopped when he realized they looked like trouble, but the tall one in a red satin basketball jacket lurched toward him, waving his arms.

"Hey, brother. Want to buy some hootcherino? Good stuff. Only thirty bucks a bottle."

As the player stepped forward, Clark saw the jacket's black basketball design. "Southeast Shootout. Juneau, 1983." Maybe the kid had been a hell of a ballplayer once, but the way he staggered showed he hadn't made any clutch shots recently. Now he had a poorly healed broken nose and split lip. His scarred hands seemed awkward clutching the bottle. "Thirty bucks," the teen said. "Around here that's a good price. Come over by the fire and Charlene will give you a free sample."

"I don't give out anything for free, aaaayyy," one of the girls called.

"She's been giving free samples for years," the other girl said, and Charlene slugged her in the shoulder.

As the teen held out the bottle, Clark shook his head. "Not tonight."

The boy's eyes narrowed. "Think you're too good to drink with me?" Jutting his chin, he tried acting belligerent but lacked any fire. He came half the distance, then stopped, squinting past Clark's shoulder.

"My dad wants to see the celebration, Perry. Why don't you go on back to your pals?"

Wade stood behind Clark where the beach sand met the black rock slope in front of the clan houses. He held a big flashlight like a club.

The school gymnasium doors were open so the sounds of drums and singing carried out to the beach. Tilting his head toward the sound, Perry straightened for a moment, then slumped his shoulders. Pointing the bottle at the school, he said, "They're all living in the past. No one gives a shit about this place or those raggedy-assed old men and their totems." He brought the bottle to his chest. "I'm leaving for good." Throwing back his head, Perry sang off-key, "Be all that you can be. In the Army."

"Hey, Perry," Charlene called. "Before you ship out, come and keep me warm."

Perry offered a crooked smile. "Soon as I finish boot camp, she's coming to join me." He pointed to Wade. "You should get the hell out, too."

Clark turned, joining Wade, and the two began walking toward the school. Higher on the hill, the last rays of summer sun glinted off the totems' crests and made the fireweed glow red.

Wade paused. "You know one of the reasons I worked on those poles?"

"No."

Wade tapped the flashlight against his palm. "Because that asshole Perry didn't like it. When I first got here he tried to whip me, but he couldn't do it by himself. The Stanley boys showed me how to fight. No one's tougher than me." He pointed to his broken tooth. "Perry and two of his buddies did that. Later on I busted his nose. It healed funny and he still can't breathe right. Now he's afraid of me."

Clark chuckled. "You fixed him good."

"I'm tough as the village dogs. Unless they fight, the little ones get chewed up. . . ." Wade's voice rose and he began to slam the flashlight against his palm. "When we were carving the totems, Perry told me he was going to come by and smash the crests with an ax. I said any damage he did to them, I'd pay him back."

"Listen," Clark said. "You don't need to do anything. The land otters got Perry." He tried placing his hands on the young man's shoulder, but Wade dipped away, his eyes narrowed.

"Maybe, if you believe Sampson."

* * *

Wade and Clark hurried back to the tribal center for the Potlatch. By the time they arrived, Sampson had already launched into a story.

"Little by little, for over a hundred years, we've been trying to get back our heritage. When we go to Celebration in Juneau and meet with all our Tlingit brothers and sisters, sometimes we feel bad because we don't have the same old button blanket tunics and carved potlatch hats and dancing sticks like a lot of other villages have. After the Navy destroyed our village the people felt so sad, some even tried to kill themselves. The Keeper of the Dog Salmon hat, the most important and powerful hat in our village, was so ashamed the hat had been destroyed that he took his canoe out into the ocean to kill himself."

Clark knew that the southern Tlingits carved the best totems, the northern Tlingits wove the best Chilkat blankets, and the villagers in Angoon crafted the finest cedar hats. To them, the crest hats were as precious as the pope's crown.

Sampson continued. "He paddled way south past Hood Bay, even past Chiak Bay. He paddled until he was exhausted and fell asleep in his drifting canoe, convinced the ocean would rise up and take him away from the misery. When he woke up, he felt a bumping and figured maybe the land otters had found him and would drown him, but as he felt more and more little bumps, he realized his canoe was moving back toward the village. This wasn't his plan! He grabbed his paddle and tried to strike the water, but he couldn't. All the Dog Salmon were around the boat. They covered that water like cheap carpet from that Wal-Mart in Juneau!"

Sampson paused and many people laughed, the women politely covering their mouths with their hands.

"He could have gotten out of that boat and walked on Dog Salmon backs just like Jesus. He kept trying to paddle but it was no use. Then he heard something—a high and powerful song—and he knew Killer Whales were singing. The song grew louder and louder until he could understand the words.

"'We will take your brother home,' the Whales sang. 'We will take your brother home,' they sang to the Salmon. And the Salmon sang back: 'We will honor our brother.'

"After that the Keeper was cheered up, just knowing the Salmon cared about him, just knowing they didn't blame him for not saving their traditional hat. When he was safely on the beach, he searched the forest for a big yellow cedar and he started carving that new Dog Salmon hat we honored today. And we honored the Keeper. That hat isn't as old as the ones our brothers in Kake and Hydaburg and Matlakatla have, but it's old.

"So it's important that even when we get downhearted, when we think our canoe isn't going to ride out the storm, we got to keep paddling; we got to keep going, and then something good can happen."

Clark wondered about the fate of the old hat. Had one of the Marines taken it home as a souvenir, lost it in a card game, perhaps sold it? Right now it could be hanging in one of the private collections anywhere in the country or stowed in a museum basement. A lot of collectors who admired masks, or paintings, or turquoise jewelry had no idea of the value of Angoon hats.

"Maybe things don't change quick like we want them," Sampson said. "Sometimes we have to wait. Now, more than a hundred years after those children were killed, I have permission from the Killer Whale clan to honor Wade by giving him the ceremonial name of Keet-heit, one of the young people burned up in the fire long ago when the Navy shelled Angoon.

"Wade here was down south a long time, gone from our people. But now he's back, and doing a lot for our village. He takes some of our elders to the Senior Center for lunch and bingo, then drives them back home after school. And he's helped me carve those totems, because my hands are all stiffened up now with arthritis. You know how that is. I've been wrapping them with skunk cabbage every night, just like you other old-timers, but I been taking white medicine, too, the way the new doctors say. A little faith in both ways is okay, I'm thinking."

Several of the other old people in the audience poked each other, and Clark chuckled.

"Anyway, he helped me with that carving. Now whenever the schoolchildren are walking to school, maybe they're a little sad and their heads are down, they can look up toward the sky and see their clan emblems on those totems. And that should make them feel good.

"So, it's time to pass on the honorary name." He signaled and Wade stood.

Clark patted his shoulder. "Hey, buddy. Good job."

Wade walked across the floor and sat on a stool near Sampson. A cafeteria table was piled with gifts. Tunics, caps, fishing reels and lures, tube socks, kitchenware, banners that said "Angoon."

"Now you Killer Whale people come up here and help with this honor." Sampson directed two dozen people who formed a semi-circle around him and Wade.

"With these witnesses standing here in support, I tell you that Wade is given the honorary name of Keet-heit of the Killer Whale people." When Sampson said the name, the people repeated it four times, signifying the four winds. Then he distributed gifts to the standing clan members. By accepting the gifts, they welcomed Wade's return to the clan.

Back straight, Wade sat still for the occasion. After they had accepted each designated gift, the men shook Wade's hand. A few of the women kissed him.

Sampson placed a bright red tunic with a black felt Killer Whale across Wade's shoulders. "Keet-heit," he said, touching Wade's forehead. "Keet-heit."

"Now he is your brother," Sampson told the standing witnesses. "When he is having trouble, when his boat is broken, you must help him. When he gets into a bad storm and his oar breaks, you must give him another oar so he can ride the storm."

.   .   .

The next morning Wade and Clark took a skiff five miles around Killisnoo Island. Wade tied up the boat, then disappeared into the woods. After a few moments, he came out carrying a small canoe. "Can you grab the oars? Leave your pack here because we're not going fishing yet."

Wade put his own pack in the canoe and they followed a shallow clear creek where bright cohos swam under the boat. A few had spawned out and lay quivering on the bank. Ravens and eagles feasted on the almost dead fish, and in some stretches, the odor was overpowering.

Upstream a quarter mile, Clark recognized the forms of collapsed buildings. From fireweed and devil's club patches, bleached rafters jutted skyward like the ribs of prehistoric mammoths. Three totems lay toppled on the ground, their emblems nothing but rotten wood. By the caches in the back, and a few smudged bits of charcoal, Clark realized they were funerary totems, erected to honor a chief's death.

"So what was this place?" he asked Wade.

"A small village. But when the people all died, it was abandoned for a long time. Then it was a summer fish camp. No one comes here anymore except Sampson."

"Do you know what killed them?"

Wade shrugged. "Sampson told me, but I forgot."

After exploring the village for twenty minutes, Clark found a couple of rusty tobacco cans and three small purple bottles that resembled old medicine bottles. He slipped them into his vest.

"I want you to see something else," Wade said.

For ten minutes, they walked along a game trail, passing through wildflower meadows alternating with stands of Sitka spruce and cedar. Finally they reached a section of stream where the water formed a placid pool. Clark thought of beautiful Creek Woman, daughter of Fog Woman, washing her long black hair in the clear water so the salmon could follow it upstream to spawn. According to the old legend, a person catching a glimpse of Creek Woman became blessed by good fortune.

"Did you ever see Creek Woman out here?" Clark asked.

"Shit, no." Wade shook his head. "All the good-looking women around here go into the cities. They got 'city eyes,' Sampson claims. I'm thinking about going there myself, pretty quick."

Payette had city eyes, Clark thought, but he told the boy, "Angoon seems good for you. You're getting along well."

Wade shrugged. "Too damn quiet. I don't know how much longer I can take it." He pointed to a faint trail near the river. "Down here."

They both scrambled down to the streambed and Wade parted a patch of devil's club, revealing a large limestone slab covered with petroglyphs. Although the figures were eroded by the elements, Clark could discern killer whales, bears, and salmon, as well as a couple of boats containing several stick figures.

"Wow, this is something!" The slab's coloring reminded him of Petoskey stones on the shores of Lake Michigan. The stones and their markings had almost the same color combinations. "Does Sampson know about these?"

"Sure. He showed me. I sat in the cold water and Sampson switched me with hemlock branches. Before letting the spirits out of the wood, I needed to cleanse myself. This place used to be where the hunters trained before the whale and sea lion hunts. I even had to drink devil's club tea. It was awful. Sampson teased me and said it tasted exactly like bear piss."

* * *

After returning to the skiff, they traveled another three miles to Wade's favorite fishing spot. When they passed a deep narrows, Clark saw two white crosses on the shore just above the high waterline. "What happened there?"

"A woman and her daughter were out fishing," Wade said. "When the little girl had to go pee, she got up on the side of the boat, then slipped off. The mother put up a distress flag and went in after her. That's what Sampson told me."

"Did they ever find them?"

Wade shook his head.

Clark listened to the boat's motor, wondering what would happen if they had trouble. Sampson or someone at the lodge would find help. Even so—the country was so wild it made him nervous. One mistake up here and the wilderness swallowed you.

Wade's favorite spot was up a channel half a mile. They left the boat and began trudging in, wearing their hip boots. Sweating freely, Clark hung his coat on a tree limb. In one meadow, they startled three deer. Clark's legs were hot and tired after the trek, but the water was beautiful: a deep green pool, a riffle, then another pool twice the size as the first. As they approached, half a dozen good-sized silvers broke the placid surfaces of the pools. The big ones looked fifteen pounds or better. Wade opened his backpack and put out an array of Blue Fox and Mepps lures. "I like silver," he said, "but some go for blue. Red and silver stripes work, too."

As Clark bent over to choose some lures, he paused, looking deeper into Wade's pack. "What's that hogleg?"

Wade took out the pistol carefully. Clark knew it was a single-action Ruger Blackhawk. "Three-fifty-seven magnum?" he asked.

"Nope. A forty-four magnum. Gary never goes guiding without it. Lots of bears. It's probably good for *Kooshdaakáa,* too."

Clark didn't like the looks of the pistol. "Be careful with that thing, Wade."

"You don't need to worry about the bears, Dad. Sampson's been teaching me how to talk them away. I wasn't satisfied with that, so Gary told me to take this pistol. We shouldn't see any bears today, though, because of those deer. They don't like hanging around when the bears are close."

They fished with stiff spinning rods and eight-pound test line. The thick-bellied silvers hit hard in the upper and lower pools. Once hooked, they made wild runs across the channel, stripping away yards of line, then reversed. Clark was feeling lightheaded, and Wade whooped like a boy at a circus. In three hours, Clark had caught and released so many fish that his arms and back ached.

Most of the fish were such spirited fighters that Clark wanted to turn them loose, but they each kept two. Clark was glad for his hefty males. They'd put them on ice at the lodge and he'd be eating Alaskan salmon steaks in Portland the next night.

As they cleaned the fish on the large-pebbled shore, two bald eagles watched intently from a spruce snag. Wade washed the fish blood off his hands, using sand to cut the slime. Then he slid the pistol out of its holster and pointed the barrel at the larger eagle. "You're too lazy to fish for yourself, old man. Just want to eat fish guts."

"Stop fooling around," Clark said. His back ached from stooping and his hands were cold. "Anyway, that fish blood will wreck up the pistol, ruin that gunmetal."

Wade slid the pistol back in its holster. "I wouldn't shoot an eagle, Dad." He sounded a little grumpy. "We better get going. When the tide shifts, it's hard running against the current."

"All right." Suddenly Clark felt very tired. The travel, worry, exhilaration must be catching up with him. "How long until we get back? I think I'll sleep sound tonight."

"You can be in bed in two hours," Wade said. "But you must be getting out of shape."

He offered to carry all four fish, but Clark insisted on carrying his own, even though he found the extra thirty pounds awkward. As he tripped on rocks and gnarled cedar roots, the fish kept banging against his chest and sides. "Let's stop a minute," he said. "I need to catch my breath."

Figuring he could use a burst of energy, he took a Snickers bar out of his pack, then tossed a second one to Wade. His arms ached from the exertion, and he decided to tie a rope through the silvers' mouths and fling them over his back, letting his shoulders carry some of the weight. "You got any rope in that pack?"

Wade jammed the rest of the candy bar in his mouth so both cheeks jutted out. After digging toward the bottom of the pack, he tossed Clark a hank of clothesline rope.

"That's the ticket." Clark hunched over the fish and ran the line through their mouths. When he tried tying the knot, his hands were clumsy with cold, but after some difficulty, he got a square knot.

"Do you think Mom and Helen would like it up here?" Wade asked.

"Sure I do." Actually he didn't think Natalie would go for it.

"No. They wouldn't like it." Wade crumpled the candy bar wrapper in his fist. "Life is hard up here. I hated it at first. And I kinda hated you for sending me so far away."

Clark narrowed his eyes, then focused on a patch of crimson fireweed. "I can understand that."

Wade hefted his pack and squared his shoulders. Instead of walking, he seemed to be waiting for an explanation.

Unsatisfactory answers crowded Clark's mind as he fumbled with his pack. Finally he got it on, more or less straight. "I'm sorry, Wade," he said. "We tried the best we could."

Clark lifted the salmon so they dangled over his back and started shuffling like a beggar with a gunny sack.

Wade lifted his own fish with ease. "You're getting to be an old fart. I said I'd carry them."

"Next time."

As he stumbled down the trail, following Wade, Clark vowed he would get in shape. When he returned home, things were going to change.

As soon as they reached the boat, Clark planned to rest. He could probably even snooze on the ride back. At least the salmon carried easier this way. Slime covered his shoulders and back, but he had a change of clothes in the clan house.

Moving quickly ahead, Wade disappeared in a dark patch of trees.

"Wade, I got to stop a minute," Clark called after him. Too tired to lift the fish again or drop his pack, he eased back against a fallen tree limb, letting the limb take the load's weight. He didn't see Wade. Damn it! He was hurrying ahead too far. "Wade!"

Exhausted, Clark felt cold doubts seep into him. What if Wade turned screwball and abandoned him here? Hell, he didn't know any of these Angoon people, not really. Another white guy swallowed up by the wilderness.

"Stupid—nothing's wrong!" He fought back the doubts that came with fatigue. He lifted his head and stared at the point where the trail entered the dark woods again, imagining that if he looked hard enough Wade would appear. But he didn't. "God damn it."

He moved away from the tree and lurched toward the gaping hole in the woods. Suddenly remembering his Filson mackinaw hanging on the tree limb, he cheered. That coat would keep him alive a long time, even if it got wet. And it made a hell of a flag. Some passing boat would see him wave the red coat.

He sweated heavily and his breath came in rasps. He slowed a bit, catching his breath. No use dying like a pudgy Oregon elk hunter, keeling over somewhere up in the Wallowas.

"Wade!" He heard a noise and lumbered toward the woods.

Wade stepped out from behind a bent tree and shouted unintelligible words. Wild-eyed, he stepped closer, raising the pistol with both hands to the level of Clark's head.

Clark saw the gunmetal gray barrel, the cavelike bore, the slowly revolving cylinder. Each chamber held a bronze-jacketed cartridge. Wade's thumb cocked the hammer and one of his eyes squinted in the old aberrant way.

"Wade," Clark thought he said.

Flame leaped from the gun barrel, as Clark started to dodge, lifting his hand as if to stop the spiraling bullet. Pain crashed against his skull and his head jerked from impact. He crumpled onto the black earth.

*   *   *

Keet-heit crouched beneath the Killer Whale crest, keeping his head low to avoid choking on the thick black smoke. Tongues of fire licked at the decorated cedar screen, blackening the design. A section of the burning clan house roof had caved in, allowing Keet-heit to see two circling ravens, their black wings spread against a pale blue sky.

As the design screen burned, his hair singed and his back scorched, but he didn't feel pain, just the terrible smell. His left leg was trapped beneath a fallen totem. He pushed against the post, his hands touching carved beaks and noses, mouths and fins. "Save me," he said, but the faces of the totem's spirits remained stolid, mute.

Bursting shells roared in his ears, followed by the screams of women and children. No one could get into the burning house. He was old enough to know that, but two other children huddled in one corner away from the flames. "Run," he begged them. "Run."

Turning black, the burning Killer Whale crest made horrible cracking and hissing noises as the flames devoured the dry cedar.

In the storage areas above the side beams, ceremonial clothes and hats charred to black. The Killer Whale hat, the most precious inheritance, had been passed down from his father's father's father and was topped by five potlatch rings and seven ermine skins. Now it was burning along with the copper tunics, cedar baskets, and Chilkat blankets.

Keet-heit thought of his father at summer fish camp, close enough to hear the bombardment, but too far away to help. Already he and the other men would have launched their boats, padding furiously toward the village and the heartbreak.

He imagined his mother and older sister running down from the berry fields. They dropped their berry baskets and ran faster until his sister stepped between hemlock roots, twisting her ankle. Still she ran, hobbling with pain and fear.

His lungs burned from inhaling smoke, and he saw the old ceremonial figures shimmering in crazy patterns from the heat. They appeared to be dancing. Their black mouths undulated in the heat, but no sounds came forth except the fire's.

Gripping a carved beak, he tried one last time to lift the post but it didn't budge. "Run to the woods," he tried to call, but choked, coughing up black phlegm. He longed for the cool sea—to be standing on the sun-washed shore feeling the breeze. Then, closing his eyes, he lay back on the hardwood floor, feeling the rough cedar planks beneath his cheek. As his flesh began to char, he remembered coming in from fishing in his father's boat, feeling the spray against his face. . . .

. . . .

A ruddy-faced Marine from the *Service* axed through the burning clan house, checking for loot. Thrusting his head inside, he saw nothing of value, so he raced on to the next burning house. . . .

. . . .

Salt water and blood. More salt water and the brassy taste of blood.

Clark tried opening his eyes but they stung and he squeezed them shut. His butt and legs were wet. Cold gripped him. Woozy. *The plane is coming,* he thought. *Have to get up and meet Buddy.* He tried opening just the right eye, to take a peek. Through a thick red film, a shadowy figure hunched over him. Wade!

Now with both eyes open, Clark saw Wade bring the gun point blank to his face. "Don't shoot again."

"I've got to get you in the boat, Dad. The tide's turning. Here, wash your mouth out." Wade held a tin cup.

Clark took a sip, then spit out water and blood. He touched the throbbing right side of his head.

"Don't," Wade said. "I finally got the bleeding stopped."

Clark was grateful to be alive but he was trying to put the pieces together. "Why in the hell did you shoot me?" The bullet must have just grazed him, knocking him cold. A .44 magnum could stop a truck.

Wade threw down the cup. "Are you crazy? Man, I saved your life!" His mouth twisted in disgust. "Climb in the boat and let's get out of here."

Clark staggered to his feet. All the gear was in the boat, but no salmon. "I don't see my fish," he said.

"What do you think?" Wade asked. "The bear grabbed them. He cuffed you a good one just as I shot. I dropped my fish, too, so I could drag you the hell out of there."

Clark rubbed his temples, trying to clear his head. Wade had shot at a bear, not him. He reached out, touching Wade's shoulder. "Thanks. I never saw a bear."

"That's right." Wade steadied Clark as he climbed into the boat. "Sampson has a ceremonial name for the bear. It means, 'You don't see him until he's standing beside you.'"

Clark touched his head again. Painful. "How do I look?"

Wade grinned. "Pretty funny. I plastered on skunk cabbage leaves to stop the bleeding and swelling. They can sew you up good at the clinic."

Clark sat and put on the heavy mackinaw. He was shivering. Had Wade killed the bear? Not if he'd dragged off the fish. "Did you hit the bear?"

Wade pushed the boat out and climbed in. He shook his head. "I'm not a very good shot, but I scared him, so he just clipped you once. Lucky he wanted those fish more than you."

"Jesus," Clark said, shivering harder.

During the trip back, he pressed the damp cabbage leaves against his head. That eased the throbbing. *Bears,* he thought.

When they could see the blue water tower and the clan houses along the shoreline, Wade said, "Dad, if anybody asks, just say I shot in the air, okay?"

"All right, but why?"

"Otherwise, they'll send out a government tracker and a warden and there'll be all kinds of paperwork shit. It might mess things up."

"I wish you had killed the son of a bitch, before it mugged me," Clark said.

"I thought maybe I'd have to, if he followed us to the boat or cut us off. I was dragging you and kept looking over my shoulder, afraid he might circle behind us, scared to death about how badly you were hurt. I strained a gut pulling you, Dad. You got to lose some weight."

*   *   *

At the clinic, the nurse was sympathetic but businesslike. She shaved the right side of Clark's head and took a few stitches. "You'll want to wear an extra-large cap for a while," she said. "And get a tetanus booster. I've called White's Pharmacy in Sitka for oral antibiotics and some pain pills." She handed him an envelope with six white pills. "Percodan. Take two when you go to sleep, one in the morning. You might have some vivid dreams."

"They can't be any wilder than what I had today," he said.

"Look at it this way. You'll have a bear story to tell your grandkids."

Somehow he was a little disappointed she wasn't making a bigger fuss over him, even if he was an outsider. "How often do people up here get attacked by bears?"

She shrugged. "Most people are smart enough to stay out of their way. The dogs get mauled, though. I sew a couple of them up every month. In addition to everything else, I'm the local vet." She handed him his cap. "I need this room now. There's a girl out there ready to pop."

The nurse took Clark's elbow and led him out to the waiting room. A young couple was waiting. The girl appeared to be about fourteen and was almost ready for delivery.

"Go right on back," the nurse told the couple. "I'll be there in a second."

Clark picked up the baby bottle the girl had set down. Cigarettes, ashes, beer caps, syringes, and pills filled the bottle instead of milk.

"Gross, isn't it?" the nurse said. "But it warns pregnant mothers. Subtlety doesn't work up here."

He waited for Wade, who had gone after Sampson. Clark could walk to the clan house, but he felt weak and tired.

When Sampson arrived, he wanted to see the wound but refused to remove the bandage until they reached the clan house. "Nurses don't like me messing with their patients. You got a genuine Alaskan souvenir," he said. "Not bad. Six stitches or maybe seven. These old eyes aren't so good." He rubbed salve onto the scalp and cheek wounds and said a few Tlingit words Clark couldn't understand. He smudged Clark's belongings with burning cedar sticks. Clark's nose tingled because the smoke smelled like that in his dream.

Wade kept talking, trying to explain the event to Sampson. "I tried yelling at the bear, like you told me, but it didn't work. Good thing I had the pistol."

Sampson put the cedar smudge into his medicine kit. "Things are changing. Even the bears don't want to listen to an old man anymore. They're hard to control, like our young people."

21

South, 1987

Wade carried Clark's bag up the metal ladder and loaded it into the small cargo area of the DeHaviland Beaver airplane. "Better let me help you, old-timer," Wade said. "Don't want you to get a hernia or throw out your back like the old geezers up here."

"That'll be the day," Clark said. He carried a carved Killer Whale dancing stick Sampson had given him and two jars of salmonberry jam, presents for Natalie and Grace. His travel vest bulged with sunglasses, disposable camera, notebooks.

Wade loaded several suitcases and sacks for an elderly Tlingit couple, George and Wilma Kanosh, whom Clark had met at the potlatch two nights before. Wilma had made certain he got an extra portion of the delicious herring roe on hemlock branches. "Good for men," she had whispered in his ear. "Help make babies."

George was headed to the Indian Health Service hospital for cataract surgery and Wilma was keeping him company. She wasn't happy with the arrangements. "I been putting in my complaints to all the Indian Health people," she told Clark while they waited on the dock for the fog to clear. "In the old days, I stayed right at the hospital with George. Same room. I ate with him, got tea and juice, delicious milkshakes. That was good service." She shook her head and clacked her false teeth in disapproval. "Now I gotta stay way out at Sheldon Jackson College. I'm stuck in this cold old dorm room."

"I think the hospital's getting crowded," Clark said. "So they can't have as many visitors."

She snorted in disbelief. "Those Sitka Tlingits get to stay right in the hospital rooms, even now. It's all politics. They're treating us from Angoon like poor relatives."

"It's clearing toward Whaler's Cove," Buddy said. "We better go while I got a couple hundred yards visibility."

"Get in," George said to Wilma. "Fog Woman's putting clouds in Raven's hat." He lifted his head. "It's clearing all right."

"Everything's foggy to you," she told him. Turning to Clark, she added, "He can barely see his dinner plate."

Clark still felt foggy himself, after being swiped by the bear, and the Percodan kept him lightheaded. He had loosened his adjustable cap so it fit over the bandage.

Clark gave Wade a hug and the young man returned it. "Be good, fella," he told Wade. "Keep helping out Sampson."

"I might be moving to Sitka or Juneau pretty soon," Wade said. "Lots of pretty girls there. Woowee! Sampson says we'll be making big money selling carvings and dancing sticks to those tourists."

"Don't spend it all in one place," Clark said. He hoped Wade wouldn't go to the city with all its temptations.

"I'm going to spend it on the girls," Wade said. "They're gonna fall in love so hard."

"Don't get too riled up," Clark said.

"If I get engaged, I'll call you, Dad. I promise. Tell Mom and Helen I love them. Okay, don't forget." He paused. "Oregon is south from here, right?"

Clark nodded. "Due south."

"Maybe I'll be coming down to see you pretty soon."

"Sounds great!"

Clark climbed into the plane, keeping his back to the dock until he blinked away the tears.

Wade helped boost George and Wilma into the plane and Clark assisted with their seat belts. "What if this thing goes down," George asked Buddy. "Where's my life vest?"

"Above your seat," Buddy told him, pointing to the deflated yellow vest.

"It's just a skin," George said, running his hands over the vest. "How's that going to help?"

"You don't inflate it until you're out of the plane," Buddy said. "This door is small, and if the vest's blown up, you might not get out. Once you're out, pull the cord and the cartridge inflates it."

Wilma repeated the directions—shouting into George's ear. "He's so deaf he can't hear himself fart," she said.

Wade clambered up the ladder and said, "Hey, Dad. If you get a new pickup, I want the old one. Okay? I can help you drive it up here. Then I can haul more firewood and stuff. It's a Chevy, right?"

Clark gave him a thumbs-up. "You got it!" He tried to imagine what it might cost to drive and ferry a pickup to Angoon.

Wade's head disappeared and Buddy closed the door. Clark took out the yellow ear plugs, but Buddy handed him a set of spare headphones. "Might see some goats or a bear going over Baranof. I'll let you know." He grinned at Clark. "Don't worry. I won't let any bears get close enough to hug you."

Wade helped untie the plane from the docks and used his long legs to push the pontoon toward open water. He waved harder and harder and began jumping up and down, shouting something Clark couldn't understand.

After taxiing away from the dock, Buddy opened the throttle and the Beaver vibrated as the pontoons rushed over the bay's rippling surface. Twenty seconds later, Clark felt liftoff. Cotton patches of fog rushed by—then clear sky, a dazzling blue that made him squint. Clark took his sunglasses from his vest and put them on. Below was the fishermen's lodge and three silver sports-fishing boats moving past Danger Point. *Incredible, the beauty of this north country,* Clark thought. Incredible also, that tonight he would be in Portland having a late dinner and talking with Natalie and Helen while Wade cleaned and packed fish at the lodge for doctors and businessmen to take home to Michigan and California.

Time and distance seemed fractured as he tried to account for the two years since he'd seen Wade, the many years he cared for the boy, the seven years since Natalie gave birth to Helen. He couldn't get his mind around any of it, so he concentrated on the beauty of the bright water, the dense green forests, sunlight flashing off the soaring seabirds.

His attention shifted to the plane's shadow, first visible on the blue water, then sweeping over a stretch of fireweed meadow. It skimmed the skeleton of the old whale-oil processing plant at Killisnoo, a tumble of ragged tin siding and a dozen concrete snags. Dense green forest hid abandoned villages where countless Tlingits died from smallpox and diphtheria, their once powerful shamans helpless against the new diseases. In Clark's mind, history fragments shifted patterns like bits of glass in a kaleidoscope.

Change, the shift of fortune, lay beyond his control. Even Wade's destiny eluded him. Clark now realized that at times he had been as powerless as the old shamans in dealing with Wade's problems. However, for the moment, Wade was balanced. Angoon seemed to be the right place, if the clan actually helped the boy during the storms. Clark had to be satisfied with that hope.

George was speaking to his wife in Tlingit and she was shouting back. Clark could tell George was worried. He turned around in his seat and smiled at them. "Everything okay?"

"He's just worried," she said. "He doesn't like to leave home."

"Tell him the operation will be fine. My mother had both eyes fixed and now she can do anything. Read books. Watch television. Enjoy wildflowers. He'll be home before he knows it and he can see all this wonderful country."

Settling back, Clark offered a silent prayer of thanks that Wade was okay, at least for now. The land otters hadn't claimed him. Still Clark worried. If something happened to Sampson, then what? Or if Wade ran off to Juneau or Sitka?

The mountains loomed ahead, lush green with alpine meadows and beautiful wildflowers Clark had photographed on the way over. Perhaps they would see mountain goats again. In forty minutes, they'd land in Sitka, and Clark planned to stop at St. Peter's by the Sea and offer thanks, then light votive candles at St. Michael's Russian Orthodox Church for Natalie's brother and Wade. The Kagitas, too, he decided. Grace. Even Emmett. Why not? Big candles, the two-dollar ones that would stay burning until he was home.

Suddenly, Buddy banked the plane to the left and Clark's stomach rolled. "What's up?"

Buddy pointed emphatically to the blue water south of them. "Killer whales, just coming up the strait. First ones I've seen this year."

He grinned and swiveled his head. "Hey, that's something. Makes your trip worthwhile."

Clark stared at the water, then saw them—black, white, and magnificent. Five orcas surged north toward Angoon—formally dressed ambassadors from another realm. Clark felt exhilaration.

Buddy took the plane lower, then leveled two hundred feet above the water. "Close as I can get," he said. "They're protected. You can't buzz or harass them."

"Do you see them?" Clark turned, tapping Wilma's arm and pointing with his own. "Killer whales."

After a moment the old woman saw them. "Keet!" she said. "Keet!" she repeated for George, nudging him in the side.

"Keet?" The old man smiled.

"Five." Four adults and a small calf. As the plane dropped lower, Clark made out two females by their smaller dorsals shaped like conning towers. From time to time, the whales shot crystalline spume into the clear air.

"Any chance of landing and cutting the motors? If they come close enough, maybe George could see."

Buddy shook his head. "I wish, but it's against the law. And there's a little too much chop. He'll have to wait for the next time."

Turning around, Clark took George's hand. "Five Keet! Heading straight for Angoon."

Buddy shrugged. "Who knows? They're chasing schools of salmon toward Favorite Bay, or maybe they'll drop down twenty miles to Harbor Bay."

Clark nodded, but he was positive the whales were headed toward Angoon. The Keet weren't late, he realized, but running on their own timetable, both natural and mythic, with no regard for the twenty-four-hour clock. Perhaps Wade would spot them a couple miles offshore while he was taking the elders up to the Senior Center for lunch. Yes, Clark was convinced, and imagined the excitement as Wade drove the red Jeep through town, honking to alert the villagers.

He thought of the people clamoring toward the beach, gathering in front of the clan houses, the nimble ones scrambling onto the roofs and sun-washed rocks for better views. "Keet!" they would shout, tugging caps lower to shield their eyes from the dazzling sun.

Years from now, the villagers would tell stories of Killer Whales coming to protect the village after the ceremony honoring the old, destroyed clan houses. Wade and Sampson would figure at the heart of those stories.

Buddy banked the plane again, taking a second pass at the whales. They were magnificent, powerful and majestic.

After taking out the camera, Clark looked through the view finder, but the whales appeared far away, so he didn't press the button. He always wanted to remember their flow toward the North—undiminished, not frozen in time.

Buddy turned the plane's nose toward Sitka. A sudden fog lay ahead and the little Beaver whined as it gained altitude to clear the banks. Clark turned back toward the whales, receding in the distance until they remained only as flecks before his watery eyes.

Clark saw their destination. The five orcas passed Danger Point and cruised the Angoon shoreline. They surged within view of the tall cedar totems—bright with sun—sentinels overlooking the village; within view of the elders and children lining the beach; within view of the popsicle signs, shiny bicycles, and warnings to keep Mom and Dad off drugs.

A boy and girl emerged from the blue house carrying a cooler full of popsicles. They passed up and down the line of spectators until they had sold out, then raced back to the house, pockets jingling with coins. Teenage mothers held up tiny children for a better view. Bright-eyed witnesses, the children pointed sticky fingers at the black-and-white messengers of blessing and hope.